The Exposure

K.E. Milligan

The Exposure

Olympia Publishers
London

www.olympiapublishers.com
OLYMPIA PAPERBACK EDITION

Copyright © K.E. Milligan 2023

The right of K.E. Milligan to be identified as author of
this work has been asserted in accordance with sections 77 and 78 of
the Copyright, Designs and Patents Act 1988.

All Rights Reserved

No reproduction, copy or transmission of this publication
may be made without written permission.
No paragraph of this publication may be reproduced,
copied or transmitted save with the written permission of the publisher,
or in accordance with the provisions
of the Copyright Act 1956 (as amended).

Any person who commits any unauthorised act in relation to
this publication may be liable to criminal
prosecution and civil claims for damage.

A CIP catalogue record for this title is
available from the British Library.

ISBN: 978-1-80074-529-2

This is a work of fiction.
Names, characters, places and incidents originate from the writer's
imagination. Any resemblance to actual persons, living or dead, is
purely coincidental.

First Published in 2023

Olympia Publishers
Tallis House
2 Tallis Street
London
EC4Y 0AB

Printed in Great Britain

Dedication

This is for my legendary Nana Kath, who never once stopped believing in me, right until the very end. She will never be far from my thoughts.

Chapter 1

She felt chaotic and frenzied. How had she got here? Where was she? What was she running from? It didn't matter. All that mattered was that she kept running, kept moving, kept pressing on forward, despite the pain. She vaguely remembered falling down, falling multiple times in fact, barely taking a moment each time to pause and acknowledge the agony shooting through her weary body – she just clambered back to her feet and ran. Her lungs felt as though they were on fire and she could feel sweat dripping down her back and off of her forehead, sometimes getting in her eyes and stinging like crazy.

She glanced around to evaluate her surroundings but couldn't make much sense of it. It felt like her brain was throbbing against her skull and she could actually hear the sound of it warping and vibrating inside her eardrums like the heavy sound of bass at a party. What the hell was in her system and playing havoc with her senses?

It was daylight and she could hear the sound of faint traffic but it was coming from beyond her line of sight – if you could even call it that. Her vision felt hazy and off-kilter at best.

There were large trees all around her that were covering the sky. The ground felt slightly damp; parts of it were light soil and parts were broken up rocks with tree trunks jutting out. That explained the many scrapes she could see collecting on her legs and the muddy state of the plimsoll-like trainers she had on.

She didn't remotely recognise the shoes she had on her feet. They looked roughly a size too big and like they belonged to a man. The waterproof jacket she had on didn't look familiar either but she was grateful for the bagginess and length of it as it covered her modestly as she stumbled through this strange, wooded territory.

Once more she fell down and, this time, she actually took a moment to listen intently for any oncoming pursuers. She couldn't hear much over the ringing in her own ears, so she took a large, calming, yet motivating, breath deep into her lungs and pushed herself back to her feet, using some nearby bunches of overgrown moss on a rock to grab onto and steady herself. She knew she had to keep moving and that to stop and pause for breath only served to heighten her chances of being caught.

How long had she been running? Time held absolutely no concept to her and she didn't actually have a goal location in mind to be running to – everything felt rushed and completely illogical. It was pure adrenaline fuelling her every move at this point; she didn't have time to question it so she continued to press on further through the trees and dirt.

Eventually the dirt beneath her feet started to become less and less, being replaced rather rapidly by more and more solid concrete. The trees started to open out and reveal more of a built-up looking area, like she was on the very outskirts of a town. The background traffic noise was beginning to get louder and she could hear what sounded like a busy road in the distance to her right. She aimed for the left, where she could see what she believed to be some sort of underpass. Though she had not a clue where it would lead to, she pelted full force towards it in blind hope of salvation.

The smell hit her first and almost caused her to completely recoil and abandon the idea of stepping foot under the grim, poorly lit, concrete structure. It had an overwhelming stench of stale urine, damp, discarded beer cans and rubbish. It assaulted her nostrils, slammed against the back of her throat and made her splutter on her own saliva for a moment. She paused to wipe her mouth and hold her breath, then ploughed straight on through, surprising even herself with her own resilience. Her erratic footsteps echoed loudly off the walls as she catapulted herself straight through the stench of the tunnel and out the other side. The fresh air that hit her was extremely welcome and she gulped it in greedily as she continued to run. It felt like a cleansing wave of purity, washing away the filth from her trachea and cascading throughout her lungs.

Onwards she must go and so onwards she went. She could see small shops starting to appear around her, mostly looking like they were only just about to open up, lights slowly flickering on and furniture being moved into place by sleepy shop owners. Thankfully, nobody seemed to notice her stumbling past messily – the very few people that she spotted were totally consumed and preoccupied with their own tasks of preparing for business. Perhaps it was a Sunday? Her very limited sense of a body clock was telling her it was fairly late in the morning as the sun wasn't yet at its highest point and was far from blazing – more like a crisp globe of cool light.

The weariness was starting to take over now. She could feel every inch of every limb getting heavier and heavier, like they were determined to pull her towards the ground and willing her to collapse. She somehow managed to remain upright and pushed past the heaviness as far as she possibly could, her legs wobbling as she staggered on forwards, until eventually she could lift her feet no more and grabbed hold of a nearby wooden bench, slowly and cautiously lowering herself onto the seat. A relieved groan escaped her throat as she felt her weight slump against the hard back of the bench. Every tiny breath she had within her exited her lungs for a moment, shortly afterwards being replaced by one long inhalation of calming, fresh air.

She very gradually leaned forwards, placed her elbows on her knees and her face in her hands whilst purposefully breathing deep, purifying breaths to try to calm the chaos circulating her mind and throbbing in her brain. She couldn't make heads or tails of any of the events that had led her here and she was far too frightened she wouldn't particularly like what she uncovered if she delved deeply into her own subconscious right now. She felt almost content with the oblivion of not knowing, blissfully ignorant and unaware of the sheer danger she'd been in mere hours ago.

From less than one hundred meters away she was being curiously observed out of a nearby shop window. Henri was peeking out through the glass at the figure slumped on the bench in front of her and was almost certain that she recognised the young woman, though she was dressed nothing like she normally did.

"Dale...?" she called out over her shoulder to the only other occupant in the shop at that fairly early Sunday hour. They weren't even open on Sundays but her and a couple of her colleagues sometimes used the space to get their own personal work done away from the noise and distractions at their various homes. Today it was just Henri and Dale doing their own thing, in their own separate corners, listening to music in the background and occasionally cracking jokes at one another when one popped into their heads.

"Yeah?" he called back from the tiny kitchenette where he

was brewing some coffee for them both.

"Is this who I think it is?" she yelled back, never taking her eyes off the young woman slumped on the bench before her.

Dale sighed, ambled through the open archway to where Henri was standing and followed her gaze to the woman on the bench. The hard realisation hit him like a sledge hammer to the chest. He immediately bolted out the door to run towards her.

"Christie? Oh my god, Christie, is that you?" Dale half yelled, half stammered, in disbelief.

She didn't even flinch or look up at him running towards her and it made him slow down his pace a little and hesitate before he reached her, feeling suddenly self-conscious and simultaneously worried for the figure in front of him. Was it even her? It certainly looked like her shape and hair colour but he couldn't see her face and she was dressed all wrong.

"Christie…?" He gingerly lowered himself in front of her so that he was squatting as close as he could get without alarming her and warranting a defensive punch in the face.

She made a tiny movement to peel her right eye away from her hand and peer at him, carefully evaluating the crouched man beside her. The look on his face was a mixture of concern and what seemed like confusion at her presence. She almost felt like she recognised him but she couldn't quite place him in her mind. It was as if she'd seen him in a dream or some far away memory and yet now he was here trying to ask her something. Was this even reality? There wasn't a single thing in her mind about this situation that made any sense to her at all.

He was sure it was her now. He would recognise those deep ocean eyes anywhere…at least the one she'd allow him to see. There was one noticeable difference though – there was nothing normal about the size of her pupil at the moment and

Dale worried about what could have possibly happened to her.

"Christie," he pressed, "are you OK? Where have you been? How did you get here?"

She didn't think it was possible but even more confusion swept over her.

"You know who I am?" she blurted as she lifted her face fully away from her hands and took him in properly. He looked so gentle and compassionate. His eyes were filled with what she could only assume was worry and he was staring intently at her as though he couldn't quite believe she was there.

"Yes, I do, I know you well. Do you know who I am?" he replied in a very measured and non-threatening or mocking tone.

"Kind of, but not really... I feel like I've seen you before but it also feels like I dreamt that. I don't know. I'm not making any sense, nothing makes any sense to me right now..." she trailed off as the air started to catch in her throat, threatening to make her hyperventilate.

He slowly and gently lifted himself up so that he could sit down on the bench next to her, cautiously placed his hand on her shoulder and soothingly murmured, "Shhhhh, it's all right, don't worry about any of that right now. The most important thing is that you're here, you're safe. I will look after you and we'll get you some help, OK? There is absolutely nothing to be frightened of; everything's gonna be just fine."

She sniffed up the bubbling liquid that had embarrassingly trickled out of her nose and nodded along to his kind words. She wasn't sure why but she felt like she could trust him, like she had perhaps trusted this man for a long time before this moment and a seemingly illogical wave of relief swept over her. Even though she was vaguely aware of the fact that she was staring at him, she couldn't seem to drag her eyes away. He was spellbinding to her. It was like she was only semi-attached to her own body and despite holding her line of vision directly at his lovely face, it kept skipping in and out of focus and she had to keep blinking to regulate it. His large azure-coloured eyes seemed to shimmer in his eye sockets, making them look like waves in a body of water and his chocolate-coloured beard looked like it was sparkling with pink glitter. It all combined to make a mesmerising sight and even though she was aware of the fact that it couldn't possibly be real, it was a mirage she didn't want to tear her eyes away from in case he vanished into a puff of smoke.

Eventually, she leaned her head to rest on his shoulder, her every action seeming to happen in slow motion and he wrapped a comforting arm around her, tentatively stroking the length of her bicep and shoulder up and down. He'd never seen her look at him like that before, as though she was completely hypnotised, and he worried what they had done to her whilst she had been missing.

They sat like that for just a moment or two and she felt a heavy sense of exhaustion sweep over her body as the toll of all that running and falling finally crept up on her.

He could sense her slumping against him so he propped her up slightly, looked into her eyes and asked, "Why don't we get you inside, get you a cup of tea that I know you love and onto a nice comfy seat that you can just melt into?"

She let out a goofy giggle at that point. She was in no right frame of mind to even form sentences and simply allowed this half stranger, half recognisable friend of a man to peel her way from the bench, prop most of her weight against him and lead her towards a nearby shop that didn't look particularly like it was open for business.

They walked until they were mere inches from the front door and Dale held it open for her, but she hesitated momentarily at the threshold, wondering if she had been swayed too easily and that this was all just a trap. Extreme paranoia teased at the edge of her already fragile mind, threatening to take over any logical judgment she had and cause her to spin around and bolt in the opposite direction.

He seemed to automatically sense her hesitation and reassured her, "It's OK, it's just me and Henri inside today – she's been worried about you too and will be over the moon to see you."

Though she had absolutely no idea who Henri was or why she would be worried, the words coming from his kind-looking face made Christie feel immediately more at ease and she stepped over the door frame and into the cosy, warm, low-lit shop.

At the other side of what appeared to be a reception area due to the large desk at the back with files and a telephone on it, there was a beautiful, pixie-like young woman looking back at her with a friendly and welcoming smile on her face as though she recognised her. She had bright pink hair that was cut into a stylish bob, suiting her pretty features perfectly, light blue eyes that were exaggerated by thin-framed glasses and was dressed for pure comfort in a grey hoodie adorned with fluorescent green and pink designs coupled with some stone wash jeans. Where she'd rolled the sleeves up past her elbows, every part of flesh that was visible thereafter was decorated with tattoos and they made her look captivating.

It was only at that point that Christie realised Dale was

completely covered in tattoos too and that this was in fact a tattoo shop. She'd been so caught up in her own manic thoughts, then so easily distracted by what a soothing and familiar effect his voice and face had had on her outside that she'd failed to register any real or extensive details about his appearance, other than the shimmering and the glitter.

Now she wanted badly to go over to Miss Pixie and ask if she could take a closer look at her artwork – she was fascinated, but the idea of dragging her body anywhere in its current heavy and slightly off kilter state was exhausting in itself so she stayed put, resting against Dale's upper body and tried her best to focus on what was happening in front of her.

Dale addressed the woman across the other side of the room, who Christie could only assume to be Henri and said, "Christie's head's a bit all over the place right now and she's having trouble remembering stuff but I let her know that this is a safe place to come in and rest a little while and we can figure the rest out later."

"No drama at all, it's just such an amazing relief to see you," came Henri's instant response. "I'll go and pop the kettle on." Then she disappeared through an archway towards the back of the shop and round a corner, out of sight.

Dale flashed Christie a grin and said, "I keep her trained well," elbowed her and then seemed to remember that he wasn't quite dealing with the same person he had known before. He shook his head, shrugged his shoulders lightly and directed her towards a long, heavily worn but grand looking brown leather couch. He gently guided her to sit down and lean into the support of both the back and the large arm of the couch so that she'd feel more comfortable, then sat himself down next to her and asked, "How are you feeling?"

She breathed in a large breath, tilted her head upwards, leaned back against the supportive furniture and considered his question for a moment, taking stock of how her body felt physically and her mind felt mentally. "Baffled," she eventually replied, gazing off into the distance and sighing heavily. "I don't really know who I am or why I'm here or how you know me and that in itself is utterly baffling."

He lifted up one of her hands from her lap and said, "I did these for you", indicating two delicate, simple tattoos on two of her fingers. They surprised her and she was impressed by how they looked – once again she'd been too preoccupied and then side tracked to even notice anything about her own appearance during her mad dash through the woods.

"They're just lovely," she crooned, in a bit of a daze.

Then he lifted up the sleeve of her baggy waterproof jacket and frowned with a furrowed brow for a split second as he noticed that underneath this baggy jacket was a black fishnet sleeve, most likely indicative of an entire outfit made from the same material hidden under the top layer of clothing. He didn't want to alarm her and quickly pushed that thought backwards as he revealed a vibrant half sleeve tattoo made up of a variety of expertly drawn and shaded designs that took up her entire lower arm. "And I did all of this, plus several others along the way."

She gasped suddenly, went completely silent and spent the next few moments rotating her arm and staring attentively at it before a glistening tear rolled down her cheek. She looked up at him, awestruck and gushed, "This is absolutely exquisite," followed by more moments of lovingly staring at it and grinning with adoration, the same way a mother would at her baby. He realised he'd been holding his breath at that moment and let out a sigh of relief. She then realised she'd probably confused him by crying over his artwork and attempted to back track on her faux pas with a light-hearted chuckle and shook her head to display her confused mindset. Henri came back into the room armed with the most appealing mug of piping hot tea Christie had ever laid her eyes on and handed it to her with a smile.

Dale stood up and pulled Henri to one side, then very quietly asked her, "Do you happen to have a change of clothes here at all? I don't know what on earth has happened to Christie in the time that she's been missing but I highly suspect foul play and underneath that jacket I think there is something that will be very alarming and triggering to her if she catches a glimpse of herself."

"Oh god, that's fucking awful. I've read horror stories about stuff like this. I don't even want to begin to imagine what's been done to her," Henri choked out. "The only issue at hand here is that, if we tamper with her clothing, we might mess with any DNA or other evidence that can be collected from it. Then they won't ever be able to catch the scum that have done this to her." She huffed irritably. "It's *such* a catch 22".

"Blimey, you know a lot about this shit, I didn't even think of that." Dale marvelled at her. "I was just thinking of keeping her from panicking, that's all."

Henri shrugged. "I watch a lot of detective shows. I just think it's best that we leave it to the experts to handle what to do from here."

"Well, I at least need to start making some calls to let people know she's alive and also get her some medical attention. Pass me the phone, please," Dale replied.

Henri spun around and grabbed the handheld landline

phone. Before she handed it over to him, she paused and asked, "Are you doing OK? I mean *really*?" She nodded towards where Christie was sitting and said, "I know that her going missing bothered you a lot more than you cared to discuss with people…" She trailed off, not wanting to seem intrusive, but also wanting to check in on her colleague and friend. She had a lot of time for Dale; he was one of the good ones and had a tendency to care deeply for the people he grew attached to.

"Yeah, I'm OK, thank you." He sighed heavily, rubbed his right palm across the top of his skin head, down the back of his neck and continued, "It's a total mind job seeing her like this but also a *huge* relief to see her alive. I honestly didn't think I ever would again." His voice choked slightly at the end of that sentence and he held out his hand for the phone.

Henri placed it in his hand, putting her other hand on his opposing shoulder, giving it an affectionate squeeze, plus a gentle rub and whispering, "I know, me neither" as she did so.

She glanced over his shoulder at Christie, who was sitting quietly nestled into the corner of the couch, seemingly off in her own little world, cradling her still steaming cup of tea. Henri wanted badly to go and give her a reassuring cuddle but managed to refrain herself for fear of setting off any unwanted traumatic responses and instead retreated backwards into the other room again.

Chapter 2

Christie was staring vacantly off into space and trying to collect any sort of remotely logical thoughts she could conjure up. It was proving extremely difficult. The way her body felt now was different to how it had felt earlier when she was pumped full of adrenaline, panic and an overwhelming sense of paranoia that someone was chasing her. The tremendous ringing and throbbing in her head seemed to have now faded away and been replaced with a low-level humming sound that was weirdly pleasant and almost enchanting. She no longer felt tense and pent up and eager to be on the move. Instead she felt cosy and comforted, like somebody had wrapped her up in a safety blanket and her skin was now nestled into the blissful luxury. She unintentionally let out a soft purr and the feeling of it vibrating through her neck and chest was almost euphoric.

Somewhere in her general vicinity she could hear Dale softly speaking into a phone and overheard the question, "Can someone be sent out to assess her as quickly as possible, please? I highly suspect she's been drugged and I'm assuming tests will need to be done. Can you inform those that do attend that she's very confused right now and also has no idea of where she's been or how long she's been missing?"

She decided to stop listening at that point and go back to her cosy thoughts of comfort and safety, whilst gazing round the room at all the colourful artwork hanging on the walls. The framed pictures dotted around her were of such a wide variety of both subjects and colours; she imagined a person could easily lose themselves in studying each and every one in great detail. She pictured a person coming into this space, feeling pretty sure that they wanted to have ink permanently etched on their body, taking a look at one of these fantastic pieces, falling in love and deciding right there and then that it was the one they wanted.

Gradually and completely involuntarily, her eyelids slid shut and she escaped for a short time into the most superb, out-of-this-world dream she'd ever experienced, taking her on a rollercoaster of vibrant colours and the glorious knowledge and confidence that she was capable of anything, like some sort of superhero.

She jolted awake to see a paramedic crouching down in front of her own knees, with her hand on her thigh, gently jostling her to arouse her from her exquisite dream. She was still on the brown leather couch, slumped a little and she felt a bit groggy, with a newly added flavour of self-consciousness at how she must appear. There was also a male paramedic kneeling down on one knee about a metre behind his colleague, efficiently getting some equipment out of a bag on the floor in front of him. He looked over and gave Christie a comforting smile, then returned to his task as the female in front of her addressed her.

"Hi, Christie, my name's Maria and this is my colleague Anthony. We're here to do a very short, simple examination on you and then we're going to take you to hospital to be fully checked over. Do you understand?" Her voice was wonderfully musical and cheerful, but her tone was entirely professional and appropriate to the situation at hand.

"Yes," was all that Christie could muster up but that seemed satisfactory enough and Maria began doing some basic checks, shining a light in her eyes, looking in her ears, listening to her pulse and timing it, all the while calling out numbers and observations that Anthony jotted down in the background. The ECG machine that Anthony had been setting up then came into play and multiple stickers were placed on her body, attached to wires that led back to the machine itself. By that point in time Christie was far too tired to care about feeling self-conscious and simply allowed Maria to quickly and efficiently place the stickers in all of the necessary spots on her skin – some of which meant fumbling around inside the over-sized jacket she had on. The reading that came back was slightly troublesome but not a major cause for concern and just further confirmed their desire to whisk her straight off to hospital.

She could once again hear Dale in the background, softly speaking into the phone receiver but couldn't quite make out what he was saying. He kept pacing up and down the length of the shop as he spoke, but he would never take his eyes off her for more than a minute or two. She felt extremely comforted by that. He clearly cared a lot about making sure she was all right and it was obvious that she had trusted him for a long time prior to all this. She'd trusted him enough to permanently decorate her body and he'd done an outstanding job and there was no doubt in her mind that there simply *must* have been a lot of bonding involved for him to have the capacity to do that.

Her mind had wandered off again and she was snapped back to reality by Maria zipping up her little utility bag, clapping her hands together and then rubbing her palms as though one stage had been completed and now they were ready to move on to the next. "Right, that's us all caught up, are you ready for us to get you into the ambulance now, hun? How capable are you of standing up?" Maria asked, both sweetly and authoritatively at the same time.

"I think I'm OK to stand. Can I just hold on to you to walk though, please? My legs feel like jelly," Christie shyly stammered back.

"Of course, you can. Here you go, take my arm and move only at your own pace. There is absolutely no rush so take your time, OK?" came Maria's helpful response. Anthony was behind her holding the door open, all of his equipment packed neatly back into its transportation bag. Christie's swirling thoughts took a mental note of just how skilled and yet delicate they had been with her. She badly wanted to reel off an elaborate speech about her gratitude for them and the wonderful job they were doing but she could barely mumble and nod for the time being.

"Would it be all right if I tagged along?" Dale paused and then added, "If that's OK with you?" as he turned and asked the question of Christie.

"Would you like that or would you rather come alone?" asked Maria, strategically placing her body so that it blocked Dale from Christie's line of sight, in a very protective, almost motherly type of stance.

"I'd very much like that." Christie gratefully accepted and nodded. She was a little blown away that he was taking the time out of his day to escort her to hospital – she knew all too well just how much waiting around is often commonplace when one is in hospital. The NHS is grossly over worked and understaffed, and any time spent trying to get treatment is a long-winded process.

She shuddered a little at the random memory shots that flickered through her brain at that point. There was nothing concrete to establish an exact time or place, but pictures of herself stuck in various different hospital beds or sitting in waiting rooms flashed at her in quick succession, leaving her with a slight feeling of dread and unease. She knew that this was a necessity though and tried her best to shake her head and erase the unhelpful flashbacks without simultaneously making herself queasy or losing her balance.

"Great, I'll just grab my jacket," Dale informed them as he strode through the archway towards the back of the shop, murmured a few words to Henri and picked up his light brown bomber jacket from its nearby hanging point. Henri rested her hand on his arm for a moment, said something quietly and reassuringly in response, then he leant in and gave her a quick hug of appreciation, letting out a long sigh as he did so. His face was showing a mixture of relief, surprise and determination, like he felt some sort of obligation to take responsibility in this completely bizarre situation.

He came back into the room, noted Maria's position on Christie's left-hand side, supporting her in an upright position and immediately went to her right side to offer his arm too, which she happily accepted.

The process of being loaded into the ambulance was swift as a result of so many hands on board to assist and the journey to the local hospital seemed very short, with Dale chatting jovially with the paramedics and making them laugh. Christie simply allowed herself to drift in and out of sleep, safe in the knowledge that these three heroes were going to take care of her.

Upon reaching the hospital the onslaught of different noises, bright lights and unpleasant smells assaulted Christie's senses all at once and she wanted nothing more than to escape back to the beautiful dreams she had been having earlier. She didn't like this place; she suddenly felt incredibly vulnerable and just wanted to hide away from everything and everyone. Thankfully, they didn't have to wait around for long at all to be seen and were ushered quickly into a separate side room on a ward, away from all the other patients. It was as though the hospital staff had already been made aware of their imminent arrival and had the room ready and waiting for them. The whole scenario seemed unusual and not like standard protocol at all.

Dale was the one answering about ninety five per cent of the questions, simply because Christie couldn't seem to focus for very long periods at a time and her response was frequently "I'm not sure" or "I can't remember". She looked totally exhausted, every bit of her usually bright, sunny glow had dimmed to a dull, almost non-existent glimmer and her eyes themselves were heavily dilated, yet her eyelids did not seem to want to cooperate with staying open or alert. In various rotations each and every doctor or nurse came and left, asking questions, doing observations, taking notes along the way and updating her medical file that was propped up in a container at the end of her bed.

Dale made himself comfortable in the high-backed armchair directly next to her bed.

Christie was finally able to break free from this unbearable setting and return to her flights of fancy amid spellbinding, swirling colours in her own, far preferable dream land.

Christie woke suddenly with an extreme jolt and she shot upright in the bed, completely oblivious to how much time had passed since she had shut her eyes and drifted away. To her left, Dale had nodded off into a gentle slumber in the armchair but upon hearing her body fling itself upwards into a ninety-degree angled sitting position, he, too, swiftly woke up and rubbed his eyes, looking a little confused.

"Dale, can I have your phone? Can you open the right app for me to record speaking a voice note into it?" she asked in an erratic and rushed tone.

He looked genuinely surprised and, glad she seemed to know who he was, reached into his pocket and retrieved a much larger and newer iPhone than she was accustomed to, tapped a few commands into it and handed it over to her. She gingerly held it a little distance from her face to avoid unwittingly spitting on it as she spoke and tried to keep her manic hand gestures to a minimum, but she wanted to get what was running through her mind recorded as quickly as possible in case it faded into a distant, forgotten memory.

"I had been held captive for a little more than three weeks. It was a little difficult to keep track of time as my quarters were purposely kept bare. I was inside a small room in what appeared to be some sort of re-purposed shipping container and there was only one person that regularly came in and out of my room after my initial capture and subsequent examination." She winced hard at the awful memory of a man taking her measurements in her lower region, using only his hand, grinning a disturbingly devilish grin at her and turning around to tell his comrades that they could get their "biggest pay out yet" for her.

She violently shook her head to try and eradicate that disturbing mental image and proceeded, "The man that regularly came in and out of my quarters looked to be roughly my age or ever so slightly younger, roughly five feet, eight or nine inches max, had a pale complexion against his mid-length, dark hair with a slim build and had a European accent that I can only guess to be something like Romanian or Lithuanian. His role was a more submissive one, like he was a dog's body or errand boy; the main work was being done by people outside of where I was staying. I could sometimes hear one sided telephone conversations and from the limited knowledge I have of other languages, I could hear them reeling out costs in Euros and account numbers in Spanish, German and a couple of other languages that I didn't recognise. The rest of the conversations were just jargon to me. The guy that seemed like an errand boy would bring me food and when he did, he looked embarrassed doing so. A couple of times he started to offer me an apology but couldn't seem to find the right words and gave up trying."

She paused for just a moment, let go of the recording button and collected her thoughts, then pressed record again and continued, "One day I woke up and things felt different. I can't explain it – there was a sense of urgency in the air like there was a looming deadline or something. When I looked down I realised someone had changed my clothes whilst I was sleeping and now I was in a revealing dress made of a mesh type material over the top of some very raunchy looking underwear. I questioned how on earth I hadn't woken up whilst being changed and then noticed how different my body felt, like there was some sort of mind-altering substance inside of me – I could feel it coursing through my veins and I felt weird. The next few actions happened in such a quick flash; it was like my body was on autopilot and suddenly full of a vast strength that I didn't realise I had. The next time that man came into my room I was waiting behind the door, took him by surprise and punched him hard in the throat. As he was crumpling towards the ground, I grabbed a fist full of his hair and slammed it into the wall, knocking him out completely. I didn't stop to check him over. I just ripped off his shoes and jacket, put them on myself and crept as quietly as I could out of the door. I found myself in a fairly long, straight hallway, where there were no lights on but I could see light shining through a clouded window at the other end. I could hear several male voices from a distance but still inside, like they had all congregated for a meeting in another room somewhere. I made my way as quickly and silently as possible down the hallway and out the door at the end, feeling sheer gratitude that it was a latch style lock, so only a key was necessary from the outside."

She let go of recording again, took a large, steadying breath and then continued, "As soon as I was outside of the door, I bolted. I took one quick look back over my shoulder and saw that my container was one of many, placed side by side in a long row, next to another older style building. It looked like we were on some sort of abandoned farmyard and the shipping containers had been brought in and placed there much later and I could only assume that there were more people being held captive in the other containers." She winced yet again at the memory of wanting to run back and offer her aid to the other victims but also knowing that she couldn't do this alone – she must run for help and she must run now! "I carried on running as fast as my legs would possibly take me. I ran past a beaten up, dark green Jeep – number plate GF69 XDB – parked up next to what looked as though it used to be animal pens and also a white transit van but I only got the first section of the registration number as there was a large mud stain hiding the final two digits – I could only make out KY10 U."

Dale looked at her with surprise and awe at that moment and she blushed a little but carried on recording, "As I neared the edge of the farmyard section of the property, I decided on following the direction that led me into some woodlands, not knowing where on earth it was gonna take me but just knowing that I had to keep running. Whatever was in my system seemed to be taking hold of me with increasing speed the more that I ran and I didn't want to end up on the ground, incapacitated and unable to defend myself so I just did my best to ignore the feelings and carried on running. My head was getting foggier and foggier as I went and I started to forget why I was running. I fell down a lot where the ground was so uneven and I couldn't focus on one singular point or goal – I was literally just stumbling my way through. The only thing keeping my mind focused was repeating the numbers from the registration plates I had seen…that was the one thing I could hold any attention on."

She paused for a moment, almost gasping for air, like the wave of adrenaline that had made her shoot upright in the first place had reached its peak and she'd moved from fight or flight mode and now freeze mode was threatening to take over again. She took another long and steadying breath in through her nose, held it in her system for four counts and then very slowly breathed it out, smooth and controlled, making her feel grounded once more.

She pressed on with recording, "After running for an unknown amount of time (it felt like hours) and falling down over and over again, I started to emerge from the wooded area and onto a more concrete terrain and I vaguely recognised the sounds and smells of a nearby town but I had no idea which town it was. I had a very faint glimmer of recognition when I looked at my surroundings but not enough to pinpoint a name in my head or confirm a direction that I should follow. I bolted through a nearby underpass and out the other side to find more and more signs of community life starting to appear and gradually my previous rush of energy and determination wore off. I sort of staggered over to the nearest bench that I could see, plonked myself down on it and had absolutely no idea what to do next. Just a few moments later, Dale had appeared in front of me and I barely recognised him, other than his face looking slightly familiar."

Dale and Christie locked eyes in that moment and gave each other a sheepish grin – her silently apologising and him wordlessly letting her know he understood.

"I'll let Dale fill you in on the rest of the details after he found me as I had officially become a space cadet by that point." She wrapped up what she had intended to be a short, concise voice note but had sprawled into several successive ones as she hadn't wanted to miss out any important details.

Holding Dale's phone out to him she asked, "Do you think you could give those messages to somebody who looks authoritative and like they'll know what to do with them for me, please?" She felt weirdly shy in that moment. He'd already done so much and stuck around in this shitty hospital room waiting for her. She felt suddenly aware that she owed him big time and yet was here asking him to be her own errand boy. The whole thing seemed preposterous and she didn't know whether to laugh or cry.

"Hold up." He stood up and reached into the pocket of his baggy, stonewash jeans and pulled out a business card. "There were some police officers in here earlier but you were completely out of it. The one who was basically running the show gave me her direct number and asked me to let her know when you woke up and what state you're in. I can text these straight to her and let her know you're back to the normal Christie we all know and love and have missed terribly…though she doesn't have to know I'll be using the word 'normal' loosely."

He winked at her and she let out a completely unexpected cackle of laughter, with a miniature snort thrown in at the end for good measure. He took the phone out of her hand and started tapping the screen furiously, momentarily glancing down at the card and then continuing to tap-a-tap-tap quicker than your standard modern day teen would when on a group chat with their mates.

"Sorted," Dale said in a mock cockney accent. He grinned at her again and jammed his phone back into his pocket. Christie looked down at the metal barrier blocking her movement from the bed and attempted in vain to find the lever underneath that she knew would release it and allow her to swing her legs over the edge to stand up.

"Here, I got it," Dale offered as he took a stride over to the bed, reached underneath the metal. There was an audible click and a slightly grating screech as the barrier swung slightly forward and then downwards, freeing her from her temporary prison. She removed the empty drip from its stand on her right so that it wouldn't tug on the IV in her hand and shimmied her lower bodyweight around to the left. She slid her feet onto the cool, hard hospital floor and stood up precariously.

"You OK?" Dale asked, holding his arms out, ready to catch her if she fell.

She seized the opportunity to wrap herself in his warmth – in what felt like the best hug she'd ever experienced. They both tightened their grip on one another. He rested his head against hers and let out a long sigh of relief. Neither said a word for a few moments, just slowly relaxing into the embrace and breathing calm breaths. Both fully appreciated the moment of solitude away from any prying eyes. She took a long inhale of his scent – like fresh cotton sheets with a faraway glimmer of masculine body spray – and it had a soothing effect on her soul. She could wrap herself up in it for hours on end.

She had not a clue what she must look like in her giant hospital gown and with unkempt hair but also realised that she didn't care one bit. She was just grateful to be here, still alive and kicking, being held affectionately by one of the few people on the planet that she trusted wholeheartedly. What a horrific and bizarre chain of events it had been to lead her to this very moment. It was quite bewildering.

Chapter 3

He gently loosened his grip a little, leaned his upper body backwards and looked deep into her eyes. He tucked a few loose strands of hair behind her ear and said, "I'm so glad you're here and you're OK. You have no idea how much I've worried about you these last few weeks."

She couldn't conjure up any words to respond and gave him a half-smile of appreciation, then pulled him back into their delicious hug.

Less than thirty seconds later the door to the side room that had been only slightly propped open now swung fully open. A bright, cheerful, smiling nurse bustled in with an observations cart in tow.

"Oh my, Miss Christie, look at you! Up and about already like a trooper, I see? How are you feeling?" the nurse exclaimed in surprise at the sight before her. She was well past middle age and cooed at Christie the way a mother would towards her daughter.

Christie let out a bashful half chuckle and joked, "Ever so slightly better than I did when I arrived!"

Nurse Sunshine appreciated the hint of sarcasm and replied, "Gosh, yes, you were in a bit of a state, darling, but look at you now. I must say I'm delightfully surprised." She started organising the various tools on her immaculate looking trolley and asked Christie to perch on the edge of the bed so that she could do her obs. Dale took a couple of steps back to allow her the space to work, looking and feeling a little awkward in the background, so he offered, "Shall I go and grab us both a cuppa?"

It was like he had read her mind. Christie felt utterly parched and nodded gratefully at him. "Tea would be beyond amazing right now," she gushed, already salivating at the prospect.

He nodded back and ducked out of the room, grateful for the distraction.

"He's been sat in here with you for hours, ya know, kiddo?" said Nurse Sunshine, who, on closer inspection of her name tag, Christie realised was, in fact, named Judy. "He mentioned that he'd called a mutual friend of yours, who is on his way here from Kent and that he'd asked said friend to contact your family, but he has sat here barely moving a muscle the entire time, answering as many questions as he could from the barrage that were fired at him by the police when they arrived."

Christie shuddered hard at that statement, wondering what sort of suspicions anyone had had of him when he'd brought her here in such a poor state. Judy noticed her reaction immediately and reassured her, "Don't you worry, darl', he held his ground and cleared things up quick and smooth as silk, then went on to charm the pants off of everyone in the room. He's a really likeable fella, isn't he?" She paused for a moment and looked directly at Christie's facial expression, almost like she was measuring her response, but Christie's mind was whirring away, trying to process all of the different scenes that were playing out behind her eyelids. This whole thing had been traumatic enough just for her to have to deal with; the last thing she wanted to do was drag anyone else into the sorry state of affairs.

Judy sensed that her mind was elsewhere and efficiently went about her checks: blood pressure, heart rate, inside her ears, mouth and a quick look over her eyes with a small torch, scribbling down all of her findings on Christie's ward notes. "I'll let the doctor know that you're awake and of a sound mind. He'll be pleased to finally get to talk to you properly."

She gave Christie's hand a gentle squeeze and looked her straight in the eye. "You've been through quite the ordeal, my dear, so I don't want you to put any unnecessary pressure on yourself. If you feel at all uncomfortable with any of the questions asked or they start to trigger any feelings of panic, I want you to be vocal about that and I can assure you he will understand. Take good care of your mind in all of this, my dear, your mental health is just as important as your physical health." Christie felt tears brimming, threatening to break loose and roll down her cheeks, as she nodded gratefully and choked on the words, "OK, thank you."

Judy then wrapped her up in a motherly bear hug, her wide arms giving her a light squeeze and a couple of gentle rubs up and down the sides of her entire upper body. As she pulled back, she gave Christie one last sympathetic and comforting smile, another small squeeze with the palms of her hands and then spun around to manoeuvre her cart back out of the door and into the bustling hallway of the ward.

For the first time in who knows how long, Christie was all alone and it shocked her just how quickly the memories of her glorified cell came creeping back in. She suddenly felt very cold and wrapped her arms around herself in as much of a comforting pose as she could, whilst the random images flashed through her mind at lightning speed. When she had first arrived there, she had been hugely disoriented, with a heavy, throbbing pain on one side of her head and a left-over bad taste in her mouth that she couldn't quite put a name to.

At one stage she had been forced to her feet and propped up against a heavy-set figure, whose grotesque body odour was poorly masked by some cheap smelling aftershave that he'd been far too generous in coating himself with. Her entire jaw tightened with fury as she replayed the physical feeling in her mind's eye of him unceremoniously yanking one side of her lovely summer dress up, shoving her legs apart with the back of his hand and then using that same large, callous hand to 'examine' her measurements between her thighs. Her entire body shuddered at the memory and she swallowed the bile down that had been edging its way up the back of her throat. He had seemed disgustingly pleased with his findings, extracted his hand and handed her back to the errand boy to place her back down on her allocated bed.

The disgusting examiner had then turned to his comrades, rubbed his hands together and informed them in heavily accented English that "They will get their best pay out yet." Then he had ushered them all out of the room.

She remembered drifting in and out of sleep and being oh so vaguely aware of other figures in the room from time to time – figures who seemed to be evaluating her and having quiet discussions amongst themselves. Then it rapidly tapered off so that the only person coming in and out of the room had been the errand boy, who said very little. He only seemed to be checking up on her or bringing her food; at first she was too petrified to even entertain the idea of consuming it for fear of what it may have been laced with.

However, the longer she remained in captivity, the more

she realised that she would need to keep her strength up if she ever stood a chance of breaking out of there. At no stage did she see it as a possibility to just accept her fate and allow this to be the end of her story. Hell no. She'd overcome *far* too much in her time for this to be it for her. It simply couldn't be. She *would* find a way out. She just had no idea when or how yet.

Chapter 4

Dale coming back into the room, armed with two steaming cups and a plastic bag full of what looked like every type of treat from the hospital's 'essentials' shop, immediately snapped her back to reality. She shook the gruesome thoughts from her head to replace them with as cheerful a smile as she could manage.

"I had no idea what you might be in the mood for but you look famished so dive in." Dale beamed at her, plonked the over filled bag down on the bed next to her and handed her the incredibly appealing cup of tea. She wrapped both hands around the flimsy, Styrofoam cup to warm herself back up and noted how his mere presence made her feel calm again.

"I'm really glad you're here, I can't thank you enough for sticking around." The heartfelt statement was all she could pull together, though she had wanted to say so much more. Exhaustion was slowly creeping back up on her, both physically and psychologically.

"Heeeeyyy, don't mention it." Dale shrugged in response like it was no big deal when actually that couldn't be further from the truth. "Like I said before, I'm just glad to have you back in one piece." He seemed to cringe a little then, as though he didn't want to seem like he was making light of a dark situation, then distracted both himself and Christie by grabbing the plastic bag and roughly tipping a few of its contents out on to the bed.

He hadn't been kidding about not knowing what to get – it was the most random variety of goodies anyone could have selected. It was like he'd grabbed one item from every shelf and hoped for the best. She let out a little raspy laugh and selected a cherry Bakewell flapjack from the display, balanced her cup between her knees and tore straight into the wrapping like a ravenous zoo animal. The first bite crumbled in her mouth and she let out a groan of appreciation, like it was the most delicious thing she'd ever tasted. He grinned proudly, chuckled and selected a Snickers from the treat mountain.

No sooner had he sat back down in the high backed armchair next to the bed, than the door swung open again and in came two police officers, both female and both looking like they meant business. Dale took that as a sign for him to get up and immediately leave but the look of sheer panic on Christie's face made him second guess his actions. He paused to ask, "Are you OK? Do you need some moral support?"

Christie took a deep and thoughtful breath and answered, "Perhaps for just a moment." She looked momentarily doubtful and then asked, "If that's OK?"

"Of course, it is," he responded without hesitation, sat back down but leaned forward so that his body was close by. He was fully alert to what was about to happen.

Both police officers looked as though they recognised Dale and were completely comfortable with the decision that had just been made without their input. One took a small step forward and positioned herself in front of Christie.

"Hi, Christie, I'm Officer Dalton," she said, placing a hand on her chest, "and this is Officer Williams," as she motioned to her colleague. "But if you like, you can call us Sue and Kate." She repeated the same two motions.

Though they were work colleagues first and foremost, it very quickly became clear as day that the two women were more like sisters. Their demographics were on opposite ends of the spectrum – Kate being mixed race, with funky, dreadlocked hair that had been woven with a mixture of colourful threads, hazel eyes that looked almost golden and appearing to be roughly fifteen years younger than Sue, whereas the slightly more senior officer was Caucasian with cropped, platinum blonde hair and extremely light blues eyes. Despite any of that, their bond was tighter than that of most blood related sisters.

"We were here earlier but you weren't of an appropriate frame of mind to speak with us so we thought we'd give you a little space to get back to your normal self and then try again – is that OK with you?" Sue was friendly, gentle and polite but it was obvious that she was also keen to do her job and do it quickly.

"Yes, that's OK." Christie nodded her understanding and acceptance but also felt grateful for the half drank cup of tea to hold onto tightly enough to keep her hands occupied.

"Great, thank you." Sue smiled tightly for one moment and then pressed on, "We received the recordings earlier and they were extremely helpful. One of the members of our squad recognised the description of the abandoned farm almost immediately based on the location of where you had appeared and been found. We sent out a large team to that location, who have since made several arrests."

"That was quick!" exclaimed Dale in the background.

Christie sat with her mouth slightly ajar, a mixture of relief and shock washing over her. They had literally taken her description, sprang into action and it sounded like they had got the results they were looking for. Christie knew better than to make any assumptions or get her hopes up too much though. She tried in vain to remain calm and not let her imagination run away with her.

"Did you find the other captives?" That was Christie's first concern. "Are they OK?" Her lip trembled then as she remembered the sheer anguish of the moral dilemma she had felt when fleeing to her own safety, whilst leaving an unknown amount of other victims behind.

"Our colleagues are in the process of transporting twelve other young women off the premises and into hospital as we speak," came Sue's rapid response, which was filled with an almost congratulatory tone.

Twelve? Twelve other women – making her the thirteenth that had been sitting ducks in this horror show of depravity. How many had there been before that? How long had this been going on for? Christie couldn't contain the tears any longer and they streamed down her cheeks in full force.

"That many? Oh my god. That's both horrific to hear about and wonderful to know that you could get to them in time." Christie shook her head and let out a large, slightly choked sigh – partly of overwhelming disbelief at the enormity of the situation, partly of relief that those women had been rescued.

"It's all thanks to your voice notes and the speed with which you got them over to us," Sue replied and also looked over to Dale to give him a nod of gratitude, which he returned with the same level of enthusiasm, not wanting to take any focus away from the subject at hand.

"Our team found both the vehicles you named on site and the culprits looked as though they were beginning to pack up shop and make a break for it. Had we shown up any later we may very well have found an empty property and had to start the investigation from scratch."

She paused for a couple of seconds just to allow that to sink in before continuing: "The number plates and any other evidence we found are now being examined and we are in the process of tracing every third party involved in this criminal ring. But for now, at least, we have several suspects in custody lined up for some extremely thorough interrogation." Another slight pause before proceeding with: "Now, it may seem a little daunting at this particular moment in time, which is fully understandable, but once you have been entirely checked over by the medical team and discharged from here, would you be willing to accompany us to the station so that you can formally identify the gentlemen we have in custody as well as give a full statement of events?" Sue's face looked grim and serious, as though it pained her to have to ask this of Christie.

"Absolutely. One hundred per cent," Christie responded without skipping a beat. She couldn't fathom a reality where she *wouldn't* want to bring these men to justice for the unthinkable things that they were planning to do with her and had clearly done to many others before her.

"Fantastic. I'm really happy to hear that and extremely grateful for your enthusiasm. Here's my card." Sue handed Christie a business card with her direct dial and email address on it. "Let me know when you're being discharged and I'll send someone to come and pick you up. I know that seems a little rushed, but it would be good to get your statement as quickly as possible, whilst it's still fresh in your mind."

Almost as though he had sensed her urgent words, the doctor breezed into the room with an overwhelmingly palpable sense of authority that emanated from him like a bright beacon of light.

He was tall, trim, yet broad and Caucasian yet freshly tanned, with salt and pepper flecks in his side parted hair and incredibly deep blue eyes. His height, broad shoulders and straight stance seemed to command respect all by themselves – respect that was only exaggerated by the white coat and title badge he wore. He scanned the room and took a mental note of who absolutely needed to be present at that moment in time, then pointedly directed his attention solely towards Christie.

"Hello, my dear, my name is Dr Malcolm Turner, but you can call me Mal." He gave her a warm and gentle smile. "I've been waiting to speak with you and to also do a full assessment of your current physical condition. How are you feeling right now? Would it be a good time to begin?" His voice was deep and full of wisdom and experience, yet he came across as incredibly personable and empathetic. It would have been difficult for anyone to refuse a request from him.

"Yes, that's fine with me." Christie smiled back at him, eager to get all of this out of the way so that she could help the police with their proceedings. She knew that doing so was going to be challenging in a raw, emotional sense but also that she wanted to give them as much information to work with as she possibly could in order to effectively bring the culprits to justice.

"Jolly good." Dr Mal clapped his hands together and spun around to address the other inhabitants of the now slightly overcrowded side room. "If I may have some one-to-one time with my patient, I'd be extremely grateful," he stated, his broad smile never faltering.

The two police officers nodded their adherence to the doctor and waved a temporary goodbye to Christie before making their way swiftly out of the door. Dale got up from his armchair, strode over to Christie and gave her a tight squeeze. She buried her head into his shoulder and took a long hard inhale of his fresh cotton smell.

He murmured into her ear, "I won't be far away at all, just holla if you need me." Then he pecked her on the cheek. "Thanks Doc." He nodded at Dr Mal before making his own swift exit.

Dr Mal turned back to Christie and looked at her somewhat affectionately, like she was a niece or other female relative that he doted upon. "Well, my dear, you have had quite the ordeal it would seem. I just want to make sure you're A OK in all aspects, both mentally and physically before I give the go ahead for you to be discharged. I want you to know that if at any stage you feel uncomfortable talking about the events that led you to being here in my care, all you need to do is say so and we can try a different approach, all right? There is absolutely no pressure on my part for you to disclose anything upsetting or triggering."

He gave her a very sweet smile that she couldn't help but return and nod at. "Now, I'm not sure how much you remember from when you were first admitted as you were, shall we say, a little out-of-it? I did some preliminary physical checks and the nurse who changed your clothes also did a check over your pelvic region and took some swabs to be analysed."

Again, Christie nodded as she did have a very vague, totally spaced-out recollection of Judy being incredibly gentle and motherly with her as she examined her and got her expertly out of one set of clothes (a.k.a. the revealing mesh dress and raunchy underwear) and into the next set (her oversized and unflattering hospital gown with big hospital pants).

Dr Mal continued, "The test results came back negative; it looks as though you've thankfully been spared any sort of physical trauma in that area."

Christie took a huge breath and let out a long sigh of relief. She had clearly gotten out just in time, before her captors or anybody else could do anything permanently damaging to her in either a physical or psychological sense, and she couldn't be more grateful for that fact. She sincerely hoped that it was the same case for the twelve other women Sue had just told her about, but then her mind started to drift off to thoughts of how ever many other captives there were before them, whom she had no doubt would have been far less fortunate. A shiver of dread juddered through her entire body as those thoughts ran through her mind and tears sprang at the outer corners of her eyes.

"Are you OK?" asked Dr Mal, a look of genuine concern on his finely aged face as he rested a large, wide hand on her shoulder.

"Yes, I'm OK, thank you. I feel very lucky to have made it out in one piece." That sentence was all that Christie could manage without unleashing a tidal wave of tears on the kindly doctor.

"That you are and it's a testament to your own courage and strength. What you did was nothing short of amazing and you should be proud of yourself," Dr Mal said with a squeeze of his hand on her shoulder and a gentle pat to follow it, before removing it altogether. "I'm quite satisfied that other than a few nasty scratches on your shins and palms, your limbs are in tip-top condition. However I am slightly concerned about the small, dark coloured bump on the left side of your scalp and would like you to go for a CT scan immediately, just to check everything over properly. I'm going to send a porter up to collect you, take you down to the CT department and then bring you back up again afterwards. All right?"

The question seemed mostly rhetorical but Christie nodded in gratitude anyway. "Great. It shouldn't take long at all. I'll get everything examined as quickly as possible and will come back to chat with you about the results."

There was a gentle knock at the door so Dr Mal took the one stride necessary with his long legs over towards it and opened it up to be presented with Christie's parents on the other side, their eyes darting eagerly between the doctor and their daughter sitting there before them, alive and well. Her father looked as though he had rushed straight there to be at his daughter's side from his job as a professional kitchen, bedroom and bathroom fitter as his casual clothes were covered in a variety of decorative substances and there was a light coating of dust in his very short grey hair. He dwarfed Christie's mum, who stood beside him looking far more put together in terms of her impeccably tasteful outfit, expertly applied make up and brunette hair that was freshly styled to shape her rounded face.

"Ah, may I assume you are the parents?" Dr Mal enquired politely, taking in their fervent expressions.

They nodded and her dad held out his hand to shake the doctor's and introduce them: "I'm Pete and this is my wife Carrie." Then Pete seemed to suddenly feel lost for words as to how to express his gratitude at seeing his daughter sitting there in one piece. It had been a rough time for them all, not knowing where she was or if she was alive or dead.

"Pleasure to meet you both." Dr Mal filled in the awkward silence. "I was just informing Christie that I'd like her to go for a CT scan to double check that everything is OK. Would one of you like to come with me whilst I make those arrangements and I can fill you in on everything that's happened so far?"

Pete gave his daughter a kiss on the cheek, a long, tight hug and said, "Welcome back," in her ear before exiting with the doctor for a man-to-man low down on the day's events. He had never been good at the emotional stuff and it gave him a sense of purpose to be walking and talking, gaining information that can be relayed to other worried members of the family later.

Carrie remained in the room with Christie, walked over to her daughter and gave her a short, gentler squeeze than what her dad had given her. Carrie wasn't much of a hugger and always appeared a little awkward when doing so, except for in the extremely rare cases that her and Pete were seen canoodling or when she had one of her grandchildren on her lap. She felt far more comfortable with her decision to sit herself down on the armchair next to the bed and ask simple questions about how Christie was feeling or if she wanted anything from the shop.

Christie gestured towards the ridiculous bag of goodies that Dale had retrieved earlier and told her mum to help herself. Carrie selected a bag of Maltesers and hungrily ripped them open to immediately distract herself from this hideous situation.

She had missed her daughter dearly and worried about her non-stop, so much so that it had caused bitter rows between herself and her husband where neither one of them had known how to handle their own grief. They had started to accept the fact that it was more than likely that they would never see their daughter again, yet now she was sitting here looking very much like her usual self, with only some minor superficial alterations.

Carrie felt uneasy and didn't know what she should or shouldn't ask about what had happened to her daughter over the last few weeks and Christie felt just as uncomfortable knowing that she was making other people feel uncomfortable.

A few short minutes later, another knock came and this time it was the porter, ready to wheel Christie off to her scan.

She was also grateful for something to do to distract herself from this weird limbo land where people didn't seem to know how to talk to her. She could understand that it was a situation none of them had ever been in and it felt like treading in unchartered waters, but the last thing she wanted was to be treated like a leper.

As they left the side room and entered the hallway, she noticed Dale a few metres away, with their mutual friend Len and his fiancée, May. Christie let out a gasp of surprise at the sight of them, waved enthusiastically, with more tears brimming out the outer edges of her eyes and then found herself gliding in the opposite direction, being expertly navigated on her hospital bed by the porter.

He hadn't said much in the room, other than a brief introduction of himself as Jimmy and he wasn't especially talkative now either. He was, however, a beautifully talented whistler and barely missed a note as he confidently alternated between pulling and pushing her bed, steering her with ease around the labyrinth of a hospital.

Just as Dr Mal had said, the scan itself did not take long at all and Christie did her best to switch her mind off from any frenzied and panic inducing thoughts. She had always been incredibly imaginative and took this as a chance to float away on a cloud of daydreams where nothing negative could touch her and she felt mightier than a superhero. In a bizarre way she felt inclined to tap into the dreams she'd been having not that long ago – how long had it been? She'd lost all track of time since the abduction, let alone since her escape. She wanted to drift away amongst all those swirling, resplendent colours that she had experienced earlier and get lost on a wave of tranquillity once more. But then, even that was a troubling thought. Her reality had obviously been bent by some sort of mind-altering substance at the time and now here she was longing for that feeling again?

For now, at least, she decided not to beat herself up about it and just accept her feelings for what they were. So what if she had garnered a small portion of pleasure out of one part of this whole ordeal? She was jolly well entitled to it after everything she'd been through. And with that, she allowed herself to slip away into an utterly blissful daydream of gorgeous, ebbing and flowing shades of multicolour and sparkles that twisted around her body. It made her feel lighter than a feather.

When she snapped out of it, she was most of the way back to her original side room, being pushed along the winding corridors by a different porter this time. She hadn't remembered leaving the CT department or meeting this new fellow and she felt slightly rude for just a moment, then reminded herself that he's probably used to wheeling patients around in a less than chatty state.

They pushed through some double doors and standing before her was her total mixed bag of visitors: Dale, one of her absolute all-time best friends, Len, and his beautiful fiancée May, plus her parents. She'd never before seen them all in the same room together and the sight of it made her let out an odd, confused giggle. The three men were all of a very similar height, each of them being only marginally taller than Christie, whereas the two women were of similar, much shorter height than the men. That was where the similarities ended amongst this ragtag collection of Christie's nearest and dearest. Seeing them all together was a mind job for her already frazzled brain.

She half waved in their direction and gave a sheepish grin.

"Hey guys." Then she felt lost for anything further to add so she just left it at that.

As soon as the porter had secured her bed back into its spot, May, who was by far the cuddliest member of the group, rushed over to her and threw her arms around her. "My god, Christie, it is *so* good to see you! We've all been so worried for what felt like an absolute lifetime." She squeezed Christie in a tight, but not suffocating way. It was the type of genuine hug that lets a person know they are well and truly loved. Her fairly long blonde hair smelled like apple flavoured shampoo and the trendy t-shirt dress she wore underneath a jean jacket wafted an aroma of jasmine fabric softener into Christie's face as she held onto her friend, gently rocking her back and forth for a few seconds. A tiny tear streamed down May's cheek as she pulled her body slightly away and looked deep into Christie's eyes with her own light brown ones, simultaneously stroking a few strands of hair behind Christie's ear in a very affectionate gesture. "How are you feeling?" she asked with a look of sheer concern.

"Tired and still kinda spacey but other than that I'm doing just fine, thank you, darling. How are you?" Though it seemed like a silly question coming from her lips at that particular moment in time, it gave Christie a vague sense of normality to be exchanging pleasantries with her wonderful friend – the woman who had seemingly fallen down from the heavens to enchant her beloved and trusted buddy, Len. She adored these two outstanding humans and felt beyond happy that they'd taken the time to travel here to see her.

May let out a little snort at the absurd question but obliged her anyway. "We're a hell of a lot better for seeing you, my dear." Then she leaned back in for another long, tight squeeze.

"All right, all right, quit hogging her." Len came over and playfully pushed May out of the way so he could wrap Christie up into the kind of bear hug that only Len could give. He smelled like Cool Water aftershave and was dressed smartly in jeans and a shirt that May had clearly picked out for him. His cropped, auburn hair had been neatly styled with a little gel and he was freshly shaven, just the way his fiancée liked. "You all right, mate?" he half asked but wasn't expecting much of a response.

Christie just nodded against his chest, her face nuzzled into his warmth, feeling one hundred per cent safe, loved and welcomed back to where she belonged. It was the best she had felt in weeks and she wanted to treasure this moment wholeheartedly. She made a mental note that on any future occasion when she feels lonely or doubtful about her own worth, she should picture this here moment and remember how wonderful it felt to have her tribe surrounding her and making sure she was OK.

She overheard her dad saying something in the background but couldn't quite make it out, then Dale laughed at whatever joke he had cracked. Knowing her dad, it was most likely incredibly dark and inappropriate, and she chuckled at the thought. Apparently the two had bonded in her absence and that didn't surprise her one bit. Her mum was pleasantly chiming in at random intervals but also tapping away enthusiastically on her iPhone, most likely keeping other family members and friends up to date on the day's events so far. She never really seemed to switch off from the virtual world, which had its benefits but also didn't seem all that healthy to Christie.

They spread themselves out in the room and started chatting, sometimes as a collective, sometimes in pairs. Carrie occasionally interjected with messages from the outside world being channelled through the phone in her hand. It was an odd scene to be amongst but felt comforting at the same time. Christie relished in the distinct lack of fear running through her body, which was something she had grown accustomed to in the previous weeks.

They were interrupted about half an hour later by Dr Mal entering the room, greeting everybody with a warm smile and carrying a folder with Christie's name printed on it, which he flipped open for more of a dramatic effect than anything else, as he quite clearly knew what was in there.

"I come bearing good news." He directed his statement straight at Christie. "Your CT results are satisfactory enough for me to discharge you. There seems to be no severe or permanent damage as a result of that nasty bump on your head. I will write you a prescription for some codeine but if you can manage without it, I would highly recommend trying to do so." He then snapped the folder shut and placed it amongst her other ward notes in its compartment at the end of her bed. "Are you ready to get out of this joint?" He winked playfully at her and gave her a devilish grin.

"Very much so." Christie beamed back at him. "You and your whole team have been nothing short of amazing. Would you please pass on my gratitude to everyone that took care of me?"

"But of course!" he exclaimed theatrically. "Everyone will be simply thrilled to see you on the mend and able to go home."

"Thanks, Dr Mal," replied Christie smiling sweetly and he laughed at her unnecessary prefix of Dr, when he had told her to just call him Mal. It made him like her even more and he secretly felt a small, internal bubble of rage towards those that had tried to harm such a delightful and charming creature. Naturally, he kept that entirely hidden from his expression – something that had taken him many years of practice in order to perfect.

As much as it would be nice to be able to go home, lay down and try to switch off from all of the day's events, Christie was also keenly aware of the need for her to go to the police station and help them with their investigation.

Len and May gave her more cuddles, said meaningful farewells and promised to come back as soon as she let them know she was ready for them. Dale followed and gave her a tight squeeze and a small peck on the cheek, feeling a little awkward with her parents in such close proximity, though neither of them were looking in their direction.

"Message me if you need anything at all, OK? I'll be right there, whatever you need," Dale said softly, looking her deeply in the eyes to make sure she fully comprehended that he would be there for her.

"I can't thank you enough for today; you really stepped up to the plate for me and I appreciate it more than I can put into words," Christie said, feeling a little shy and inarticulate.

"Any time," Dale replied with a genuine and heartfelt grin on his face. "I'm just so glad you're back." One more squeeze of her shoulders, a quick handshake with Pete and a kiss on the cheek for Carrie, then Dale had swiftly exited the building.

Christie watched him walking away for longer than necessary and felt a twinge of loss in the pit of her stomach. She laughed that thought away immediately and shook her head in disbelief.

She quickly distracted herself by going about the business of changing her outfit. Carrie had incredible foresight and had packed a bag of necessities for her before coming to the hospital, including a change of clothes (a comfy t-shirt dress, cardigan, tights and her favourite pair of Doc Marten's boots), plus a toiletries bag filled with a variety of goodies to freshen up with and a hairbrush. She thanked her mother profusely for being so well prepared and used the toilet attached to her side room to tackle her appearance. It was the first time during the course of events that she had actually bothered to properly evaluate how she looked in a mirror and it was beyond weird. Her long blonde hair was a little scruffy, but not in a horrendous fashion. It had obviously just taken a bit of weathering whilst she was bolting through the woods and continually falling down. The hospital gown absolutely drowned her but she was much happier in that than she had been in the earlier outfit. The most jarring thing was her extremely vampy eye make-up. It must have been applied at the same time as she was 'dressed up' for whatever horror show her captors were planning on shoving her into and that thought alone made her grimace. She grabbed the make-up removal wipes out of the toiletry bag and scrubbed it off quickly and efficiently, then splashed her face with delightfully cooling water and gazed back at her normal self in the reflection. That felt a lot better, like she'd done a little bit to erase the filthy intentions of those terrible men. Having a bit of a strip wash, spraying deodorant and then climbing into her familiar clothes and beloved boots felt even better, like she was piecing herself back together bit by bit.

  She emerged from the cubicle looking and feeling much fresher, once again thanked her mother and got straight to business using Carrie's phone to put in a call to Sue to let her know that she was on her way to the police station so sending a car wasn't necessary. Then the three of them left the hospital and climbed into Pete's work van to make their way there.

Pete dropped off Carrie and Christie, telling them to let him know when they needed picking up again and drove off to take care of some other business. That was her dad all over. He was one hundred per cent reliable and dependable but he always liked to be on the go and didn't much care for waiting rooms or small talk. Carrie and Christie hadn't always seen eye to eye in the past, but the one thing she would always give her mother credit for was that she was there for her when the shit hit the fan. Carrie was one to spring into action and be there for the ones she loved, solid as a rock, whenever the occasion called for it and, in that moment, Christie could not be more grateful for that fact.

Upon entering the station, they were greeted by Sue and Kate in as cheerful a manner as was appropriate for such a grim situation. Sue reconfirmed very gently with Christie that she was still comfortable with identifying the gentlemen in custody and completing her own statement of events, whilst Kate asked Carrie if she would like any refreshments and led her to a comfortable chair in the waiting room. There were stacks of various magazines for Carrie to devour and she also had her trusty third palm, a.k.a. her iPhone. She settled in and politely accepted a cup of coffee, whilst Christie was led down the hallway with the more senior officer.

She was led into an interrogation room and told to make herself comfortable, whilst Sue poked her head back out of the door and called down the hall asking Kate to bring them both cups of tea also. A little bit of light-hearted banter ensued and it was clear the two of them had a tight knit bond that would no doubt be incredibly rewarding in this line of work.

Christie's mind wandered off into what it would be like to be a police officer and having to deal with such horror stories on a regular basis. It certainly wouldn't be her dream job and she marvelled at the strength it must take to remain impassive and detached from the subjects of their day-to-day cases.

"Thank you so much for coming to see us so soon after being discharged, Christie, you truly are a warrior." Sue looked directly into Christie's eyes as she spoke, gave her an appreciative smile and placed her hand on top of hers for just a moment before withdrawing it again to open up a file in front of her.

Christie nodded in acceptance of her gratitude. "I want to be as helpful as possible."

"Wonderful," came Sue's response, "We currently have five men in custody and as I'm sure you can imagine, none of them are being particularly cooperative." She rolled her eyes for dramatic effect, though it was clear that in reality she was harbouring an innate desire to bring these men to swift justice for their actions. "There is one who seems like he might be slightly easier to pressurise into submission than the others and he's the thread in the tapestry that I'd like to focus on picking at." Christie chuckled slightly at that analogy and once again marvelled at the type of character it would take to be good at this job.

Kate reappeared with two steaming mugs of tea, plus a bottle of Pepsi Max wedged under her arm, all of which she placed on the table and sat herself down next to Sue. "The line-up is prepped and ready to go." She addressed Sue but kept her body language open so as to make Christie feel included and alerted to what was about to take place.

"Great, let's just let Christie have her tea and we'll—"

Christie interjected, "No, I'm happy to go now and get this over and done with." She resolutely stated.

"Well, then let's do this." Kate slapped the table with her palms, pushed her chair back and held open the door for the other two women to exit. It was even more obvious that she wanted to see these men behind bars as quickly as possible.

The station was quite a small one and so the walk down the corridor was relatively short, which thankfully meant there was no time for any panic to set in.

"Usually with our line-ups we'll place a number of decoys in there so that we can be sure we've got the most accurate choice of suspect from the witness," explained Kate, her enthusiasm radiating off of her, "However, it's a bit different in this case because we found all of these men on the property where you and twelve other victims were being held, so it's obvious that each and every one of them had some level of involvement in the monstrosity that was taking place there. Now it's our job to figure out what level that was and what they can be charged with."

Christie nodded her comprehension and braced herself for the fact that she would soon be face to face with her captors once more, albeit from behind a protective, one-way glass screen. She gave herself a mini mental pep-talk and focused on breathing, deep and slow, in through her nose and out through her mouth.

They stopped in front of a door and just as Kate was about to open it, Sue placed a hand lightly on her shoulder and said, "Hold on." Then she turned to Christie and switched her hand from Kate's shoulder to hers. "Are you ready?" she asked.

Again, Christie simply nodded back and then swallowed back the rising saliva that was collecting at the back of her throat.

Sue nodded at Kate and she opened the door, strode through and held it open for them to follow. They all lined up next to one another and turned to face the glass, with five men standing on the other side, all of varying heights, weights and ages. There were two that looked similar enough to perhaps be brothers but there was a significant age difference between them; the rest were a mixed bag of ethnicities and appearances. After standing a couple of metres away from the screen and in line with the police officers either side of her, Christie took in one long breath and breathed it out in a very controlled, measured way before taking a large step forward and then a wide side-step to the left, so that she was face to face with the first man in the line-up.

He was incredibly tall and broad; he looked like he would be suited to a job in security because he posed such an intimidating figure. His hair was a dull brown, past shoulder length and tied back from his face in a ponytail. You would be forgiven for finding him quite handsome, though his eyes were cold, his complexion alabaster and his expression made of stone. He didn't look like there was an ounce of compassion for anyone or anything inside of him. Christie studied his face for a moment and had a mental flash back of him shoving the errand boy and yelling something at him in an Eastern European tongue. Those were the two that had the brotherly-like facial similarities so perhaps that explained how the younger and seemingly more passive man had become involved in the sordid affair – perhaps it had something to do with family loyalty?

Christie shook her head harshly and immediately told herself to stop analysing or even going so far as to try to excuse any one of their reasons for taking part in this horrific and demoralising activity. She had a job to do and she must remain focused.

She moved on to the next one, who was far shorter but still taller than her five-foot eight figure by perhaps an inch or two. His heavy-set frame was unmistakable as the man that had callously 'examined' her when she had first arrived at the farm of doom. A shiver ran straight up from the bottom of her spine to the back of her neck, making all the tiny hairs on her body stand up. She swallowed down the bile that had crept up from the pit of her stomach and looked intently at all of his features – from the dark, soulless eyes, the nose that looked like it had been broken more than once, the mocha-coloured skin, to the jet black hair that had been slicked back with far too much styling gel and the matching coloured, slightly overgrown and unkempt moustache. She recalled his unwashed and poorly masked by cheap cologne odour and it made her stomach churn. The words he had used to describe her to his comrades made it churn even harder and made her blood boil at the same time.

She dismissed that memory and took another side-step to come face to face with the errand boy. The last time she had seen him he was crumpled on the floor of her 'cell' and she had robbed him of his jacket and shoes. She felt zero remorse for that. She had done what she needed to do in the moment and it had paid off; she'd earned her freedom and in turn helped to set twelve others free. Why was she even bothering to mentally justify it?

Once more, she shook her head in disbelief. Yes, those actions were completely out of character for her and she normally shied away from any type of violence or wrong doings towards others, but in this case the situation had very much called for her to strike. She wasn't ashamed and she did not feel guilty. She felt proud. She'd risen to the challenge and she'd owned it. She took the time to look him carefully up and down, noting the extreme facial similarity between him and Captain Stoneface, even down to the similar hairstyle, though his was a couple of inches shorter. However, that was where the similarities ended as this man was only marginally taller than herself, very slight and almost effeminate, plus far younger, perhaps in his very early thirties at the most.

What a life to choose, she thought, feeling her lip curl in disgust at this man's obvious herd mentality.

She slid along to the next one, a bald man with skin the colour of dark chocolate and menacing eyes that were too big for his svelte face. He was about an inch taller than her "Examiner" and in excellent shape, as though he virtually lived at the gym. She recalled seeing him in the background on that first day of captivity, but he had said nothing and then also left the room silently when the others had departed.

The final man was another Caucasian, but with more of a peachy colour than the alabaster brothers. He was tall, perhaps an inch or two shorter than Captain Stoneface, like they had been placed at each side of the line-up to book-end it. He had dirty blond hair in a crew-cut style that was neatly shaved around the edges and his eyes were a light hazel colour but the most notable thing about his face was the large, deep scar that ran from one corner of his mouth and up towards his cheek bone, like someone had been trying to slash all of the skin away and leave him faceless. Christie shuddered at the mental images that thought had conjured up and tried best to place him in her memory. Just like the bald, black man, she recalled seeing him in the background but he had recited no lines in this ghastly theatre production.

Once satisfied with her study of the men, she turned back towards the two patient and yet eager police officers and addressed Sue. "I think I'm done here. Can we go back so that I can sit down now, please?" she enquired politely.

"Absolutely," came Sue's immediate response and she held open the door for Christie to exit and start making her way down the corridor towards the original room they had been sitting in.

There was still a little bit of warmth in her mug of tea and Christie barely skipped a beat before enjoying a huge, delicious gulp as soon as she sat back down. The familiar feeling of it warming her insides was delightfully comforting and she closed her eyes for a few seconds simply to take a breath and enjoy the moment.

"I know that must have been extremely difficult and we really appreciate you taking the time to look at them all closely." Sue's words brought Christie back to full consciousness. "The next part is that we would like you to describe to us, in as much detail as you can recall, how it transpired that you ended up being held in captivity by these men. Do you remember them abducting you? Is there anything you can tell us about the stages you went through from when you were first abducted, then to being held and then to escaping? Literally any memories you have of the whole ordeal will be useful so take as long as you need and don't leave anything out, no matter how insignificant it may seem." She paused for just a moment to allow Christie to nod her understanding and nicely capped it off with: "After that it's *our* job to piece it all together and build a strong case against the bastards; you can go home and try your best to get back to some form of normality. How does that sound?" She gave Christie an earnest and sympathetic half smile, as though she knew all too well that things would be far from normal for her for a very long time.

"That certainly sounds manageable and like I said before, I want to do everything I can to be as helpful as possible." Christie genuinely meant it but her voice came out sounding a little robotic. It dawned on her just how much she was missing her own bed in her own little room in her beaten up, neglected HMO.

Sure, it was a galaxy away from palatial living, but it was her safe space, her nest, with her own little creature comforts. She longed to pour herself a cosy hot chocolate, put something goofy and hilarious on Netflix, cuddle up to her teddies and pretend like the last few weeks had been nothing but a horrific nightmare that she'd just woken up from. Yet here she was and she knew she had to get her head in the game, tap into the darkest parts of her memory and dig deep for all of the relevant information that she could bring to the surface and present as evidence.

Come on, Chris, you got this, she said to herself internally with no outward sound, look at all you've survived and how God damn resilient you are – you just got to get over this next hurdle and then you'll be allowed some peace.

She shook her head, bounced her shoulders up and down a couple of times and then angled her head from side to side so that each ear was close to each shoulder a couple of times, almost like she was giving her brain a mini jostle and a workout before getting started. It was all psychological, but it made her feel slightly more pumped and energised, plus the caffeine from the tea was nicely working its way into her system.

"Let's do this." She nodded one sharp nod at the officers, signalling she was ready to go.

"You're amazing." Kate grinned at her and switched on a recording device next to her on the desk that Christie hadn't even noticed until that point. This was where it got real. Kate then spoke precisely and coherently, listing the three people in the room, the date, the time and describing what was about to take place.

Now it felt even more real.

"As best to your recollection as you can manage, please describe the events that took place that led you to being held in captivity at the abandoned farmyard off the A125." Kate's instructions to Christie were clear.

Christie took one long, deep breath, closed her eyes and took herself mentally back to the evening she was taken. "I was on my way home from a gorgeously long power walk. The weather had been outstanding all day and I finished work a little early so I had decided to make the most of both that and the fact that there are so many big parks close to where I live. I had walked for hours and by the time I was getting close to my home, it was beginning to get dark. I had my headphones on full blast, and only just heard the final few steps of someone with heavy sounding shoes coming towards me from behind. I barely had a chance to turn my head to one side when I felt a large thud on the left side of my scalp and the pain shot through me instantly, leaving me incapacitated and unable to defend myself.

"It all happened so quickly. I could feel my body heading downwards towards the ground entirely of its own accord, but it never made it there as somebody's arms were suddenly wrapped tightly around the width of my body, catching me and simultaneously dragging me. From somewhere else, perhaps another person was there, I can't be sure, someone put a dark material bag over my head. It smelled damp and musty, like something or someone else had also had their head jammed into it at some point before mine was. I remember trying to scream but the moment I did, the bag was pulled tighter and the material filled my mouth, completely muffling any sounds. I started to smell something chemical-like and the arms that were wrapped around me grew tighter too, making it even harder to make a sound. My body felt heavy and uncooperative, then my legs totally buckled underneath me and I felt myself being dragged along the grass, my feet unable to get myself standing upright. I've never felt so utterly helpless and completely fucking terrified."

The alarming feelings washed over her anew and she took a moment to pause and collect herself. The officers patiently waited, wanting to put zero pressure on her.

"I could hear only faint murmuring in the background and it wasn't in a language I recognised. I could only tell that it was some variety of Eastern European based on how I've heard people speaking in the shops close to where I live and in movies and stuff." That sounded wishy washy at best in her mind, but she would rather give her own brand of narrative than nothing at all.

She pressed on: "The next thing I knew I was being lifted and I couldn't tell how many arms were on me but it was definitely more than one person and I was placed laying sideways in a vehicle of some sort – it felt like a van due to the amount of space I could sense around me. I could feel only a small piece of carpet between me and the vehicle floor and I felt somebody else climb into the back beside me, but they didn't touch me. They just sat somewhere else in my nearby vicinity. Whoever else was there slammed the door behind us and then climbed into the front seat to drive away. I could only just make out some very muffled talking coming from the front section of the vehicle and I could feel myself slowly drifting out of consciousness. I started to panic more and willed myself to stay awake and alert. I kept lightly tapping my head against the floor to try to spike some adrenaline and jolt myself into a vigilant state but it was useless and I soon lost the battle against sleep."

Christie polished off the last tiny sip of her tea before continuing, "The very next thing I remember was being inside my new cell – the shipping container where they held me prisoner. I realised I had been lying sideways on the bed with my legs dangling over the side, as though I had been sort of dumped there temporarily. I felt somebody lifting me up and propping me against somebody else, who proceeded to take my body weight against his and wrap his right arm around my waist to hold me up. After seeing that line-up just now in the other room I can confirm that the one propping me up was suspect number two but I failed to see who had lifted me off the bed." She then went on to describe in detail her disgusting violation by the man in question and what he had said to the rest of the men in the room upon completing her 'examination', using very colourful language as she did so. She felt herself grimace and squeezed her legs tight together, folding one on top of the other and clamping hard.

"I can vaguely recall seeing suspects number one, four and five standing at the back of the room. Four and five said nothing, one said something in response to what two had just told him but I couldn't make out what it was. I was so groggy and also trying not to vomit. I was then shuffled back over to the bed and casually dropped there like a discarded rag doll. The one who had dropped me looked me up and down for a few grotesque, cringe worthy moments, like he was half making sure I didn't make any sudden movements and half contemplating something more sinister, then he turned and all of the men proceeded to make their way out of the room. I remember feeling terribly cold and exhausted, so much so that even shimmying my way under the sliver of a blanket they had left me was a job and a half and I slipped into an extremely deep sleep for an unknown amount of time.

"The next time I woke up I looked at my watch and could see that it was 4pm but it's an analogue one so I had no idea if it was the next day or even the day after that. I felt foggy and stiff all over, like I'd been laying in the same position for quite some time. As I was swinging my legs over the side of the bed to attempt to stand up and stretch, suspect number three from the line-up entered the room quietly, carrying a tray with a sandwich on a plate, a carton of juice and a bottle of water on it. He looked embarrassed and nervous when he saw me sitting up, placed the tray on the floor next to the bed, stood back upright again and looked directly at me as though he wanted to say something but then thought better of it and scuttled out of the room." Christie let out a light and ironic chuckle at how ridiculous that entire scene looked in her memory.

"I stood up slowly and walked around the room to examine my dwellings. Someone had repurposed it to make it into a place where someone could stay for a substantial amount of time if they needed to as there was a fully functioning toilet at one end and a sink next to it, plus a shelf unit standing next to that with some toiletries stacked on it and a couple of towels. It was like it was a not-remotely-subtle way of instructing me to keep myself clean and presentable." She shook her head in disgust and felt her lip curling up at one side.

"I mean don't get me wrong, I did take full fucking advantage of the cleaning supplies but because *I* wanted to, not because I felt obligated to." She felt the need to justify herself and had no idea why.

"The coming days and weeks were all very much the same routine and it was both tedious and yet frightening at the same time. I kept track of the days by scratching a tally chart on the bed post with a tiny piece of discarded charcoal I can only assume someone had accidentally trodden in with their boots, dropped out of their pocket or kicked in by mistake, who the hell knows? I had tallied up 23 days on my last count. I only recall seeing that one man – suspect number three – coming in and out of the room to deliver food and drinks, plus changes of underwear every day and changes of clothing every third day.

"On several occasions I demanded answers from him but kept a distance between us just in case he lashed out or anything. He refused to answer those questions each time and mumbled the words 'I'm sorry' without looking me in the eye and then scuttling off again. In a way I started to feel sorry for him but was also infuriated by the fact that he clearly knew what he was doing was all wrong... He *knew* it and yet he continued to do so like a god damn pathetic, herded little sheep." As she felt the blood boiling underneath her skin and the rage rising up in her chest, she placed her hands flat against the table, stroked its smooth, cool surface back and forth a couple of times to steady her nerves and took another long and calming breath.

"The first two days I outright refused to even take a bite out of the food that was brought to me as I had no idea what it would be laced with. I drank the juice and the bottled water as they had come in sealed packaging but I was too scared to eat the food. By the third day I was utterly famished and also fed myself the logic that if I stood any chance of breaking free from that hell hole, I would need some strength to do so. I ate only a quarter of the sandwich as a test and nothing untoward happened so the next time I was brought anything I ate it all. I filled my days with strength training exercises that I've been taught previously at post-injury physiotherapy and also at gym class. I knew I had to try to keep myself in peak shape to fend off any oncoming attacks – even if they outnumbered me when it came, I would go out fighting, I wasn't gonna just fold like a motherfucking napkin when the shit hit the fan and all came to blows.

"Each of the coming days seemed to blend in to each other. I could occasionally hear voices on the other side of the wall but the door was always locked and there were no windows in my cell to attempt to climb out of. On one occasion I heard a man standing directly outside of my door and I could hear him making multiple phone calls in a variety of different languages. The only two I recognised were Spanish and German. I could hear him reeling off numbers but the only thing I could think of was that they may be account numbers or phone numbers. I'm not sure. I could regularly hear footsteps up and down what I later discovered to be a long hallway outside of my door but at the time I had no spatial awareness other than my immediate surroundings. I had no idea how many people were coming in and out or what the rest of the layout was like.

"The next event of any substantial difference was the day I woke up in different clothing and subsequently escaped. When I woke I was lying flat on my back, which I never do to fall asleep – I prefer to either be on my side or lying face down on my stomach. My head was making a kind of warping sound from the inside and my eyesight felt strange; it felt like I was bobbing up and down on a ship or something. I could barely get my eyes to focus at first. Something in the air felt strange. I could hear louder voices on the other side of the wall and the sounds of multiple people's footsteps moving along the hallway from one end to the other, then a door closing and the voices becoming far more muffled and quieter. When I looked down at my own body and could finally get my eyes to focus, I was absolutely repulsed by what I saw. Whilst sleeping or whatever type of coma I had been induced into, someone had changed my clothes and I was now donning a set of raunchy black underwear that looked like it had come straight out of a sex shop, with a short, black mesh dress with half sleeves barely covering my modesty. It was such a shock to the system and I felt a surge of adrenaline sweep its way through my body, like a fight, flight or freeze kinda feeling, and I swiftly urged myself to air more towards the fight and flight options but my brain was also whirring in a panicked state. I jumped up to my feet and waited behind the door, ready to pounce the next time it opened.

"I didn't have to wait that long I don't think. It was hard to tell with my mind being so chaotic, until the errand boy, or should I say, suspect number three came through the door. I waited until it had closed behind him and he turned around with a look of total shock and horror on his face to see me standing there and I punched him straight in the throat. I think I must have punched him pretty hard because he doubled over immediately and couldn't seem to catch his breath. I seized the opportunity to grab a fistful of his hair and slammed his head into the wall, then he crumpled like a piece of paper to the ground. I didn't feel like there was enough time to check his pulse or anything. I simply ripped his shoes off his feet as well as the waterproof jacket he was wearing off his body and messily transferred it all onto myself. My hands were trembling really hard but I pushed through it to get myself ready to bolt, stepped over the errand boy's unconscious body and very slowly and quietly opened the door just a crack, trying to peer out with my foggy eyesight.

"I could see or hear no movement in the hallway but I could hear voices from behind a closed door somewhere else in the nearby vicinity. When I looked in the other direction, I could see a clouded window at the end of the hallway so I slipped out of the door, placed my back against the wall and side-stepped my way towards it, trying to remain vigilant and alert to any oncoming attack. I fully expected somebody to see me and come hurtling towards me to capture me again but no one came and I somehow made it to the door. I couldn't believe my luck to be able to open the latch from the inside and once I'd established that no one was on the other side, I made a break for it and started sprinting as fast as my feet would carry me. I briefly looked over my shoulder at one point, just to take note of what I was fleeing from and when I noticed the number of other shipping containers all lined up side by side, it dawned on me that there were other hostages too. I faltered at that point, wracked with guilt for leaving the others behind, but managed to convince myself that I would be no use whatsoever running back and trying to free them by myself. I needed to get some help. I needed reinforcements to come and swoop in and save the day." She noticed a light tear had trickled down the side of her right cheek at the memory of how much guilt she had felt for abandoning the others.

Kate grabbed a box of tissues from the side of the table and placed it in front of her. "You're doing great," were her simple words of reassurance.

Christie gratefully grabbed a tissue, wiped the escaped tear plus the small bubble of snot that had begun to form inside her right nostril and continued, "As I ran, I was trying desperately to mentally note down any distinguishing features or objects that I saw. Memorising the number plates was easy as I've always had a thing for recalling numbers or patterns, plus I found that if I continued to repeat them over and over in my head it gave me something to focus on other than the terror running through my mind. I didn't know where I was running to but knew I just had to keep moving forwards and the repetition kept me somewhat lucid whilst I did.

"I remember reaching the edge of the farmland and entering some woods, then I remember falling down and picking myself up repeatedly until I got to the other side. All the while, I could see weird, multi-coloured, swirling effects around me and sparkles too – everything seemed to be glittering but I didn't want to pause and let that overcome my attention because I knew that if I stopped and succumbed, then I may be captured again and who knows how mad they would be when they caught up to me? I just kept running and running until my body could run no more.

"By that stage I had made it through a terrible smelling underpass and out to what I now recognise in hindsight as Romford, but at the time I had not a clue where I was going to end up. I stumbled over to a nearby bench, collapsed onto it and buried my head in my hands, not knowing what to do. That was when Dale found me and took me to the safe haven of Vogue

Vintage Tattoos, where he works. He and Henri took care of me and then Dale came with me to the hospital. All of that part of the story is a giant blur, but when I properly came to in my hospital bed, I could remember all of the events that led up to me being there clearly, so that was when I made the voice recordings that Dale sent to you." At that point Christie felt as though there was little more to add to what she had already presented, let out a long sigh, clasped her hands together and placed them on the table in front of her, as if to signify that that was the end of her story.

"Thank you, Christie. That was an excellent amount of detail," said a thoroughly impressed Sue. "Can you give us a pinpoint location for where you were abducted from, please?"

"Yep, it was shortly after I'd entered Old Dagenham Park and I went in through the entrance nearest Vicarage Road. The direction they pulled me in must have been back towards that road – there's a small spot where cars can pull in to either drop people off or pick them up," Christie responded, hoping that it was helpful in being able to track down where other people had also been snatched from. Who knows how many people had been taken before she was and what their fate had become? Would this case blow open an entire trafficking ring and would that lead to more victims being located in whatever faraway places they had been shipped off to? Her mind could barely comprehend the magnitude of such a thing and the massive ripple effect it would have.

"Brilliant. Thank you." Kate was busy scribbling down tiny snippets to be able to pass on to their colleagues for immediate action so Sue was asking all of the questions. "You can confirm that you saw all of the men in the line-up but only suspect number three said anything directly to you?"

"Yes, that's correct, if you could even classify that as talking to me." Christie added bitterly, "Coward."

Kate visibly nodded and let out a little grunt at that point. Ever since meeting her it had been obvious to Christie that she seemed to harbour an incredible amount of disdain towards the perpetrators of this particular case and she couldn't help but wonder if there was some sort of personal connection there.

"Right, I think that's enough for us to be working with for now," Sue stated, largely because she was aware of the fact that this had been an incredibly taxing day for Christie. "You must be exhausted and I would like you to go home and rest up. What you've done today is nothing short of amazing and you should be incredibly proud of yourself. Yourself included means that you've saved thirteen women's lives already and who knows how many more we're going to uncover with the information you've provided us with?"

Christie blushed and gave a little half shrug. "I can't take all the credit – your team swooped in at lightning speed and got immediate results, plus Dale was so quick to act too and if it hadn't have been him that I woke up next to in the hospital I wouldn't have felt so at ease in demanding the phone to make the recordings in the first place. We all had a part to play."

"That's very humble of you, my dear, and thank you for your kind words. I'll make sure I pass them onto the rest of the team." Sue nodded at her both proudly and affectionately. "Now, if you remember anything else at all that you think might be relevant, it doesn't matter how small or insignificant it may seem, please call me and let me know. We may need to call you back in for further questions at a later date as the investigation unfolds; will that be OK with you?" she asked politely, though she was about ninety nine per cent sure she knew it would be absolutely fine.

"No problem whatsoever, anything you need," Christie enthused.

Kate wrapped up the recording with a little sign-off message and switched off the machine. She beamed at Christie and thanked her warmly, calling her a warrior and making Christie blush even harder. They then escorted her back out towards the waiting room, where Carrie was sitting, poised and polished, with a copy of Closer magazine in one hand and propped up against her knee as she flipped through the articles, looking bemused. She looked up to see the three women enter the room, immediately closed the magazine and placed it neatly back in a nearby rack that was spilling out with a variety of slightly battered looking reads, stood up and greeted them with a polite smile.

"All finished?" she asked, her look switching from Christie to the officers and back again.

"All finished. Thanks so much for waiting for me, Mum," Christie responded with an appreciative smile.

Sue handed Carrie a business card 'just in case', shook her hand, thanked her and also told her there were a number of hotlines that both her and Christie could call if they were struggling psychologically. Kate overheard her say that, went over to the reception desk and retrieved a pamphlet of numbers and services for victim support, then helpfully handed one to both mother and daughter.

"Please, please, please do not suffer in silence if all of what's happened starts to feel too heavy to cope with. We have some amazing services at our disposal and you should take full advantage of what's on offer to help you at any stage." Kate pleaded with them as though she had seen the worst-case scenario of another person's mental health taking a nosedive before and she wanted to avoid that happening to them at all costs.

They all said their thank yous and goodbyes and Carrie put in a call to Pete to come and pick them up straight away.

"I noticed a little café just over the road as we were pulling into the station earlier – let's go and wait in there for your dad. I highly doubt he'll say no to a sausage roll and I would love a decent cup of coffee." Carrie gave her daughter a playful smile but she felt anything but playful in that moment. She was still trying to mentally process all that had taken place in the last few weeks but felt the need to hide behind a mask of nonchalance for the sake of Christie's well-being. What on earth had happened to her in the time she was gone? It didn't bear thinking about.

The one and only saving grace was that she'd had a quiet word with the nurse whilst Christie had been wheeled away for her CT scan and had thankfully been given confirmation that there was no evidence of rape or sexual assault. Just because it hadn't happened yet didn't mean it wasn't going to at some stage if she hadn't escaped. Carrie felt pure rage starting to bubble beneath the surface.

She quickly shoved those thoughts to the back of her mind, led Christie towards the main road ready to cross and felt a sentimental wave wash over her when her daughter linked her arm to do so. She never had liked big roads and for just a nanosecond she saw Christie as a small child holding her hand whenever she was scared. Her throat choked almost inaudibly and she swallowed it down undetected.

They entered the café and both caved almost immediately to the temptation of freshly baked carrot cake presented gloriously in front of them like it was the winning entry of a bake-off style competition. Carrie ordered two slices, a cup of tea for Christie, black coffee for herself and a takeaway sausage roll for her husband, then they made their way over to the window seat so they could keep an eye out for his imminent arrival, whilst also indulging in a little people-watching.

"Hal's been messaging non-stop asking about you," Carrie informed Christie after they'd both taken their first scrumptious bite of cake.

Christie perked up at the sound of her big sister's name and washed down the cake with her tea so she could respond, "I thought about Hallie and the kids all day every day whilst I was away." Then she laughed at her own words as she'd only ever used them that way before when talking about people who'd either just got back from holiday or been incarcerated by the justice system. This entire situation, however, felt incredibly *un*just. "Thoughts of seeing them again were my motivation to get the hell outta there. I couldn't bear the thought of the kids growing up without their cool Auntie Christie being a terrible influence on them." She sniggered and Carrie returned the grin with a little snort added in as she remembered how Christie took great pleasure in encouraging the kids to act goofy and silly every time they were together.

"Hal took the news of you going missing really hard." Carrie felt the need to inform her daughter of how much she had been missed by the rest of the family. "She had to take a couple of days off work. She was in pieces. It didn't help the way they dramatized it all over the news. There was a huge media circus about it and a lot of uproar from people who felt passionate about the subject. I'm telling you all of this now to prepare you for what's coming – there are no doubt going to be a lot of people that will want to hear your side of the story. We were told very early on that the likelihood of finding you was slim at best."

Carrie paused and closed her eyes for a moment as though she was remembering the moment she had been given that piece of information. When her voice reappeared it had faltered ever so slightly and the raw emotion behind it was unmistakeable: "We were told that there had been many similar cases to this one in and around Barking and Dagenham, the last one had been closer to Becontree and then the perpetrators had gone quiet for a few weeks. None of those victims had ever been seen again and their families were devastated. They appeared in force to tell their individual stories in an attempt to spark up the search parties again and hopefully find their daughters – it was always women that were taken and they were always young, attractive women who appeared to live alone or with people who wouldn't particularly miss them if they were gone. It was like the abductors had stalked them and profiled them long before they snatched them, then picked the perfect moment to do so. It was sick." Carrie shuddered with a look of sheer disgust on her face.

"That's heavy. Is Hal OK now?" Christie hated hearing that Hallie had been so broken by the news that her little sister had gone missing. Hallie *never* took time off work; she was an extremely dedicated nurse, who felt pride and passion for her job and worked harder than most to care for her patients. This must have been a huge blow to cause a reaction like that.

"Oh, she's over the moon! She didn't know what on earth to tell the kids and the thought of even having that conversation with them was tearing her up inside. She was barely eating or sleeping. It was like talking to a robot when we facetimed her.

A robot who sometimes cried." That thought seemed to hang in the air as they both digested the conversation in silence and absentmindedly chewed on their carrot cake.

It didn't seem to have the same great taste now and Christie put hers back down on the flower patterned, china plate, having only consumed a third of it. Instead she sipped her tea gently and pondered the ripple effects that all of this had had. She felt incredibly glad that the other twelve captives found after she had escaped would no doubt be with their families and loved ones now, catching up on endless hugs and kisses, tears being shed left, right and centre. But that feeling was a double-edged sword and she couldn't help but wonder how many other families were out there pining away for the women they had lost to these ghastly men.

It was a lot to process.

She hadn't even noticed Carrie clicking away on her phone. "Your dad's just pulled up round the corner," her mother announced and they rose in unison. Carrie neatly stacked and lined their cups and plates up on the table to make it easier for the waitress to collect. They both called out a pleasant "Thank you" towards the server behind the counter and headed for the door.

"Do you want to come back to the flat with us?" Pete asked, unsure of how much his daughter needed her own time and space or needed to be around her family. He longed for her to say she would join them at their flat but also didn't want to put any pressure on her when he had just got her back. He waited in awkward and eager silence whilst she considered her options.

"Yes, please, I'm not sure if I'll stay the night but I don't feel like being alone just yet." Christie confirmed after having glanced at the clock. It was midday but she had no idea what day it was. The days and weeks had lost all meaning to her and all she could cling to was the digits on Pete's dashboard in front of her.

"Good." Pete nodded. He was a man of few words and he felt satisfied with her response. He started up the van, roared the engine a couple of times and then pulled out onto the busy road with a confidence that Christie had always admired but Carrie always cringed at because she was a nervous passenger.

Back at Pete and Carrie's luxurious and modern looking flat, surrounded by all of the latest technological creature comforts, Christie nestled herself into the corner of their long, beige, and leather sofa and rested her weary body completely into the arm and head rest. Carrie brought her over a cup of tea, put the TV on and flipped to one of the music channels as she knew how much her daughter was comforted by background noise at all times. Christie felt herself drifting off into sleep and didn't waste any time fighting it, simply allowing her heavy eyelids to make their way towards each other and her whole body to slump further into the comfort of the couch beneath her.

Chapter 5

She woke with a loud gasp of air. Her chest felt tightly constricted and it took a few seconds to catch her breath. Her eyes darted around their surroundings, trying to make sense of where the hell she was and who was breathing heavily in the room, close to where she was laying. Her mind spun into a jumbled frenzy and she had to work hard to calm herself down enough to properly take in the objects around her.

It was OK. She was in her parents' flat. She breathed a little deeper. Her dad was asleep at the other end of the sofa, head tilted backwards, mouth gaped open as though he was catching flies. She breathed a little more slowly. She was safe; no one was going to harm her. Two long, deep breaths in through the nose and out through the mouth.

She couldn't see her mum but assumed that Carrie had gone to her room to lay down. When she glanced over at the TV she noticed the channel had been changed and the news had just started. Her breath caught slightly as the very first news story that was reported on the show was of her escape from captivity and subsequent hospital stay. It was hard to focus on all of the various screen shots. There were photos of her flashing on screen that had obviously been used for search parties when they were still trying to find her, an extended film clip with a panoramic view of the exact location that she had been snatched from, slowly winding up with a beautiful female reporter describing the days' events in an over-the-top, yet sombre fashion, using highly emotive words purely for dramatic effect.

When the clip cut back to the studio, the newsreaders assured the viewers that they would bring them the latest updates as the story unfolds.

It was beyond weird hearing her story being reported by somebody else and from an entirely different perspective. They had barely even scratched the surface with what limited information they had so far and Christie's mind went straight into overdrive about how much questioning was going to be done – both of her and of any other witnesses over the coming weeks. She wondered how respectful and sensitive the reporters would be, given that it was such an emotional and disturbing subject matter.

Then she let out a loud snort to herself, rolled her eyes and shook her head because she knew that anyone trying to get any titbits of information to present on the media was going to be *far* from sensitive about it. She envisioned a flock of vultures circulating her, swooping in to peck at her dignity and snatch away any pieces of information that could be sensationalised in an over-the-top fashion for the sake of boosting media ratings or making sure her story went viral. The thought left a bad taste in her mouth and she leaned forward to retrieve the now cold, half drank cup of tea that Carrie had left on the coffee table in front of her just for something to wash it down with.

Pete stirred from the other end of the couch and looked confused at having woken up there. He looked at her through half open, bleary looking eyes, trying to make sense of the scene in front of him for a few seconds, the cogs almost visibly turning inside his skull, then gave her a warm grin of combined recognition and relief.

"All right?" he asked, as always, a man of few words.

"Yeah, I'm all right." Christie grinned only half-heartedly

back at him, feeling a little unsettled by thoughts of an impending media circus gate-crashing her life and disturbing her inner peace. "Do you think you could take me home, please? I really just wanna curl up in my own bed with my tunes on and make some sort of attempt to get back to normality. Though if this is anything to go by–" she nodded at the TV screen where her story had re-appeared once more after a brief round of adverts "–I very much doubt my life will be anything remotely close to normal for a *very* long time." She let that thought hang in the air whilst Pete gazed over at the screen and recognised the story immediately.

"If that's what you're sure you want." No matter how reluctant Pete was to see her go, the last thing he was going to do was impose a different form of captivity on his daughter after all she'd endured. "Can you do me a favour though?" he asked and then didn't wait for a response before continuing, "We've got a spare phone for you to use for now. Can you just drop me a text a couple a times a day to let me know you're still about?" He was kind of trying to make it into a joke but fully meant what he was saying. He felt a need for reassurance of her whereabouts and safety like never before.

"Of course." This time Christie's response came with a genuine, full and slightly emotional smile. She felt sincerely cared about and whilst that was such a beautiful feeling, it now came marred by the realisation that her loved ones must have gone through utter hell whilst she was away.

"Come on then, I'll let your mum know." Pete got up stiffly from the low height of the sofa and wandered down the hallway to let Carrie know that they were leaving and that he would be back soon. Carrie unexpectedly came back into the living room and handed Christie an older version of her iPhone.

"Here, I put a pay as you go sim in it that I still had left over from the last time your phone was stolen. I can top it up online and you can use that until your new sim and phone arrive." She helpfully instructed Christie, ever-prepared as always.

"Thanks, Mum," Christie just about managed to say before Carrie gave her a brief but tight hug, her arms fully encompassing her daughter's body in a way that she wasn't accustomed to from her mother, then she kissed her sweetly on the cheek.

The drive back to her HMO in Pete's van was surprisingly jovial and distracting. Pete was excellent at steering any conversation onto something more pleasant and light-hearted and he had Christie roaring with laughter for the first time in weeks. It slightly pained her sides and made her face ache, but it was the best kind of pain, which left her feeling both joyous and knackered at the same time.

As they pulled up next to the house Pete surprised her by getting out of the van instead of just letting her get out like he normally did. He walked around to the passenger side as she got out, wrapped her up in a tight and long, drawn-out bear hug, then kissed her on the cheek.

"Don't forget to text me," he reminded her.

She nodded back at him and confirmed, "I won't."

They both said "Love you" in unison and then cracked up for a few seconds before walking in opposite directions – him back to the driver's side of the van and her towards the neglected house she felt relieved to have in her sights for the first time in what felt like months.

Once inside, Christie made a beeline for her kettle and switched the radio on at the same time, feeling gratitude for the fact that none of her housemates were stirring nearby. The house was blissfully quiet. She busied herself making a cup of delicious Options white hot chocolate and changed into some comfy pyjamas adorned with Ariel the Little Mermaid designs, then climbed into bed to devour her treat.

Though it was difficult, she tried her best to ward off any swirling, chaotic and nightmarish thoughts of the events of the last few weeks and simply focused solely on breathing, slowly and deeply, whilst allowing the music in the background to transport her to fond memories of much happier and cheerful times.

She had long ago started practicing 'mindfulness' and used this as a tool to remember all of the things in her life that she felt thankful for: her freedom, her health, her family and friends, her strength and resilience against all odds…. She kept on adding to the list until she drifted off into sleep, wrapped snugly in her cosy duvet and watched over by her teddies.

She woke startled, panting and covered in sweat, her duvet twisted around her body like a large, hungry snake constricting its prey. It took a few seconds to wrestle herself free, flip the entire cover in half so that it was now only partially covering her body and place her hands on her chest to try to calm her breathing. Her dreams had been a demonic barrage of grotesque images, distorted faces and a feeling of inescapable constraint that she had bucked and kicked against to absolutely no avail.

Her jaw felt like she had been clenching it non-stop for hours and had now settled into a dull ache. Was this how she was going to find herself waking up every day from now until the end of time? The thought didn't bear thinking about. She rubbed the sleepiness out of her eyes and attempted to massage her achy jaw but that was of absolutely no use.

Instead she pushed herself away from the bed and wandered over to the kettle to make a cup of tea, mentally patting herself on the back for always keeping some Coffee Mate in her supplies, just in case of times when milk wasn't readily available. Whilst that was brewing she sent a quick text to her dad that read: "Morning! This is your notification that your daughter is still about" with a winking emoji and an "xx" at the end.

He quickly responded with a "Thank you", a thumbs up emoji and returned her "xx".

That felt odd but nice. This whole episode seemed to have spawned an entirely new dynamic within their family unit. She retrieved her iPad from underneath the bed and returned to a seated position underneath the covers, rested her tea on the windowsill and logged on to the crazy world of online media to see what was going on out there.

She felt a little bit of nervous dread creeping in but curiosity far outweighed that and she began by flicking through the ridiculously large amount of messages she had waiting for her on her social media accounts. There were so many heartfelt tributes to her from friends, far and wide, begging and praying that she would soon be found and returned safely, then these were later followed by a wave of messages expressing their relief at the news that she had escaped and returned to society. People kept saying things like "Let me know if you need anything at all, I'm here for you" and whilst that was a lovely sentiment, it seemed kind of redundant and lacking in any genuine substance.

Or perhaps she was simply over-thinking everything right now? How were people really expecting her to behave or respond at this time? Was she even expected to or would people have the good grace to respect her privacy for a while? This was unlike anything she'd ever gone through and she had no bench mark of appropriate behaviour or list of ways in which she should be conducting herself. She decided to post a blanket "Thank you" on her Facebook page, letting people know that she was OK but asking them to give her a little bit of space to come to terms with everything, then made a conscious effort to log out so that she wouldn't receive any further notifications until she was good and ready.

She focused a little bit of attention on her Instagram page, purely because in the past that had been the main way she and Dale had stayed in touch and she sent him a direct message letting him know she was safe and sound in her own home and her own bed, with a little tea cup emoji and a smile.

He replied almost instantly, as though he had been attached to his phone all morning and she realised the likelihood that he would have been hounded by people wanting to hear his side of the story. That thought made her cringe and she hoped that it hadn't been too invasive for him, then she remembered how well he had supposedly handled himself when being questioned by the police as to where he fit into Christie's reappearance and felt confident that he would show resilience against this too.

She felt like she was overthinking every minute detail right now – it was like a sensory overload, having gone from a space where nothingness filled her days to suddenly being thrust back into the real world where everything seemed to move at lightning speed. And this wasn't even technically the real world; this was just the digital world and she was merely playing catch up. What was going to happen the moment she stepped out of the door and had to face crowds of people? At that moment she could fully understand how and why people ended up suffering with agoraphobia. The idea of having to set foot outside was kind of terrifying and she wanted to curl up in the foetal position with her bears and not face any of it.

"Hey you! Thanks for letting me know. I've been worried about you." Dale's response snapped her out of her reverie, "How you holding up?"

"I'm doing all right, cheers." She tried her very best to sound light-hearted and happy when in reality she felt like there was a large, heavy weight sitting directly on her chest, making it difficult to breath. "It's just a little strange being back here and wondering what life is going to look like in the outside world." Christie had always felt like she could be completely honest with Dale and not be judged for what came out of her mouth, or in this case, typed with her fingers.

"I get that. Just remember you have so many people around you for support, myself included." He added with a winking emoji, "Any time you need to vent I'm here or if you just want someone to crack a dumb joke to take your mind off things, I'm your man." His earnest words radiated with compassion and she felt humbled to have such a sincerely kind and caring soul in her life.

"I seriously can't thank you enough for everything," was the best she could do in that moment to try to portray just how grateful she was. She knew it fell horrendously short of what she really wanted to say but she was too overcome with emotion to try to find better words.

"Pleasure to be of service, M'Lady," Dale quipped and Christie let out a loud and unexpected cackle.

They'd always had brilliant banter and she replied with, "Why thank you, my good Sir."

She then clicked off of that page in order to focus her attention on some news updates. This was something she wasn't remotely in the habit of doing – she felt the world was far too sucked in by media propaganda, feeding into people's fears and using those fears to herd them like lost sheep. In a way she preferred to live in her own little bubble, untainted or swayed by public opinion on most things.

This time it was different though. She was the subject matter of a widespread news story that had no doubt received an enormous amount of coverage whilst she was away and she wanted to prepare herself for what was to come. She felt trepidation at the looming onslaught of attention to her usually peaceful and tranquil life but knew deep down that it wasn't something she could run and hide from. She knew she would have to face up to it with as much strength as she had faced every other curveball life had thrown her way.

She took a deep, calming breath, jiggled her shoulders up and down a couple of times and logged on to the daily mail website first, basically taking a stab in the dark at which outlet to choose from. She was shocked by the sheer volume of different articles relating to this case alone. It was like it had taken over the news entirely, as more and more victims spoke out about their personal experiences, more and more family members of both the victims that had been found and of women who were still missing came forward to speak and the amount of the general public leaving comments on each article was also growing exponentially. It was mind boggling and bizarre to be viewing all of this for the first time considering she had lived the experience for the last few weeks and yet now found herself observing it all from a completely different perspective. She flicked from article to article, a lot of them with accompanying video clips of news reporters conducting interviews and watched each and every one of them. She felt compelled to hear as much of the other victims' stories as possible and also reminded herself to take what the reporters were saying with a pinch of salt as they obviously wanted to tease out the most shocking and disturbing aspects of the story in order to embellish it in the media.

She began by watching a couple of feel-good clips of families gathering around the hospital beds of those victims that were awake, well and recovering from the ordeal, with the help of the dedicated NHS doctors and nurses, sharing hugs and kisses and speaking into the camera with words of thanks for all those involved in locating their missing relatives and returning them safely to where they belonged. Christie then clicked on another video of a feisty looking young woman, covered in large, deep purple and blue bruising across her face and chest, standing outside the hospital, where she'd clearly just been discharged from. She had three men of varying ages and a woman flanking her, all with similar facial features that indicated they were related and all looking incredibly solemn as the young and beautiful, injured woman gave her responses to the questions being fired at her. She had a burning look of rage in her eyes as she described a harrowing story of her own failed attempt to escape captivity.

"You mentioned you weren't as lucky in your own escape attempt," came the concise and well enunciated voice of a male reporter, hidden from view, with both his microphone and several others pointed towards her, "Could you elaborate on that a little, please?"

"Sure, a couple of days before I was found by the raiding officers, I tried to make a break for it myself," explained the dark tanned skinned, green eyed, young woman, with a thick, Essex accent. "I caught one of the men, the younger one that normally brought me food, trying to fucking inject me in my neck with something and before he could, I backhanded the motherfucker by the side of his head and shoved him hard to the ground. The little wimp let out a bitchy cry for help in some other language and two of the bigger guys came running in to beat the shit outta me." Every time she swore, the editor had beeped it out but it was fairly obvious which curse word she was using each time. "They didn't hold back as you can see." She moved her head from side to side and rotated her body so that each angle of her neck and chest could be seen by the camera and therefore the viewers at home as well. The camera operator zoomed in to show the full effect of the dark bruising and then zoomed out again to her grim looking facial expression, full of contempt.

"At that point I felt like it was pointless, like I was done for, and I would never be found. I had no idea what those bastards were planning on doing with me and I felt helpless and alone." A shimmer of a tear threatened to roll its way down the side of her heavily bruised cheek, but she wiped it away defiantly, not wanting to come across as weak or emotional. Instead she looked directly into the camera and clearly said, this time with no swearing, "I wanna send a message to the woman who broke out and got us all help. Thank you so much from the bottom of my heart, you absolute diamond. And a huge thank you also to the police squad, who came in quickly and tore that place apart, the medical staff here at Queen's for patching me up and to my beautiful family, who never ever gave up hope."

The older, shorter woman with neatly braided hair standing next to her put her arm around what looked to be her daughter.

They exchanged grateful looking, warm smiles and one of the men, who was taller and only slightly older looking than she was, placed his hand protectively on her shoulder, which she then placed her opposing hand on top of. It was clear as day to see that their tightknit family bond had been strengthened even further by this traumatising and drawn-out ordeal.

Christie felt her own tears brimming and simply allowed them to freefall down her face as she was thankfully not standing in front of a camera, but safely tucked away under her cosy duvet for the first time in far too long. Once again, she mentally counted her lucky stars that she'd been able to fight her way out in one piece and get help for the others.

There were a couple of more video interviews that weren't quite as heart-warming in the same fashion, but still good news stories regardless. They were of young, previously homeless and drug addicted women, who had been snatched from the street and placed in captivity. There were no family or friends that had missed them and sent out search parties and thus, there was nobody by their side when they were subsequently placed in hospital after being found. One of them was clearly still quite incoherent about the whole affair and hooked up to multiple drips that were working hard to flush out her system. The other was a pale and extremely skinny, yet still delicately pretty woman, who was a little more aware of her surroundings and what had happened to her in the weeks leading up to her rescue. She sat on the edge of her hospital bed, politely answering questions from the sole reporter in front of her.

"How did it feel to be held against your will for so long?" asked the mature sounding, feminine voice from outside of the view of the camera.

"At first it was a nightmare. I was withdrawing badly 'cause I'm an addict. I've wanted to get off the stuff for a while now but when you're on the street, it's all that'll get you through the night." She candidly opened up, seemingly fearless of the views of her audience. "Then all of a sudden I was in this little room, rolling around on the bed and sweating 'cause I was clucking. I felt like climbing the walls but I was so weak too. The hours felt like days and the days felt like weeks.

"There was a skinny, young fella who brought me food that I didn't touch and also some sort of medication, which I did take. It slowly made me feel a little better physically but mentally I felt so depressed and alone. I just sat in a corner crying a lot of the time." She shook her head momentarily, seemingly in a dazed and far away mind set, remembering her own isolation and wondering how her life had come to this, then blinked her eyes a few times and continued, "It got easier the longer I was in there and I started to tell myself that even this was better than being out there on the street where anything could happen. It was the only thing that kept me going and I just sat and waited to see what my fate was gonna be. Then next thing I know, I'm being broken out by the cops and they brought me here to get better."

"Did that make you feel relieved?" pressed the reporter.

"I was surprised to see them and they all treated me so nicely. It wasn't the same as my other experiences with the cops; they all seemed happy to have found me still alive and kicking, then when they put me in their car, they were really gentle and kept telling me everything was gonna be OK." Her tone was demonstrating genuine shock at having been handled so carefully by the authorities, like it was something she was far from used to.

The camera was then angled so that both the mature, sophisticated reporter and the young, fragile woman were in view but only the reporter looked directly into the lens and spoke passionately: "*Both* of the homeless women found and rescued have now secured a bed space via the well-known charity for vulnerable females, Solace. There, they will receive all of the support they need to get their lives back on track after this horrifying incident and this support will continue throughout the coming months to ensure their recovery is both long and sustainable. *All* of the women that were found as a result of the police raid on the abandoned farm will be provided with specialised, ongoing one-to-one counselling, as well as regular group therapy if they would like to utilise it."

That was music to Christie's ears, not just for herself and her own mental health, but for the rest of the victims and also their families. She knew all too well the danger of leaving any type of trauma unaddressed – in the past, unresolved issues had come back to haunt her in extremely non-subtle manifestations. The sooner they all put in the work to address the atrocious events that had taken place over the last few weeks, the better for everybody.

She flicked over to other related pages, read more articles and watched more videos. Public opinion on the whole affair was an enormous spectrum of completely differing perspectives, arguments, ideas of who was to blame and what should have been done and when by the authorities. She didn't understand the logic of playing the blame game one bit. People do bad things every day and it's not up to the rest of us to start pointing the finger and shifting the responsibility onto others. Really the most important issue that needed to be addressed was recovery from the unfathomable ripple effect that this nightmare had had. Lessons needed to be learned and acted upon to ensure cases like this one are stamped out before they have a real chance to take root and go so deep at any point in the future.

She was suddenly stopped in her tracks by the haunted, ghost-white look of a young, stylish and impeccably polished female reporter standing next to the very same abandoned farm on which she had been held captive. The entire backdrop looked like a town's worth of people had descended upon it and tore it to shreds. There were holes in the ground, piles of freshly dug soil next to them, digging machinery on the outskirts of the farm now that had clearly been hard at work before that, multiple witnesses to the action milling around, all with grim looking expressions on their faces. The female reporter ever so gently wiped a stray strand of her neatly styled, straight, brunette hair away from her forehead but the dramatic effect of that tiny action made it seem like she had been sweating profusely due to the stress of the ordeal of being there. She looked solemnly into the camera and in a slow and careful tone described the scene behind her, where five decomposing bodies had been unearthed throughout the course of tearing the farm apart for evidence.

Christie gasped hard and couldn't seem to close her jaw back together with the shock of it, so she placed her hand over her gaping mouth and tried harder to focus on what was being delivered by the reporter.

"Medical staff and police are now working hard behind the scenes to identify the five female victims so that their families and loved ones can get the closure they both desire and deserve. It's been a weighty and incredibly distressing day for many onlookers as the shocking findings have been uncovered." As the reporter finished her sentence, the camera swept over the mutilated graveyard and focused on the sombre faces of nearby witnesses, some of whom were still shedding tears and appeared quite shaken by what they had seen.

The reporter then handed the story back over to the two newsreaders sitting comfortably in their studio, far away from the painful scene and they further added that ongoing searches were taking place as a result of evidence found within the main building at the farm. They had uncovered and seized a decent amount of computer equipment, which was now being digitally hacked into in an attempt to find out where any previous victims had been shipped to once they had been either sold or traded by this hideously immoral trafficking ring. They had the most specialised I.T. staff flexing their highly tuned skills to decode as much information as they could possibly get out of the machines and feed it back to the police.

Christie's mind boggled at the sheer volume of people involved in working on this case. Not only was there the super-fast acting task force that had descended upon the abandoned farm as soon as they had received her voice recordings; then the team involved in the line-up and questioning (and probably a whole host of different stages in between that she knew nothing of) and now a host of specialised tech nerds breaking into the seized computers and storage devices and filtering through all of the evidence. Then what? A whole troop of other officers assigned to locating the victims, arresting their buyers, most likely uncovering more and more criminal circles as they went along and taking them down too?

She shook her head in amazement and wondered hopefully that they must get major job satisfaction from cases such as this. Surely it's the type of work that would earn a person a commendation for their efforts? She sat and pictured the various law enforcement staff going home to their families and telling them over dinner how hard they'd worked and how it had gotten results.

Her mind further wandered to the prospect of them actually being able to hack into specific details about previous transactions made, thereby allowing them to follow a trail that might lead to the recovery of further victims. She pondered what they would have been through after they had been sold to the highest bidder and what kind of traumatised mental state that would leave them in. A harsh shiver ran through her entire body as she decided that it was highly likely that what they had been subjected to was far worse than what she had suffered. The outfit she had been dressed in before she escaped was a clear indication of what was going to be expected of her on the other side of her own 'transaction'. How many other women had been put in similar costumes and shipped off to serve beastly men, performing grotesque and degrading acts at their beck and call? The thought made her wretch a little and she suddenly felt very cold.

Before she found herself tumbling down a rabbit hole of sickening thoughts, Christie gave herself one of her infamous self-pep talks, reminding herself of the victories so far. Breaking herself free and even managing to throw a couple of punches in the process – this was something she had *never* done as violence was terrifying to her and she avoided it at all costs. She successfully got helpful evidence to the right people in the quickest time possible with twelve other victims being freed as a result. The finding of five bodies was absolutely tragic but it did at least give their families closure as opposed to a lifetime of not knowing. Now there was the chance that further victims may be found and rescued; plus the gang of despicable traffickers had been stopped in their tracks and thrown behind bars. If that delightful list of achievements wasn't worth celebrating, then she had no idea what was.

She suddenly realised she had been staring at the screen for hours, reading through such a vast variety of articles and watching news clip after news clip. It had left her eyes feeling dry and sore, plus she felt the need to get up and do a few yoga poses to stretch her stiff body out.

Once suitably flexed, she made herself a cup of tea and picked up the phone she'd almost entirely forgotten about off the bed. There was a message on there from Carrie that had been sent an hour and forty-seven minutes ago, simply asking, "How are you feeling? xx"

She started to type out a reply but only got a couple of words into the first sentence when the phone rang and 'Mum' flashed up on the screen.

"Hey, I was just replying to you," Christie answered the call with.

"Yeah, I know, I saw the animated speech bubble on my screen and I figured it would just be easier to call," replied Carrie.

"Everything OK?" asked Christie, wondering what the sense of urgency was all about.

"Everything's fine. It's just that we've had a call from the powers that be at Romford police station. They wanted your number but when I asked what it was regarding, I said no to that request until after I've had a chance to speak to you to gauge where your head's at right now." That sentence made Christie's stomach drop and an enormous feeling of dread fill the gap.

"Go on..." She left her request at that, bracing herself for what was about to come next.

"It's nothing to panic about. It's just that they are intending to hold a press conference to address the current media circus that's built up around your case. They wanted to ask you how comfortable you would feel being personally involved and answering some questions from the reporters," Carrie carefully explained, "Please know that this is *not* required of you; this is *your* choice to make and nobody would judge you if you simply said no because you need privacy right now, OK?"

Christie took a long, deep breath and let the oxygen sit inside her lungs for a few seconds, carefully weighing up her options and trying to picture what it would be like to stand in front of a crowd of people firing questions at her. She had no idea how unbridled they would be in their desperation to hear her raw and vulnerable side of the story. Would they respect her boundaries at all? Should she have boundaries? Or should she lay it all bare for the world to hear? People should know the dark and twisted things that other humans are capable of. But they should also hear the light at the end of the tunnel, the fact there *are* people out there willing to put their neck on the line to help their fellow man. People needed to hear the amazing effort that had been done to take the evidence she had provided and turn it into a highly effective rescue mission, plus were now extending that effort even further, leaving no stone unturned, no victim left behind.

"Christie?" Carrie sounded slightly worried on the other end of the call and Christie realised she'd been holding her breath for much longer than she'd originally anticipated. She let it out in one long, controlled stream from her nostrils, loud enough to be heard on the other side.

"Absolutely," she said resolutely, "One hundred per cent I

would like to be involved."

"Are you sure? Like I said, nobody would judge you for saying no." Carrie seemed to be doing her best to talk Christie out of it but she also knew how strong willed her daughter could be. When Christie made up her mind about something, she was a force to be reckoned with if you were going to attempt to stand in her way. They had clashed over their own stubborn natures many, many times in the past and this time she decided that she wouldn't force her opinion on this warrior of a woman that had not only survived such a horrific ordeal, but come out of it fighting and with her head held high. She marvelled at the person her daughter had matured into.

"Yes," replied Christie, "I'm not afraid to stand up and tell my story. Who knows who it might help?" It was more of a question to herself that she had said out loud, her inner voice urging her to do all that she possibly could to provide assistance to those that needed it, comfort to some and closure to others.

Hell, she didn't even care how many viewers utilised this platform as a source of entertainment – if it got people talking about the nightmare she had gone through and therefore putting in preventative steps to stop similar situations from taking place then she would happily cater to that insatiable human need or desire for gossip, for a good story, for the shock factor of the capabilities of a twisted mind to spawn an entire operation of evil deeds and recruit others to assist them in carrying those deeds out.

"OK, I'll let them know and we can make arrangements together." There was a slight pause from Carrie and she added, "If you like?" She wanted to make sure her daughter was comfortable every step of the way.

"That would be great, thanks, Mum." It dawned on Christie just how much she appreciated the fact that her mother was being so considerate of her feelings and not just wading in to take control of the situation, as she always had done in the past. In that moment she felt truly loved and cared for, like if at any stage she felt like she wanted to hide away from the world, she would have somewhere to turn to and do that. She wasn't *going* to do that, but it was nice to have the option.

"No problem, I'll call you back after I've spoken to them, OK? Love you." She signed off the call to go about making arrangements. The concept, in itself, was completely alien to Carrie. Calling up to arrange a press conference? Life sure did take some funny twists and turns.

Christie got up, took a long stretch and decided to shower and make herself presentable in order to face the day feeling fresh and prepared. She always liked to blast Kiss 100 on the radio whilst she got ready and enjoyed the light-hearted banter amongst the DJs whilst they played uplifting music that she could shake her hips to.

She got about two songs in and realised the music wasn't remotely reflecting her mood at that stage, switched the radio off and instead opted for her "Deep" playlist on Spotify, that contained an entire spectrum of styles and artists, but mostly aired towards heavy metal, rock ballads and indie. That felt far more fitting and she busied herself washing and drying her hair, applying some light eye make-up and getting dressed. It felt unbelievably good to be doing normal, routine things, like little by little, she was piecing herself back together and it wouldn't be too long until she was back to her normal self.

That thought was quite short lived as she wandered through to the kitchen to wash up her mug and took a glimpse out of the large window that looked out on to the main road. She gasped loudly at the sight of swarms of reporters waiting outside on the street below the first floor window. How long had they been standing there? Who'd given them her address? How brutal and imposing would they be when it came to bombarding her with questions? The thought of celebrities being terrorised and utterly traumatised by the paparazzi sprung to mind and shocked her to her very core. She didn't feel even a tiny but prepared for this, certainly not alone anyway.

She backed slowly down the hallway towards her bedroom in a little bit of a daze and made a beeline for her iPad when she got safely behind her closed and locked door.

She logged back on to her Instagram account and sent a message to Dale, "Hey, have you been hounded by any reporters over what happened?" she asked, feeling about ninety-five per cent sure that she already knew the answer. She left the app open and waited nervously for him to write back, all the while her brain going into overdrive about what her life was going to be like from now on. She laughed ironically at her earlier naivety about getting herself back to a sense of normality.

Nothing was ever going to be normal again, at least not the way she had known it. For the last two or three years she had lived a fiercely independent life and kept herself to herself, only letting a *very* select group of people get close in order to protect her own boundaries and sense of inner peace. Now there was an entire troop of people waiting just outside her front door, ready to pounce and seize the opportunity to infringe upon her privacy – one of the few things she treasured and protected the most. A wave of relentless anxiety swept over her and settled itself in the pit of her stomach. Her breathing started to get slightly more erratic and she felt herself having to work hard to try to control it and return it back to its normal rhythm.

A few minutes passed by and her breathing had become less weighted and arduous. She saw a message notification pop up from Dale in response to hers: "Yeah, a lot actually. I'm sure they've been a lot worse with you though. Are you OK?"

"I've only just seen a crowd of them outside my house; I haven't actually talked to them yet," Christie explained, "Mum called earlier and told me they want to set up a press conference and I sort of left that in her hands to arrange." She added in a gritted teeth emoji to represent her own nervous state.

"I've been approached about that too," Dale added, "I guess they'll come back to me and let me know the date and time your mum has set it up for? I dunno." He inputted a shoulder shrugging emoji.

"I'd like it if you were there too, that'd make me feel heaps better." Christie surprised even herself by so openly admitting how vulnerable she was feeling. She was normally incredibly guarded about those things and liked to put on a brave face under any challenging circumstances. With Dale it was different, she felt completely at ease letting him see that she was worried and would rather have someone she trusted by her side.

"Then I'll be there whether they want me to be or not," he replied decisively.

Christie's jaw unclenched and she grinned from ear to ear, a large sigh of relief escaping her lungs and her shoulders returning down to their natural, relaxed position. It suddenly felt a lot less scary and she no longer felt like making a mad dash out of her bedroom window, scaling down the back of the house and into a nearby alley way that led out onto a different cul-de-sac. She felt like she could hold her head high and face whatever questions the world had to throw at her.

"You have no idea how much I appreciate that," she responded with a hugging emoji at the end of her sentence.

"Any time," he responded immediately, "I mean it, Christie, you need me, and you let me know. I'll be there."

Those words made her feel overwhelmingly looked after and she felt a few tears spring up at the corners of her eyes. Where once she would have rolled her eyes, shook her head to shrug off the oncoming tears and light-heartedly told herself to stop being such a soppy cow, she instead allowed them to roll down her cheeks and merely accepted that she was going to be on a rollercoaster of emotions for the foreseeable future.

It was important to remind herself at all times that she was only human and what she had been through was enough to bring down the strongest willed people. She was allowed to be raw, messy and even gave herself permission to be highly strung if that's the way she felt. She needn't hide what she was going through or be ashamed by it and most importantly, she reminded herself that she *must* reach out for help when she needed it. She didn't have to face any of this alone and trying to do so would most likely be to her own detriment. Why on earth would she want to make life any more difficult for herself than it had to be? She needed to let her guard down and allow those that cared for her to do just that – care.

With that resolution in mind, she picked up the phone and dialled Pete's number. Her parents' mobile phone numbers had both been permanently etched on her brain since the age of ten or eleven, which was extremely useful in emergency circumstances. It rang three times before he answered, "Is everything OK?" His voice sounded slightly urgent.

"Everything's fine." Christie reassured him, "It's just that there is a huge group of reporters outside my house and I felt a little nervous going out there alone." She suddenly felt very self-conscious and once again had to remind herself that this was an important part of her individual healing journey – getting used to asking for help from those around her. "Do you think you could come and get me when you've got a spare moment? No rush or anything."

"I've actually finished a little bit early today and just dropped Tom off at Harold Wood station," Pete replied in reference to his trainee, the sounds of traffic echoing in the background, indicating he had her on speakerphone in his van. "I can be there in about fifteen to twenty minutes so if you wanna pack a bag and stay at ours for a couple of nights…or really, however long you want, then feel free. It's your call."

He was trying his very hardest to sound nonchalant but inside he was hoping and praying that his daughter would take him up on that offer. He wanted her close by and had hated every part of dropping her off at her unsecure, dingy, little HMO yesterday. She needed protection right now but he didn't want to force that on her for fear of her shutting him down and defiantly digging her heels in. Granted, he did have a lot of respect for his daughter's strong-willed nature, but there was a time and a place for it and now was not that time. Now was the time to allow him to support her.

"Thanks, Dad. I'll see you soon. Love you," she responded and hung up the phone, then immediately emptied the backpack she normally carried her work things around in and began filling it with a couple of changes of clothes, some make-up and a few toiletries. She knew she could get away with packing light because her mum always kept spare underwear, pyjamas, toiletries and hair styling tools at their place for when she stayed over for a night or two. That had been only on very rare occasions up until this point, but now she was incredibly grateful for her mother's ever-prepared quality. Plus she knew she'd be in for a treat on the dining front as Carrie happened to be an exceptional cook and even Pete had recently been learning a few culinary tricks from his wife. She actually felt genuinely excited about the prospect of having all her needs catered for, even if only for a little while and also under incredibly abnormal circumstances.

Roughly twenty minutes later, she received a text from Pete saying he'd parked in the road opposite her house and to come downstairs so she followed his instruction and met him at her front door, backpack slung lightly over her shoulder, ready to make a quick dash through the crowd, over the road and into his van.

"All right?" She nervously grinned at him as she opened the door to see him standing directly in front of her, surrounded by loud and quite invasive reporters, all shoving their microphones in her direction and yelling out a barrage of mixed questions. It was hard to decipher one singular question in order to respond and the clicking and whirring sounds of nearby cameras was too distracting to even attempt to focus.

"Yeah, you ready?" he asked hopefully and when she nodded back at him he spun his body around to face the reporters in a fatherly, protective stance.

"We would appreciate some dignified privacy at present," he announced, practically and without hesitation, "A press conference is being arranged so that you can all ask your questions one at a time." He left it there and made a straightforward arm gesture to signify that he wished them to clear his path and allow him to take his daughter out of that situation. The reporters in front and either side of him only moved a fraction out of the way and so he took a large, confident step forward, simultaneously grabbing Christie's hand and leading her forwards too.

Some of the reporters took the hint and slowly drifted backwards and away from the rest, others lingered but looked a little awkward doing so, then one boisterously determined male reporter forced his way from the back of the group to the very forefront, shoved his microphone in front of Pete's face and asked, "Sir, what are your personal feelings towards the men currently being held by the police over the abduction and captivity of your daughter?" His tone was unapologetically aggressive and body language indicative of a fellow who was not remotely phased by the idea of ruffling a few feathers in order to get the results he wanted.

Pete stopped in his tracks, looked the man directly in the eye, then he shifted his gaze towards the camera operator that appeared to be accompanying this narcissistic reporter. He took one pointed step towards the reporter, as though he was squaring up to him, ready to take him down, but instead faced the camera lens and said, "I hope they get their come-uppance."

With that, he shut down any further questioning by ignoring any of the follow-up, feverish shouts from the rest of the crowd, tugging Christie through the mania, across the road and into the relative safety of his large, black VW transit. He buckled himself in, made sure Christie was too and revved up the meaty sounding engine before assertively pulling away and forcing the crowd to retreat backwards and away from them.

"Well, that was something!" he joked and cackled darkly after they got a couple of minutes into the journey back to his and Carrie's place.

Christie chuckled. "You could say that." She shook her head and then added, "I really appreciate you coming to get me and for fighting my corner."

"That's what I'm here for," he said with a nod and a shrug, seemingly unflappable but she knew deep down that he honourably and affectionately liked the fact that she had asked him for help. He *wanted* to be there but on her own terms.

By the time they got back to the flat it was late afternoon and Carrie was in the process of tying up her workload too. She had been working from home ever since the COVID-19 travel restrictions had come into play and it looked like that would be her arrangement for the foreseeable future seeing as though her job role was so admin heavy. It suited her just fine no longer having to deal with public transport to get to the city five days per week, plus she had a penchant for online shopping and being at home allowed her to take deliveries far more efficiently.

Somewhere in the middle of working and finding out that Christie would be coming over, she had started preparing a delightful smelling meal for them all to sit down to together. The aroma of chicken stuffed with garlic and camembert and wrapped in bacon wafted down the hallway as soon as they stepped over the threshold to enter the flat.

This place was previously a place that made Christie feel trapped and like she had to walk on eggshells the entire time she had stayed there. She'd always felt on edge and like she wasn't really welcome, so getting away from there and seeking out her own treasured independence had been a massive game changer for her and she'd flourished as a result.

Today, however, this place did not make her feel edgy or constricted. She did not feel the need to break free from any metaphorical shackles; she felt calm, cosy even. She felt like a student coming home from university to settle back into the home life that they'd missed dearly during term time. She knew very well that it was just a temporary measure until things on the outside world died down a little but it was such a wonderful feeling that she didn't waste her time over analysing any of it.

Carrie had yelled out a "Hello!" and an "I'll be with you shortly" from her office space and the sound of her tapping away on her keyboard had been the only audible sound coming from that vicinity for the next half an hour or so. Pete and Christie made themselves comfortable on their luxurious couch, with cups of tea in mismatched mugs and Pete was distracting her as best as he could by providing a highly insightful commentary on a TV program where couples bought derelict buildings in obscure locations and made them over before selling them on. It was a subject matter Christie knew absolutely nothing about so she relished in hearing her dad speak so passionately about what he would do differently if he was in that situation.

Carrie came through to the living room to join them and let out a big, dramatic sigh, as though the day had weighed heavy on her shoulders.

"Tomorrow morning is when the press conference will take place. Is that OK with you?" she directed at Christie. "I've taken the day off work so I will be there with you the entire time, as much or as little as you need my involvement, I'll still be there."

"That's great," replied Christie, totally impressed by the speed with which Carrie had been able to pull those arrangements off. "The sooner I get it outta the way, the better in my eyes. Dale said he's been approached about it too – I'll message him in a minute and find out if they've contacted him with the time and location."

Carrie snorted. "I bet he's been inundated with nosey reporters wanting to know the ins and outs of your relationship with him and how you ended up outside the shop he works in." She then looked at Christie a little too closely, as though she was inspecting her reaction and waiting for some sort of giveaway.

"Yeah..." Christie let out her own drawn-out sigh and her shoulders slumped. "I've been worried about that; it makes me feel bad that his life may be being massively intruded upon by anybody just 'cause he helped me."

Carrie scoffed loudly at that. "Don't you for one second feel bad about any of this. We're all just glad to have you back and we will all deal with the media circus as and when it unfolds around us. And hey, worst case scenario, it's free publicity for the shop," she added in a pragmatic tone. "We'll leave here at 8:30 and go to Romford in a cab. I'm not wasting any unnecessary time on public transport – it's too risky right now." Her tone had switched to business-like, then she went through to the adjoining kitchen area and busied herself preparing the accompaniments to the lovely chicken dinner.

Christie pulled her iPad out of the backpack she'd discarded on the floor next to the couch, opened up her Instagram and messaged Dale, "Yo, we're hitting up Romford in the morning for the press conference. Did anyone contact you?"

He replied seven minutes later, "Yeah, your people called my people." He added a winking emoji and she let out a loud cackle. Pete glanced over with an interested expression but was then swiftly distracted by a commotion on the TV involving the accidental knocking down of the wrong section of a dining room wall and let out his own hysterical laughter.

Christie composed herself and replied, "Ha! See you tomorrow."

To which Dale wrote back, "See you then."

Chapter 6

Later in the evening, they sat down to the first family dinner they'd had without the need for a special occasion, such as Christmas or a birthday, in a very long time. It was a mixture of calm, peaceful quiet, with the occasional compliment to the chef and an overall sense of weary relief. The events that had led to this tranquil moment had taken their toll on all three of them and they retired to their beds almost immediately after the meal was over.

Before she went into their bedroom, Carrie promised Christie that she would message Hallie and let her know of what had gone on, then tell her that they'd put in a joint facetime session tomorrow, after they'd had a chance to recover from the press conference. That filled Christie with an enormous amount of joy – the thought of seeing her big sister, and hopefully her beautiful kids too, was something that always brought her a great deal of happiness.

Christie slept a lot more soundly than she had done the previous night but still woke up in a panicked sweat, which was exasperated by the change in her surroundings. It took her a few minutes to collect herself and her manic thoughts, as she could feel liquid running down the back of her neck, all the way to the base of her spine and droplets of it making their way from her forehead down the sides of her face. She felt sticky and kind of gross but ultimately grateful for the scene around her. It was nice to wake up and not feel imprisoned, defeated, lacking in hope and simultaneously terrified for the future. She counted each and every one of her blessings – freedom being at the very top of that list.

Pete had already left for work and both Carrie and Christie got themselves ready for the day ahead in separate rooms with only minimal interaction in between. They were both a little disappointed, but not remotely surprised, to see a gaggle of reporters waiting for them outside the main entrance to the block of flats and it was a minor struggle to push their way through to the patiently waiting cab that had parked mere metres away in order to provide the easiest transition possible.

Carrie had placed a call to the police station ahead of their departure and as a result, Sue and Kate, the officers that had originally questioned Christie, were there waiting for them with welcoming smiles plastered on their faces. They were given hot, caffeinated drinks and taken to the closest interrogation room to sit and chat informally about what was going to take place. It was apparently something that the station itself had to be 'home' to on a fairly frequent basis, particularly during such high-profile cases as this one, so there was a large board room dedicated to the event. There would be a long desk situated at one side of the room with places for Christie, Dale and Carrie to sit, accompanied by the officers at either side, like book ends. They would have microphones placed in front of them at the table so that everything they said in response to the questions asked could be heard clearly and recorded.

"Try not to be too phased by the recording aspect of it," added in Kate, spotting an alarmed expression on Carrie's face. "Just be as natural as you can and respond honestly. People are keen to see what it's like from the victim's perspective; they're not here to trip you up or point fingers. The recording is so that it can be transcribed later. We want you to be authentic...but watch the swear words," she added, winking at Christie, who chuckled mildly as she did have a tendency to swear a lot and Kate had become privy to her terrible potty mouth during her interview.

There was a short, sharp knock at the door and another police officer poked his head into the room. He was a young, androgynous man, who looked better suited to being a member of a boy band and seemed very enthusiastic about being involved in any part of this case, as though he was trying hard to earn his stripes.

"Excuse the interruption, Ma'am, I've brought along your third witness, as instructed," he informed Sue, looking akin to an eager puppy expecting a pat on the head.

"Cheers, Gherard," Sue replied affectionately, "Bring him in."

Dale entered the room, politely thanking the young officer as he breezed past him, and Kate retrieved the extra chair that had been pushed into one of the corners of the room and placed it at the end of the table, next to Christie. He greeted the two officers and Carrie with a handshake and a "Nice to see you again", then turned his attention to Christie and gave her a brief hug and a peck on the cheek before sitting down in the chair next to her. They exchanged relieved grins and it was obvious that they were genuinely happy to see each other.

Sue repeated what Kate had said about the recording purely for Dale's benefit and he nodded his understanding, then she added, "We've let the reporters know that the main purpose of this press conference is for us to handle the majority of the questions." She gestured between herself and Kate. "We've encouraged them to ask us about the success of the raid, the numerous arrests, the seizure of property, the upcoming trial and so on. However, they will obviously want to get some more gossipy tit bits from the three of you, and I want you all to know that you are under no obligation to answer anything that makes you feel remotely uncomfortable."

At that point she placed a hand gently on top of Christie's, which was resting on the table and looked her in the eye with a pointedly serious expression. "You are not a source of entertainment – you are a survivor and a hero. Do not let anyone push you for answers to things that are only serving to dramatize what you've been through. Give them as much or as little as *you* feel comfortable with and we'll handle the rest."

Christie nodded and said, "OK," feeling glad for the reassurance and almost familial protection from the two female officers, but also a little apprehensive. She decided to keep that part of herself under wraps and paint on her warrior face, as though all of this was no big deal.

"Great." Sue rose from the desk and Kate swiftly joined her in an upright position. "We're going to go and make sure everything and everyone are prepped and ready to go. You guys wait here and Kate will come back to get you in about ten minutes or so."

They began to walk out the door and Carrie asked if she could use the toilet quickly, so they led her out as well to show her the way to the facilities.

As soon as the door was shut, Dale turned to Christie and said, "Come here and give me a proper cuddle." A boyish grin spread across his handsome, kind face as he stood up and spread his arms out. Christie's expression morphed into a beaming grin and she didn't hesitate for a second before standing up to accept his earnest gesture, tucking herself neatly into his shoulder and allowing his arms to envelope her completely.

"It's really good to see you," was all she needed to say and they stood quietly, breathing peacefully against each other's bodies, taking in the scent, the warmth and enjoying the embrace for a couple of minutes.

Eventually he softly rubbed her back three times before pulling his upper body away to look into her eyes. "How you feeling? ...*Really?*" He heavily emphasised the "really" part of the question.

"Ummm... a bit overwhelmed but I can handle it," came her truthful response. She wouldn't admit that to anyone else but felt safe to do so with him.

"I know you can. You're without a doubt one of the toughest women I know." He gave both her shoulders a tight, sincere squeeze. "Just don't put any unnecessary pressure on yourself, OK? I've got your back and those three seem to have it too." He nodded at the door behind her.

Carrie and Kate must have been making their way back to the interrogation room at the same time as they both appeared at the door and it became immediately clear that it was show time. All four of them left the room feeling slightly nervous and fell into silence as they walked down the corridor towards the large board room. The tension in the air was almost palpable.

They entered to be greeted by the flashing of cameras, the whirring of recording equipment and the growing murmur of the audience in front of them. There was a raised stage with a long desk situated on top facing the crowd of reporters, allowing the five speakers to address the throng from a slightly elevated vantage point and also allowing more people to cram into the audience.

Sue had risen at the opposite end of the long desk she had

been sitting at, waited for the four newcomers to be seated first, addressed the crowd of reporters to let them know they could begin their line of questioning and then sat down herself.

The first few questions fired were surrounding the raid of the abandoned farm. The reporters wanted to know all of the details about how they were able to locate it so quickly and strike so efficiently when all of the previous search parties that had been sent out for the victims had fallen flat.

Sue precisely and factually described the process of providing Dale with her contact details at the hospital, receiving the voice notes via WhatsApp after Christie had woken up and recorded them, playing them to her team and one of their most recent recruits recognising the description of the farm, then the running of the number plates through the system and how it had led them to identifying two of the men that they later found at the farm itself. Everything had linked up perfectly once they knew where to look and from there it had been the uncovering of one stone after the other.

More and more questions were fired regarding the other captives that were found, the deceased bodies that were unearthed, what was being done to support their families and what was being done to trace the victims that had been trafficked to a number of unknown locations. Both Sue and Kate handled the barrage in a cool and concise manner, alternating between which of them would answer depending on who had the most up-to-date information relating to each question. It was almost like a choreographed performance between them, a well-practiced dance to entertain the hungry masses of gossip seeking media professionals.

A tall, Caucasian, athletic looking male reporter who

seemed to tower above most of the crowd directed his enquiry towards Carrie: "How did it feel when you found out your daughter was alive and well?"

"I was utterly shocked at first," replied Carrie, "We had been told on several occasions that the likelihood of us ever seeing her again was extremely low, that there had been a number of similar cases that had been left unresolved and I just didn't see how Christie's case would be any different—"

The reporter cut her off before she could finish what she was saying, "You mean you'd given up all hope of ever being reunited with her?"

"Not *all* hope," Carrie clarified, a faint shade of crimson suddenly flushing in her cheeks, "It just seemed like the odds were stacked against us and it was awful. I spent the first week in uncontrollable tears and not being able to sleep at night. I was forced to try and get used to the fact that the next time we heard anything about her it wouldn't be good news."

Carrie's voice broke a couple of times whilst attempting to answer that question. She had wracked herself with all manner of guilt after Christie's disappearance and this was simply wrenching all those feelings back to the surface. She felt flustered and embarrassed by the oncoming threat of tears in such a public setting, especially one that was being filmed. She cried so very rarely and when she did, it was in private, even away from her husband's view. Now she was sitting in front of what suddenly felt like a global audience and the feelings of panic started to rise up in her chest.

The reporter started to push another question in her direction and Sue immediately cut him off. "Let's move on to another line of questioning now, please," she said with a slightly raised left eyebrow and a stern tone, similar to that of a teacher telling off a wayward pupil. The reporter nodded humbly, backing down.

Further back and to the right, a tiny, Asian female reporter, who was barely visible due to her disadvantage in height, aimed her question towards Dale. "Sir, did you have any inclination of the state Christie was in when you found her, based on how she presented? Were you aware that she was heavily under the influence of narcotics?" The question had a vaguely accusatory tone to it. What was she implying here? Was she trying to villainise the man who had come to Christie's rescue and gallantly refused to leave her side until he was sure that she was in the best hands possible and that he was no longer needed? Dale's face looked pained in that moment, as he recalled how confused and frightened Christie had been that day. He had wanted to wrap her up in a protective cocoon where the evils of the world couldn't touch her and even the mere thought of somebody wishing to cause her harm was sickening to him. He'd told her before that he'd never met a stronger, more resilient woman than she was and he had meant that but seeing her looking so fragile in the moment when he had ran up to her on the bench outside the shop had been a terrible shock to his system.

"Yes, it became clear very quickly to me that Christie wasn't herself," he replied, choosing his words carefully, "I didn't know what had been done to her or what was in her system to make her behave the way that she was behaving. The fact that she couldn't even remember who I am was alarming as we've spent a large number of hours together at the shop whilst I've tattooed her. You learn a lot about a person during that process and the woman I met on the bench was not the Christie I know." He paused and looked at Christie with a sympathetic smile, which she returned to him.

She was so grateful for him being there for her in that moment and this was the first time she was hearing the experience from his perspective. It was hard to imagine herself coping as well as he did if she'd have been presented with that same situation in reverse. He handled it like a total pro and she reminded herself to make sure he fully understood just how much she appreciated it.

Dale continued, "I'm just so relieved that she managed to somehow find her way to the shop where I could get to her and then get her the help she needed. I shudder to think what on earth may have happened had she ended up anywhere else in the mind set she was in." He visibly grimaced and the flashing of the cameras highlighted the haunted look on his face as he pictured the worst possible case scenarios.

"If she was as out of it as you're describing, how do you suppose she was able to make it in one piece to the bench outside Vogue Vintage? It's a little *too* much of a coincidence, wouldn't you say, given your history with the victim?" came the obnoxious voice of a stout, middle aged, male reporter close to the front of the crowd. He was wearing a mocking expression that looked as though he didn't buy a single word of Dale's story.

Murmurs rippled through the crowd, the flashing of the cameras picked up speed and microphones jostled against each other to get the best vantage point to pick up his response to the intrusive and almost accusatory questions.

"I can't answer that. I'm no scientist." Dale shrugged casually, cool as a cucumber. "The mind's subconscious is a powerful thing and Vogue Vintage is obviously a place where Christie feels safe. Perhaps she's part homing-pigeon?" he joked.

A tremor of stifled laughter rumbled through the crowd and Dale humbly half nodded in appreciation. He really was the master of winning over any crowd he addressed and Christie beamed at him in admiration.

"Christie, we've heard a few testimonies from the other victims that were found awaiting their fate on the abandoned farm, but this is the first time we'll have properly heard from yourself, a.k.a. the heroine of this story," began an impeccably dressed and manicured, slim, black, very attractive reporter about three rows back from the front. She flicked her shiny black curls away from her face for what seemed to be dramatic effect as she addressed Christie, clearly aware of the numerous cameras that would capture the moment she obtained a statement from the main person everyone wanted to hear from. "What can you tell us about the day you were able to escape? How were you successful where others had failed?"

Christie's expression shifted to a look of surprise and bewilderment as she tried best to figure out how to answer that. It hadn't occurred to her that she was being viewed as some sort of victor where other people had supposedly lost. In her mind that was kind of a warped way of looking at the entire situation, though she knew all too well that those words had been chosen purely for entertainment purposes. The media was a well-oiled machine in getting the juiciest parts out of every story and maximising on them to keep people's interest soaring high.

"It was pure luck on my part," was the best Christie could think to offer as her answer, "Timing just so happened to be on my side that day and I ran into few obstacles after I'd made a break for it. I don't know what had changed, but I could sense that something big was about to take place and the rest of the men were too preoccupied with whatever that was to keep a mindful watch over my room. They probably thought I'd be too out of it to function properly but I guess adrenaline took over and enabled me to power through." She shook her head and shrugged at the end of her sentence to display the fact that what she had stated was pure conjecture on her part. She didn't know the real answer to why she had been spared by fate and how she had managed to pull it off in her clumsy, confused and highly panicked state.

"Do you think your abductors were gearing up to sell you on to the highest bidder?" The question was so bold and unbridled that it didn't seem fitting to have come from such an exquisite face as that same reporter with the beautiful curls, yet she stood proudly straight faced, awaiting an answer.

Christie paused to let that thought sink in for a moment and it dawned on her that everything could have gone so much differently had she not bolted when she did. At this very moment in time, instead of being at this table addressing reporters and telling them of her successful escape, she could be in the hands of some sort of demonic predator of a human, in a far-away location where no one would ever find her and she would be lost forever, forced to take part in all manner of grotesque activities. The air felt tight in her chest and her entire body developed a cold, clammy sweat. It trickled down her back and she noticeably shivered.

"It could very well be possible," she finally managed to say over the giant lump that was now occupying her throat.

"How do you feel towards the men who did this to you?" The same reporter relentlessly pressed on.

The rest of the crowd appeared to have fallen into silence, other than the noise of their equipment. They seemed almost awe struck by the tenacity of this one stunning and forthright woman in trying to get the most emotional response she could out of the gentle and traumatised victim she was pursuing.

"I feel... very mixed feelings. At first I was filled with anger at what they had done to both me and to the rest of the victims. I wondered how on earth they were able to sleep at night knowing the devastation they had caused to so many people and how many lives had been upturned by their actions. I've tried to process it in my mind and make sense of it. I've wondered what could have driven them to behave so callously, what trauma they had possibly experienced in their own lives to allow them to justify their behaviour in their minds.

"Was this a finger up to someone who had abused them? Were they doing it out of desperation to rectify their own poor life situation? Or was it simply greed? There are so many questions swirling in my head at any one point in the day and I don't have the answers to any of them." Christie let out a long sigh and bowed her head, feeling suddenly drained and overwhelmed.

"If you could give a message to those men, right here and now, what would you say to them?" The reporter further pressed. She wasn't letting go of the bone she had dug her teeth into for one second.

Christie couldn't even find the words and merely sat there shaking her head as she tried to formulate a sentence. It was impossible. Every time she opened her mouth to begin, she faltered and closed it again, until she realised she must look like a fish gulping for air once it had been ripped from the water it had been leisurely swimming in and decided to give up on trying to answer.

"I think it's time to move on to a different line of questioning now," stated Sue with a stern look at the outspoken reporter. She gestured towards a portly, middle aged, greying Asian man with glasses that were too tight for his round face purely because he had been polite enough to raise his hand. "Yes, sir?" she enquired.

"What can you tell us about the vandalism and suspected riots either already taking place or due to start any moment now in Becontree?" asked the gentleman, pushing up his glasses as he addressed Sue.

There was a prominent jostle amongst the crowd as they shifted their attention and stance towards the commanding police inspector at the end of the desk. Sue seemed entirely unperturbed, despite the rapid spreading of the gossip like wildfire. She had only received report of these incidents moments before heading into the press conference and hadn't had a chance to get as much information from her colleagues as she had wanted. She liked to be prepared and right now she felt pretty damn far away from that.

"I can't tell you very much at this stage, as I have yet to hear the full report myself," she replied in a matter-of-fact tone. She wished that would be the end of it but she knew far better from previous experience.

The Asian reporter pushed further, "Is it true that a large, angry mob have discovered a family business associated with two of the men you currently hold in custody over the abductions related to the case we are here to discuss today? There have been rumours that this family business is actually a money laundering front to cover up all manner of criminal activity, including drug trafficking, prostitution and weapons dealing. How accurate are those rumours? How justified is the mob in their current attack on the property?"

This was all brand new information to Christie and made her mind go into overdrive. Could it be the two men that looked as though they were possibly brothers – the errand boy and Captain Stoneface from the police line-up? Was their involvement in this just one of many different facets of a much larger organisation that solely relied on evil and debauchery to fund itself? How far did this rabbit hole tumble down into a nightmarish world where wickedness and corruption reigned supreme and nobody was safe from being snatched at the nearest opportunity to be held against their will and forced into situations they would never have chosen to enter? She felt completely overwhelmed by the enormity of such an idea and her head felt light as she tried her best to compute it all at the same time.

"At this stage the word 'rumour' is entirely appropriate and a taskforce of police officers have been assigned to both assist in calming the so-called mob that is currently attacking the shop in Becontree, as well as probe deeper into what started this dramatic turn of events. We don't have any solid proof of what has been going on there, *yet,* but I can assure you that we will get to the bottom of it as soon as physically possible and bring all of the relevant parties to justice." Sue clearly enunciated each word to ensure her message was well received.

"When you say 'bring all of the relevant parties to justice'", began another, male reporter with rosy cheeks very close by to the Asian gentleman who was the last to fire a question. He was a fairly young, white and otherwise non-descript fellow, who appeared to be a little out of his depth, trying to hold himself up amongst the heaving crowd around him. "What will become of the vandals to this property? Will they be convicted of arson?

Surely you can understand their outrage?" he asked.

There was a distinct rumble of agreement amongst the reporters as it became clear that the majority of them could empathise with what was apparently taking place at this nearby fictional business that was in actual fact a cover up for the worst types of human behaviour. It seemed like an almost medieval way of thinking. Like it was OK for a mob to form and torch a building because they had discovered bad men doing bad things inside and felt that it was up to them to punish the perpetrators. Surely there were morals that governed against such behaviour? Or was it simply deemed appropriate to repay the vile acts that had been committed by this much larger than anticipated criminal ring?

"As I stated earlier," Sue was beginning to get a little impatient but on the surface remained calm, collected and authoritative, "At this stage it is mere rumours and until both myself and my team know more about the situation, I can't possibly provide an accurate or up-to-date comment." She glanced quickly around the room and noted the overly sensitised and hyperactivity of the crowd in front of her. It was clear to her that nothing more of any use was going to be achieved by feeding them any more information and she leaned slightly forward to speak directly into the microphone in front of her. "I think we have made a great start today and have now reached a suitable level of helpful questioning. Continuing any further would be pure conjecture on my part. Ladies and gentlemen, thank you very much for your time and patience today. Myself and my colleague Kate–" she motioned towards her work sister "–will be available at a later stage to provide in depth answers as the case develops."

And with that, she flicked a switch to the side of her at the end of the table that disabled all of the microphones that had been set up in front of the five seated people. She looked to her left and began to rise, nodding at the rest of the witnesses in a motion that indicated they should all begin to make their way towards the exit.

Carrie, Christie and Dale all visibly let out a sigh of relief in unison which appeared to be almost choreographed. Under any other circumstances it would have been quite comical but it was obvious that this event had put all three of them under a level of stress that none of them deserved.

Neither Sue nor Kate particularly enjoyed press conferences, but they had grown accustomed to how forthright and intimidating reporters could be. One of their least favourite things to do was to put witnesses through this type of ordeal, especially when they had already been through so much and their nerves probably felt frazzled.

All five of them spilled out into the corridor and Sue closed the door behind them, the crowd still heaving on the other side and various reporters failing to quit on the idea that they could still fire questions at people who were walking away from them.

Christie felt both shocked and exhausted. What type of person did you have to be to hold down the job of chasing after gossip to feed back to the hungry public? Why were people so fascinated by bad news and constantly seeking out the worst things to either read or report on? This was one of the many reasons she had never bothered investing in a TV and neglected to stay up to date with politics or global affairs. Sure, it would appear to an outsider that she lived in her own little Christie bubble, but up until recently that had been an extremely positive and light-hearted place to live. She loved to see the best in people and to promote a happy-go-lucky view of the world around her, not get bogged down with the depressing or mind-numbing aspects of existence. Her biggest hope was that she would someday be able to grasp that back.

Right now, she felt a heavy weight on her shoulders and she knew it would be some time before that let up. All she could do at this moment in time was to take each day as it comes, not put any unnecessary pressure on herself and to hold her hand up and ask for help if she needed it. That last one would be the most difficult by far. She had become so used to being self-sufficient when it came to looking after her own mental health and it was an extremely rare occasion that she opened up to people when she was struggling. She had become the master of self-pep talks and knew how to dig herself out of any hole.

However, this felt like more than just a shallow or temporary hole. This felt more like a huge and winding black hole which threatened to suck her in at any moment, dragging her so far down into its depths that she couldn't make her own way back up to the surface for air. It terrified her and she consciously reminded herself that she was safe, that she was amongst people who cared about her, that she could get through this one day at a time.

Dale's hand at the base of her spine shocked her out of her reverie and she looked in his direction to realise that he had obviously said her name a couple of times and had no response.

She blinked hard and shook her head a little. "I was miles away," she explained and gave him a half smile.

"I can see that...you OK?" he asked, gently stroking the lower half of her back and offering his own reassuring, sympathetic smile.

"Yeah...pfft...that was a mind job and a half!" She tried to shrug it off and make light of it but they all saw straight through her act.

Kate grabbed hold of Christie's trembling hand and held it tightly between both of her dark caramel coloured, soft and feminine hands, giving it one gentle squeeze and then continuing to hold on. "Remember what I told you before about needing any counselling or support along the way? Do not be afraid to reach out, even if it's to one of us or to a mate or family member. The absolute worst thing you can do is keep any of this bottled up so make sure you let *someone* know if you're struggling." She rubbed the top side of her hand back and forth a couple of times. "Understood?" she asked, looking her directly in the eyes and making it clear she wasn't intending to let go until she had received confirmation.

"Understood." Christie nodded and genuinely smiled back at Kate, a tiny tear threatening to spill from the corner of her eye. She wasn't remotely worried about crying in front of them anymore. She felt gratitude that they were here to support her and make her feel cared for.

"Good stuff." Kate beamed back at her and then turned her attention to Dale. "It goes for you too ya know, Mr Funny Man." She gave him a little wink and a nudge. "I've already seen first-hand how often you like to turn things into a joke or make light of a dark situation, but if at any stage the onslaught of media attention becomes too circus-like and chaotic and you feel like you need some support then please feel free to reach out to us or use any of those numbers I gave you when we met at the hospital."

"I will do, thanks, Kate," Dale replied with his charming, boyish grin and as soon as Kate turned her attention to Carrie to give her a few words of encouragement and check her emotional levels, Dale turned back towards Christie.

"Seriously, make sure you take on board what she's saying – you've been through an absolute shit tonne of drama and nobody expects you to just bounce back to the normal, smiley, ray of sunshine that everyone associates with your name. Take your time to process and if part of that process is yelling at something, hitting a punch bag, going a bit crazy on the ice cream consumption or crying your eyes out for a bit, you just go ahead and do that. Do it for as long as you damn well please until you feel better."

He was looking directly into her eyes and in that moment Christie felt like he could see into her soul, like he was reading her like a book and knew all too well that she would suffer in silence trying to deal with this by herself. He always had an innate ability to read her better than most; even the subconscious messages that she seemed to transmit without even noticing, he picked up on those without batting an eyelid.

"I will." She nodded back at him and offered a sheepish grin.

"Good. Make sure I'm way high up on the list of people you reach out to. I've said it before and I'll say it again and again and again – I'm here." He felt the need to drill that message into her to make sure it sank in and she appreciatively accepted.

They all said their goodbyes and the two police officers headed back down the corridor into the throng of the station, whilst Carrie, Christie and Dale went in the opposite direction towards the exit.

"Do you need a lift, Dale? My husband is just outside waiting to pick us up," Carrie offered politely.

"Nah, I'm all good, thank you, my mate's out there too – we had already made arrangements and then I messaged him as soon as this little shindig came to an end." He gave her a warm squeeze on her shoulder as a show of appreciation, then pulled Christie into a brief but sincere bear hug, followed up by a gentle kiss on her forehead. "Talk to you soon," he added as they all parted ways.

Carrie spent the entire journey back to the flat filling Pete in on the events of the press conference, making the occasional snide comment about how 'pushy' and 'nosey' some of the reporters had been. Pete chimed in with the odd comment, such as "Well that is their job!" but mostly allowed her to vent and release some of the stress she had clearly pent up during the whole process.

Christie sat quietly listening to her mum rant about what had taken place as she always enjoyed hearing stories from another person's perspective. She had been sitting at that very same table, listening to the exact same questions and hearing the variety of responses, yet her experience had been an entirely different one. Where she had become quite overwhelmed by the enormity of what her escape had then led to uncovering in terms of criminal activity that was, up until now, completely concealed from the public eye, her mother had zoned in on the news-hungry and egotistical arrogance of the reporters and felt offended by the intrusion on her emotions. People's perspectives were fascinating. The subject rapidly turned towards the rioting and arson that was supposedly happening nearby after the discovery of a money laundering family business used to cover the tracks of the abductors and all of their wrong doings.

"Have you heard about any of this?" Carrie asked Pete.

"I have actually," Pete confirmed with a slightly grim expression, "It was fresh news on the radio earlier when I was leaving work to come back and pick you two up. Apparently someone got wind of the names of two of the men in police custody right now and recognised them as being part of this local family owned shop near him. I think they said it was either a newsagent or one of those Eastern European mini supermarket type shops that you see scattered all over the area. Anyway, something didn't sit right with this fella and he started doing some digging and whatever he found wasn't particularly savoury or moral in the slightest. They didn't give the full details as to what he uncovered or how he uncovered it – I guess that will come out later. Either way, rumour spread, as it always does, and it didn't go down well amongst the locals – particularly the friends and family of the other victims found and *especially* amongst those related to the victims who have yet to be found."

"God, I can imagine!" exclaimed Carrie, in disgust. Pete continued, "Yeah there's a lot of angry people out there now all swarming together, egging each other on and causing a right mess of the property. They've smashed all the windows in, looted it, torched it and then stood outside screaming in a sort of mini protest. They're really wound up that this has been allowed to go on for so long and no one has done anything about it yet. Plus this isn't where their protests and mob mentality are gonna end – they reckon that shop was just one of a chain of shops owned by the same family and as we speak they're on a bit of a witch hunt to uncover the rest."

"It sounds messy and although I'm not condoning their violence, especially if anyone innocent was hurt in the process, but to be honest, I can understand their outrage and sometimes when a person is that angry or hurt, all they can think to do is lash out," Carrie said, quite reflectively. It was almost as though she was speaking from her own experience of lashing out or perhaps as a witness to someone close to her behaving in that manner.

Her words hung in the air for some time as they all sat quietly digesting their thoughts for the rest of the journey. Once back inside the safety of her parents' flat, Christie made a beeline for the long, extravagant and comfy couch to lay her head down and rest. She wanted to be close to the background noise of her parents pottering around, chatting, doing normal, everyday things and regardless of what the subject of their conversations were, she liked hearing their voices nearby. For the first time in many, many years, she found it soothing and drifted off into a much needed, peaceful sleep.

When she woke she could smell freshly brewing coffee and hear the noises of her mum tidying up in the kitchen. No one had bothered rousing her to move her from the couch and into the bed in the spare room and she couldn't remember the last time she had slept so well. Both her mind and her body must have been thoroughly exhausted for her to have not woken up once during the night. She stretched her long limbs and it felt wonderful to feel all of her muscles slowly flexing and waking themselves up at a leisurely pace. For a very brief moment in time she felt utterly content and blissful.

However it wasn't a remotely lasting feeling as the memories of the last few days and weeks didn't hesitate to start seeping back into her mind like a poisonous vapour making its way into any nooks and crannies it can spread its way through to infect everything it touches. Her vision was rapidly skewed with mental pictures of the place she had been held captive, the various characters she had come into contact with along the way, heavily focusing on the errand boy and how she had assaulted him in order to set herself free. Then suddenly a heavy barrage of all the faces of the other victims she had seen so far in the news reports she had devoured: some looking well and relieved to be free, some looking enraged and bitter with obvious battle scars, some looking like they had not a clue what had taken place with dazed, confused and faraway stares, some with only a name and no face as they were either still missing or had tragically been found dead.

She shivered hard and the tremor ran all the way from one end of her body to the next. Was this how she would always wake up now, regardless of how well she had slept the night before? Was she forever doomed to be plagued by the same grizzly memories repeating themselves and bringing a daily fresh round of hell to squash her inner peace? It didn't seem fair in the slightest. Not just for her, for everyone involved.

None of this had been fair.

She immediately recognised the anger and sense of injustice starting to build up inside her chest and had to remind herself that, though she was fully justified in feeling that way (in fact she had more right to do so than some of the people in the outside world that were taking matters into their own hands!)...Though it *was* justified and one hundred per cent understandable on her part, it wouldn't change anything. All it would do is make her bitter, twisted and filled with an unquenchable rage because it's not like she could or would seek her own form of revenge.

She saw revenge as a pointless and hateful act that only served to lower a person to the same standards of whomever they were seeking their revenge on. Plus she was too gentle, too caring and usually a very calm type of person. She actively sought out tranquillity and encouraged diplomatic responses to any situation she was going through. She aired towards serenity and spent a great deal of time nurturing her own composure. The events that had taken place threatened to come in and bulldoze over all of that and turn her into an either emotional wreck or even an odious, traumatised or hostile creature with no means of adequately processing those feelings and turning them into something productive.

She had to remind herself of who she was and what she stood for and to not let any of this change her character or rob her completely of her entire identity. She had already lost a lot in terms of both time and her formerly unwavering positivity and optimism. She didn't want to lose any more of herself as a traumatic response and decided right there and then to work hard to not let that happen.

They would not steal her shine or dampen her spirit. She would come back from this like a phoenix rising from the ashes and figure out a way to help others do the same. That was why she was still here – to be a shining beacon of light and hope to those still captured by the darkness and choosing to remain dwelling in it despite being set free. She felt compelled to reach out to them and let them know that everything was going to be OK.

Carrie abruptly waded into her line of vision and it became clear that she had been trying to get her daughter's attention for some time, but to no avail. "Are you here in the land of the living?" she half joked, but as soon as the words left her lips she instantly regretted them and tried her best to snigger her way out of it. Inwardly she reprimanded herself for being so insensitive, but outwardly she covered her blunder with as cheerful a smile as she could muster up and let Christie know there was fresh coffee if she wanted some.

"Thank you, I'd love a cup," Christie replied, indeed snapping herself back to the land of the living and actually finding her mother's horrendous choice of words mildly amusing in an obscure way.

Carrie busied herself pouring a delightful smelling cup of coffee for her daughter in a Winnie the Pooh mug and had even gone to the trouble of getting in some oat milk for her as she knew it was Christie's favourite. Little details like that were what made her who she was and was how she showed affection. She wasn't a hugger or someone who would rub your back and tell you what you wanted to hear. She was an action taker, a forward thinker and a planner. She remembered minor specifics and acted upon them to show that she had been paying attention.

She placed the mug in Christie's eager grasp and sat down next to her on the luxuriously long couch.

"So, I've had a call from a television producer," she began, and Christie stopped in her tracks to hear the rest of what her mum had to say. "They want to get you on the morning show for an interview about what's happened."

"Holy shitballs," exclaimed Christie, a little dumbfounded. "And what did you say?" she asked, feeling almost every hair on her body stand up to attention as she awaited the response.

"I told them that I would ask you but that if you say no, then they must respect that," came her reply. No nonsense, no wiggle room or space for negotiation. When Carrie said something, she meant it and she would stand by her word until the end of her days.

Christie nodded enthusiastically. "Thanks, Mum. I really needed that," she told her, with extreme gratitude coupled with a strong sense of relief. "I mean I most likely will say yes and go through with the interview, but I didn't wanna feel forced into it, ya know? I want it to be on my own terms and because what I have to say will prove useful as opposed to just pure entertainment."

"And that's exactly how you should respond any time anyone asks you to do anything after all of this mess. You should take the time to sit and ask yourself if you really feel OK doing it or if you're just doing it to appease others or placate the masses. You have to look after number one right now, Christie, 'cause I can guarantee you the reporters won't consider your feelings. They'll trample right over you to get to a good story. You need to be wary of people's motives and intentions, observe their actions as well as their words and only go along with what you feel comfortable with." Carrie felt the need to drill into her, no matter how harsh it sounded, as she knew all too well how laid back and easy going her daughter could be and right now that would only serve to her detriment.

There were people out there clambering over themselves to get a piece of what Christie had to say. She wanted desperately to wrap her up in cotton wool and hide her away until the mania passed but she knew that all that would do was create a feeling of resentment. She had to let her daughter make up her own mind whilst still trying her best to steer her away from danger. It wasn't the easiest job in the world when dealing with such a headstrong woman but she recognised a lot of her own traits reflected back to her when she looked at her daughter and there was a distinct feeling of respect and appreciation as a result.

"Right, well I'll wait an hour, give you a bit of space to think and come and ask you again before I call them back, OK?" Carrie gave her daughter's knee a brief and uncharacteristic squeeze, then rose from the couch and disappeared down the hallway to her own room.

Christie rummaged around in her backpack for her iPad, couldn't find it and briefly panicked before realising it was right in front of her on the coffee table and laughed at her own scatter brain. She clicked onto the messaging section of her Instagram page and opened the previous conversation between herself and Dale.

"Hey, I'm guessing you've been asked about the morning show interview too?" she typed in.

A few moments passed before his response came, "Yep. They asked me if I'd do a joint interview with you and I asked whether or not you had agreed and they said they were still waiting."

Christie sat there nodding at the screen and then realised that he would have no idea she was doing that whilst mulling things over in her mind so she simply typed a puzzled looking emoji.

He immediately responded with, "Don't say yes just to please anybody else, Chris. Do what's right for you." He ended it with an OK emoji, followed a moment later with a hugging one.

She grinned a wide grin at that and was grateful for the fact that he couldn't see her. "Thanks, love," she wrote back, "I was already half decided that I would say yes but knowing you'll be there too actually makes it a lot easier to say the full yes and to mean it."

"Cool. You can be the superstar heroine of the story and I'll be there as your acting bouncer if anybody tries to get fresh with ya." He added a wink at the end.

Christie cackled loudly at that and enjoyed the feeling all

the way through to her inner core. He had always been able to make her laugh hard, even at the most obscure things and she treasured that about their relationship. In the past she had confessed deep and dark secrets about herself to him that he had had a beautiful way of putting a positive spin on, then in the moments when they could be silly and laugh like school kids she could also rely on him to take full advantage. "Ha! Will you even back me up if I go into full diva mode and start making ridiculous demands?" she joked.

"Yes, Ma'am," he replied, "They'll have to tend to your every whim and desire before they can get past me."

Christie chuckled and felt light as a feather for the first time in far too long. "Cool. I guess my people will call your people and I'll see you soon."

"See you soon, Wonder Woman," was all he needed to write to leave her beaming from ear to ear and she closed the app before practically skipping to the shower.

After washing all the sleepiness and previous stresses away, Christie let her mum know that she would go ahead with the interview and left it all in her capable hands to arrange. It was nice having her there as a buffer to the onslaught of current demands for her time, almost as though Carrie had unintentionally become her PR manager and was now fully thriving in the role. Christie was happy to hand the reins over to her and let her be the filter because she knew that Carrie wouldn't let anyone walk over her and push her into doing things she didn't want to do. As Dale had casually joked, it seemed quite necessary right now to have a team of people acting as a defence barrier before they could get access to her. She didn't care if that made her appear aloof or even slightly egotistical – she needed extra protection from the seedy intentions of the outside world and would relish in accepting it from those closest to her.

She decided to sit and have a little catch up online with her nearest and dearest. At the very top of that list was her darling friends Len and May – the pair of them were two of her most favourite people on the planet. She'd known Len a few years longer and during that time, they had formed a spectacularly strong bond where they could tell each other anything and supported one another through the highs and lows of this rollercoaster called life. May had been a very welcome addition to the mix, bringing Len an untold amount of happiness and stability and really affirming in Christie's mind that there is someone perfect out there for everyone. It reassured her that she was not in fact destined to walk these earthly planes alone forever, that she too would someday find the one that was meant only for her, exactly when the time was right. She lived in hope.

She re-opened an old group chat on Facebook messenger between the three of them and typed: "Hey, thanks so much for travelling all the way in to see me the other day. I know I've been a bit quiet since. I just wanted to let you guys know how much I appreciate it and have missed you both beyond belief."

"Oh, Christie!" came May's reply almost instantly, "Don't you worry about that one bit, we completely understand and will be here for you whenever you need us. We missed you so very much and are just super happy that you're back! xx"

"Yeah, mate," chimed in Len, "Don't worry about a thing, we'd drive to see you any day of the week, you mean the world to us and we'll do anything for ya."

Christie couldn't help but smile broadly as she could

almost hear their voices in her head as she read the words on the screen.

"Thanks so much guys. Things have been a bit crazy in these parts and I'm still trying to wrap my head around it all. It's like being a celebrity and it's next level strange. I'm not used to being centre of attention at all," Christie explained, though felt like the picture she was trying to paint for them fell a million times short of her actual lived experience of it.

"I can only imagine!" began May, "Your face has been all over the news for weeks and your story gained a huge online following because your disappearance reignited former search parties that had died out when they proved fruitless. Your friends and your work colleagues were relentlessly sharing your missing person's listing all over social media and campaigning hard for more people to join the search for you." She must have been typing furiously fast as she went on, "When the news emerged that you had not only managed to break free but had directed the police to the exact location of the remaining captives and helped them be rescued, the story went viral within less than an hour. People have been following it all over the world."

This part was news to Christie and she had no idea how to respond. She realised then just how well protected she had been by her parents, who had somehow managed to keep the media circus at bay as much as they were able to do so, only letting parts of it filter through so that she was only somewhat aware of its presence and threat.

"What a mind job," was all she could put together in a measly effort to show that what May had said had registered for her to mull over.

A couple of minutes passed before Len wrote, "It'll ease up

eventually, mate. People are fickle and attracted to things that grab their attention. The best thing you can do is look after number one right now, don't let the outside world get to you or consume your thoughts. They'll all move on once enough time has passed and you can try to get back to some sort of sense of normality." He tried his best to sound genuinely reassuring and calming but in actual fact they all knew that his words were rather optimistic. This story was going to be newsworthy for a very long time as it seemed to have opened up a Pandora's Box of shocking and depraved underground criminal activity and the more time that passed, the more terrible, frightful, long-hidden secrets were exposed.

May picked up where he left off: "He's right in that you need to look after number one right now, but please don't feel like you're alone in that. We're here to look after you too, plus I'm sure your family and other close friends feel the same way. Don't be afraid to reach out when you need anything – we were all terrified that we'd lost you forever and the fact that we have you back and have the chance to show you how much we care means the world to us. Remember that in any time that you're feeling low or lost or intimidated by what's going on outside."

Christie let out a long sigh and typed, "I will. Thank you, I really appreciate that."

Both Len and May wrote their own versions of "any time" and "we're just a phone call away" before Christie clicked out of the chat section of Facebook and on to her profile page out of curiosity. There she was inundated with posts dedicated to her search party that implored people to share far and wide to increase the likelihood of her being found. There were messages of sympathy from total strangers in the comment boxes, where friends of friends of friends had gone out of their way to turn this into a huge campaign to 'Bring Christie Home'. It was touching and also bizarre that people who didn't even know her had been getting involved. She noticed that she had been tagged in numerous video interviews where her close friends, colleagues, even her favourite teacher from school had appeared on the news describing to the general public what type of woman she was and why it was so despicable and unfair that she had been snatched from them. Christie began to cry when she heard all of the beautiful things they were saying about her kindness and compassion. It was the type of thing you only hear in full about a person after they've passed away and people are reading messages out at their funeral. Yet here she was listening to them speak of her as though she was already gone. The word surreal didn't even begin to cover it.

Christie shut down all of the pages she had clicked open and put away the iPad for now. She needed a breather from watching people effectively mourning her and went through to the kitchen to make a cup of tea. Just as she was pouring in the milk, Carrie appeared through the doorway and let her know that the TV producers had asked her to make an appearance the very next morning. That sounded good to her, at least she would have the afternoon to mentally prepare herself and then get it out of the way as quickly as possible. She had absolutely no idea what to expect but also no intention of trying to guess what might happen as it would no doubt unnecessarily raise her anxiety levels to sky high extremes and that was the last thing she needed.

Her afternoon surprisingly flew by with her mum making arrangements in the background for them to be picked up ridiculously early in the morning, cooking herself and Christie a delicious lunch and later on when Pete returned from work, they all sat down to a cosy family dinner. Time had returned to a much more normal feeling pace and the whole afternoon/evening was exactly the type of comfort that Christie had needed to return her emotions to a steady, even level.

The next morning was an entirely different story. Christie had actually bothered to set an alarm clock for the first time in weeks and waking up to that shrill sound was an odd combination of confusion as to what on earth the racket was coupled with desire for more sleep, but also a weird feeling of motivation to be up and about, getting things done to a schedule the same way her former self would. She hadn't had a specific reason to be woken up in so long that it felt nice having a goal and going about the routine of getting herself ready to go out. That part was entirely minimal as she had been given instruction from the team at the TV studio to arrive in no makeup and simply clean hair, which thoroughly intrigued her and she wondered how they would make her up to appear on camera.

Carrie and Christie were picked up at 4am by a driver in a black, electric powered Lexus with tinted windows to create a sense of privacy. Even at that ridiculously early hour there were reporters milling around outside her parents' flat and Pete had had to escort them to the car, acting like a human shield to any unwanted questions being fired at his wife and daughter. He was tough enough to hold his ground and cut off any advances before they had a chance to get started and exerted an air of confidence and authority that made the majority of people back down when he rose his voice. There were a couple of reporters that challenged this anyway but all he needed to do was say,

"No comment," before making his way back to the flat to get ready for work.

At the TV production studio they had to go through multiple layers of security to gain access to the building, which filled Christie with reassurance and relief. Had her life really come to this? A need for extreme levels of protection before she felt remotely safe and at ease? She hoped with all her might that things wouldn't always be this way.

Once they had been signed in they were treated how Christie would imagine A-listers were treated, being offered any type of refreshments they desired and seated in a luxurious waiting room to later be called for hair and make-up.

Dale appeared at the door about ten minutes later and strode sleepily into the room. He looked like he had literally rolled out of bed, into the nearest crumpled, creased skater style t shirt, baggy jeans and his trademark funky, colourful trainers, then fallen back to sleep in the car on his way here.

Despite all of that he still looked incredibly handsome and nobody could resist his boyish grin as he politely greeted everyone he came across.

Carrie excused herself to go and find a toilet, leaving Dale and Christie alone for a few moments. "I guess you're not much of a morning person, huh?" Christie giggled as she made her way over to Dale's open arms and wrapped herself up in his warmth.

He rested his head on top of hers and closed his eyes. "You guessed right," came his weary response but he was still grinning so she knew he wasn't too begrudging about being dragged out of bed at this hour. They remained still, both enjoying the embrace and breathing comfortably against each other in unison. Slowly, Dale leaned the top half of his body backwards and looked into her eyes, keeping his arms in place, wrapped around her.

"You feeling OK?" he asked.

"Yeah, I'm OK, thank you." She smiled back at him. "The last few days have been absolutely mental but the best thing that's come out of all of it is that I feel ridiculously loved and cared for by way more people than I could have ever expected." She nestled back into his chest and he rested his head against hers again.

"And that's exactly how it should be," he replied.

A couple more minutes passed by with them standing alone and enjoying their hug before a young woman, dressed all in black casual clothing with a couple of random hair clips attached to the bottom of her shirt, entered the room. She was tiny in both height and width, had radiant porcelain skin with a hint of blush, loosely tied back, brunette hair and dazzling blue eyes that were incredibly perky considering the hour. "Hey Christie." She didn't seem remotely phased by having to interrupt their embrace; she looked more enamoured by it than anything else. "I'm here to grab you so I can do your hair and make-up."

"See you on the other side," Dale joked, untangled himself, gently nudged Christie in the direction of the tiny stylist and made himself comfortable in one of the plush armchairs in the waiting room.

Christie was whisked away down a few winding corridors and into a room dedicated to getting people 'camera ready'. On the way she learned that the tiny stylist was named Sylvia and took an instant liking to her as she seemed to have no filter when it came to expressing her opinions on anything. Sylvia directed her into a tall black chair that had been raised up from the ground so that when seated, Christie was of a much more similar height to Sylvia when standing.

Directly in front of her was a Hollywood style mirror with lightbulbs around its circumference that lit up every minor detail on her peach skin. An array of make-up brushes, pallets, glosses, liners, basically every type of make-up imaginable littered the desk in front of the mirror and attached to the side were multiple containers filled with hair styling tools and sprays. *Now* she felt like an A-lister.

Sylvia spun the chair around so that they were eye to eye. "I have no idea what the last few weeks have been like for you, Christie." Her tone had become entirely serious. "And quite frankly, it's none of my business so I won't ask you to tell me anything. However, this is a *very* busy studio, with all manner of people coming through here in a continuous flow and your story is the hottest thing in the press right now. There will be those who have no respect for other people's boundaries that will want to grill you, there will also be some who look up to you and admire you, who will simply want to express that and there will be a *lot* of people who stare." She paused for a moment to allow that to sink in and Christie nodded as she processed Sylvia's information.

"I want you to know that it is one hundred per cent up to you how much or how little you give away to anyone who asks. You are your own woman and *you* are in the driver's seat here. Well, the stylist's seat." She chuckled and rolled her eyes, then continued, "My point is that you needn't feel like you owe anybody anything. You're here of your own accord and it's your right to decide what you tell to whom and if you need anybody to step in and ask people to back off, I'm your woman." She winked. "I can be quite feisty when the situation calls for it." She spun Christie back around to face the mirror and addressed her reflection: "Sound good?"

"Sounds good." Christie beamed back at her.

Sylvia expertly went to town on firstly making Christie's face look perfectly blemish free, smooth and radiant, transforming her eyes so that they stood out the most without looking over-the-top and styling her hair so that it looked voluminous, yet naturally so. She hadn't been kidding about the number of people vying for Christie's attention throughout the process and even though she had been pre-warned about it, Christie still found it quite jarring.

Initially it began with a group of female panel show hosts making a beeline for her when they spotted her from across the room. They were all perfectly lovely and gave her sincere compliments about her bravery and resilience. Each took a separate turn to wish her well and politely moved on. The next few people that came through were clearly in a rush to get from one room to another and kind of yelled their compliments at her in passing, which felt *very* odd and Christie half waved and nodded her gratitude at them. Sylvia shook her head and tutted at them but carried on working her magic.

"My, my, my." A senior gentleman with broad shoulders who towered over Sylvia came and stood next to them so that he could address Christie's reflection in the mirror. His accent was incredibly posh and well spoken, with a gravelly voice and a slight wheeze, but his physical stance was as strong as a man half his age. "You're the gutsy woman who managed to break free from those low-life, trafficking predators, aren't you?" It wasn't remotely clear who this man was and he seemed to have no regard for what anyone thought of his choice of words. Perhaps that was a privilege of reaching his stage of life – that you no longer had to give a damn what anybody thought and could go about your day saying whatever you want to whomever you damn well please.

"Yes, sir." Though Christie was initially slightly taken aback by how brazen this man was, she was also slightly curious about where he intended to go with this and whether or not it would reflect the general consensus of the public.

"Bloody good show, my dear, a bloody good show. You sure showed them that they had no right to mess around with young women's futures like that. It's absolutely revolting that they think it's acceptable to steal a woman off the street, lock her up, fill her system with drugs and then sell her on. Utterly disgusting if you ask me. But well done you for standing up to such depravity." He enunciated each word clearly and fervently so that it would truly express his feelings on the subject.

"I look forward to hearing your views on the matter and hopefully what you have to say will bring about a much needed change in how the authorities tackle such an obviously long standing ring of crime. Something needs to be done to stop this type of abomination from ever happening again. My prayers will be with you, my girl." He took Christie's hand in his and placed a completely unexpected, gentle kiss on the back of it, the way she had only seen in old style movies. With that, he strode out of the room and on to spread whatever words of wisdom he had for the next person.

"Who was that guy?" Christie asked Sylvia after he had left.

"I'm not exactly sure, ya know?" Sylvia was still staring after him in the direction he had vacated the room, rubbing the handle of a comb against her chin in thought. "I've seen him loads of times in different parts of the studio but he's never spoken directly to me and he seems to have an air of authority about him that makes me think you shouldn't speak to him unless he speaks to you." She shrugged and turned back to her masterpiece. "I guess maybe we'll find out later," she suggested and went about finishing the task at hand.

Christie felt like a new woman once she had been dressed in an outfit picked by Sylvia purposely to make her look like her regular, everyday self, whilst also being smart enough for television and she thanked her profusely for both her work and support throughout the transformation process.

"It's my pleasure," replied Sylvia, "Now go and show the world what a total badass you are." She gave Christie a playful jab on the shoulder and they both giggled as they approached the entrance to the original lavish waiting room she had picked her up from. There they found Dale and Carrie cheerfully chatting as though they had known each other for years and Christie was a little taken aback by that. It usually took her friends much longer to get her mum to warm up to them and yet here she was eating out of the palm of Dale's hand.

"You're up next, sunshine." Sylvia pointed at Dale and he politely excused himself from his and Carrie's conversation, pulled himself up into a standing position and before going anywhere with Sylvia, he turned to appraise Christie.

"Well, don't you scrub up well?" He grinned and attempted to give her a peck on the cheek but was stopped in his tracks by Sylvia's palm on his shoulder, acting as a barrier to his advances on her masterpiece.

"Oi, back away from my art, pal, you can save your sentimental mumbo jumbo for *after* the recording," she stated firmly but with a tone full of jest and a wink at the end to prove it.

With that, he gave her a mock salute as though she was an army captain and followed her lead down the winding corridors, towards the styling studio. Christie sat down next to her mum to wait to be told what the next steps were. She'd never done anything remotely like this before and she felt a little like a sheep being herded from one place to the next.

"You really do look lovely," Carrie complimented her, looking pleased with the choice of plum coloured mini dress that was a perfect blend of smart and casual, black opaque tights and Christie's favourite blush patterned Dr Martens boots.

"Thanks, Mum. I feel fresh as a daisy." Christie beamed back at her.

"Well, that's good. It's important to be in a positive frame of mind before taking on a feat like this." Carrie was forever the cautious pragmatist in any situation and felt it her duty to mentally prepare her daughter for what she could already foresee as being incredibly emotionally taxing. She had a keen eye for detail and took it upon herself to be continuously evaluating her surroundings and what was being communicated in her near vicinity. She had overheard snippets of conversations about video evidence coming to light of the current riots and arson that were taking place as a result of the discovery of several money laundering businesses, all linked together and acting as a cover up for the criminal activity of multiple gang affiliations, each holding their own position in a widespread lawbreaking syndicate that went further underground than anyone had originally anticipated. It was as though, beneath the surface, the entire borough of Barking and Dagenham was built upon and operating on an infrastructure of lawless networks and that this had been the case for many years up until now.

New evidence was coming to light on an hourly basis and police raids were uncovering more and more hidden bunkers filled with weapons, drugs, even hostages that had been trafficked in from Eastern Europe to be put to work illegally for long hours and paid a pittance of a wage to survive. It was the lowest, most depraved displays of human greed being exposed and showcased to the world with every new discovery.

"Obviously I can't predict what's going to be asked of you and what you are going to find out during this interview," Carrie continued, "But I think you need to be aware of the fact that there is *a lot* of unrest out in the public at the moment; there are a lot of very angry people acting out against what they see as a massive governmental failure to protect its own citizens." She placed her hand on her daughter's knee. "I don't want you to feel frightened by what you are shown; you are safe now and don't need to worry."

Christie appreciated her mother's sentiment and knew all too well the type of mind set she usually occupied. Though Carrie was pragmatic, she also had a tendency to air more towards the negative side of any story and anything that she had overheard would likely have sent her mind into overdrive so the fact that she was sitting patiently and trying to reassure her daughter must have been no mean feat in itself. She had no idea what this interview was going to entail and decided to go into it with zero expectations – much like she did with every other situation in her life. That way whatever did happen, she would just deal with it on the hoof and not waste any of her precious time overthinking it.

"Cheers, Mum. I'll be all right." She gently rubbed the back of Carrie's hand a couple of times and they both removed themselves from each other's grip soon after that. They had never really had a very touchy-feely type of relationship and both felt slightly awkward with the brief alteration to their usual routine.

Dale re-appeared looking rejuvenated and stylish. Sylvia had swapped his jeans for some slightly smarter ones, but stayed true to his laid back look, plus dressed him in a sleeker, dark coloured t-shirt that wasn't heavily creased. Like Christie, she had left him in his own shoes to keep in-line with his own funky, colourful flare, but he was now well-groomed and practically glowing with it.

"Well, don't you scrub up well?" Christie threw his earlier compliment back at him to appear playful but she genuinely meant it. She thought he looked handsome as hell.

"Why thank you, M'Lady," he replied with a mock bow and they both chuckled but kept the distance between them intact so as not to perturb Sylvia's handy work.

Almost as though he had been waiting eagerly in the wings for the return of Dale, a very young, trim, fairly tall man came breezing into the room with a clipboard propped against his body and a headset on his head. His clothing could only be described as fabulously flamboyant and his attitude was chipper, but also driven and motivated to adhere to a schedule.

"Good morning my two stars of the show." His large, turquoise eyes dazzled as he took in the freshly rejuvenated appearances of Dale and Christie before him. "My name is Timothy and I am here to give you an overview of what's about to take place, plus introduce you to your morning show hosts and get you mic'ed up and ready for action."

He made the whole affair seem glamourous and appealing, which was a breath of fresh air for Christie's weighted mind, and she immediately liked him. Dale shared that sentiment and graciously offered this new charming, bubbly entity a handshake, saying in return: "Pleased to meet you, Timothy. Obviously you won't be needing an introduction on our part."

"No, no, darling, you're quite right – I've been waiting for you both with bated breath. Come, follow me." He spun around with the grace of a dancer and sashayed in the opposite direction, towards a room lined with large cameras, microphones, a ridiculous amount of wires criss-crossing each other over the floor and various crew members milling around making adjustments to the set and their equipment.

Dale and Christie followed and listened as intently as they could to his instructions, though it was incredibly difficult with so many things to distract them along the way. Christie had been an audience member of a TV recording once in the past, way back in her teen years, but that studio had been miniscule in comparison to this one. There was so much to take in and it was difficult to keep her mind focused on the task at hand.

"You two are going to be seated over on this side." Timothy gestured towards a long, modern looking, bright red couch on the right; to its left were two similar style arm chairs in bright orange. "And that's where Holly and Phil will be seated." He gestured to the left. "Ah, speak of the devil!" His gaze had switched to the people approaching from behind Dale and Christie and he enthusiastically ushered them over so that he could revel in making his introductions amongst the most important people in his schedule today. "Christie and Dale, please meet your hosts and interviewers, Holly and Phil." It practically rhymed and sounded cheerfully sing-song in Timothy's effeminate voice.

Holly was tall, slim but with curves in all the right places, had beautifully styled, long blonde hair and wore a figure-hugging jade green dress with matching heels. Phil was a few years older than Holly, with silver hair and a cheeky, handsome quality about him and was sharply dressed in a tailored, cashmere-coloured shirt with black trousers and dress shoes. They all responded to each other with bright smiles and handshakes, making pleasantries about how nice each of them looked. It was oddly familiar because the two hosts were obviously well known and recognisable to the masses, but now so were Dale and Christie. There was no sense of intimidation on anybody's part as a result; they all simply treated it as though it was an average, everyday meet and greet.

Timothy then led Dale and Christie over to a large table adorned with a wide variety of highly technical recording equipment, whilst Holly and Phil went in a separate direction to finish preparing themselves for the show. Two crew members came over at Timothy's beckoning and went to work attaching tiny wireless microphones to the front of Dale and Christie's clothing, tapping them and murmuring comments into them which were supposedly being fed through to their own inner ear devices.

It was seriously impressive to observe but all of a sudden things had also become very real and Christie could feel a distinctive knot forming in the pit of her stomach. Almost instinctively, Dale seemed to notice her breathing become more rapid and shallow so he placed a calming hand at the base of her spine.

"You OK over there?" he gently probed with a reassuring half smile and empathetic eyes.

Christie took a large, deep breath and nodded back at him. "Yeah, I'm OK. Just processing it all." She attempted her own half grin but fell a little short and abandoned the idea.

"You got this." He leaned in and broke Sylvia's rules by planting a light kiss on her forehead. "And *I* got *you.*" He then lightened the mood with a playful, tender jab to her upper arm and she couldn't help but giggle. It was practically impossible to maintain any negative emotions when she was in his company and she adored that about him.

The pace of activity quickly sped up and they were soon being ushered over toward the bright red couch, instructed exactly where to sit, at what angle, how loudly to speak and to not do so too quickly, to instead take their time and consider their responses to each question. They were given a list of definite questions, likely questions and informed that they would also be subject to some video footage of the protests and arson taking place as a result of the ongoing findings of the case so far. They were asked how comfortable they felt with all of the above, asked to sign a waiver and then reassured if at any stage they felt discomfort or unease, then all they had to do to inform the crew was lightly tap their own left shoulder with the forefinger of their left hand. The production team would be watching out for this and would immediately move the hosts on to the next question or topic via their inner earpieces.

Before they knew it, the hosts were seated next to them, the cameras were all lining up into position and they were being counted down by a voice somewhere at the back of the room.

Phil and Holly took it in turns to greet the viewers and describe the variety of topics that were going to be covered on the morning's show. They were both poised and perfectly timed in their delivery and it was obvious that they had an incredibly tight knit relationship in both a personal and professional sense.

"We have on our couch today two people who have won

the hearts of the nation and quite rightly so, I might add," remarked Phil, "Thank you both very much for being here and welcome to the show."

Christie smiled and nodded back to him, feeling a little shy, so Dale picked up the slack. "Thanks for having us," he replied.

"Christie, your story is one of extraordinary courage and resilience against all odds. The whole country was shocked by your sudden reappearance after being so extensively searched for and the best part was that you made it back to reality relatively unscathed. How on earth did you find the strength to achieve such a wondrous comeback?" Though Phil seemed genuinely interested and it was clear that the choice of words were popular opinion of the events that had taken place, Christie was slightly jarred and confused by the mental image he was projecting as it wasn't remotely close to how it had played out in her mind.

She exhaled a long breath and considered her response. "It's odd to hear it described in that manner because to me – it wasn't a well thought out or planned act in the slightest. It was impulsive and purely adrenaline fuelled...I literally stumbled my way out of there feeling utterly lost and bewildered. Looking back on it, I'm surprised I made it back in one piece." Christie's candid statement received nods of understanding from her hosts and Holly took her turn next.

"It's a miracle that you did." She addressed Christie with sincerity. "And also that you were somehow subconsciously drawn to a place where you knew you would be safe. How did it feel to come face to face with your friend and tattooist after being held captive by a group of strangers in a seemingly hopeless situation for more than three weeks?"

Christie let out a sheepish laugh. "Well, I barely recognised him at first!" She gave Dale a playful nudge. "It was the weirdest thing; I had this man crouched in front of me who's face looked like it was something I'd either dreamed or seen in a movie at some stage. It was like recognising someone but from afar." She felt like her words weren't adequately describing the bizarre feelings that had taken over her body that day and she tailed off.

"And he somehow managed to convince you that you did, in fact, not just know each other but also trust one another whole heartedly?" prompted Phil.

"Yeah, thankfully my outstanding ink is an inarguable testament to how much I trust this man." Christie beamed at Dale and he smiled back with a humble head bow.

"It really is beautiful artwork." Holly came across as genuine when she admired the resplendent colours and intrinsic shading of the tattoos on Christie's arms.

Dale and Christie said thank you in unison and they all shared a good laugh. It was a delightful ice breaker and both guests seemed to fully ease the slight tension they had been holding in their shoulders and relaxed into the interview.

"So, you'd been hurtling through the woods after escaping an utterly nightmarish prison cell..." Holly was painting a visual picture for the avid and loyal viewers. "You were now face to face with a trusted friend for the first time in weeks. How did you describe to him what had happened to you and why you had ended up there?"

"I don't think I really did...?" Christie half stated and half asked. "I think I just rambled a load of barely coherent nonsense and Dale thankfully realised I wasn't my usual self and took it upon himself to get me the help I so desperately needed."

"Can you tell us a bit more, Dale?" Phil chimed in.

"Sure, I've known Christie for about three years now; we had a couple of mutual friends and our shared circle has grown over time because she's spent a lot of time with me in the Vogue Vintage shop where we've got to know each other very well. When you spend that amount of one-on-one time with a person and you're being trusted to permanently alter their skin, it has a side effect of bringing down any barriers between the pair of you. I find *a lot* of my clients are very open with me.

"Now, I'm not usually one to reciprocate that feeling; my role almost becomes similar to that of a therapist when I'm tattooing someone. They feel comfortable enough to open up to me and I merely listen whilst they either vent their problems or tell me the inspirational reasons behind their tattoo design." Dale paused for a moment and looked briefly at Christie's striking face as she listened intently to what he was saying. "However, with Chris it was different; it was a two-way street and I felt comfortable telling her deeply personal things about my life and my past too. She has a non-judgemental quality about her that makes you feel safe in opening up to her and knowing that what you share will stay between the two of you."

Christie blushed a little and truly appreciated his kind words.

"That's incredible, no wonder she seemed to be magnetically drawn to that specific spot, right in front of Vogue Vintage and it was just pure luck that you happened to be in there on a Sunday," evaluated Holly.

"Yeah, it's not every Sunday that I'm in the shop, 'cause we're not open for bookings on a Sunday and it's usually a day when I like to relax and put my feet up if I haven't got any other plans," explained Dale.

"What made that Sunday different?" enquired Phil, with an interested look on his face, almost as though he had some insider information that nobody else was aware of.

"Well, I was taking the time to do some sketches for a client I was booked in with the following week and the shop was a perfect location for my buddy to come and pick me up from at lunchtime as we were due to go to the opening of his brand new music venue in Camden," revealed Dale.

"So you cancelled important plans with a friend to take care of Christie that day, is that correct?" Phil surmised.

"Yeah…he was pretty mad at me at the time but since this whole case has blown wide open and he's seen my face all over the news, he gets it and we're cool." Dale shrugged.

"That sounds like a great friend," Holly inputted and then asked, "Christie, did you know anything about this?"

"No!" Christie exclaimed a little shriller than she had intended to. This was brand new information to her and had an enormous ripple effect on the outcome of the story. "I had absolutely no idea and this changes everything."

Her words tumbled out of her at an only just coherent speed. "If you hadn't bailed on your mate and I hadn't woken up in hospital next to *you* specifically, I very much doubt that I would have felt comfortable enough to demand a stranger's phone to start rambling my descriptions into a voice note in front of them. It was only because it was *you* on the receiving end that the cops got the info they needed to perform their raid as quickly as they did and find the other twelve victims still alive and mostly unharmed!"

Her voice had taken a slightly higher pitch as she feverishly explained that his choice that day had had its own ramifications. If it wasn't for him, the fate of those women could have been entirely different and all of the discoveries that had been made afterwards about the colossal underground crime syndicate in Barking and Dagenham may have remained unexposed for many years to come. "You're a true hero!" She blurted out at the end.

Now it was Dale's turn to blush ever so slightly, which was a very rare occurrence for him. "I wouldn't go that far." He tried to act nonchalant and only semi managed to pull it off.

"She's quite right, Dale," Phil interjected with a serious tone. "If you hadn't changed your, I must say rather exciting sounding plans and been there for her the way that you were that day, this case could have ran into a dead end. The men behind the whole affair may have packed up all of the evidence and ran by the time the police had arrived – who *knows* what would have become of those twelve women at the abandoned farm and further still, there would be nowhere *near* as many leads to follow up as a result and those all important discoveries of affiliated underground gangs may have never taken place. At least not for many years to come, as they would have surely been spooked by Christie's escape and gone to greater efforts to cover their tracks." He was essentially reiterating everything that had already been said but adding his own exaggerated flare and suppositions onto it, purely for dramatic effect for the viewers at home.

"It seems the two of you are a force to be reckoned with in this tale of heroism." Holly's spin on it was very kind but a little fanciful as she was clearly trying to sensationalise their roles in the ordeal.

"Quite right, Holly," agreed Phil, "and we have some wonderful clips to show of the other victims that were found that fateful day, showcasing the results of their ongoing recovery. Let's take a look."

The first video shown was a mixture of interviews with the dark skinned, green eyed victim that Christie remembered from the news clips she had watched on her iPad the day after returning home, interviews with her family and short scenes of her putting together her own new charitable venture that aimed to help vulnerable females that have been victims of crime. Her bruises had faded well but were still in the healing process and simply added to the effect of the message she was trying to promote into the camera lens. She had taken her own horrific experience and turned it into a non-profit organisation that would act as a venue for victims to receive counselling, psychotherapy, attend group sessions in occupational therapy, wellness activities and be referred to other services relating to their recovery from trauma. It was only in its very early stages and she had high hopes for turning it into a well-rounded, holistic approach that would take a victim from their most vulnerable state and allow them the time, space and resources to completely rebuild their lives from scratch into something far better than they ever could have imagined.

The feisty, passionate victim, who had now introduced herself as Lacey, spoke with confidence into the camera and emitted a defiant attitude towards anyone who thought it was acceptable to treat women in any type of violent or dehumanising way. She came across with a strong, almost protesting style against those oppressive forces that would drag its victims down into a pit of despair that they felt unable to escape from. It was hard not to be entirely enraptured by her charismatic, 'voice-of-the-people' manner as she spoke from the heart and let the viewers know that it was "OK to reach out for help". A couple of her family members gave their own brief comments about how proud they were of her and also sent out messages of thanks to all of the people who had made this new, improved version of Lacey possible.

Next up came a video of the two previously homeless victims, who had since become good friends as they embarked on their journey together in a women's refuge in South London, ran by charitable organisation, Solace. One of them was more vocal than the other and spoke on both of their behalf, but the second one seemed more than happy to allow her new friend to take the lead and remained passive and shy in the background of their interview, only giving short answers when directly spoken to. The camera followed them around on a tour of their accommodation at the refuge, plus the large and naturistic grounds it was situated on.

The more confident one, known as Pat, described how they were receiving medicated treatment and talking therapy for their issues with addiction, taking part in vocational courses to both keep them occupied and to improve their chances in the "real world" once their stay in the refuge had come to an end and even finding joy in activities that had never appealed to them when they were too busy chasing their addictions.

"I've come to realise I'm quite the dab hand at crocheting or knitting and Debbie is a green fingered wonder!" Pat quipped.

She went on to describe how welcoming the staff and other residents at Solace had been to them and how much she felt like this was a turning point for both of their lives. Then she rounded off the interview with a sincere and heartfelt thanks to those that had dug them out of the hole they were in and placed them on the road to recovery. The words that she used made her sound like the experience had led her to discovering her own deep-seeded faith and she seemed like a completely different woman to the one that had been found locked away in a shipping container on an abandoned farm not so long ago.

In the final video all twelve of the victims had been placed together in an obviously contrived but incredibly emotion inducing line up, where they all wore big smiles and waved at the camera with gusto. Their family and friends were gathered to the sides and in front of them, cheering them on and also waving at the camera as it panned across them for full effect of the numbers of people that had benefited from this case being blown open the way that it had.

It had indeed been a lovely way to begin the show and everyone in the studio was internally celebrating, some had tears rolling down their faces and some were simply grinning from ear to ear as they fully emerged themselves in the entertainment of what they were being shown. So far, the picture painted of the story had been nothing but heart-warming, with many neatly wrapped, fairy tale-like endings.

The camera panned back to Phil and he began by rounding up what a pleasant experience it had been to see the former captives and their families doing so well, then his expression notably darkened as he began the next segment of the story: "As always, it is our job to report the good news *and* the bad and the next topic we have to discuss is not remotely pleasant or easy to hear about."

Christie bristled and Dale placed his hand on top of hers, rubbed it gently back and forth and then left it there, not giving a damn whether or not that was in line with appropriate televised behaviour.

"That's right, Phil." Holly took her cue. "The ongoing reports of violent acts of protest and arson against a number of properties said to be owned by the family of two of the men currently being held in police custody in relation to this case are getting more and more worrying by the day." Her expression conveyed this concern perfectly and one would be forgiven for mistaking her for a highly trained actress. "What started off as an attack on just the one shop has multiplied into a large and angry mob who seem to be banding together to destroy several family-owned businesses in the borough because they believe them to be money laundering decoys for a network of affiliated gangs."

"The following videos are disturbing and violent in places and are only to be watched at the viewer's discretion," warned Phil, looking solemnly into the camera lens.

Christie gripped Dale's hand and braced herself for the carnage.

The first video showed a violently heated crowd of people filling the street outside what had previously been an Eastern European mini supermarket but was now barely recognisable amongst the debris of its former shelves, stock and shattered windows. There were still fumes of smoke filtering out from where it had been torched and the fires had died down. It had all been filmed on a member of the public's android phone so the shot was extremely shaky and not well panned out, but that just served to give it an accurate and real-time account of the pure outrage and disgust that hung in the air. People were livid and shouting hateful, xenophobic chants in unison about foreigners coming into the country and pillaging British society.

It cut to a more professionally filmed interview of one of the crowd members, who had been pulled to the side away from the main swarm of activity to give his personal view of what was taking place. He was a middle aged, slightly rotund and red faced, white man with a heavily cockney accent and he slurred into the camera, "I don't know who these people think they are, coming into our country and snatching our women off the street like dogs." He paused to swallow down an obvious belch, then continued, "Our poxy government had allowed this to go on for too long and it's time somebody stood up for the little man. We've all gotta unite and rise up against this disgusting violation of our rights. We ain't gonna allow it no more!" He finished by raising his fist up in the air to be greeted by the background noise of loud cheers to his speech emanating from the crowd behind him on top of an underlying melody of glass smashing, bins being tipped over and people jostling each other to get closer to the action.

The next video appeared to be shot from a headset attached to a member of a police raid and it quickly became clear that they were targeting the basement of a shop. The nominated camera operator stood slightly back from the front of a row of armed raiders and filmed as two men at the head of the troops used a large metal ram to break down the door. It took a few heaves and slams against the door, then once they were inside the room the camera captured walls lined with heavy weaponry and a few men scattering away from them, trying to break free but being tackled and held in place by members of the raid. Handcuffs applied, the suspects were then lifted to their feet whilst they continued to struggle and fight, then dragged one by one out of the room by the police. It was still a fairly shaky and certainly a poorly lit shot, but slightly steadier and more comprehensive than the earlier android phone recording.

As the camera went around the room slowly to capture all of the evidence, it exposed the basement as being deceptively deep and piled high with stacks of boxes filled with tightly packaged white powder, other packages filled with dull, green processed cannabis leaves, containers filled with miniature plastic bags containing various types of pills and more weapons of differing styles and power. It was like something you would see in a violent, thriller type movie, not a scene you would commonly associate with being below a local shop in Becontree.

Another video was filmed in a similar style but the police raiders were entering a different basement. What they found was harrowing as the camera panned across rows and rows of camp beds all in very close vicinity to each other. Some of the inhabitants had already been removed and were being processed by the cops, but the last few that remained were malnourished, unkempt looking Eastern Europeans, who looked alarmed and confused by what was happening around them. They varied greatly in terms of demographics and shockingly included small children being shielded in a protective manner by what appeared to be their mothers, all trembling fearfully; some crying and some yelling, but most subdued into a terrified silence.

Police members had wrapped blankets around those that would accept it and were gently trying to usher them towards the door, however, some were clearly too traumatised to understand and tried to resist the aid they were being offered. They were seen lashing out and screaming in turmoil, not wanting to be caught and later punished by their captors. It was utterly gut wrenching to watch as they lost their battle against the help purely because they were too frail to fend off any advancements. They withered and gave in to being taken away from their prison, crying helplessly in their native tongue and looking completely downtrodden.

The camera continued to be walked around the dwelling by the police raider operating it in order to capture the squalid conditions the captives had been held in. The camp beds were small, slim, rusted and unclean, each with a shred of a blanket – none of which appeared to have been washed in some time and only a select few had barely an excuse for a pillow. There were meagre possessions scattered around, clearly of more sentimental value than monetary and with no means of storing them safely. There were two separate rooms attached to the main bedroom: one contained two urinals and a seated toilet, the other contained three shower heads – the type that one would typically find at a gym or swimming pool, no cubicles or shower curtains, so absolutely zero privacy and a pathetic supply of soap. Clearly if one of the captives had wanted to maintain any sense of personal hygiene, they would have had to have done so in full view of everyone in the room and make do with what was on offer to scrub themselves clean. It was as though whomever was holding these people here wanted to keep them looking shabby and unkempt, like they would somehow use that to their advantage. What kind of horrific manipulation was taking place as a result?

The final shot returned to the protesting mob and panned across them from a higher vantage point than before. The crowds stretched back further down each angle of the cross junction they were on and they continued to chant antagonistic, racial slurs, coupled with yelling out grievances at the state of the British government. In the background a variety of destructive noises could be heard, even more glass shattering, signs being torn down and storage boxes kicked over, car horns in the distance where they had blocked off an entire junction with their protesting.

They didn't seem remotely close to letting up on their mission of hatred any time soon; more accurately it seemed to be growing exponentially with the increasing amount of media coverage they received. The more attention they garnered from the rest of the world, the more it spurred them on to create even more destruction and violence.

The camera cut back to the studio where Phil and Holly sat with appropriately grim expressions – Holly being slightly more on the emotional side with tears brimming the corners of her eyes. The colour had completely drained from Christie's face and she sat frozen, only her shallow, rapid breaths acting as an indicator that she was still present. Dale wore a solemn look and was gently rubbing his thumb across the back of Christie's hand. He could feel a slight tremble coming from her body and he wanted more than anything to wrap his arms around her, hold her tight and tell her everything was going to be okay.

"Some gut-wrenching footage there to display the aftermath of what has been exposed in the borough of Barking and Dagenham due to evidence that has come to light following the police raid on the abandoned farm on the A125 just over a week ago," Phil summarised in a grave tone for any viewers that had just tuned in. He shifted his position towards Dale and Christie. "How do both of you feel watching that and knowing that your heroic actions have led to such a vast depth of criminal activity being uncovered, but most importantly, more human lives being spared from the grips of these corrupt gang affiliations?"

Christie still appeared to be in a state of shell shock so Dale piped up, "It's truly appalling to see the state of the place those people were being held in. My thoughts go out to them and their families. I honestly don't know how you can justify treating people that way." He shook his head unhappily, trying to make sense of what he had just seen. "I mean you hear horror stories about this type of thing or you see stuff in the movies, but to find out that it's been happening in real life and so close to home is a real shock to the system and a tragic wake-up call to the depravity of certain segments of humanity."

Christie had begun shaking her head beside him, listening to his thoughts and feeling her own bewilderment about how this could be happening right under people's noses. None of it was fair and her heart bled for those poor souls that had been snatched from their home countries, shipped here illegally in who-knows-what kind of traumatising manner and held for an unknown length of time in a dark, dingy and filthy room full of other prisoners. How petrified they must have felt! How confused, angry, miserable – basically the entire spectrum of negative emotions – must have been their ongoing mental status and you would forgive them for wanting to give up hope.

"W...w...what will become of the hostages that were found?" Christie's lip trembled as she stammered over her words.

"At this moment in time, they are being processed thoroughly by the police to find out how they came to be in this nightmarish situation and to figure out how best to help them moving forwards," Phil assured her.

Holly took over: "They will leave no stone unturned in finding out the truth and the hostages will not be penalised in any way; they will get professional help for what they've suffered and be given options as to whether they want to remain here in the UK or return to their home countries." She seemed also sincerely concerned for the wellbeing of the victims of such a heinous crime. It was clear in her eyes.

"First and foremost they will be interviewed in depth to find out how far this criminal activity stretches, not just here in this country, but also overseas. All of the perpetrators exposed along the way will be brought to justice." Phil was now speaking into the camera to ensure the viewers that all political avenues were being explored and that every aspect of the case was going to be investigated in full before any decisions were made. "As you can see from the footage of the protests currently taking place in Becontree, and we're now being told, in other areas across London too, there is a lot of social unrest due to people feeling as though the British government has let them down and allowed this to go on without intervention. This is not entirely the case as it has nothing to do with immigration standards in this country. Sadly, the hostages we saw in the third video had been trafficked here illegally so that those strong and capable enough to perform manual labour would be put to work every day on a variety of sites owned by the organisation at the top of this lawless network. The rest, mostly women and children, were dropped off daily at various hotspots across the borough and instructed to sit in the same spot and beg for loose change or dropped off at rail stations and instructed to walk up and down the train carriages with a cup in their hand, asking passengers for money. They would be picked up at the end of each day by their captors, fed a barely substantial meal and taken back to their fetid den to rest for the night before doing the same the following day."

"That's simply awful," stated Holly and paused for just a moment to let that thought sink in before continuing, "But the good news is that now that so many people have been rescued; they are in the right place to receive all the help they need to recover from what they've been through. They will be given the best treatment, care, advice and options about how they want their lives to proceed. It's going to take a *lot* of work, but it will be so worth it in the grand scheme of things." Though she was correct in what she was saying, it was an incredibly optimistic way of looking at things and also entirely unlikely that the victims and their families would share in that same viewpoint.

"Christie, given that you are the only person here to have had any physical contact with several of the men involved in all of this," began Phil, "What is your view on the type of person it takes to commit such monstrosities on such an enormous scale?"

Christie pondered the question for a couple of seconds and swallowed down the lump in her throat before answering, "As Dale said before, you cannot possibly justify treating another human this way. It's disgusting and it should never have even crossed a person's mind, let alone expanded to involve as many widespread gang members as it did. It makes me wonder how on earth a person is recruited into this type of organisation. What trauma have they been subjected to in their own lives that makes them believe it's acceptable to behave in this manner…?" She shook her head in disbelief, blinked her eyes and held them shut for a couple of seconds, then re-opened them before continuing, "It's one thing snatching a person who has a sliver of a chance of fighting their way back out again, it's another kettle of fish entirely to capture such vulnerable and fragile people as those we have just seen. I mean they obviously weren't always that way but just look at what they've been reduced to. It's the lowest form of cruelty imaginable." She lowered her head and slumped her shoulders at the wickedness of it all.

"I make you quite right there," Phil stated, nodded his head in Christie's direction, thanked them both for "joining them on the couch this morning" and then turned back towards the camera to wrap that portion of the show up before they would go into an ad break. Holly joined him by reading out a list of support numbers that the viewers could call if they had been distressed by any of the topics they had discussed so far, then Phil took over again to read out the show's social media pages for viewers to get in touch and express their own viewpoints on the story.

Dale and Christie received warm handshakes and sincere thank yous from their gracious hosts, before being whisked off the set by Timothy so that the show could continue without them.

"Guys, that was exceptional," he praised Dale and Christie once they were away from the recording equipment. "I know that must have been a particularly painful process, especially during the second half, but you did really well in maintaining your composure and I salute you." He had such a whimsical manner that it was hard not to feel slightly comforted by his compliment. "I'll take you back to the waiting room, where some refreshments have been laid out for you, so just help yourselves and I'll make arrangements for your travel assistance to be allocated."

Dale and Christie nodded in acceptance and followed Timothy's lead back to the waiting room, not really knowing how to fill the silence along the way. Just outside of the doorway, he thanked them for their time, bid them farewell and sashayed back in the other direction to continue with his busy schedule.

They were slightly out of sight of the inhabitants of the

waiting room and Dale turned to look Christie in the eye. "That was heavy," he said and pulled her into his arms, resting his cheek on her forehead.

About a minute passed before her voice came out muffled against his shoulder, "There's so much hatred spiralling out of control out there." He leaned his top half back slightly so he could hear her better. "Do they really think that responding to evil with acts of revenge is the right way to go about it? All that's gonna happen is that more people are gonna get hurt – some of them completely innocent and maybe even unaware of what was happening in their family. Or maybe they knew but were intimidated into silence. Who knows? It's just... it's scary and it doesn't look like it's gonna go away any time soon. It's like my escape has spawned an entire movement of malice and retribution. I don't want my name to be associated with people fighting or seeking vengeance on one another. Why do people have to turn on each other? Why can't we all try to pick up the pieces together and make it right?" She was rambling a little now and Dale could tell that her mind was whirring out of control.

"Hey, shhhh." He comforted and rubbed her back up and down three times. "Don't for one second believe that you could have helped prevent this outcome. This level of political unrest has been building up for a *long* time. People have been frustrated as hell with the government for God knows how long and they just wanted an excuse to channel that anger somewhere. This seems like a pretty perfect opportunity to do that so of course they're gonna milk it for all it's worth. It is *not* your job to worry about any of this. All you gotta worry about is your own wellbeing right now, OK?" He placed both hands on her shoulders and gave her a tiny shake as though that motion would drum his words into her.

A tear rolled down her cheek as she nodded and replied, "OK."

He wrapped her back into a tight, protective and caring hug and held her there for a few minutes, feeling in absolutely no rush to let go of her and move on to the next task of the day. He was still in awe of the fact that she had made it safely back in one piece – he had thought for sure that he would never see her again and that thought had hurt him right down to his inner core. The three or four weeks that she had been missing had been torturous for him and he counted his lucky stars for being there, in that moment, having her wrapped safely against him and having the privilege to take care of her in her time of need.

Eventually it was Carrie that disturbed their moment when she came out of the door to the waiting room, making her way to the toilet.

"Oh, there you are!" she exclaimed, breaking them out of their spell. "I've been wondering when you were going to make your way back here. Are you all right?" she asked but didn't wait for an answer before animatedly continuing, "I was able to watch the whole interview on a small screen just through there." She pointed towards the other end of the waiting room where a little 'viewing section' had been segmented off with a flat screen and two armchairs. "There were quite a few of us crammed in there because everyone was keen to see what was going to happen, but they graciously let me have the prime seat. You both did really well. I know that must've been tough, especially watching those videos in the second half. Even I was welling up at those poor people in that horrific cess pit of a basement that they've been shoved into."

"Yeah, I'm not gonna lie, that part wasn't the most fun I've ever had," Christie joked as she untangled herself from the hug she had been so enjoying.

"At least it's out of the way now, ay?" Dale suggested but they all knew that that was far from the end of what they were going to have to deal with over the coming weeks, months – who knows, maybe even years.

Whilst Carrie excused herself to go and use the facilities, Dale and Christie decided to go and make the most of the refreshments that had been laid out for them. The spread was absolutely glorious and they filled their boots with the likes of freshly brewed, Italian coffee, English breakfast tea, pastries and fruit platters, allowing themselves to forget, even if only for just a brief moment in time, all of the drama that was unfolding around them. They sat quietly together, happily chewing, sipping and digesting before any more chaos hit them like a sledgehammer.

Chapter 7

Back in the borough of Barking and Dagenham, a huge police task force had been allocated to calming down and breaking up the ongoing protests taking place on Martin's Corner in Becontree. It was a lengthy job and required a lot of manpower as so many of the participants were incredibly militant and their vengeful mind set was deep seeded and relentless. They weren't about to give up without really making their feelings known on what had been allowed to continue right under their very noses, in their own neighbourhood, where their kids went to school and their relatives walked the streets thinking that they were safe when, in fact, nobody was safe. The blowing open of this case and the exposure of such a widespread network of affiliated underground gangs had been the realisation of the public's worst nightmares and their feelings of fear and unease had turned into spiteful anger and the only way they felt like they could make their feelings heard was by lashing out.

Over the coming days multiple arrests were made over the acts of arson that had taken place and all that did was make the general public even angrier at what they saw as a huge injustice because they felt they were fully justified in their actions against the money laundering businesses that had been discovered.

More importantly, there had also been a large number of arrests of various gang members and several family members of the two brothers that were still being held in police custody following the raid on the abandoned farm that Christie had originally escaped from. The arrests weren't simply taking place in the borough of Barking and Dagenham but stretching over to the neighbouring boroughs and even some further afield in various parts of London as a result of leads being followed and distant gang members being tracked down.

Due to the fact that they had been present from the beginning, Sue and Kate were placed at the head of the elite task force allocated to interviewing these gang members and they relished in the idea of being able to break this case even wider open and get right down to the root cause of all of the evils that had been taking place for such a long time. They had both invested a lot of overtime in what had already been achieved and had no desire to take a break from it any time soon. The work sisters were dedicated to seeing this through to the very end and getting the best possible outcome they could to ensure the safety of the citizens under their jurisdiction.

After a great deal of interviews that had produced measly results due to the interviewees being too afraid to snitch on other gang members for fear of retribution, it was starting to feel hopeless. People would rather serve time in prison than discuss the heinous acts they had witnessed purely because they had seen the extent of what the perpetrators were capable of. They not only wanted to look after their own skin, but that of their families, friends and anyone remotely connected to them because they knew that everyone they loved or cared about would be at risk if they spoke of the monstrosities they had seen.

"Do you think we'll *ever* be able to crack *any* of them?" Kate half huffed, half whined at Sue in reference to the witnesses they had been interviewing unremittingly, whilst they filled their coffee mugs in the station kitchen.

Sue let out a long and weary sigh. "Eventually. One of them has to give us something. Regardless of whether they mean to or not, the second they give us even a snippet of information we need to pick at that stray thread until it unravels." She had a steely look of determination in her pale blue eyes, despite the deep-set dark circles that had started to form underneath them through lack of sleep.

"God damn family loyalty is strong in this lot. No wonder it's been kept hidden for so long when everybody's too afraid to say a word." Kate shook her head and rolled her golden hazel eyes, then took a large and very much needed gulp of her extra strong coffee with two sugars for an extra buzz.

"Yup," agreed Sue, "Are you ready for the next round? From what I'm told, this one may be slightly more open than what we've experienced thus far, but I don't wanna get either of our hopes up so let's keep an open mind. This one apparently has aspirations of going back to his home country of Poland, collecting the family that he still has there and moving them all on somewhere else. If there's *any* chance that we can strike a deal, let's see what he has to offer us."

Kate immediately seemed to perk up when she heard this, gulped down the rest of her coffee, quickly placed her mug in the dishwasher and said, "Let's do this."

They strode single file into the interrogation room emitting an air of confidence and authority and sat themselves down opposite their next witness, a muscular and fit looking white man in his mid-thirties, named Marcel. Kate went about her routine of switching on the recording equipment at the side of the desk and introducing them all for the sake of being played back later on, then settled back into her seat, allowing Sue to take the reins.

"Mr Kowalski, can I call you Marcel?" Sue asked politely.

"Sure," Marcel replied, opening his palms briefly and then retracting them again into loose fists, sat on top of the desk in handcuffs.

"Thank you, Marcel. What can you tell us about your arrest yesterday outside of the basement of the shop on Martin's corner?" Sue continued.

"Let's get this straight." Marcel had a notable Polish accent but his English was excellent and his tone abrupt. "I'm nowhere near as deeply embedded in this organisation as a lot of the men you arrested at the same time as me. I'm actually pretty new to it and I only took on the role when I lost my former security job thanks to all the Covid closures and I couldn't get work anywhere else."

He was referring to the huge amount of redundancies that had been made as a result of the global Covid-19 pandemic causing numerous businesses in a wide range of industries being forced to close their doors. A lot of businesses had re-opened since then but the large debts incurred had meant that staff had only been brought back to their previous roles if they were absolutely necessary to the running of the business. Many people were still in dire financial crises and it was understandable that some were venturing into industries that they had no former experience in.

"So, you're saying you don't feel as much loyalty to the organisation as the others, is that correct?" surmised Sue.

"No, I don't. But that doesn't mean I'm not aware of what may happen to me as a result of me telling you what you want to know. So tell me, what can you do for me to make sure that I am safe, that my family in Poland is safe, that we can move on with our lives unharmed and get as far away as we can from anyone that has any intention to make an example of what happens when you talk about things you're not supposed to talk about?" Marcel was clearly not going to give them anything until he had reassurance of protection from the organisation that he wanted so badly to disassociate himself from.

"Based on what I've read in the notes from your arrest, it would appear that your crimes are not as terrible as the other members of the organisation—" Sue began, but was rapidly interrupted by Marcel slapping his palm against the desk.

"I am *not* a member of that organisation," he spat out, almost aggressively, then took a deep breath, swallowed hard and composed himself. "My apologies, I didn't mean to snap. I just…I do not want to be associated with them anymore and I want you to know that I never got involved in what they were doing. I'll admit I was aware of some of it, only some of it, not all of it. I was *not* aware of any of the people trafficking and I am disgusted to find out about that." He let out a long sigh and buried his head in his large, sweaty palms. "I have daughters, ya know? I can't bear to imagine…" he trailed off, shaking his head.

"OK, Marcel. I believe you. We'll take this slowly and you can tell us all that you know," Sue continued reassuringly. "What I was *going* to point out was that because your crimes are actually very minimal in comparison to the members of the organisation, it will allow us the opportunity to offer you a certain level of protection from any repercussions from any outside parties, *if* you agree to fully cooperate and tell us everything you know. Do you understand?" she asked, completely matter-of-fact.

"Yes. I understand." Marcel nodded, "I want you to help me get my family out of Poland and to another location. A secret location, where nobody can track us. For that I will tell you anything you want to know."

Sue nodded back at him. Thankfully another member of the team had already received an almost identically worded request from Marcel during a preliminary interview with him earlier in the day and had started putting into action the necessary paperwork behind the scenes. "My colleague is just preparing a document for you to sign as we speak, which will confirm our dedication to re-homing you and your family in the very southern part of Sweden in exchange for your cooperation on all matters related to this case. Your family will be moved there first, whilst you remain here as long as is necessary to gain all of the information we need from you, so at least they will be safe from being tracked down. You will be under the protection of our tactical team at all times to ensure your own safety until we can fly you over to be with your family. Do you accept these terms?" she asked, entirely business-like on the outside but inwardly harbouring a strong sense of empathy toward his family.

She had read his file before coming into this interview. He had a wife of five years back home, and two young daughters – one two-year-old and one three-and-a-half-year-old. He had come to the UK seeking better wages to send back to them and had been planning on returning home to them within the year, but the COVID-19 pandemic had thrown a spanner in the works, meaning he'd had to accept work in the only place he could find it and that was what had landed him in the seat before her.

He had committed some fairly minor assault offences in his

duration of working for the organisation and when he was arrested he had been found to be carrying an illegal weapon. However, Sue genuinely believed him when he claimed to not know about any of the abducting and trafficking of people. She had always had an exceptional ability to read people – it was what also made her a highly skilled poker player – this man was sincerely disgusted when he spoke of the crimes that he had only been made aware of after his arrest.

Practically on cue, a young, slim, very pretty admin clerk entered the room carrying a document to hand over to Sue. She was smartly dressed but her shirt was far too baggy for her slim line figure, her hair was dishevelled and pulled back into a ponytail and her glasses kept slipping off her face as she moved. She looked like she had worked sixteen hours straight with no break as she placed the paper in front of her senior.

Sue thanked her and Kate grabbed her hand just before she had a chance to leave the room "Thank you, Sienna," she said with a warm, affectionate smile, "Now, *go. Home.* And do not come back for at least one day. That's an order. You've well and truly earned a breather."

Sienna smiled shyly, nodded her head and tucked a stray hair behind her ear, "Thank you, Ma'am. See you on Thursday." She scuttled out of the room and closed the door almost silently behind her.

Sue quickly read over the document, scribbled her own signature on the final page and swivelled it around for Marcel to do the same, handing over the pen to his open palm. He took slightly longer to read it over, English not being his first language and clearly wanting to be thorough, then he signed his name too, feeling satisfied and relieved. The tension noticeably dropped out of his shoulders and he eased his bulking frame back into the cool metal of the chair.

"Wonderful, thank you very much, Marcel. Why don't you start by telling us how you came to be hired by the organisation?" prompted Sue.

Marcel cleared his throat and began, "I've been in this country a couple of years now. Shortly after my wife gave birth to our second daughter, I realised that the money I was earning at home wasn't going to be enough to survive on and I have a few friends here who said I could stay with them if I needed to travel over and work for a while, send money back to the family, ya know?" He seemed to feel the need to fully justify his desire to support his family, despite that being the most obviously honourable and dedicated thing that a new father could do.

"At first I was hired by an agency who provided me with several jobs – all in security. They would rotate their workers regularly to keep things constantly in motion and I liked it. I would sometimes be working night shifts as a doorman to clubs or pubs, sometimes on building sites where they didn't want people to come in overnight and steal the machines or supplies, sometimes even in shopping malls. It was always different and that kept it interesting. I'd work a contract for three months at a time and then move on to the next place." He smiled at some distant memory. "My wife was happy because she could buy all the things my daughters needed and have some left over for herself. She likes pretty things and I like to be able to give those to her."

He shook his head, realising that he'd gone off topic. "When the pandemic hit UK shores, the work quickly dried up. I was easily dispensable and had no right to claim benefits here.

I looked into it. I managed to get pre-settled status after I went through the process of a EUSS application but that wasn't enough. You need to have been in country for five years before you qualify for settled status and even then, all it would really help with is getting some benefits paid into my account. The amount I would get would be totally inadequate to send home."

His breathing and speech had got more and more rapid, then he took a long breath, wiped his forehead and released it in one, drawn out exhale, clearly trying to steady his own nerves. "A friend of a friend heard about how desperate I was when we were all out drinking one night – I was kind of drowning my sorrows, ya know? I felt helpless. He gave me his phone number and told me to meet him the next day by Becontree train station 'cause he knew a guy who could give me some temporary work. He said if I proved myself as reliable and trustworthy the work would continue on a rolling basis and he said the money was great. He didn't tell me much more than that; it was all a bit cloak and dagger, like I wouldn't really find anything out until they knew I could be trusted.

"My first job was unloading boxes from different trucks into a warehouse on the outer skirts of Barking. It was pure grunt work but I didn't care. I was happy to be doing something and nobody asked any questions of each other or why we were there. There were a few of us that all seemed to be in a similar predicament – we'd lost our jobs and were just trying to make ends meet any way we could. It was nice to know I wasn't alone in that and I kept my mouth shut about how I'd got the job – we all did, we just worked and had a bit of a laugh without getting too friendly or nosey." He rolled his eyes and shook his head at how ridiculous that sounded considering what he knew now about the types of materials he had been unloading.

"The money they paid was excellent and all off the books, so I was very happy with the amount that I could send home and so was my wife. Things seemed to be looking up and I felt relieved. I was doing that for maybe three or four weeks and then an opening came up in a position more similar to what I had been doing beforehand in security. Again, they assured me it would always be different—"

Kate interrupted, "They?"

"They from higher up in the organisation," explained Marcel, "I still was not trusted enough to meet anyone important and I liked it that way. I didn't really want to know anyone, I just wanted to do my hours, collect my cash and go home." He was very firm in his explanation of how little he had wanted to be involved. "I was given my instructions from that same friend of a friend that I mentioned earlier. He told me his name is Andrei, but that probably isn't true. He wanted me to come and work as part of his crew, told me not to ask any questions and to just accompany them as a security detail. We would go to different locations depending on what was needed each week and all we were asked to do was patrol the grounds of each location, make sure no outsiders could get in and whoever and whatever was inside was protected. I was given a gun so I knew they were up to something they shouldn't be, but I had no idea how far this thing went, I promise you." He buried his head in his hands at that point, clearly struggling with his own inner turmoil about the role he had maintained in all of this foul play.

"No one is blaming you for wanting better for your family, all we need from you is as many details as you can give us about those higher up in the organisation," Sue reassured him in a calm and patient manner. "What you can provide us with could be extremely valuable in putting a complete halt to the criminal activity that has been going undetected for so long. Together, we could stop anyone else from getting hurt."

Marcel drew his face away from his hands and took another long, steadying breath before continuing, "On one of the later and quieter shifts that I did with just Andrei, we were so bored and had nothing to do and it was one of the only occasions he told me more than necessary about the organisation and the people at the top. He told me that it had been started a long time ago and as it had developed alongside technological advancements, it had grown in size but had stayed run by the same family since the beginning. He said the man that had been in charge for the last couple of decades had passed away a year ago and that his widow had been in charge of decision making since, but that her role in any of it was kept top secret from anyone who isn't immediate family or very, very close friends. I can tell you with almost certainty that this woman is the mother of two of the men you currently hold in police custody. I can also tell you that she has a third son who is integral in the running of the organisation and the last I heard was that he had ran off somewhere to hide. If you manage to find the mother, I doubt very much that she will talk but she's the one holding the reins and getting access to her will surely lead to getting access to other people who may be more susceptible to outside pressure."

"Can you think of anyone who may be able to get us access to her or to the whereabouts of the third son?" asked Sue.

"That's the thing, everyone is very, *very* scared of what will happen to them if they open their mouth. For me, this is a huge risk, even though I know I haven't given any specific names or ways to find them, just pointing you in the right direction means that I'm going to have a major target on my back. I just want to get away from here and get into a position where my family will be safe and we can just forget about any of this," replied Marcel.

"We understand. Like I said earlier, we will be putting steps in place to move your family first, but we will need you to stick around for a little while to give us as much information as possible. Would you be willing to view a line-up of some of the men we arrested at the same time as you, to see if you can spot Andrei or anyone else that you think might be able to answer some more questions for us? We will also need to consider whether or not you will be useful when this thing goes to trial. Your identity would be concealed from those on trial at all times if that's the case and we would only consider putting you through that if it's absolutely necessary, I'm just warning you ahead of time that it may come to that," advised Sue.

"I can pretty much guarantee you that if you question Andrei it will be like talking to a brick wall. He's absolutely terrified of the organisation's higher-ranking members; it was obvious when he told me as little as he did. No names ever, no specifics, he only ever spoke of them like they were some sort of all-knowing, all-powerful force to be reckoned with. I will point him out for you if I see him in any line-up, I'm just sayin'," Marcel assured them.

"Thank you, Marcel, we'll leave it there for now but may have some more questions for you later. You've been a great help so far. I know that must have been a tough decision to make, but you've done the right thing and we will do our best to keep you and your family safe from any backlash," Sue offered him with genuine gratitude. He was literally the only one who had given them anything to go on and he seemed sincerely troubled by the fact that he had had any type of involvement with such a vicious and cruel group of people.

After dismissing Marcel to his holding quarters and arranging for him to be kept under supervision, but not treated like a prisoner, Kate set about instructing her colleagues to do some more intensive digging into the ancestry of the two brothers they had been holding in custody since the original raid on the abandoned farm Christie had escaped from. It was less than two weeks since that day and yet in her mind, it felt like a lifetime since she had met with the trooper of a woman that she had come to view Christie as, despite her slightly emotional and fragile state the day they had met her.

The more that came to light about this case and the perpetrators involved, the more astounding it became to Kate and her colleagues that this delicate looking, kind and compassionate woman had actually fought her way free from the imprisonment she had been subjected to. She had seized the opportunity, punched a guy in the throat, slammed his head into a wall, stripped his shoes and jacket for herself and then ran for it. She was something else. And not only that, but in her chemically induced haze, she had somehow managed to memorise details of the crime scene to feedback to the cops and help rescue the rest of the prisoners she'd been forced to leave behind.

Sue, in the meantime had gone to fetch suspect number three or as Christie referred to him, the errand boy, from his cell because she figured that he would be slightly easier to put pressure on than his mammoth, cold and expressionless brother. The younger of the two seemed to be harbouring at least some guilt about what he had done, whereas his brother showed not a single shred of remorse. Either he was incredibly good at hiding his feelings from the outside world, or he just didn't have any. Sue had seen it on a few occasions where a criminal had been through so much trauma in their own upbringing that they felt completely detached from any type of human emotion or sentiment. When she had looked into his icy, vacant eyes she had recognised that same reaction in him.

His brother, on the other hand, appeared to be a different story entirely and that was the stray piece of thread that Sue had her sights set on unravelling. She had seen a look of true remorse on his face when they had very first questioned him after the raid on the abandoned farm and at the mention of Christie's name, she had seen something else – an extremely pained look. Like perhaps he was hiding stronger feelings for her than he would like to let on or would want anyone to believe, especially not his brother or any of the people he was working for. Sue had to remind herself not to get her hopes or expectations up too much because it was clear that family loyalty had been drilled into him, most likely from a very early age, so it would have been all he'd ever known as he was still relatively young. Still, it was certainly worth a shot and Sue would take *any* shot she could at getting to the people at the very top of this corrupt and malicious organisation that had wrecked so many lives to date. She wanted to be part of the total destruction of the entire network, like a metaphorical wrecking ball to all of the evil they had spread and to make sure it stayed wrecked, never to be rebuilt or reformed.

Sue and Kate let their little friend stew on his own in the interrogation room for a short time whilst they re-filled their coffee mugs for what felt like the hundredth time that day and their trusted colleagues in the admin team collected more details as per Kate's request.

"Seriously, after we break this case I'm gonna need a full blown caffeine detox!" joked Kate. "My nervous system is shot to pieces with all these long hours."

"I think my system's too far gone now – if I were to give up the caffeine for even a day my body wouldn't know what to do with itself and I reckon I'd end up rolling around like I was withdrawing from the hard stuff," Sue retorted.

They each took a sip and sighed loudly, then laughed at how in unison they both were. They'd been through so much together but this was, by far, the biggest and most important case they'd handled and it just seemed to keep getting bigger and longer the more that was exposed at each and every turn.

"Who knew it was gonna go this far, ay? I feel like every single lead we follow up just uncovers more and more evil and debauchery at every turn. It's like a giant, tangled up web, that when you think you've undone one knot enough to make the whole thing unravel, all it does is tangle up a different set of knots." Kate's mind was buzzing and starting to go into overdrive.

"We've had this chat before, my girl." Sue was ever the calming influence. "Don't allow yourself to get overwhelmed by the complexity of it all and get bogged down with worrying about how we'll ever find a way out. Just pick at each and every knot, one at a time, showing care with each one and being as thorough as you possibly can. The rest will eventually fall to pieces; patience and resilience are key," she said intentionally slowly, a pure Zen master.

Kate was practically bouncing now that the caffeine and sugar combination had kicked in and she couldn't resonate with how cool and steady her work sister was being. "Are we ready to do this?"

She practically snatched the mug out of Sue's hands and loaded both of them into the dishwasher.

Sue placed a soothing hand on Kate's shoulder, then gently spun her around to face the exit. "Yes we are."

They strode confidently down the corridor, collected the relevant file from the admin department and entered the interrogation room, giving away nothing with their expressions.

Once inside, they politely greeted the errand boy, whose real name was Luca, and took their seats at the table facing him. Kate switched on the recording device and gave her usual introductions into the machine, then handed the reins over to Sue.

"Mr Balan, welcome back. May I continue calling you Luca?" Sue began formally.

"Yes." Luca barely looked her in the eye when he responded. He looked nervous and sweaty, as though the walls were closing in on him and he felt trapped.

"Thank you. Luca, I wanted to get to know a little bit more about you, if I may?" Sue continued, "Why don't we start with what it was like growing up in your household? I understand your family are Romanian but that you were, in fact, born here in the UK. Is that correct?"

"Yes." All Luca was giving away was an incredibly tense and agitated vibe. It made Sue wonder if perhaps he was withdrawing from anything.

"So you've been here your whole life? Or did you travel back and forth somewhat?" Sue already knew the answer as she had read his file thoroughly – including travel details from his passport that a member of her admin staff was able to extract using the home office app on his work phone. All she was doing was trying to lull him into a false sense of security and get him to open up to her.

Luca made a half-arsed attempt at shrugging his shoulders and shifted his weight around in the metal chair, looking extremely uncomfortable. Despite his bedraggled appearance, where he had obviously suffered a few sleepless nights, there was something relatively attractive about him. He had piercing blue eyes that looked ocean deep and like they stretched far beyond the surface, hiding a multitude of secrets away from any prying outsiders.

However, he also looked like he hadn't eaten in days and Sue noticed that his cheekbones were far more prominent than they had been when he was first arrested, as though he'd dropped a considerable amount of weight just by being in custody.

Sue pressed on, "What's your relationship like with your brothers?"

Luca looked directly at her then, knowing immediately that she had discovered it was his family at the bottom of all of this. It hadn't taken her long. He had hoped and prayed that somehow the family would have managed to stay underground and unexposed; after all, they had done so long before he was born. What was so different now? Who had opened their mouth? How much did this woman or any of the other cops know? A large bead of sweat ran down the side of his face, barely missing his eye. He could hear a gentle, yet shrill ringing in his ears and his breathing got shallower and more rapid.

Kate noticed the change in him as soon as it happened and kindly pulled a tissue from a box next to the recording equipment and handed it over so that he could wipe his brow. He looked at it for a few seconds, suspicious of her gesture, then hesitantly snatched it from her hand with an awkward and apologetic look on his face, before dabbing his overheated forehead and wiping away the excess fluid that had now cascaded down the side of his neck.

"I see there's quite an age gap between the three of you." Sue glanced at his file that was open in front of her, though that was purely for show as she had already memorised the most important details from it before they entered the room. She had a flare for detail and always liked to stay informed ahead of time. "Between you and Augustin, the other Balan we have here in custody, there's eight years and between you and Gabriel there's a whopping sixteen years!" Sue exclaimed in a slightly over the top fashion. "I imagine you must have felt like you had a lot to live up to, theoretically being the runt of the family." She was trying to push his buttons now and induce some sort of outraged reaction from him. "Did they push you around a lot growing up? It must have been difficult with your dad being so engrossed in his business as much as he was. I mean, who could you turn to for support or to back you up when your brothers were being too heavy handed?"

Luca balled his hands into tight fists, crumpling the sweaty piece of tissue in the process. "My father was a great man," he said through gritted teeth.

"Was he? Tell me more about him," Sue ventured, but was met with a cold, hard stare from Luca. She waited for a minute and tried again, "What about your mum Olga? Do you get on well with her?" Though he had bristled when Sue referred to his mother by name, he continued to hold his jaw firmly closed.

"All right, how about we leave the family stuff behind for now and talk about your job on the farm instead?" Sue's voice remained even and consistent, giving absolutely nothing away about how much she wanted to grab both his shoulders and shake the answers right out of him. "Did you like working there? It's quite an attractive piece of land when you take the unsightly storage containers out of the equation. What did your role entail?"

Luca's gaze had now lowered to the table in front of him, his head hanging in shame as he remembered the months he had spent there, tending to the needs of the women that came and went. At first he had made the terrible mistake of letting a couple of the women see his weaker side. He'd tried to apologise to them on multiple occasions and explain that he didn't want to be there, that he had just been following orders.

That had ended badly, with one of them trying to seduce him so that she could ultimately make her escape when she had him in a compromised position, the other launching a raging attack on him when she had identified his vulnerability and wanted to use that to her advantage. Both of those women had met their bitter end at the hands of his colleagues on the farm as a result and that was a guilt that he would carry with him for the rest of his life.

After that he had made a conscious effort to remain completely detached from any of the women he tended to. He refused to say a word to them and mostly avoided any eye contact as he went about his duties of bringing food, drinks and fresh clothing into their rooms, whilst removing any dirty laundry and waste. He was much like a room attendant at a hotel in that sense, though they at least had the dignity of cleaning rooms whilst they were empty. He abhorred having to face the prisoners every time he stepped over the threshold to do his job. They looked at him with such disdain and he didn't feel like he deserved that. He hadn't put them there for crying out loud! He didn't want to be the one absorbing *any* of the blame for what was taking place there. He was merely following orders to avoid his own beating. None of it was fair. He remained still and quiet, mulling over his thoughts with a sullen expression on his face.

"You must have seen a whole variety of women coming onto the farm, only to be shipped off later right?" Sue interrupted his trance, "Then there was Christie. The one that got away. What do you suppose was different about her?" Both Sue and Kate studied Luca's reaction intently and they weren't disappointed.

At the mention of Christie's name he noticeably blanched and his entire body seemed to stiffen, seemingly awaiting a pummelling from some unseen force.

Sue and Kate exchanged glances and Kate briefly interjected, "Do you know what became of Christie once she broke out of the farm?"

Luca leaned forwards in his chair and raised his eyes to meet Kate's at that point, searching for answers with a look of deep seeded urgency in them. He had unwittingly found himself caring for Christie during her time at the farm. He had no idea what was so different about her – she seemed gentle and radiated a sweetness that none of the others had. She had questioned him in the first couple of days but not aggressively, more like she was trying to wrap her own head around how any other human could be capable of inflicting such crimes against their fellow neighbour. He had had no answers for her, though he wished he had.

He wanted to reach out to her and explain everything, to hold her, to somehow be her knight in shining armour and set her free. She had quickly given up trying to seek any explanation from him and barely acknowledged him when he entered her room, always making sure there was a distinct distance in between them whenever he did, showing her suspicion of an imminent attack on his part. How ironic that the attack had eventually come from her and she had caught him off guard before making her own break for freedom. It was quite poetic really.

"She's doing well, all things considered," Kate said dryly, "She's a tough cookie, that one."

Luca felt a wave of relief wash over him and his demeanour relaxed as he slumped back into the chair. He was glad she had made it out in one piece and Kate had been right when she said the words "all things considered" – it was some sort of miracle that Christie had fought her way through the surrounding woods on the outskirts of the farm. He knew how dense they were after managing to get himself lost in them on more than one occasion and the fact that she'd made it to the other side in the drugged state his colleague had put her in was practically superhuman.

"You're glad about that, aren't you?" asked Kate, "You cared about her, didn't you?"

Luca let out a weary and satirical laugh, tilted his head back to gaze at the ceiling for a few seconds, shook his head back and forth then very slowly leaned forward and placed his forehead on top of the backs of his hands, with his palms resting on the table. He remained still, the only slight movement in his body was his calm and measured breathing. He looked almost peaceful, like he was in danger of falling asleep right there at the desk in the interrogation room.

Sue decided that was all they were going to get out of him

at that point in time. Perhaps he would be more open to questioning at a later stage, once he had rested, whatever withdrawals he was suffering had subsided and they had gathered more information to be able to put pressure on him. All they had at this point were the names of his family members that were still at large. The mother would be simpler to track down than the missing older brother, but both were an absolute necessity to truly blowing this case wide open and getting justice for all of those that had been harmed along the way. Kate wrapped up the recording and grabbed one of her colleagues from just outside in the corridor to escort Luca back to his cell.

There, he collapsed face down on to his bunk and almost immediately fell into a deep, all-consuming sleep, Christie's exquisite face at the forefront of his mind as he drifted off into the abyss.

"He's not quite ready yet, but I think we can break him at some point." Kate had a look of deep concentration on her face as she summarised what had just happened in the interrogation room, gently stroking her chin as she did so.

"I think so too," agreed Sue, "Did you see the look on his face when I asked what his role at the farm entailed? It's obvious he didn't want any part of this – he was forced into it out of some bizarre, warped sense of family loyalty. I can see that it's been eating him up inside and if we can find a way to play on that, we can pull it apart and potentially get something helpful from him."

"We need to find the mother," muttered Kate.

As if her words had conjured a magic spell the very moment they left her lips, a stout, well past middle aged, greying black man entered the room carrying a slip of paper.

He, too, looked as though he had been working serious over time as his large spectacles were covered in smudges, his shirt unbuttoned at the collar and slightly overhanging his trouser waist. He handed over the slip of paper to Sue and said, "We have a development for you, Ma'am."

Sue glanced down at the note where she saw various scribbles of address information, a time of raid, a list of suspects that had been found, arrested and were on their way to the station for questioning. The most notable name on that list: Olga Balan. A flush of excitement ran through her entire body and she showed the note to Kate.

"Olga Balan is on her way here now?" she asked of Frank, the deliverer of the good news.

"Yes, Ma'am." Frank nodded with glee at being the one to provide such prized information.

"Right on, Frank." Kate raised her hand to high five him and he gratefully accepted the motion. "Could you prepare the relevant file and as soon as she's arrived and has been processed, bring her straight to one of the interrogation rooms, then come and let us know, please? I wanna catch her off guard before she has time to think up any type of strategy."

"I sure can," he replied and practically skipped down the corridor in the opposite direction. He was rather spritely for an older gentleman and it was plain to see that being a part of solving this case meant a lot to him. He had always come across as a big family man – his desk was littered with happy, exuberant photos from graduations, weddings, birthdays and so on and these photos were populated by a high percentage of female family members. Seeing what happened to the victims of this case must have sparked all sorts of horrific mental images in his head of how it would feel for one of his own to be snatched from him unexpectedly with the aims of trafficking her off to some distant, unknown location under the 'ownership' of a ghastly tyrant. He was relishing in his own ability to play a part in the righting of so many wrong doings and bringing the perpetrators to justice.

It took a little while for Olga to arrive and go through the motions of being entered into the system so Sue and Kate did what they always do whenever the opportunity presented itself – they retreated back to the office space that they so rarely enjoyed sitting in and only made use of when necessary. They both much preferred to be on the go and only utilised it for admin purposes, phone calls that needed to be made with zero distractions or private meetings with important members of the hierarchy. However, they had also made some adjustments to the space so that, when they worked ridiculously long hours, they could comfortably take a nap on top of either one of the two soft couches they'd placed along two of the walls that didn't face each other. They stashed a box with a couple of pillows and light blankets, plus some essential toiletries for freshening up afterwards. Both of them crashed into a deep sleep as soon as their heads hit their pillows and they only woke to the shrill sound of the office phone ringing, which they knew signalled the go ahead for their interview with Olga.

The time was now upon them to come face to face with the matriarch who sat at the head of the organisation behind this vile scandal. They entered the interrogation room wearing serious faces and not knowing what on earth to expect when they sat down.

Olga sat before them, completely free from any type of giveaway expression, just entirely placid and unruffled.

Everything about her was tiny – her height, her width, her limbs all seemed to have been shrunk in the wash or downsized by a computer mouse. She was in her late seventies, heavily wrinkled, with smooth, grey hair that rested in a tightly wound bun at the base of her neck. Both her make-up and her outfit were pristine and she clearly cared extensively about her appearance to the outside world. She sat in a position that would imply she had once been given etiquette lessons on how a woman should and shouldn't hold herself in society in a distant, gone-by era.

After Kate had done their introductions into the recording machine, Sue began, "Good afternoon, Mrs. Balan. May I call you Olga?"

"I prefer Mrs. Balan," came Olga's aloof reply.

"Very well, Mrs. Balan, do you understand why you have been brought here?" continued Sue, unperturbed by the brusqueness of her suspect. She was met with stone cold silence from Olga, who simply stared back at her through those same icy eyes that she shared with her son, Augustin, who was sitting silently in his cell in this very same building.

"Are you aware of the charges that two of your sons are facing as well as the charges that are currently being compiled against yourself?" Sue pressed.

Olga sat feeling nothing but contempt for these two righteous women before her. They knew nothing of what she had been through and what they thought they knew about the organisation was so horrendously skewed that she didn't feel like she could possibly communicate with them. They were entirely one sided in their opinions and ignoring all of the intricacies that made her network so masterful and essential to the running of society as they knew it. They had no idea how much the pillars of civilisation rested on the actions of those that were willing to go the extra mile, bend the rules, take the risks in order for the rest to live in this idyllic little bubble of morality and honour. What a joke. There was no honour in ripping apart what she had worked so hard to maintain and keep hidden away from the outside world. All they were doing was cutting off their nose to spite their faces but she wouldn't be able to explain that to them in a way that they would remotely understand.

"Mrs. Balan, don't you want to at least try to help your sons? Telling us the truth could make all the difference in their sentencing." Kate tried to appeal to her motherly side.

Olga had drifted away in her own memories by that stage and Kate's words barely touched her periphery. She was back in her heyday where things made more sense to her and she felt untouchable by any negative outside influence. She was with her beloved Marius, the father of her three boys, but only Gabriel, their oldest, had been born at this stage. She was the wife of an extremely powerful man who commanded the respect of an elite crew of men in Romania and his prestige was growing exponentially the more networking and business he did with neighbouring companies.

When she had originally met Marius she had disliked him in every way imaginable. Her union with him had been against her will – much like the women whose faces were currently all over the news for being rescued from their imprisonment on the abandoned farm, she too had been snatched from her hometown of Uglich in Russia and trafficked into Romania to be married to her winning bidder. She had heard horror stories of this type of thing happening in towns nearby but she had been dismissive of the idea and never envisioned herself falling victim to such an immoral act.

When she had first arrived in her new, luxurious home she had tried more times than she could count to escape and flee home to her family. She wanted nothing to do with the man that had forced her into this dreadful, though gloriously lavish dwelling, but all of her attempts failed and she found herself imprisoned against her will in a fairy-tale like palace that most young women could only dream of.

Over time she had gradually accepted Marius' advances and slowly came to love him. She later found out that he had taken it upon himself to visit her parents back in Uglich to offer them a vast sum of extra money on top of what he had already paid for Olga's sale. They had accepted and told him to wish their daughter the best of luck in her new life. From that moment she had vowed to make the best of what had seemed like a truly awful situation and fully embraced her new role as the wife of this powerful, distinguished, highly respected man. She had come to realise just how devastatingly handsome he was and before she knew it, he had become her everything and their family unit had grown into the embodiment of an almighty stronghold on the society beneath their feet.

These two pathetic women that sat in front of her with their silly questions knew nothing of what it took to reign supreme over as many people as she had done in her time, once with her beloved Marius by her side and now completely solo. She had shouldered the burden of maintaining the organisation in his honour when he had passed away from liver cancer over a year ago and her intent had been to pass it on to her eldest son when she parted these earthly planes. She could already feel it in her body that she didn't have much longer to go and she had been busily preparing all of the 'handing over' documents and making sure all of her affairs were in order.

Now everything she had worked for was in turmoil, two of her sons were in custody and her eldest had gone on the run. How had it come to this? She felt devastated and deflated on the inside but there was no way she would reveal any of that to the outside world, so she remained completely composed and held herself together, obstinately refusing to answer any of the questions presented to her.

"You know, if you actually open up to us and tell us what you know, there is a chance we can help you and even better, help you help your sons," Kate said through ever so slightly gritted teeth, trying her best to appear both professional and helpful towards this woman that she had taken an instant disliking to. Really the last thing she wanted to do was bargain with her but she felt it worth a shot at getting the stubborn old mule to confess to what she had done. "It must be painful to know that two of them are sitting in this very building, locked away, awaiting the news of what will become of them. Meanwhile, the other is fleeing for his life as we speak and you have no idea when you'll ever see him again. Don't you wanna see if you can help repair some of the damage that Christie did the day she escaped?" That second part was a stab in the dark to try and test Olga's reaction and the elderly woman broke her composure by spitting on the ground at the mention of Christie's name. She had a look of pure disdain on her face as she did so, the hatred burning visibly behind those characteristically icy irises.

Kate saw that opportunity and pounced on it, "It must feel like a bit of a slap in the face, having a young, beautiful, caring and compassionate woman be the one that brings down the tyranny of the organisation that has been so far ahead of the game for so long and completely hidden from the watchful eye of the authorities. How did it feel when you found out that she was the one to expose you all? That someone so sweet and gentle could turn out to be the metaphorical David to your Goliath?" She enjoyed every moment of trying to make Olga squirm, trying her hardest to rattle her cage and break that seemingly impenetrable stone wall she had built up around herself.

Olga merely shifted her body weight in her metal chair, uncrossed her legs and then re-crossed them on the opposite side. She blinked a very long blink, sighed loudly and pointedly, and then re-opened them with her frosty glare.

On any other day, she had a set of rosary beads around her neck that she would remove, wrap around her wrist and stroke the cross pendant that was at the bottom back and forth as a self-soothing and calming measure. She couldn't do that now because they had made her remove the beads when she had been processed by the station staff in case she had any suicidal ideations. As if she would risk her soul for the sake of escaping this situation! It was laughable to her but also pissed her off to no end that they had taken her beads from her. They had belonged to her darling Marius and even back when he had worn them, she had always stroked them whenever she felt stressed. He could read her like a book; whenever he sensed her anxiety or stress he would take the beads off, gently wrap them around her wrist and kiss the back of her hand in a silent "Take these until you feel better" kind of gesture. Now she just rubbed her thumb back and forth against the side of her clenched fist until it started to become quite raw under the pressure of her fury.

Sue attempted to play good cop, which was an entirely new dynamic for her and Kate – they usually played good cop/bad cop in opposite roles to this. She wasn't used to playing nice, "What would make you feel more comfortable about opening up to us? How can we make this process simpler and beneficial to all?" The words left a bad taste in her mouth as she didn't like to tip toe around someone who was so obviously evil at their very core and completely unapologetic about it. In fact, she probably saw her actions as justified in some disgustingly distorted manner. What on earth had happened to this woman in her life that made her think her behaviour or her family's behaviour was acceptable in the slightest? She swallowed down the bile that was threatening to rise up the back of her throat as pictures of the victims unintentionally ran through her mind.

Once it had become clear that Olga was not going to budge on her silent stance or provide any help whatsoever, both Sue and Kate decided it was time to wrap things up and have Mrs. Balan escorted to her own cell to think about the way things had turned out for her. Hoping that it would inspire any sort of change in attitude was far-fetched and they both knew that but there wasn't much else they could do at that moment in time. Now their best bet was to locate the missing brother and bring them all down in one fell swoop. If he was left out there to his own devices he could very well start picking up the pieces of the broken up organisation and start fresh elsewhere.

This thing spanned over multiple countries in Europe – who was to say he hadn't already fled there and was putting steps into place to rebuild from scratch? They had no idea how many contacts still remained underground and unexposed since the original breakthrough raid on the abandoned farm. How simple would it be to lay low for a little only to re-emerge as a newly branded organisation with partial old members and new recruits working side by side to learn from the mistakes made here and put processes in place to ensure they never repeat them? That concept was more terrifying than anything. The need to find Gabriel and *any* of his concealed associates was imperative.

After giving their instructions to the admin team to keep digging for any more intel they could find that may possibly help them on their quest whilst also handing out instructions to the tactical team to continue searching every nook and cranny across the borough of Barking and Dagenham, its neighbouring boroughs and stretching out further afield as necessary, the work sisters decided to call it a day to give their bodies some well-earned rest. They knew that they would function far better once they'd indulged in a brief period of R'n'R, though neither one of them was under any illusion that they would be able to fully switch off from thoughts about the case. There was just so much that still needed to be dug up and processed before they could even take this thing to trial and get justice properly served. However, it was worth being thorough and making sure anything remotely close to this was never allowed to happen again.

Chapter 8

As time progressed and further police raids continued to take place, more and more gang members were arrested and brought into custody to figure out how deeply they were involved in the organisation and all of its wrong doings. It was utterly shocking just how many people were taking a cut from the money earned during the course of the worst acts of human exploitation imaginable. It seemed like the underworld of crime and gang affiliations was in actual fact holding up the rest of society on its seedy shoulders. The more that came to light and was plastered all over the daily news, the more political and social unrest there was amongst the general public and this movement seemed to be gaining more and more followers by the day. It was now being reported on across the globe and the faces of all those involved were now commonplace in the national media arena. Everybody seemed to want a piece of the action and to sensationalise the story as much as they could in order to get the highest ratings. People were actually entertained by the suffering of others and it was sickening to those that simply wanted to put this whole sordid affair behind them and move on with their lives.

Though Christie had returned home to her decidedly shabby HMO in Dagenham, things were far from being back to normal for her and she wondered if they ever would be. Certainly not whilst the trial was still looming anyway and that didn't appear to be coming into action any time soon as they were still working hard to bring in *all* of the guilty parties and every time she checked, those seemed to have multiplied. She had been advised by her GP to take a substantial amount of time off work, which she hated because she absolutely adored her work in the charity sector but was also aware of how necessary it was. She was no good to anyone else unless she was feeling completely OK herself so it was important to take stock of her own needs first.

For now, all she could do was attempt to make the best of a bloody awful situation and throughout the process of it all, try to remain authentic to her true self instead of getting too caught up in the media circus that appeared to be following her every move. Now she had a greater understanding of what those troubled celebrities she had read about in the past were talking about when they described how being followed by the paparazzi was too heavy to deal with and how much they struggled to cope with it all. It was such an intrusion on a person's life to be continuously hounded for the sole purpose of satisfying the gossip needs of the masses, but Christie tried her hardest to remain respectful and composed whenever she was faced with the task of answering the questions that were fired at her non-stop.

Both Sue and Kate had been very sweet in their constant checking up on her, whilst also letting her know that they were still working hard behind the scenes to bring everyone involved to justice. Christie felt like she had gained life-long friends in the seemingly superhuman pair of relentless policewomen and she appreciated their efforts no end.

She had also been contacted by a number of the other victims that were rescued as a result of the raid on the abandoned farm as they wished to express their gratitude for her having the strength to do what they hadn't been able to do for themselves. They had now formed their own exclusive support network and regularly chatted via a group chat on WhatsApp to keep tabs on how they were all coping with the residual nightmares, PTSD symptoms and the excessive attention they were getting from the media.

There were certain good aspects about having a famous face – Lacey was a perfect example of that as her charitable venture to help female victims of crime had garnered a huge amount of support and had come along leaps and bounds from its humble beginnings. She was currently in the process of signing tenancy agreements for multiple buildings in different neighbourhoods that would act as bases for her charity to run their support groups from and as safe spaces for women to find shelter from ongoing crime or abuse. She was flourishing in her role and was now also giving inspirational talks to widespread audiences about how to turn trauma into something positive.

Hearing about Lacey's mounting success made Christie think hard about ways in which she too could turn what she had been through both during and after her abduction and imprisonment into a constructive and encouraging tool for other people to utilise in getting over their own struggles. She had been approached by numerous TV shows and publishers who wanted to buy the rights to her story and turn it into something more glamourous and dramatized but she hadn't found the right fit yet. She wanted someone to tell the nitty gritty truth about her story, not simply turn her into a superhero style heroine who had battled the forces of evil with her impressive strength and intuition. That didn't suit her one bit and she wasn't about to 'cash in' on her experience just to appease the production companies.

She would wait until someone presented her with an idea that told people the ugly facts about the world in which they lived, what to look out and prepare for, how best to bounce back from having the worst kind of human behaviour inflicted on you for no reason other than the fact that you happened to fit the mould of what they were actively seeking. She shuddered as she remembered what they had had in store for her – what would have become of her had she not had the bottle to take action that day. She thanked her lucky stars for her own courage, coupled with the adrenaline rush that had surged through her body in that moment. It got her where she was today – totally free.

Whilst Christie was at home feeling all of this gratitude for her freedom, safety and ability to potentially help others in the future, in a police station in central London a very different story was unfolding from the perspective of another victim of the organisation's trafficking antics.

Victoria was a stunning, tall, slim woman in her late twenties, with cascading, russet coloured hair, porcelain skin and the graceful appearance of a ballerina. She had been brought home to London from Hungary after being tracked down by a combination of all of the police forces involved in investigating this case. They had travelled to various different countries in Europe and managed to trace six further victims to date. Unfortunately, two of those had been found to be deceased when they raided the various properties they were being held captive in; the other four had been flown home as quickly as possible and were going through all of the motions of processing before being reunited with their families. It had thus far been quite a huge success story, with three of the captives being absolutely delighted with the turn of events and looking forward to seeing their loved ones again immensely.

Not Victoria. She was utterly fuming that she had been dragged back here against her will from the land and the man that she had fallen for during the last eighteen months of being held there after her sale to the highest bidder.

She had already gone through one round of intensive questioning by the police force that she had come to resent so deeply. She had grown quite rude to them the longer the process went on as they couldn't seem to get it through their thick skulls that she hadn't wanted to be "rescued"; she had wanted to be left alone to enjoy her current life with her husband and the friends that she had made along the way.

She sat alone in a non-prison like holding room at the station that was still technically like being imprisoned. She had been left there to cool off after a rather angry outburst where she had taken her frustration out on a police officer who was only trying to do their job. She did feel repentant about that as this particular individual had seemed very sweet and helpful but she had been pushed to her snapping point and they had been caught in the crossfire. All she had to keep herself company were thoughts of her devoted husband and she longed for him with every fibre of her being.

When she had been located, she was living in an enormous mansion in the Hungarian countryside, where she had multiple luxury vehicles at her disposal, a housemaid, a butler and she could essentially click her fingers to demand anything she wanted. She didn't do that; she hadn't become spoiled by her newly found riches and possessions, but she had grown accustomed to the lifestyle she had been living and she had fallen head over heels in love with the man who had purchased her at auction.

It hadn't been an intentional thing. The event of her being sold and shipped off to Hungary had happened so quickly that she had barely had a moment to realise what was going on. Between being snatched from a street close to her home in Chadwell Heath in the later hours after going for some drinks with her work colleagues, it had taken just three days to complete her sale and load her onto a boat headed towards Europe. She had spent the entire time blindfolded with her wrists and ankles bound, only being allowed to remove the blindfold to use the toilet and even when she did, the men who were transporting her remained concealed underneath balaclavas to protect their identities.

She hadn't seen a single face for the duration of her journey before being handed over to her new owner – she had heard voices along the way but they were in a language she didn't recognise and they only spoke around her in short bursts of instructions when necessary. All of the worst possible case scenarios had ran through her mind whilst being carted off to some unknown location to meet her mysterious fate. She had wept and felt so devastatingly alone and helpless. She couldn't see a way out of this and slowly grew to accept that this was it for her.

When she had arrived at her new mansion of a home, she had been taken to her private quarters where an older, yet still ravishingly beautiful maid with jet black hair and cream coloured skin, dressed professionally but also functionally, had immediately began tending to Victoria's styling regime. She had ran her a bath, prepared her lavish evening outfit and laid that out on the four poster bed for her, arranged a selection of beauty potions, elixirs and make-up products on the dressing table with all of the necessary tools to use them to their maximum effect. In a sense she had dressed Victoria up as though she were a doll, a mere plaything for her master to have his wicked way with. They had gone through this entire process in almost silence, with only the occasional instruction from the maid in English with a heavy Hungarian accent. Victoria had been far too terrified to argue, kick up a fuss or outright refuse to be tended to in this manner. She felt edgy, alarmed and so deeply confused, with no idea whatsoever what was going to happen to her that night or if she'd even make it through to the following morning in one piece.

Her first meeting with Sandor had proven to be far from the petrifying, degrading experience she had envisioned. It was actually quite the opposite. She had been led down a grand set of winding stairs, carpeted with divinely soft and expensive looking material and as she approached the bottom, she could hear a very light orchestral song being played from a distant location. He had been waiting at the very end of the staircase to greet her, dressed in a tailored dinner suit, with his hair and goatee beard styled to perfection. He smelled intoxicatingly good and was breathtakingly appealing in every sense of the word, holding his hand out politely for her to accept and to join him in an evening of overwhelming romance and carefully pre-thought out gestures.

Victoria had felt like a princess and allowed herself to simply let go and get swept up in the magnificence of it all. Who was here to tell her otherwise or to judge her decisions? Nobody. Nobody except this gorgeous man who stood before her, offering her the world if she would only consent to being his.

During their relationship she was considered to be his subordinate in all of their roles and interactions, but she had no qualms with this; she liked to feel like she had a purpose in life and this finally felt like it fit. It suited her to be his and she made the very best of what he had to offer her too. His business kept him occupied for most of the day almost every day but that was just fine because his colleagues had wives that she was introduced to and they all soon became exceptionally tight-knit because they had all essentially taken on the same role with their husbands. They were all picture perfect and happy to dress up and be put on show at banquets, balls, whilst attending shows and other black tie events. None of them saw this as degrading, humiliating or sexist in any way because they had all come from a background that they had deeply hated and wanted to escape from for a variety of reasons. They had all confided these reasons with one another and it had served to make their bond even stronger.

Victoria had picked up basic Hungarian quite quickly through their combined tutelage but they all shared English as a common trait because not all of them had been born there. In Victoria's case, she had confided in her new girlfriends that back at home in the UK she had been the victim of sexual abuse at the hands of her stepfather for many years and she hadn't been able to break free from his grasp because every time she tried, he would badly assault her mother, who was completely unaware of what he had been doing to her daughter for so long. She had tried and failed time and again to involve the police or social services because whenever it came down to it, he would use the threat of violence against her mother to make her retract her complaint. The services appeared to grow tired of repeating the same cycle of starting an investigation only to have it later retracted, particularly due to her lack of evidence as her stepfather was a master at covering his own tracks and making sure he had a false alibi ready for any occasion.

Her poor mother was suffering early onset dementia and deteriorating rapidly, which wasn't helped by the fact that her husband was plying her with alcohol all throughout the day in order to keep her mollified. It had been tearing Victoria apart to watch her mother go through this as well as suffering her own abuse at his hands and she had often wondered what her life was even worth to anyone.

In being purchased by Sandor she had come to realise just how much she was worth to the right person – he had saved her from her dreadful fate and whisked her away into a splendid new lifestyle that she would be a fool not to appreciate. That was how she saw it anyway and as she opened up to her new friends, they all congratulated her for her wonderful good fortune as they too had been rescued from their own individually traumatic situations.

They even encouraged her to confess all of this to Sandor and when she finally took that leap, he had proven to be incredibly supportive and had pulled her into his lap, wrapped her up tight in his strong arms, and rocked her back and forth whilst she had sobbed and told her nightmarish tale. Then he'd carried her to bed and laid with her, stroking her hair for hours whilst they bonded over their family history and what had brought them to where they had ended up at that moment in time. She had never felt closer to another human being in her life and she knew then that she would never love another man the way that she loved him.

All of the reminiscing left her weeping uncontrollably and she let her head rest on the side of the armchair she had been sitting in only to drift off into a weary sleep, wishing with all her might that when she woke up this would all have been a terrible nightmare that she would later laugh about with Sandor.

Meanwhile, in an interrogation room in that same police station in central London, two police officers were being told a completely different story from another one of the victims that had been located in Europe after being tracked down as a result of the developments made in this case.

Tara was a petite, attractive woman of half-Filipino descent, also in her late twenties, with thick, luscious black hair that fell most of the way down her back and dark brown eyes that radiated with sheer ferocity. When she had first arrived in the interrogation room she had been presented with one male and one female officer but at this moment in time her pure hatred for *all* males stood in the way of her being open and cooperative with them. She had demanded to speak to only women moving forwards and they had complied to make her feel as comfortable as possible. Now that they had gone through their introductions on the recording, she took a deep and steadying breath before she began.

"I was snatched from my hometown of Upney one night when I was making my way home after having a particularly long shift at Barking hospital. I was knackered and wasn't really paying too much attention, plus I had my earphones in and my playlist blaring so I didn't hear them coming. It was so quick. I had no time to react or put any of my self-defence moves into action. I'd been taking classes for about six months up until that point and for what? They were useless to me." She shook her head remorsefully and continued, "I had walked from one entrance of Mayesbrook park – the one closest to the Roundhouse pub, gotten all the way to the other side and was close to the exit nearest Clare gardens but suddenly there was a material bag over my head and arms pulling me in close to a large, heavy, hard body. His arms were wrapped so tight around me and I could tell that he was both tall and broad so no matter how much I struggled, I didn't stand a chance. My earphones fell out and I heard two male voices talking to each other but only a couple of words here and there and in a language I didn't recognise. They dragged me kicking and trying to scream against the bag and loaded me roughly into what I can only assume was a van as I heard the door slide shut behind me, with one of them joining me in the back, the other went round to the passenger side and got in there. Next thing I know, I'm in my little prison cell which looked like once upon a time it had been a storage container of some sort but now it had a loo at the back and a basin, plus stuff to get washed with.

"I had the pleasure of being 'measured for size' by a grubby man who stank and then was left to my own devices for the next week or maybe two – I can't remember now – with only one of the men coming in daily to bring me food, drinks and changes of clothing.

"One day I woke up and was no longer in that place; I was in transit somewhere else, blindfolded, bound at my wrists and ankles and gagged. I had no idea how long I'd been out for. My head felt groggy, as though I had a raging hangover or something worse. I could tell that I was on a boat of some description 'cause I suffer with terrible sea sickness and that was what had woken me up. I started to heave against the gag that was over my mouth and my whole body started to convulse where my vomit had nowhere to go. Somebody nearby pulled it off and I threw up all over them, which made them yell at me in disgust, like *any* of it was my fault." Her teeth were gritted now and she had to pause for another calming breath.

"Take your time, you're doing great." Kelly, a white and

slightly plump faced police officer with a bright ginger bob-style haircut, round, dark blue eyes and a warm, friendly smile gave the back of Tara's hand a couple of gentle rubs of encouragement.

Tara half-smiled back in appreciation and continued, "The rest of the journey is hazy at best. I felt weak, empty and queasy the entire time. I drifted in and out of a restless sleep and was transferred from boat to vehicle and driven to my new prison in the dark.

"When I came to I was in what I can only describe as a sex dungeon. I had been dressed in an outfit made of PVC that left nothing to the imagination and was extremely uncomfortable and I had been splayed out on a four-poster bed with my arms and legs stretched out, my wrists and ankles held strapped in place to each one of the four corners. It was the most terrifying and yet humiliating moment of my entire existence. There was nothing I could do but just lay there and wait for what happened next. I cried for what felt like hours but was probably no longer than twenty minutes as I didn't hold back. I was no doubt very noisy and alerted my captors to my consciousness. I sobbed uncontrollably, wailing loudly and thrashing against my restraints but it was no use, then I just laid there and prayed over and over again. I prayed for my life to end right there and then. I didn't want to know what 'they' had in store for me and I knew no one was coming to save me. Why couldn't it have just ended there?" She suddenly yelped, with tears rolling down her face.

Veronica, the second police officer with ebony skin, chiselled cheek bones, tightly curled black hair that was cropped short against her head and large, dark brown eyes, retrieved a handful of tissues from the box at the side of the desk and handed them over to Tara without saying a word. She appeared to be struggling with her own emotion at seeing this beautiful, tortured woman breaking down in front of her and had chosen to swallow down her own feelings out of respect.

Tara gratefully nodded at her, accepted her gesture, and wiped the stream of tears that had taken over her composure for a moment, gave her nose a little blow into the tissues and crumpled them up into a tight ball that she proceeded to squeeze as though it was a stress-reliever.

She continued, "It wasn't long until I met my 'owner', whose name I only know as Tariq because that's how other people addressed him – he never introduced himself to me. He barely spoke to me at all in the months that I was there. I don't even know how long I was gone for – all he would do was order me around in a language I don't understand, grunt at me, manoeuvre me how he wanted me and groan when he found the right spot. That was literally my role in this whole sordid experience – I was like a human sex doll to him and he didn't just keep me to himself; he shared me around his friends too. He took me to orgies at least once per week and they would pass me around like I was a joint at a party." She blushed at that moment, realising her error of admitting to smoking weed on record and was met with sympathetic smiles and shoulder shrugs from both of the policewomen in front of her. She sniffed and carried on, "The orgies were horrific. They would vary in size and participants and each person that had their way with me would push and tug me around at their pleasure, forcing me to perform acts on them against my will and violating my body in every manner possible. Some of them were gentler with me than others, like they actually wanted to see me enjoying myself. More often those were female participants or more effeminate looking men, but even so, they were still forcing me to do things I did not want to do." It was as though she felt the need to make that clear, as though she felt plagued by some sort of bizarre guilt for taking any sense of pleasure in such an overall demoralising and degrading experience.

"I tried in vain to escape more times than I was able to keep track of. The stately mansion he kept me held in was full of long winding corridors and I scoured every single one of them for any type of escape route – I had in my head that I would stumble across a secret passageway or something, ya know, like you saw in movies when you were a kid? Like someone would move a book on a bookcase and the whole thing would spin around to reveal a hidden room or a tunnel or whatever? I must have tried every damn book on every damn shelf in that place and searched every surface and every corner for some sort of clue as to where I was. I didn't even know where I was!" She slammed her palm down on the table at that point, her inner rage bubbling over to the surface. "I didn't even know what country I was in until I had been found and was being transported back here! Isn't that a joke? *That's* how hidden away I was from the public eye. I was just his filthy, smutty little secret." A visible shiver ran through her entire body and she took a moment to re-compose herself.

"There were security cameras all over the property that would track my every move. I could hear those swivelling positions whenever I moved from one side of the room to the other or walked down any of the corridors. I can still hear them now even though I know they're not here; it's like they're permanently etched on my ear drums. Regardless of whether I had been left alone or was surrounded by people, I would seize any possible opportunity to make a break for it and snatch back my freedom but all that did was proceed to turn Tariq on even more because he could 'punish' me with his stupidly vast range of tools built purely to inflict grotesque cruelty against another being. He had whips, floggers, paddles, everything that you could only conjure up in your worst nightmares and he relished in any chance to take them out and teach me a lesson.

"A few times he did it in full view of his gross 'fetish friends' and they would watch and get turned on by it. I saw a few of them masturbating when they were audience to such events and it made me feel sick to my core. Nothing was off limits when they were all together: no holds barred, no safe words, no tapping out. You just had to take what was given to you." She sat for just a few seconds in silence, processing her thoughts and when she spoke again her voice broke, "I thought I would never get out of there. I thought for sure I would die in that place, either through a failed escape attempt or at the hands of another, I didn't know. To be honest, I didn't care. I wanted so badly for it to be over. It wasn't a life. It was a nightmare."

She bowed her head and the tears began free-falling so she leaned forward and placed her face against her palms, elbows propping her up against the desk. Veronica pulled the entire box of tissues so that it was directly in front of Tara and discreetly wiped her own single, lone tear away before Tara had a chance to spot it.

"You've done really well, Tara, thank you," began Kelly, sensing that her witness would be needing a break to recuperate soon. "If you would like to leave it there for today and we'll let you know if we have any further questions tomorrow or thereafter, then that's absolutely fine with us."

"Thank you." Tara smiled appreciatively back at Kelly and

Veronica. "This has been a really, *really* long day. I just think I need to get some decent sleep and I'll feel much better. Do you think you could find out if anyone has been able to get hold of my mum yet? I can't even begin to imagine what she's been through for the last few months... how many months was I missing for?" she asked, still feeling utterly dazed that she had had no idea until a few hours ago which country she had been held in – turns out it was Northern Portugal and she had been transported there via Gibraltar – and she was still clueless as to how long she'd been gone for. The days had a tendency to blend into one another when you were stuck in a demonic penitentiary and all that kept you going was your own personal quest to find a way to escape.

"I can certainly do that for you, my dear," confirmed Kelly and she cringed when she added, "You were gone for just shy of six months."

"Six months. Six damn months of my life in that absolute hell hole." Tara shook her head in despair and another tear rolled down the right side of her face. "Mind you, considering I thought that I would *never* make it outta there I guess I should be grateful." She laughed darkly.

Veronica reached out and clutched her hand, looking her directly in the eye when she spoke, "Do not for one second feel like you need to play down what you have been through. You just go ahead and take all the time you need to be mad or sad or disgusted or offended or whatever you need to feel to get yourself through this. I've got a list of numbers that I'm going to give to you later on after you've had a chance to rest; they're for a range of counselling and support services that I want you to make the most use you possibly can of, OK?

"I've also heard of a brand new charity that's been opened up by one of the other victims in this case that I'm going to find out the details for. Her story doesn't come close to what you've been through, but she's gone to great lengths to reach out to female victims of any type of crime and I'm sure you'll be able to build up a strong network around yourself if you seek help there. You are not alone anymore Tara; I'm just so sorry that you had to feel that way for as long as you did." She smiled sympathetically at her before letting go of the stronghold she had on her hand.

They wrapped up everything in the interrogation room and the two police officers escorted Tara back to a comfortable and discreet waiting room away from the hustle and bustle of the rest of the station so that they could go and find out if her mother had been located and informed of her daughter's return. They didn't have to look very hard, as it turned out Tara's frantic mother had already made the journey to their station and was chomping at the bit to see her 'baby girl'.

Tara was a spitting image of the youthful looking Jasmine and the pair of them ran straight into each other's arms as soon as they laid eyes on one another. They sobbed uncontrollably into their opposing shoulders for several minutes, Jasmine stroking her daughter's hair and repeatedly lifting her head to kiss Tara's cheek, then returning her face to her shoulder to cry some more. There weren't any words adequate enough to express the relief they both felt right there in that moment as they clung on to each other, so they just quietly wept and hugged until they were both exhausted. They then collapsed together onto the comfy couch in the waiting room and Kelly fetched them some steaming hot tea from the station kitchen whilst Veronica went to grab all of the support leaflets she had promised Tara only moments beforehand.

After returning to the waiting room armed with refreshing hot drinks and a vast array of different pieces of information to sit and discuss with the newly reunited mother and daughter, they both relished in providing a nicely wrapped up mini support session for them. They let them know just how many charitable organisations, support centres, helplines and tools they had at their disposal to help them both in their recovery from such a life changing and traumatic ordeal. The entire time Tara sat nuzzled against her mother's shoulder and Jasmine wrapped a protective arm around her daughter, stroking her hair up and down like she was trying to somehow erase the last six months from her brain entirely with the motion. It was obvious that going through this utterly disgraceful experience was going to bring the two closer together than ever before. They would lean on each other at every possible opportunity and never let any amount of time or distance come between them again.

After giving an overview of what the next steps would be in terms of calling Tara back in at a later date, if necessary, as and when more information about the case came to light, plus potentially needing her to give evidence in court, they very gratefully gave the women permission to make their way home and ordered them some transportation for that purpose. They personally took the time to make sure Tara and Jasmine were safely and comfortably in the back of the squad car to escort them back to their cosy little two bedroom house in Upney and took great pride in being able to do so because seeing the two of them reunited had been one of the more pleasurable outcomes of this sordid ongoing case. They had witnessed some of the most depraved and gut-wrenching evidence in their police careers to date and it had been incredibly draining on both of them mentally, which in turn led to physical exhaustion.

Back in the station kitchen, Kelly and Veronica were filling their mugs – Kelly was going through a phase of drinking an extremely overpriced 'slimming tea' that wasn't particularly desirable to the taste buds but the supposedly 'authentic and traditional' combination of oriental herbs gave her a bit of a buzz in the process of drinking it. Veronica preferred black coffee that she brewed so strongly, in her individual French press, that her colleagues referred to it as rat poison and only ever asked to steal some from her out of a desperate need for an instant caffeine fix.

Kelly absent-mindedly stirred half a teaspoon of honey into her tea, whilst staring at the wall and let out a long sigh. "That was intense," she muttered.

There was a moment of radio silence coming from her teammate and she glanced over at Veronica to discover her beautiful comrade shedding a couple of tears.

"Oh, love!" Kelly exclaimed and wrapped Veronica into her large bosom to comfort her. Veronica accepted the warm gesture with sincere appreciation and wrapped her slender but muscular arms around her caring and compassionate work friend's back.

She stayed put with her face pressed against Kelly's shoulder for a couple of minutes, let out a succession of gentle sobs, then pulled her upper body away so that she could wipe her own tears from her face before they soaked Kelly's shirt. "You're not kidding there; that was *beyond* intense. I'm surprised I managed to keep it all together in that damn room!" She shook her head and marvelled at her own ability to remain professional whilst face to face with such a devastating evidence-giving session.

"I know, me too, we both deserve a frickin' medal for that class act," Kelly joked and offered Veronica a high five, who laughed and hit her up top.

"At least we got the joy of seeing her mum reunited with her baby girl though. That part made it all worthwhile." Veronica shrugged as she replayed the beautiful scene in her mind of Tara and Jasmine literally running into each other's open arms. It had been like something straight out of a cheesy Hallmark movie but so much better in real life.

"Absolutely!" Kelly nodded with extra zeal. "That part will stay with me forever and I'm really glad I got to experience it with you."

They both grinned at each other and went back in for a shorter but still very touching cuddle, both rubbing one another's back and finishing it off with a gentle squeeze in unison.

As they extricated themselves from their conjoined grip, one of their admin colleagues came into the kitchen to hand over a document regarding their other victim, Victoria.

The skinny, effeminately handsome colleague in his mid-thirties and of Japanese descent offered them a look of pure empathy as he said, "I hope you guys are feeling strong enough to deliver some bad news to a woman who's already in a very bad place right now." He looked like he hated every part of delivering that piece of paper and that verbal message to them in what was clearly a hugely sentimental moment for the pair, nodded his head out of respect and then exited stage left as quickly as he could without breaking into a full sprint.

Kelly glanced down at the piece of paper he had handed her, inhaled sharply, holding her breath for a couple of seconds, then sighed deeply and passed the paper over to Veronica, who also took in its contents.

"Oh my," she said and covered her mouth.

It was confirmation that Victoria's mother, who had suffered a severely debilitating case of early onset dementia, had passed away roughly three months after her daughter's disappearance from Chadwell Heath eighteen months ago. Her husband, Victoria's abusive stepfather, had not only commandeered the property they had lived in, despite it being in his deceased wife's name and rightfully owed to Victoria, but he had also moved in a woman much closer to Victoria's age within just two weeks after the funeral had taken place.

Clearly he had been having an affair with the younger, incredibly naïve and easily influenced woman, then shacked up with her at the first possible opportunity he had been given. It left a vile taste in both of the police officers' mouths and they looked at each other with a mutual feeling of disgust and dread.

"I was already not looking forward to dealing with Victoria and now this?" Veronica's shoulders slumped as she heaved a weighted sigh.

"C'mon, babes, we got this." Kelly gave Veronica's shoulder a supportive squeeze. "Let's go and get this next bit out of the way so that we can officially take off the next couple a days for some much needed and very well deserved R 'n' R." She hated trying to sound so blasé about it when on the inside she was feeling extreme sorrow for the already severely woeful Victoria but she did her utmost to make it sound convincing for the sake of both of their sanity. They polished off their drinks and tidied up after themselves before heading down the corridor into the interrogation room Victoria was patiently waiting in, ready for the next round.

"Hi, Victoria, how are you feeling?" Kelly began after Veronica had gone about her usual routine of introducing them all into the recording equipment.

"Shit. Thank you *very* much," spat out Victoria, unapologetically, "I've felt like shit ever since the moment your *officers–*" she emphasised the word officer with a look of pure loathing on her face "–forcibly removed me from my beautiful home, my wonderful life, my beloved Sandor and carted me back to this hell hole of a country against my will." She slumped back into the metal chair and folded her arms like a sullen teenager and glared at the two policewomen in front of her.

"I'm very sorry to hear that, Victoria, I'm sorry that you've had to go through any of this," offered Kelly with sincerity. "Our task force was merely following instructions and you were being held in that house after being sold to Sandor in an illegal trafficking transaction—" she started to explain and was rapidly cut off by Victoria leaning back forwards and stamping her right foot hard against the ground to get the most audible effect.

"I was *not* being held. I *wanted* to be there. I love him. I love all of the wonderful things he's given me and I adore my life there. Why wouldn't I? Did you see the place? Did you see him? Every part of it was breath taking in comparison to my repulsive life here." She swallowed down the taste of bile in her throat as a memory of her stepfather's former abuse flashed through her mind. She envisioned him creeping into her bedroom late at night after her poorly mother had fallen asleep in a drunken stupor that he had induced her into, then doing the most utterly degrading things to his stepdaughter, forcing himself on her and leaving her alone weeping into her pillow in the foetal position as soon as he was satisfied. "I do not want to be here. I did not need rescuing. I want to go back and I want it now."

"I understand why you'd feel that way, Victoria. I really do." Kelly gave her a remorseful half smile. "I had a little look over your file earlier and what I saw in the reports and then later on the retraction of those reports about your stepfather was not remotely pleasant at all and again, I'm sorry you've had to go through any of that. Unfortunately, I have to deliver some bad news to you before any one of us would feel right about you making a decision on your next course of action."

Victoria stared at her, silently bracing herself.

"I'm afraid your mother passed away roughly three months after your disappearance," she said with a sorrowful tone, "My deepest condolences." She grabbed the box of tissues from the side of the desk and slid them over so that they were directly in front of Victoria.

The stunning, ballerina-esque woman sat and stared at the box of tissues with her mouth slightly ajar for a solid two minutes that seemed to span on for much longer. She had been so caught up in all of the traumatic events of the last couple of days that her poor mother had only fleetingly entered her mind, then had been quickly replaced by stronger, more pressing feelings of longing for her precious Sandor. How could she be so selfish? What a disgraceful daughter she had been to so easily pack the memory of her mother neatly away in its own little compartment of her subconscious. She had practically wrapped all details of her former life up in a tidy little bow and shoved them to the back of her mind so that she could focus solely on her new and fabulous life amongst the upper tiers of a whole different society, a society where she was admired and respected.

Had her mother realised she was gone? Had she missed her? What had the final moments of her tragic life been like? Had she been in pain or slipped away silently and mindlessly into the next dimension?

She leaned forward very slowly and carefully placed both elbows on top of the table, followed by her face into her palms and began to weep silently. Her tears seemed enormous and relentlessly flowed into a puddle on the desk in front of her. She had never felt such extreme grief and regret as she did in that moment, knowing that her mother had left this world not having a clue whether she was still alive and well and certainly not knowing how much she had loved her, even despite her rapidly deteriorating sickness.

Right now she would give anything to be able to hold her mum's hand and be softly stroking her hair, telling her everything was going to be OK as she slipped away into her final rest. As morbid as that was, at least it would have given her some closure knowing that her sweet, gentle, severely poorly mum was no longer being subjected to the will of her grotesque husband and she would now be at peace.

"I hate to have to bring it up at a time like this." Kelly's words snapped Victoria out of the trance she had slipped into and she looked up at the policewoman through streaming eyes. "But as a result of your mother's passing it means that there will be solicitors wanting to get in touch with you to discuss her property. I *completely* understand if you do not feel at all ready for that, but I thought it would be best to make you aware of it now before they start bombarding you," Kelly explained.

"What's happened to mum's house since I've been away?" Victoria stammered through the frog in her throat and grabbed a handful of tissues to wipe away the tears and snot that had collected on her still beautiful face.

"Currently it is being occupied by your former stepfather and his... girlfriend." Kelly cringed at having to use the word girlfriend to describe what was clearly a very toxic partnership.

Victoria's eyes bulged. "Girlfriend," she said in pure and utter shock. It wasn't a question. She wasn't hoping to find answers here. She just wanted to say it out loud so that in a weird way it would make it real and not just some crazy idea she'd conjured up. That sick bastard had a girlfriend and they had the audacity to be living in her mum's home. *Her* home!

Surely it would have rightfully gone to her unless he had managed to convince her mother to sign it all over to him and to be fair, she wouldn't put it past him. She shook her head violently, trying to erase his face from her memories. She didn't have time to think about him right now. She wanted to grieve for her tragic loss; she needed to cry and sob and say a few words in private to her mum's spirit up in heaven. She knew she would be listening. She felt an uncontrollable need to wail at the sky and let her dear mum know that she would always love her.

"Are you OK?" asked Kelly. "I know it's an awful lot to take in for one day."

Victoria nodded once and then sat staring at the puddle of tears on the desk in front of her. If she squinted her eyes a little she could imagine it as a vast ocean, like the one between her and Sandor right now. She thought of him sitting alone in a prison cell back in Hungary and her swimming across the vast ocean to emerge the other side in France, hitchhiking her way across Europe and banding together a group of his most trusted comrades to break him free. It was all just foolish flights of fancy but she didn't care. She wanted so badly to be wrapped back up in his welcoming and comforting arms.

"I think we should wrap it up for today and re-convene when you've had a chance to process everything and feel ready to discuss your next steps." Veronica offered her an escape, even if it was only a temporary one. She could see that they weren't going to achieve anything further by keeping her trapped in this room and she could feel the anguish radiating off of the slender woman's body. "A room has been booked for you in the Ibis hotel that's at the end of this street, so you will be comfortable enough to shower and rest, but also close enough to call the station if you feel distressed at any stage. Don't be shy about using that – you've been through a terrible ordeal and our officers will be happy to come and ease any anxiety you feel, OK?" Veronica's voice was soothing and understanding.

"OK." Victoria nodded. She couldn't wait to get out of there and retrieve the phone from the satchel she had been wearing when they had grabbed her from the sprawling gardens of her stately mansion home. She always carried a charger with her in preparation because she liked to stay connected to her beloved Sandor so it never left her satchel unless it was in use at any point in time. Everything she had on her person when she was taken had been left under the care of the station staff but she had every right to have it back now as it wasn't like she was a suspect of anything. She was now chomping at the bit to obtain her meagre possessions back, get to her room and charge her phone so that she could see if there was something... *anything*... from anybody back home that would let her know what had happened after she had been carted away from the life she loved.

Veronica wrapped up the recording in the interrogation room and the two police officers steered the silent Victoria to an empty waiting room nearest reception so that they could give the staff their instructions to give their devastated witness everything she needed and make arrangements for a couple of squad members to escort her to the Ibis and check her in. They attempted to offer her a sympathetic and heartfelt goodbye but it was lost on Victoria's vacant stare and they respectfully left her alone in her reverie whilst she awaited her next move.

"That was fucking awful," Veronica blurted out as she collapsed into a chair back in the station kitchen.

"Don't I know it?" Kelly collapsed into the chair next to her colleague and they both sat for a few minutes replaying the ghastly scene in their heads over and over again.

Eventually Veronica broke the silence: "I'm gonna leave my paperwork 'til tomorrow. I can't focus on anything right now. My brain feels like scrambled egg."

"Mine feels like mashed potato." Kelly half chuckled at her dear work friend, feeling her conundrum. "Let's go home and recharge our batteries so we can come back and face this head on with fresh eyes and a keen spirit."

"Amen to that," Veronica agreed with fervour and the two of them rose wearily from their respective chairs, gave one another a truly earnest, long hug and a little peck on their opposing cheeks, then headed towards the locker room to grab their personals and get going.

Victoria, meanwhile, had gone through the motions of being checked into the Ibis, a mere five doors down from the police station by her two police escorts and thanked them politely before closing her door to the outside world and making a beeline for the nearest plug socket so that she could connect her phone. A gleeful yelp slipped out of her lips when she found the plug socket to have its own USB port so the non-UK plug attachment to her phone charger was irrelevant and she hungrily shoved the cable straight into its connecting point in the wall. She sat on the floor next to it, willing it to power up quicker and as soon as it did, it began vibrating incessantly, notifying her of the eighteen messages that had come through the network since she had been seized close to two days ago now.

She had barely had any grasp on time and day since her entire world had been turned upside down; the whole thing had felt like a strange, topsy turvy nightmare that had whizzed past all of her senses without her being able to properly process any of it. Every single negative human emotion had ebbed and flowed through her body at the various stages of the whole debacle and she felt completely exhausted from it all but she somehow pulled together the strength to read through the texts that were being transmitted through her phone line in order of being sent.

The first two were obviously before word had got out that she had been taken as they were from her girlfriends back home asking her what she was planning on wearing to the ball they were attending that night in honour of one of their husbands being promoted to a higher-ranking position in parliament. It seemed so unimportant to Victoria now but it had been all her and her friends had discussed for about two weeks prior to that. It was going to be an event to remember and there would be photographers snapping pictures of the entire night to include in both the local and national newspapers so they simply *had* to look perfect.

The next few were all clearly after the news of her snatching by the British police and Sandor's subsequent arrest had come to light as they were an array of mournful messages from all of her closest friends letting her know of their devastation as well as assuring her that their husbands were working tirelessly to get Sandor's name cleared and his freedom secured. They willed her not to fret or worry and repeatedly said that they would not rest until she had been returned to the land she belonged, surrounded by the people who adored her.

At that moment Victoria had to put down the phone and take a breather. All of the emotions that she could feel being transmitted through texts from her friends, coupled with the heartbreak of losing her mother and simultaneously longing for her treasured husband seemed to hit her in one go, like she had been drop kicked right in the centre of her chest. She curled up into a ball on the floor and sobbed uncontrollably for at least an hour. She lost track of the time in the process and the tears just flowed from her relentlessly until there was nothing left in her to cry out.

She crawled her way towards the bathroom like a wounded animal and used the sink as a means to pull herself up off the floor and gaze at her own reflection in the huge bathroom mirror. She looked horrendous, drawn in the face, had deep, dark eye circles and puffed up eyelids from all of the crying. She splashed some cold water on her face to try and ease the swelling then dried herself off so that she could return to her phone.

When she opened the final three messages she felt a giant wave of relief wash over her from head to toe. They were from Sandor – he had called in some favours from his friends in the right positions and had been allowed to return home without any charges being pressed. He would have to pay a hefty fine for partaking in trafficking activity and his reputation amongst the upper tiers of Hungarian society had taken a fairly substantial beating but he said he didn't care about any of that.

All he cared about was the welfare of his cherished wife and it was eating him up inside not knowing how she was coping.

He wrote: "This has been a terrible and trying time for all of us, but I want you to do your very best to stay strong for me, my Angel. I promise you it won't be long until this is all a thing of the past and you are right back here with me to take care of you for the rest of our lives. I will never let anything even remotely close to this happen to you or to us again, my love. Hold tight, I will get you out of there if it's the last thing I do. I'll see you soon, all my love, always. Your Sandor xxx"

She didn't think there was any more fluid left in her to come out but fresh tears rolled down her cheeks as she read through his beautiful words. She could hear his glorious voice in her head as she read and imagined his arms wrapped around her body, holding her tightly close to him as he promised her the world and meant every bit of it. She adored him as much as he adored her; they belonged together and nothing was going to keep them apart. All this would do was make their bond even stronger than it had been before and even more committed to displaying a united front to all who bear witness to their reunion.

She decided that was more than enough tears for one day and made her way to the kettle situated on the desk near the TV and made herself a Galaxy instant hot chocolate to take to bed with her. After consuming its velvety richness, she wrapped herself up tightly under the blankets and fell into the deepest sleep she had succumbed to in a long time, where she had a mixture of dreams of her younger, healthier mum chasing her gleefully through tall grass and daisies, blended in with visions of Sandor's handsome face welcoming her home with open arms.

Chapter 9

Less than twenty miles away, hidden in a bunker deep underground that had once been used to hide and shelter from air raids during World War II, a bitter, dark and twisted soul was sitting alone and stewing in his own vengeful thoughts. He didn't know exactly how much time had passed since the raid on the abandoned farm that was one of many of the properties owned by his family and had initiated a huge chain reaction that had proceeded to bring down the family's organisation in a catastrophic domino effect.

Piece by piece he had watched his empire crumble and his army be taken captive. He had quickly made the decision to flee to the safety of this bunker whilst he put steps in place to make a purposeful return to his former position and seize back what was rightfully his. At this moment in time he had no idea how he was going to do that as, according to his last intel update two days ago, the raids were still ongoing and there was a relentless police hunt out looking for him to drag him into custody. Extremely few people knew of the existence of this bunker and he just had to trust that they would have the good sense to keep their mouths shut over its whereabouts and allow him the space and time to come up with a solid strategy.

For now he would have to bide his time until the perfect opportunity presented itself for him to make things right. He just hoped and prayed that they hadn't been able to locate his mother in all of the madness. He had made arrangements for her to flee separately from himself to a different location up in the midlands and he had entrusted the duty of making sure this took place to his right-hand man, Stefan.

He had paid Stefan a huge sum of money to hide his mother, drive her up to her new temporary and secure home, make sure that all of her needs had been taken care of and to stay close by in a separate house to keep a watchful eye on her and make sure nobody could get to her. He trusted Stefan with his life as they had served time together in both the Romanian armed forces and in a couple of stints in prison. They were brothers not in blood, but in bond and he was the only one that could be trusted with such an important task so he had left it in Stefan's capable hands to execute and had made a break for his own freedom before the cops could close in on him.

Now he sat and he waited, going a little bit madder with each passing day and looking forward to emerging from this confinement to be able to take back his power. He thought back to the original news stories of the raid and how they'd celebrated the ferocious young heroine that had escaped the evil clutches of the bad guys and pointed the authorities in the right direction to track them down so that the remaining captives could be located and set free. He remembered hearing about her memorising number plates and that being a significant lead in being able to track down further evidence and expose multiple members of the organisation as well as the buildings they occupied for business purposes.

He kissed the back of his lips in a derogatory gesture, he had picked up from his comrades over time, shook his head with disgust and muttered out loud, "Memorising number plates…who the fuck does she think she is? Fucking Rain man?"

He huffed loudly, stood up and started pacing the length of the bunker up and down like a caged animal. When he was able to get out of this damn prison he was going to find her and make her pay for what she did. He didn't care if he had to wait a lifetime to take out his revenge. He would wait until the timing was absolutely perfect before he tracked her down and took everything away from her, just as she had done to him.

First and foremost, he would need to ensure his mother's safety and as many other family members as possible. It was a terrible shame that Augustin and Luca had been caught in the crossfire during the raid and taken into custody. He felt remorse about that but also knew that they were fully aware of the risks involved with taking part in any work for the organisation before they had agreed to sign up. He had mentally prepared them both on an individual basis for the dangers that such a line of work imposed on their lives and they had made up their own minds to be a part of it.

Granted, Luca had taken a little more persuading than his brother Augustin. He was a gentler soul than the two older brothers and a little bit of a 'Mama's boy' so treating women like they were objects to be sold at their leisure didn't come naturally to him at all. In fact the final breaking point in convincing him to agree to be a part of the organisation had been getting Olga involved to charmingly explain how much their sick father would appreciate the knowledge that they are all working productively together before he dies. He could go to his final resting place safely assured that his organisation would continue to flourish and provide for them all and to see all of his boys working together in perfect harmony. What a joke that was!

Olga could always be relied upon to put a sweet, innocent

spin on things – no matter how vile or corrupt the subject matter at hand.

After that he had left the running of that particular show mostly up to Augustin whilst he took care of all other physical aspects of the business. Ultimately the power was in Olga's hands to make the big decisions and it was his job to execute those decisions as he see fit. They *all* had their roles to play and they all stuck to those roles with fierce unity. It was why the organisation had ran like clockwork for so long, completely hidden from the majority of society, whilst they all went about their pathetic, shallow little lives, blissfully unaware of the hard graft and sacrifice it took to hold everything together behind the scenes. They seriously had no idea how much their idyllic little society relied upon the criminal underbelly that supported their entire infrastructure and that he had worked so hard to maintain.

His pacing slowed down and his body grew weary as the earlier adrenaline rush from his irate thought patterns subsided.

Thankfully he had had the foresight to stock the bunker high with canned goods, bottled water and even a generous amount of scotch to help him fall asleep when his PTSD symptoms were taking over. Now seemed like an extremely deserved time to pour himself a large glass of scotch and to retire to his military style camp bed.

Tomorrow was a new day. He would put on a disguise and drive the beaten-up Ford Focus he had stolen, repainted and had the plates switched over to the nearest Wi-Fi hotspot where he could use his unregistered sim card to log on and check for any updates on the situation surrounding his family and the organisation. He wondered just how much of it had been exposed and which parts he might still be able to salvage before it was too late, then had to remind himself that he shouldn't get carried away with making plans until he had a better grasp on the current situation. It was hard though; it went against everything he had spent years training for – he always liked to be prepared and to have a strategy in place before undertaking any course of action.

Tomorrow he would be going into uncharted territory with the hopes of doing some preliminary recon over a situation that he had very little information on, particularly how much had happened since he'd gone into hiding. It made him slightly anxious at what he was going to find but the scotch helped mask over those unwelcome and totally unhelpful feelings so he proceeded to gulp down three large mouthfuls and re-fill his glass before surrendering to sleep.

Chapter 10

It was a fresh new day in the central London police station where Kelly and Veronica were arriving to start their shift. They had spent the last twenty-four hours fully recharging their batteries and winding down from the chaos of the previous fortnight and felt better in every imaginable way.

Veronica had had a chance to spend time with her two precious, young sons and had smothered them with more affection than they were used to as a result of her own exposure to such horrific and terrifying evidence over the last few days. Her sons had, of course, milked every opportunity with their 'extra cuddly mummy' and she had relished in giving in to their every demand.

Kelly had made the most of taking her sleek and beautiful greyhounds on the longest walk they'd had the luxury of having in far too long and they had enjoyed the vast open space of South Norwood country park under the glorious sunshine, where there was no media interruptions to remind her of the tragedies she'd seen.

"Hey, girl, you ready to get back into the swing of things?" Veronica greeted Kelly cheerfully as she came into the station kitchen, where she had already started setting up their drinks of choice.

"I sure am," Kelly replied, "I've already been over and requested a couple of squad members to go and pick Victoria up from her hotel – if she's ready that is. I told them to leave her be if she's not feeling up to it."

"Too right. That poor woman needs to grieve. I can't even begin to imagine how I would cope with hearing that news about my mum. But then again, my mum's an angel – I dunno what I'd do without her, full stop." Veronica shivered at the mere thought.

"Yeah, your mum's pretty rad, not gonna lie," Kelly agreed.

Just as they were heading towards the seated area with their hot, caffeinated drinks in tow, the effeminate Asian guy from the admin team came to find them wearing a perplexed look on his face. "I just had a message from Callum – he's one of the guys we sent over to pick up your witness from the Ibis," he started to explain, "He said she's not there."

"What do you mean she's not there?" asked Veronica, "Did they check properly? She might have just gone for a walk or something."

"I'm pretty sure he checked with the hotel staff because he was concerned when she didn't open the door. He said they said she had walked out early yesterday morning and not come back. He and his colleague, Sandra, are on their way back now to give the full details but he wanted to call ahead and alert you to the situation."

"Ok, thanks very much for letting us know." Veronica nodded at him as a way of letting him know he could get back to what he had been doing.

"Shit. This can't be good;" Kelly broke the shocked silence they had momentarily slipped into.

"Hmmmm." Veronica acknowledged Kelly, whilst still mulling over her own thoughts. "Now that I think about it, I can't say I'm remotely surprised. Imagine being in her situation – being torn away from this incredible life that you've spent the last eighteen months making the absolute best of, torn away from the man you loved and brought back to a land in which you were abused ...I know, I know... allegedly abused–" She corrected her own sentence before Kelly could interject "–by a man who had a hold over your own mother and *then* you find out your mother passed away whilst you were gone and you had no idea? Man. What a mind job. There are very few on this planet that would know how to process that barrage of woe in a healthy and functional way."

"So where do you think she might have gone? Or is that just a dumbass question?" asked Kelly.

"I reckon she's either already found or is planning to find some way of getting back to her husband," concluded Veronica, knowing all too well that her work chum already had the same thought in mind. It was, after all, the only logical thing to do.

"I think so too, but we can't exactly rely on that as a fact. There's every possibility that she could have gone to track down the former stepfather and is now planning on taking revenge on him in some way, or demanding her mother's house back, whilst also warning his new girlfriend about what a monster he is. We just have no idea where her head's at right now."

True to his word, Callum appeared as they were discussing the various possibilities of Victoria's AWOL status. He was an excessively tall, trim and relatively handsome white man in his late thirties with mousey brown hair and a matching coloured, bushy beard. "Hey, I just wanted to give you guys a briefing of what happened at the hotel before I go write up my report," he offered, helpfully.

"That's great, thank you very much," Kelly replied and

pushed a chair away from the table they had been seated at, indicating for him to join them.

Callum gratefully accepted the seat and explained, "Sandra and I – that's my colleague, she's just gone to inform our manager of what went down so that they can dispatch other members of the team as they see fit for follow up. We went straight to the room number we were given and knocked on the door several times. There was no response and we couldn't hear any sounds coming from inside the room; no TV on, nobody moving around. We then went and asked at reception whether or not anyone had seen Victoria going in or out of the room and if so, what time and was she alone or with anybody.

"It took a little while for the hotel manager to find one of the room attendants, who confirmed that she had seen Victoria very early yesterday morning – she described her as having left in somewhat of a brisk fashion, though she had clearly taken the time to wash and dry her hair. The room attendant said she checked over the room after seeing her leave and thought it was odd that there were no personal belongings left behind, due to that room booking remaining open on her list.

"After that she let us into the room to have a little look around and she was right. It doesn't look like Victoria intends to return. Sandra requested that we could see the footage from the CCTV cameras leading in and out of the hotel and we saw Victoria leaving the building solo and in a bit of a rush."

"That's extremely helpful. Thank you for taking the time to be so thorough," Kelly responded with a half-smile that hid her genuine concern for the welfare of their missing victim.

"No problem. You need anything else, just give me a shout," Callum rounded off his summary and rose back up from the chair to make his exit. On his way out he grabbed one of the pastries that had been left in a box on the counter for the staff to help themselves to and a couple of napkins so that he could eat it on the move.

"So she left solo. No one was there to pick her up," noted Kelly.

"Doesn't mean she hadn't already made arrangements with someone via phone. I noticed that when she checked her little satchel bag in upon arrival here, there was a phone inside and a charger for it too." Veronica replied.

"She came prepared," Kelly concluded, rising from her chair too because she knew they were going to need to spring into action immediately and work alongside the taskforce allocated to tracking her down. She wasn't just aware of the need; she was also aware of her own desire to find the missing woman and make sure she was OK. She'd been through an awful amount of uproar in such a short space of time and Kelly's heart bled for her.

Veronica followed suit, clearing away any mess from the table as she went, "We need to find out what happened to her husband back in Hungary. If there's any chance that he may have been able to shake off the charges he faced – you know how it goes when you're wealthy and you have all the right people in your back pocket." She rolled her eyes at the implied discrimination against anyone who couldn't afford to buy their way out of a crime. "We don't know how far his influence stretched. He could have called in a few favours from his fancy friends and gotten out of jail free despite having bought a woman against her will and marrying her further down the line. It's not exactly right but it is entirely possible," Veronica surmised.

"That we do," Kelly agreed, "We also need to find out the address of where her former stepfather is currently shacked up with his new squeeze, plus the phone numbers and addresses of any of Victoria's old friends – you never know, she could have simply gone to track down an old gal pal or whatever." Though both of them highly doubted that last statement, they knew they needed to cover all the bases and not leave any stone unturned.

Meanwhile, Victoria herself was touching down in a private aircraft overseas in her beloved Hungary. The last twenty-four hours had been a complete blur, but in all of the best possible ways in comparison to the utter nightmare that had been the rest of her week up until that point.

She had woken up early the previous morning and checked her phone to find the most touching and caring messages from Sandor asking if she was OK and telling her just how much he was missing everything about having her close to him. Despite publicly being a distinguished, well respected, silent type, who commanded authority effortlessly, with Victoria he was incredibly sentimental and never shied away from expressing his adoration of her. His poetic words via WhatsApp made her heart sing and she felt instantly rejuvenated from having cried herself to sleep the night before.

She typed back to him: "My darling, you have no idea how hard these last couple of days have been without you. I cannot wait until I can be with you again."

His reply was practically instantaneous. "Oh good, you're up!" He inserted a little kiss emoji. "I've been dying to talk to you; is it OK to call? Are you alone or under supervision?" he asked.

"I'm alone – the police booked me into a local hotel and

left me here," she assured him.

Moments later, her phone started buzzing and his handsome profile photo popped up on her screen, making her internally gush as though she were a lovesick teenager. She answered, "Good morning, my love."

"*Aaahhhh!* It is amazing to hear your voice, my sweet Angel. Did you sleep OK?" His voice was as smooth as velvet on the other end of the line.

"Kind of. I had a few nightmares but I was so exhausted that the sleep I did manage to get was very deep and restorative. Are you OK? What happened after they took me away?" she asked with concern.

"It was a bit of a nightmare," he confirmed, "I was arrested and thrown into jail for having purchased you illegally. They made the whole thing sound so horrendously sordid, like I'd been holding you prisoner for the last year and a half." He tutted loudly, then continued. "You would tell me if I had made you feel in any way like you couldn't leave, right?" he asked, sounding genuinely paranoid.

"Yes, I would have," she replied vehemently, "But you didn't. For the first time in many, *many* years, I felt like I finally belonged somewhere and that was all down to you and the outstanding life you provided me with. I don't care *how* you got me there – what you did for me after I arrived was what made me fall for both you and my beautiful new home."

"OK. Sorry. I've just been losing my mind a little bit over here thinking that maybe I *had* been this terrible demon that had ripped you away from your family and forced you to stay here just to satisfy my needs. I never, ever want you to feel like you're obligated to be with me. I want you to want me because you truly love me," he explained sheepishly.

"And I do. You needn't worry about that for a second longer, my love. I promise, I am yours because I want to be," she reassured him.

"So... may I assume that you are willing to cooperate wholeheartedly in my rescue mission?" He was half teasing, but also knew full well that she would be taking a risk in doing so and felt anxious at having to put her through any more stress than what she had already suffered.

"Of course. You may!" She squealed with glee and had to resist the urge to start clapping like an excited child. "Do you have a plan already?"

"I'm in the process of trying everything up at my end in terms of transportation, but I have already made arrangements at your end for you to be picked up. I just need you to get ready and to find a way to get to London City airport. Can you do that? Do you have your bank card with you so you can hail a cab?" His words were coming out in a flurry of excitement at this point and she could hear it in his voice.

"I sure do. I have my passport with me too thanks to the oh-so-helpful police raiders that took me away," she drawled sarcastically, rolling her eyes despite the fact that he couldn't see her.

"Brilliant. Go get showered and ready to make your way there as quickly as possible. Make sure your phone is fully charged. I've given your number to my colleague who will be at the airport to collect you. I'll text you his number as soon as we have hung up. He's a good man – his name is Adrian and you can trust him. He has clear instructions to bring you back to me without a single hitch. Do not tell anybody where you are going or that you have anyone meeting you to take you away – they will only stand in your way and this is *your* decision, not theirs. If any of the hotel staff ask you where you are going, just tell them you need to get some air or that you're doing some retail therapy. Nothing more." Sandor's voice had switched to business like for a moment and then he returned to sentimental: "I can't wait to see you, baby, this experience has just further confirmed in my mind that I cannot live without you."

As soon as they had hung up Victoria had sprang into action to make herself as presentable as she possibly could considering she didn't even have a change of clothes to work with. Thankfully she'd had the foresight to give her underwear a good scrubbing using the hotel shower supplies and left them to dry overnight on the radiator and had used the bathrobe as her nightwear. She washed her hair in record time and blow dried it effortlessly into its usual voluminous, bouncy style, got dressed, gathered up her measly possessions and practically sprinted out of the door in a whirl of anticipation.

She refused to even glance in the direction of the hotel reception desk as she left the building, not even to offer a polite 'good morning'; she just wanted out of there as quickly as she could and wasn't about to let anything or anyone get in her way.

Once outside, she expertly hailed down a cab as though it was second nature to her, gratefully climbed in the back seat and ordered her cockney cabbie to take her the quickest possible route to city airport.

In the interim she received a text containing Adrian's number and decided to send him a text to say, "In a taxi and on my way to the airport, see you soon. Victoria."

He replied less than two minutes later to say, "Great, call me when you arrive and I'll come and find you."

London traffic was over the top chaotic but she didn't care

anymore; she was on her way home to the man and the land she loved. Nothing could touch her now and pure relief washed over her from head to toe as she relaxed back into the comfort of the cab seat. She remembered the dream she had had the night before of her younger, healthier looking mother chasing her through the grass, looking happy and carefree. She decided that was how she would rather remember her mum than the poorly, deeply confused woman with a drink problem she had become with the help of her arsehole of a husband.

She would tell Sandor all about how he had commandeered her mother's property after Victoria had left and even somehow managed to bag himself a young girlfriend. The poor cow. What kind of issues and low self-esteem must she have in order to willingly accept a man like that into her life? Perhaps there was some way she could help her whilst also stripping her former stepfather of what was *not* rightfully his? These were all just suppositions on her part and didn't particularly matter in the grand scheme of things. All that mattered at this moment in time was getting her beautiful backside on a plane to her husband.

Upon reaching the airport she instructed the cabbie to find a nearby cash point so that she could pay him with a very generous tip involved for both his speediness and his avoidance of bombarding her with pointless casual conversation when that would have been the last thing she needed. After he had driven away with a huge grin on his face and a friendly wave, she put in a call to Adrian.

"Good morning, Victoria," Adrian answered ever so professionally, "Whereabouts are you?"

From that point onwards it was like someone had hit a fast forward button on her every move and before she knew it, she was on a private jet heading towards Hungary in extreme luxury. She enjoyed a delightful in-flight continental breakfast of fresh fruit, Danish pastries and Italian coffee. Then when it passed noon she even treated herself to a glass of champagne as she felt like she deserved it after all she'd been through.

Before taking her first sip, she raised her glass in the air and toasted her mum's memory, telling her how much she loved her and how sorry she was for not being there to see her off. She knew in her heart that her mother was now in a much better place and made a commitment to her to live her life to the fullest in her honour.

On the other side of the flight Sandor was ready and waiting for her with open arms and she ran to him as though they were characters in a romantic movie that were being reunited after years of separation. It was a magical, fairy tale-like moment and they both clung on to one another without a single other care in the world for an unnecessarily long amount of time.

"I have so much to tell you," Victoria whispered to her love when they finally pulled away from each other's grasp.

"Me too. Let's get outta here," Sandor replied, taking his Angel under his wing and leading her towards the elegant black Bentley with tinted windows he had been chauffeured there in.

Chapter 11

Back in Romford, the police station was the elevated flurry of activity that had been commonplace ever since the case had first come to light. The energy of the staff was tangible as they flitted in and out of the building to either chase up fresh leads or update their admin tasks on ones they had just returned back from duty on.

One squad member had a particularly pressing matter to discuss with Sue and Kate and was dashing frantically from room to room to try and locate his senior colleagues with the news. He found them just as they were leaving the locker room and despite it being the early afternoon. They looked fresh and well rested, which he took as an excellent sign because he knew that they would need to be alert and ready to receive what he wanted to tell them. He scampered up to the pair like an excited puppy would to its owner when they first arrived home after a long day at work. He knew very well who they were, but he doubted that they would know him, as it hadn't been long since he'd joined the force and this would be the first time he'd addressed them directly.

"Good afternoon, Ma'ams." He blushed a little at not knowing whether or not that was a common plural to use, but it at least got their attention so he shrugged it off and waved the papers he had in his hand at them.

"I was a member of the police raid that recently took place on the basement of a shop in Becontree where we found a large amount of people who had been trafficked into the country illegally so that they could be put to work in various locations without the appropriate immigration papers. I'm sure you're already fully aware of it?" he began.

"Yes, we are," confirmed Sue, "Do you have some further developments to report to us?"

"I sure do." He nodded enthusiastically as he spoke, "It's quite a lot to process; do you have a few minutes to sit down with me so I can discuss it with you?"

"Absolutely, my dear. What's your name?" asked Sue.

"Thank you. I'm Zane," he replied, placing his hand on his chest and smiling politely.

"Nice to meet you, Zane. I'm Sue and this is my colleague, Kate. Why don't you follow us?" she instructed and they all marched down the corridor towards the first empty interrogation room where they could talk freely.

Once inside, Zane sat down opposite his two female senior officers ready to show them how serious and thorough he could be whilst also being enthusiastic about his job. Even in a seated position he towered over them – he had the height and physique of a professional basketball player, which was something he enjoyed practicing in his spare time but this was where his real passion was. His combination brown/turquoise eyes were glowing with excitement, making them stand out from his mixed race complexion and it was an effort to keep his deep voice measured and paced at a rate where he could explain everything adequately.

"It's been a bit of a process to speak to each of the individuals we found in the basement underneath the shop, mostly due to the fact that they speak a variety of different languages and we've had to source the different interpreters, then hold the lengthy interviews and then figure out where best to place each person from there," Zane started to explain.

"Of course, it must have been a very difficult task." Sue nodded as she spoke.

"It was, yes, but it's been totally worth it," Zane gushed and then remembered his professionalism and mentally told himself to rein it in a bit. "One of the men found has been interviewed at Dagenham police station and what he had to say was *very* interesting. The interpreter has agreed to accompany him for another interview with you two, if you think it will be necessary but I can give you a brief outline of what he said so that you can make that decision for yourselves."

Both Kate and Sue nodded in unison and Zane continued, "He was brought here with his wife and their two children – a ten-year-old girl and a seven-year-old boy. They had been promised a better life over here and though they knew it was technically illegal, they agreed to take the risk because their lives back in Romania had been extremely poor and they were barely able to sustain themselves in their home country.

"According to him, the police force over there can be incredibly brutal if they find anybody sleeping rough on the streets and this family could no longer afford the shanty accommodation they had been living in. They were struggling to make ends meet and so when they were offered a way out and essentially everything on a silver platter, they thought it would be the end to all of their worries.

"He gave a long description of how they were transported over here by boat and also talked in great depth about the roles they were each given once they had arrived, but what I think you will find most interesting is how he talks about his seven-year-old son having autism and not only overhearing a conversation that he shouldn't have, but memorising the coordinates of a top secret hideout, where a man named Gabriel has been staying since shortly after the case exploded."

Both female officers sat bolt upright at hearing that final piece of information. "Have those coordinates been looked into?" demanded Kate.

"Yes, Ma'am," Zane replied gleefully, "We have a task force on their way there now to see if they can find the man in question." He knew very well that there had been an ongoing hunt for the third brother – the missing piece of the puzzle and that the outcome of this raid could provide even bigger developments.

"Excellent. This is very good news, Zane, thank you." Kate grinned back at her dashing junior officer.

"You were correct in your assumption that we would like to speak with the interviewee ourselves. Could you start making arrangements for that immediately please?" Sue instructed.

"Absolutely," confirmed Zane, "I'll get straight on it and in the meantime, here are the notes that were sent over from the original interview." He rose from his seated position, bid them both farewell and exited so that he could set about the task at hand.

It wasn't a huge amount of time before the victim in question and his interpreter had been transported to Romford police station ready to be interviewed by Sue and Kate in full. Though they had done a great job at the Dagenham police station, they had been absolutely swamped by the sheer volume of victims to process and each interview needing to be translated was taking up much more time than they had to spare when chasing up leads needed to be done immediately.

There was every chance that the exposure of Gabriel's secret hideout may have come too late as a result of this but an entire tactical team had been sent to extensively search the coordinates they had been given and even if he wasn't there at their time of arrival, the place would remain under surveillance for the foreseeable future in case he, or anybody else, planned to return.

Sue and Kate sat opposite their witness, a middle aged, white gentleman named Florin, whose appearance was quite shabby and he was obviously malnourished, yet he still had a rugged, handsomeness about him. He had dark grey hair that was a little overgrown around his earlobes and neck, plus a thick moustache that needed a good trim and his clothes were both creased and filthy. His interpreter was quite the opposite: a very neatly polished and perfected Armenian woman in her late thirties with long, copper coloured hair slicked back into a ponytail and stylish, thick rimmed glasses. She wore business attire coupled with very expensive looking jewellery and all it did was make her look like royalty sitting next to her lowly client.

Kate went about the business of introducing them all into the recording equipment and the interview took place at a slow enough pace to allow for pauses and translations to occur after every question and answer.

"Thank you very much for your time, Florin, I know this must be an awfully stressful time for both you and your family so we really appreciate you coming here to talk with us," began Sue. "Could you please describe how you came to be in captivity in the shop basement in Becontree, what you were forced to do once you came to this country and any other information that you think would be useful about who did this to you?" she asked.

After hearing the translation Florin replied, "Our lives at

home in Romania were very, very poor and we had basically run out of options as to what we could do next. We were on the verge of losing our accommodation because we couldn't afford the rent – I had been struggling to maintain regular work and even the work I could get was barely enough to cover our bills. My wife was trying to juggle a low paid job as a cleaner, plus caring for our two children, one of which has more needs than the other one. We couldn't afford proper healthcare over there so we didn't exactly know what was wrong with him. It's only been since coming to this country and hearing the opinions of other, more knowledgeable people that we think he might be autistic. Either way, it means he needs a lot more attention than our daughter and it was putting a strain on all of us." He paused to clear his throat and seemed to be struggling for a moment with the admittance that his son was a burden to them. He loved his son dearly and hated to convey to any outside parties that his little boy was hard to handle, but that was the sorry state of affairs as he knew it.

He continued, "We lived in a shanty town that was full of other families in a similar situation to us and we were all good friends who tried to look out for one another but we were all struggling badly financially. One day one of my friends told me that his cousin had been offered work in England and that when he had accepted, they shipped his whole family over here to make a better life for themselves. It sounded *very* interesting to me as we had all heard the stories of how much better the system is in England for people like me. In Romania, if you are found to be sleeping on the streets the police will beat you until you are coughing up blood. They don't care about your age or gender; they will shamelessly tear you apart just because they can. The government doesn't support its weakest citizens and we are simply left to fend for ourselves or die trying. I did not want this for my family and I was tired of fighting so hard to try to keep us all alive and fed.

"I started asking more questions about who had offered my friend's cousin this promise of a fresh life. In fact it wasn't just me; there were several of us that would whisper amongst each other about how we wanted out, how we would do anything for the chance to break free from the oppression and start over. It wasn't long until I was approached by a man named Gabriel who wanted to know how badly I wanted this opportunity. I practically leapt at the chance and he seemed very happy with this. He told me that he would help me but only if I kept our arrangement a secret and if I get my whole family ready to depart within twelve hours of talking to him.

"Though he was cold and straight to the point in the way that he spoke, he was also quite charming and painted a picture of a much nicer experience in England, where people worked together and helped each other and were taken care of by the people in charge. Of course I agreed, he was offering me the world on a silver platter." Florin smirked and shook his head. "I had no idea what I was getting myself or my family into." His voice cracked a little at the end of that sentence and Kate dragged the tissue box so that it was sitting directly in front of him. He looked up at her with tears streaming at the corner of his eyes. "Multumesc." He nodded and accepted her gesture.

"What was it that you had unintentionally got your family into?" Sue asked with a sympathetic look.

"We were brought here under the cover of dark' it all seemed very back handed and there were no officials to check us over or accept us into the country so I knew that what we were doing was illegal. Every time we changed modes of transportation we had material sacks placed over our heads so that we had no idea where we were and the journey was terrifying. My boy spent almost the entire time weeping and it was heart breaking to listen to. My wife and my daughter were terrified into silence – the only noises I heard from either of them were to soothe my boy through his trauma.

"We got here in what must have been the very early hours of the morning and shown to our new room, which was the same room we were later found in during the police raid. We shared the space with rows and rows of other families – some of them I recognised from home but no one that I was particularly close to, most of us were complete strangers from different countries. I can only guess that they did that on purpose – to stop us from communicating too much or getting too friendly. We were there for one thing only – to be their slaves and they didn't want anything getting in the way of that.

"There was that one main room packed full of camp beds, with next to no space for any personal belongings we had managed to bring along with us. Not that they were worth much; it was more sentimental items than anything else. There was a toilet room with absolutely no privacy between the urinals and the seated toilet and also a shower room, again with no way to hide your modesty from each other. If we wanted to be clean we had to expose ourselves to anyone else in the room and the cleaning supplies were limited so there was often arguments between people trying to wash themselves. Though we were all in the same boat, it didn't stop us being pissed off about it and sometimes taking it out on each other.

"That first night, we were ordered to rest so that we could start work the very next day. I barely slept all night and I knew all too well that my family didn't either. We were so tired but so scared and we didn't know what was going to happen next.

"When dawn broke we were abruptly awakened by a man barking orders in a range of different languages and told to get ready for work. They handed out bags to each family with a pitiful excuse for breakfast inside, which we had to wolf down and then head towards the front of the room to be given instructions on where we were going. They split us all up to do different things and my boy began to wail uncontrollably. The man in charge that day – they changed who was in charge on a regular basis, but that day it was a man named Stefan – he slapped my boy a couple of times to try to quiet him but all that did was make it worse and he was screaming by that point. I jumped in front of him before he could slap him again and explained that he has certain needs and he's not like other little boys. I begged him to let him stay with his mother, my beautiful wife, I got down on my knees and pleaded. I told him that I would personally work any amount of hours necessary to pay back their understanding in this matter.

"He turned around and discussed this with two of his colleagues and I overheard him telling them that they would have to change my wife's role and that her and my boy would now be placed somewhere called Faircross, where they would have to stay put and beg for spare change from strangers, then later be picked up again and brought back to the room. You can imagine the relief that washed over me when I heard one of his colleagues say that they would get better money for my wife in her original role – as a sex worker." The tears were streaming out of Florin's face much quicker now, "She is just so beautiful to look at and they knew they would get a lot of custom for her. But for that moment in time, they had to settle for the fact that she came as a pair with our son and put them to work as a team."

He wiped the tears and dripping snot from his face, his hands trembling a little as he did so and continued, "It was a short-lived relief as they later found a routine whereby they could have her and my boy begging all throughout the day, pick them up, drop our son off with me and his sister, then send my wife back out to tend to their customers on her own.

"I could tell they were starting to groom my daughter for a similar role. Though she is only ten years old, she has already started to develop and she looks older than she is. It won't be long until she is passing for a sixteen-year-old and they were already planning to cash in on that fact. For now they had her walking up and down the trains with a sign hand written in English that begged the passengers for money to feed her family. They would take her away with several other kids in the morning, drop them all at different stations and pick them up again in the evening to bring them back to the room.

"They seemed to favour her over a lot of the other kids because of her good looks and they had bigger ideas for her future within the organisation. She didn't realise it yet. She's so sweet and doesn't know the wicked ways of these men. They would show her extra attention and affection when they were around her and I could see that she was starting to enjoy it. You hear about these things – when young girls get kidnapped and they grow attached to the one that kidnapped them.

"I kept telling her not to trust them but I could see that she didn't want to hear it. She didn't trust me very much anymore. After all, I was the one that had brought her here – why would she? In comparison to their jobs, mine was nothing. All they had me doing was grunt work, offloading boxes from vehicles and into different storage places, sometimes warehouses, sometimes basements. I felt like I'd been given the easiest job whilst my family had been punished for my bad judgement. I would have given anything to turn back the clock." Florin leaned forwards and placed his head in his hands that were propped up by his elbows on the desk.

"If you need to take a break at any point, Florin, please let us know," Kate offered.

"No, thank you, I'm fine, it's hard to relive what we went through to get us to where we are now. This has been going on for months and I did not think we would ever escape. I thought there was no way out and that I would watch my daughter become a sex worker, just like her mother had been forced to be." He sniffed, shook his head a couple of times, blinked hard and proceeded, "In the most tragic way we had gotten used to our new roles and each day seemed to blend into the next. Then one day everything was different and we weren't told why. The men in charge seemed agitated and more tense than usual, things got even stricter and the way we were transported to our jobs became even more secretive.

"Very quickly our working hours were cut back and we were spending more and more time in the room, isolated from the rest of the world. I took advantage of this time to spend with my family and we would curl up together on one camp bed as it was closest to the wall and we could lean our backs against that, all huddled up under our skimpy blankets and my wife would tell us stories that had passed down through the generations in Romania.

"On one of these occasions my wife and daughter fell asleep before me and my son and so I sat up with just him asking about how his day had been. He confessed to me that he had overheard a conversation that he shouldn't have when he was coming back from the toilet room. He had heard one of the men in charge saying that Gabriel had got wind of his brothers being arrested on a farm and he had now gone into hiding, then he read out the coordinates of the exact location for his colleague to give to someone else but told him he must tell only that one person – no one else. My son is very special in that when he hears rows of numbers he remembers them and it almost becomes like a game to him to try and figure out all of the different sums he can make out of them.

"Like I said before, I had never known this condition has a name until we came here and I had been talking about my family to one of the men I was on shift with. He had described his autistic brother as being the same as my boy when they were growing up. Unfortunately his brother passed away twenty years ago, but my colleague remembers him well and talked fondly of how particular and peculiar he was. When he described his strange habits, I found comfort in the fact that there were other people out there just like my boy, that he wasn't alone and maybe someday he would find others to connect with.

"Anyway, I asked him to tell me what the coordinates he'd overheard were and I wrote them down because I knew they may be important. The fact that it was Gabriel's name he had overheard and that there had also been mention of the brothers' arrest meant that something big had happened and we would all have to brace ourselves for what the next stages were in our captivity. I kept the piece of paper with the coordinates on it folded up in my pocket and it was only one day later that the police raided the basement we had been held in. Because there were so many of us, it took probably two or maybe even three days before my turn to be interviewed came up. I'm not sure. It was such a strange and chaotic time for all of us. I gave the coordinates over to the policemen that interviewed me and they were extremely grateful. They thanked me a lot and told me they were going to get their men straight on it. That made me feel a little better. At least I had done *something* worthwhile in all of this mess."

"You can certainly rest assured that you have done something *extremely* worthwhile, Florin. You should also give that message to your little boy – that his exceptional memory could be the key to us solving a very important part of a very big puzzle." Sue reassured him with a warm smile. "For now, let's leave it there so that you can go back to your family and get some good food, some decent rest and you can start looking forward to a better standard of life than what you have been subjected to for far too long."

Chapter 12

In a small café just off the A123, close to the outer skirts of Ilford, Gabriel sat alone, wearing multiple layers and heavy padding to disguise his physique, a scruffy wig and a baseball cap to disguise his dark brown buzz cut and kept his sunglasses on despite being indoors. He had parked the stolen Ford Focus a few streets away and walked there so that he could access their Wi-Fi in as much anonymity as possible and get a very much needed update on how the situation had unfolded since he had gone into hiding.

He had ordered a black coffee just so that he could be seated and not disturbed, then chosen the spot nearest the door so that he could make a quick escape if anybody did happen to recognise him. He would pay in cash so that he could not be traced and he had an unregistered sim card to use in the second hand smart phone he had picked up from a pawn shop the same day he had fled from his home.

He logged in and scrolled through article after article that only served to make his blood boil with greater ferocity with each page that he landed on. The organisation had suffered a huge amount of loss and he was both devastated and fuming at the same time. Sweat was running thick and fast from the top of his body all the way down his back and he struggled to refrain from throwing his coffee mug through the window or tipping his entire table over in a fit of rage.

His mother had been found, arrested and was being held in custody for questioning before she would later face trial and in the same report that described her capture he had learned that his dear friend and non-blood related brother, Stefan, had fallen at the hands of the police whilst trying to protect Gabriel's mother. Stefan had been loyal right up until his demise and Gabriel was pained to have lost him under such gut-wrenching circumstances after decades of considering him his truest ally.

He saw his own mug shot plastered across several web pages and descriptions of the ongoing search that was taking place to bring the third brother to justice. He laughed ironically at the amateur dramatics behind the wording of each story. It was all filled with sensationalised propaganda that painted his entire family as wicked, evil demons with no sense of decency or moral compass.

In his mind the traditional government could be seen as no better; every aspect of it was corrupt and feeding off the lower levels of society for its own advancement. He shook his head in disbelief.

Everything he had worked so hard to build and maintain, particularly after the tragic loss of his father, had all gone to hell and what did he have to show for it? Nothing. He had very limited options as to where he could go from here and who he could turn to. He wasn't completely empty, but also not far from it.

What he wouldn't do to chase down the little bitch that started this entire chain of events and ring her neck. He pictured wrapping his thick, strong hands around her throat and watching the life slowly drain from her eyes whilst her attempts to struggle against his grip became more and more feeble – then he had to pause for a moment to try and control his breathing as he could feel his temper beginning to slip into the danger zone.

He would have to come up with a new plan of action seen

as the first one to get his mother to safety as quickly as possible had completely failed. He wondered what was going through her mind as she sat alone in her cell, knowing that two of her sons suffered the same fate as her and the third was now a fugitive. He knew her well enough to know that no matter what they threw at her during the interrogation process, she would maintain a dignified silence and not utter a single word about any of the places she knew he would run to. She would keep her mouth shut about all of it; he knew that she would rather die or rot in prison than incriminate anyone that she cared about and he loved her immensely for it.

The next few pages he landed on were filled with pictures of Christie's face coupled with articles describing her supposedly incredibly brave tale of heroism and he couldn't stand to look at her anymore so he decided to head back towards the bunker in the hopes that it would still remain unexposed. He couldn't think of anybody that both knew of its whereabouts and would be foolish enough to hand this level of highly guarded intel over to the authorities.

He drained the remnants of his coffee, left his cash payment with a generous tip behind on the table and exited the café as swiftly and covertly as possible to make his way back to the stolen Ford Focus. His mind was a whirling frenzy of chaos as he drove the thirty minute journey to the bunker.

Flashing images of the people that he felt he had let down kept appearing in his mind's eye –his mother, his brothers, his comrades and all of the people who looked up to him and admired him for stepping up to the plate and filling in the gaping hole that his father had left behind. He had wanted so badly to honour Marius Balan's memory and to make his dearly departed father proud. Perhaps, in his haste to live up to such a notorious and legendary man's standards of business, he had overlooked something, some flaw in the system that had allowed it to be brought down so catastrophically.

He mulled over that for a few minutes and then laughed bitterly because no, that couldn't be it. He had masterminded everything, every single detail with military precision – this was all that bitch Christie's fault and he vowed to repay her for all that she had overturned.

He came closer to the bunker and slowed the car right down so that he could properly take in his surroundings before pulling up too close to it. He examined all of the nearby vehicles with a keen and methodical approach and he knew almost immediately that something was wrong. He spotted a couple of unmarked, blacked out vans parked on either side of the road a short distance from the hidden entrance to the bunker and his former training in the forces all came screaming back to him. Somebody was either in the process of, or just about to raid his safe hole.

He immediately made the decision to turn around and drive away but made sure that he did so in a calm and carefully measured manoeuvre, so as not to draw any unwanted attention to himself. He drove just until the ringing in his ears began to ease up and pulled over into a large service station to attempt to rationalise his own thoughts and piece together some form of plan of action. Who had let slip about his refuge? How much more had they let slip in the process?

He slammed his palm against the steering wheel and soon realised just how violently he was shaking. He reached inside his inner jacket pocket and pulled out a sterling silver hip flask that had been engraved with his father's name and the dates of his birth and death, took a long and thirsty swig of the scotch inside and murmured a prayer for guidance. The scotch rapidly warmed his belly and lessened the shaking so he took another swig for good measure and sat for a few minutes slowing down his breathing.

Though he had very few options left in this country, he wondered if perhaps he might seek refuge in one of his colleagues or client's overseas abodes. He had a variety of numbers stored in a small, black notebook that he carried on his person at all times. If ever it came to the stage where he himself was arrested, then he would destroy its contents before the authorities could get their hands on it as he would always remain loyal right until the very end.

He started with a colleague of his in Belgium that he had been dealing arms with for many years – it was one of the aspects of the business that his father had allowed him full rein over very shortly after his recruitment due to his expertise in such equipment.

The phone rang for the longest time and there was no option to leave a voicemail at the end so eventually he hung up and tried another number. The second call was to one of the many drugs suppliers he had on his books; this one in particular being in Poland. Though the drugs aspect was more his brother, Augustin's forte, he had personally built up an exceptional rapport with this gentleman due to their shared military background, love of scotch and distaste for committed relationships. It had been a number of years since he'd seen this comrade but once upon a time they had spent many raucous nights out tearing up the local gentleman's clubs in Poland, making sure everybody they encountered along the way knew who was boss and knew to come to them with any business transactions. This man had the local politicians and police force eating out of the palm of his hand and Gabriel knew without a doubt that he would be safe under his protection.

He dialled the number excitedly expecting to hear the familiar gruff voice at the other end immediately offering him an escape route but the automated voice message advised him that this number was no longer in use. That was a bit of a blow; he had no idea what the circumstances were behind that number being disconnected but his mind couldn't help but go into overdrive considering all of the potential possibilities. Had this been a recent thing since the exposure of the organisation and its long-standing criminal activities? Had his comrade either been captured himself or decided to disassociate himself with any member of the group that he had once so actively engaged with, not to mention enjoyed doing so? Or had this been a simple clerical error? Would he ever be able to make contact with him again? Even with his first call – had his arms dealer seen an unknown UK number flash up on the screen and decide that it wasn't worth the risk of answering?

He took another swift gulp from his engraved hip flask to steady his nerves, then tried another seven phone numbers with very much the same results. People were either not answering at all, their phones were switched off, or the numbers had been disconnected. This was not good at all. He was starting to feel more and more alone, desperate and could feel the panic rising in his chest.

He stepped out of the vehicle and took in a gulp of the brisk air to try to soothe the tight feeling in his chest and practised the breathing techniques he had picked up to employ when faced with his PTSD symptoms, then paced up and down a few times to get his blood circulating around his system better. He came back to the car and rested his crossed over arms on the roof, then laid his forehead on top of his arms, almost like a child would when they were calming down after a temper tantrum, but in his case it was less a case of anger that was overwhelming him and more a feeling of being abandoned and lost.

He wasn't remotely used to feeling so helpless – he was normally the one in charge, the one that people looked up to and sought out for instructions on what to do next. Yet here he was, not knowing who he could turn to or where he could go, what he could do. He gripped onto the set of rosary beads hanging around his neck that his father had given him shortly before his first military deployment in Bosnia and held them tight for a few minutes, stroking them back and forth, asking for guidance on what to do.

A moment of clarity washed through him and he opened the car door back up, reached for the phone that was lying face down on the driver's seat and his little black book of contacts. He dialled one more number and held his breath as he heard the foreign ringing tone on the other side.

Eight long rings later, Sandor answered: "Sandor speaking."

"Sandor, how are you? I hope everything is well with you and your family." Gabriel wasn't even a tiny bit accustomed to offering such meaningless small talk during any conversation – not even with those he was closest to, let alone with a former client with whom he hadn't spoken in over a year.

"Hello, Gabriel." Sandor had had an inkling about who would be on the other end before he answered. "I've been partially expecting to hear from you."

"I can believe that. I guess you've heard just how bad it's been over here?" Gabriel asked.

"Over there? How things have transpired over there have been the furthest thing from my concern, Gabriel. Things over *here* have been dreadful for me *and* my beautiful wife, as I'm sure you can imagine." Sandor didn't waste any time sugar coating the situation. "Thankfully I have been able to exert a certain amount of control, with the help of my most trusted allies and put steps in place to return to a relative sense of normality, but things will never quite be the same again. I'm even considering moving elsewhere and starting a fresh. Time will tell."

"I can only offer my condolences for any of the trauma that you and the lovely Victoria have been through, my friend. We have all been through a huge amount of devastation and it is at times like these that we all need to stick together and help each other out."

"What is it that you need, Gabriel?" Sandor got straight to the point.

"I'm seeking refuge," Gabriel began to explain, "As soon as the initial event occurred that started this whole chain reaction of events. I put plans in place to secure my mother away from everything that would connect her to the organisation, whilst I myself went to a secret, hidden bunker and laid low for several days. I had hoped that things may have died down somewhat whilst I was in hiding and at the very least, I would be able to make the journey up towards where my mother was going to be concealed and we would escape together overseas so that we could regroup and eventually start to rebuild.

"Every one of my plans thus far has failed and I emerged

from hiding to find out that mother is in police custody, as well as my brothers, being interrogated whilst awaiting trial. My bunker has also somehow been located and raided in the interim and I am desperately looking for somewhere else to go." He took in a deep breath and let out a long sigh. "Sandor, can I please come to your abode in Hungary in order to avoid being captured? I will keep myself completely out of sight and I won't allow anybody to find out who I am or where I'm hiding," he pleaded, another concept that was entirely alien to him.

"I'm afraid not, Gabriel." Sandor was firm in his refusal. "Things are *far* too tense here as it is and I need to keep a low profile myself until it all calms down. You coming here is not an option, however, I do own several other smaller properties across Europe, the closest to you if you wish to be overseas would be the one on the coastline of Normandy. I could send you the address and you will have to make your own way there. Or if you think you can remain concealed in the UK and wish to try that, I have some friends in Southeast London, who *may* be willing to help. All I can do in that respect is put in the calls to determine whether or not they are able to accommodate you on a short-term basis and then I can let you know what they say."

"I would very much appreciate that Sandor, thank you. I do not wish to put you in any compromising position; it's just that I'm utterly desperate," Gabriel explained, feeling just as alone as he sounded. It wasn't like him to be so candid about his own weakness, perhaps he had been a little too eager with the scotch. "Will you let me know as soon as possible? I will only be using this number to contact anyone on for now."

"I will be in touch. Take care of yourself." Sandor hung up, leaving Gabriel staring at the phone in his palm and wondering how on earth it had come to this. How had he gone from being such a powerful and foreboding figure in the eyes of so many to feeling like a lost little boy who'd been separated from his parents in a shopping mall or something, panicking, not knowing who to turn to, reaching out in desperation for a kind face and a shoulder to cry on.

In some respects his lone wolf style of living paid off in that he had no sentimental connections to outside parties that he would need to worry about or protect from all this madness. However, it also made him feel incredibly isolated when the shit hit the fan. Who was there to hold him and tell him it would all be ok? Not a soul on the planet.

He sighed a heavy sigh and rubbed his forehead wearily with both hands whilst mentally listing off the places he could potentially go to nearby just to get his head down until Sandor got back to him. There was a supremely concealed storage space in Marks Gate that had been used as a kind of staging post for shipments to be transported to, unboxed, sorted through, repackaged and then placed in different modes of transport to be taken to where they would be distributed from. Marks Gate seemed a little too close to home though and he weighed up the likelihood of that being just one of the many places the police had raided since the original exposure of evidence at the abandoned farm.

Every single time he replayed that shattering incident in his mind it reignited the overwhelming rage he felt for Christie and he had to remind himself that his anger would be of no use to him in this situation – he should reserve it for a moment that requires an adrenaline rush, a fight, flight or freeze type of moment in which he would always choose the fight option. That was just his nature, indoctrinated with years of military conditioning.

Where else could he go? He needed somewhere that nobody would be able to connect the dots to and he sat strumming his thick fingers against his now stubbly chin, wracking his brain for any forgotten entities that had long gone unneeded and unused. He reeled off an enormous mental list of past lovers and their variety of locations and then shrugged that idea away almost as quickly as it had emerged; there was absolutely no way he could put his trust in any one of them. They were simply gold diggers or status hungry, they hadn't cared about him on a personal level, and much less had he cared about them. Anyway, it was more than likely that a huge majority of those with any type of connection to his past had either already been sought out by the authorities for questioning or they had come forward of their own accord in order to get a slice of the media action. He shook his head in disgust.

Following that line of thought brought Gabriel to an epiphany as he recalled one of the many lovers his father had taken during the course of his marriage to Olga, completely off the radar. Most of those had only been fleeting dalliances that had ended in a sizeable pay off to the lover in question, or on the very odd occasion out of necessity, said lover would mysteriously disappear.

However the woman that popped into his head now had been different. She had been loyal to Marius until the very end and as far as Gabriel was aware, had never spoken a word of their affair to this day. What they had had was unique and beautiful and though it had been disrespectful to his own mother, Gabriel had understood why Marius behaved the way that he did around this woman and fallen for her as deeply as he had. It had only been when he was diagnosed with second stage liver cancer that he had made the decision to end things with her because he knew his time left on the planet was limited and he had a vast amount of loose ends to tie up before he departed from these earthly planes. It would have been far too complicated to keep her on the scene whilst his family was going through such a dramatic and heart-breaking upheaval; he knew he had to let her go and live the rest of her own life to its fullest. Marius had taken time and care to end things amicably with her and made sure that she was financially secure for the rest of her years – in fact he had been *incredibly* and some might argue, over the top generous in such matters because leaving her had been one of the hardest things he had ever had to do.

Gabriel recalled seeing the life drain even quicker from his father's eyes after the day that he had officially ended that relationship. It had been the final nail in the coffin, to think of it so callously. There was no doubt in Gabriel's mind that Marius had loved Olga deeply, cared for her unreservedly and valued her immensely for the fact that she was his loyal wife and the mother of his children; however, the other woman in his life had unexpectedly stolen his affection right down to his inner core and losing her had stripped him of the virility that kept him attached to his own body.

It wasn't too much longer after that until Marius had become bed ridden, a mere fraction of his former self and only capable of barking orders from a horizontal position. Gabriel had detested seeing him that way and only visited out of a sense of dependability, not remotely because he had wanted to do so. He would go to his father's bedside and update him on all aspects of the business that needed his attention and would promptly leave. They never discussed the emotional side of Marius handing the reins over to Gabriel, that wasn't their style; it was just the natural order of things and they preferred it that way.

When Marius had finally slipped away, Gabriel had compartmentalised any information he had about his father's infidelity and never brought it up with another soul. Now might be the time to unlock that little box in his subconscious and ask the last person anybody would ever expect for a favour.

He turned to the final page of his little black book and found the number he was looking for. She hadn't been placed in alphabetical order like the rest and he hadn't written down her name either, just her initials – M.J. He dialled the number and held his breath.

"Hello?" Her elegant and quintessentially upper-class British voice sounded a little confused at not having recognised the number on her screen.

"Mary. It's Gabriel." He had never called her before and had no idea what the protocol was in this bizarre situation. "I hope you don't find this too much of an intrusion."

Mary took in an audible breath and let it out in a long, drawn out exhalation. "My goodness, I was not expecting this at all. How are you, my dear?" Her head shaking at how ridiculous a question that was at that particular moment in time was also audible. "I mean, that's a very silly question, I know." She laughed a little uneasily. "Let's call it a knee-jerk reaction."

Gabriel appreciated her forthrightness and chuckled a little himself. "I've been better!" He attempted to make light of the intense, dark cloud hanging over his head.

"Of that, I have no doubt, dear one," Mary sympathised.

"Believe me when I say that I never, *ever* thought I would

be making this call and I have exhausted all other avenues that I could think of before doing so," Gabriel explained.

"Well now, don't you just know how to make a woman feel special?" Mary quipped and they both laughed for a moment at the obscenity of the idea.

"You have no idea how much I've needed to laugh, Mary, thank you. These last few days have been nothing but tense and it's been driving me slightly insane." Gabriel opened up to her once the laughter had died down.

"I can only imagine. So tell me, why is it that you're calling? What do you need?" The fact that she was even asking what he needed from her, what she could do for him at a time like this, blew Gabriel's mind a little bit. Here she was being genuinely loyal to Marius' family long after he had put an end to his devotion to her – even some of his so-called closest comrades had not been so openly available to him.

"Somewhere to hide on a very short-term basis." Gabriel knew she would appreciate his blunt statement as much as he had appreciated it from her.

There was a brief pause whilst Mary was performing some mental calculations, then she asked, "Do you remember, roughly six years ago now, there was a golf course very close to Epping forest that you picked your father up from?"

"Yes, I know exactly where you mean." Gabriel's heart was beating slightly more rapidly now, he could sense that she had a plan of action in mind and he felt totally enamoured by that concept.

"Are you able to get there within the next hour?" She was keenly aware of the need for swift, decisive movements.

"Yes, I can." Inwardly Gabriel felt giddy and wanted to

clap like an excited toddler, outwardly he was all business and matter-of-fact.

"Meet me there and we will get you somewhere safe. But my dear Gabriel, this can only be for a very short time. Do you understand?" Mary was ever the organised pragmatist.

"Of course. I will see you very soon." Gabriel had to fight to keep the sheer glee out of his voice by that stage.

"See you soon —" Mary began.

"Mary?" Gabriel interjected before she had a chance to hang up.

"Yes?" she enquired.

"From the very bottom of my heart, thank you." For the first time in a very long time, Gabriel felt sincerely humbled by her kindness and he wanted to convey that without sounding too corny.

"You are most welcome. See you soon." A click signalled the end of the conversation that had all at once lifted Gabriel's spirits out from the depths of doom and into a more motivated and confident state of being. He felt rejuvenated and full of vigour as he put the stolen Ford Focus into gear to begin his journey towards salvation.

Upon arrival in the golf course car park, Gabriel instantly recognised Mary's sleek, black Toyota Supra and felt rather sheepish pulling up to park a few spaces away from such a stunning vehicle in the beaten up machine he was operating. He quickly reminded himself that that was the last thing he should be concerned about, cut the engine, took a deep breath, made sure he had all of his limited personal belongings safely in the non-descript camping-style backpack he had brought with him and exited the car.

He expertly and covertly removed the number plates from the stolen Focus and tucked them under his arm before striding confidently, but not too quickly, over to the Supra, mindful of the fact that anybody could be witnessing his movements from any position right now and he did not want to draw any attention to himself or to his kindly Samaritan. He got into her car in as nonchalant a fashion as he could possibly manage and looked over at her radiant beauty –she had barely changed at all since the last time he had laid eyes on her almost three years ago now. The only real difference was a minor change in her luxuriously thick raven coloured hairstyle; she now had a very flattering fringe cut in that emphasised her striking, model-like facial structure. Gabriel guessed her to be roughly ten, perhaps a maximum of fifteen years older than himself – his father had fallen for a much younger woman – and yet she was more breath-taking than most women half her age.

"Hello Mary. Once again, thank you for your kindness." Gabriel kept it simple.

"Don't mention it." She smiled sweetly at him and batted her practically luminous green eyes. "Let's get out of here." With that, she expertly put the car into gear and drove away as though she was a racing pro, which only served to make her even more attractive.

They drove for slightly more than half an hour, mostly down winding country lanes and it comforted Gabriel to know that wherever they were headed to, it was a remote destination and not just that, even he had no idea where they were going so nobody else would for sure. He knew that back when the affair was still going on between Marius and Mary, she had kept it completely secret from any of her closest friends or family as she said it had been none of their business and he respected her enormously for that.

In the background was a gentle instrumental playlist running through the car's impressive sound system and they both sat quietly letting the notes drift through the air, soothing their souls from the inside out. They arrived at a delightfully quaint country house at the end of a sprawling gravel driveway, which was ideal under these circumstances as it meant that it would be difficult for anybody to sneak up on them unexpectedly.

They wasted no time going into the lavishly decorated and furnished dwelling, where they could make themselves comfortable and have a heart to heart about all that had transpired over the previous disastrous fortnight. Gabriel knew he would be able to be nothing but truthful with Mary, but also felt nervous about how she may feel about the organisation's activities considering its awful portrayal across the media. In fact, with that in mind, he was surprised she had been so willing to accommodate him at all. She poured him a glass of Glenfiddich, as she had remembered his drink of choice matched that of her former lover, poured her own preferred glass of Taittinger Brut Prestige rose wine and they eased into the comfort of opposing couches in her grand living room.

"Let's make something clear," Mary began, "I do not expect to hear any explanation from you as to what happened that led you to be here. Back when your father and I were an item I knew that his business dealings weren't exactly above board and I didn't feel it was in my interest to know anything about them. I adored your father for the man that he was below the surface and his business was nothing to do with me." She took a gentle sip of her wine before continuing, "It would have been the natural order of things for you to take over the running of the business after his departure and I offer you the same respect. You do not need to feel any obligation to tell me any of your business and in all honesty, I believe that the less I know, the better."

Gabriel nodded his understanding. "That's very gracious of you."

"Good. That's settled then. All you are is an old friend who has come to stay for a short time until he can make other plans." She raised her glass towards him in on offer of salutation. He clinked his glass against hers in recognition and they both took a sip to seal the motion.

Chapter 13

Back in the Romford police station the raiding taskforce had returned to report their lack of findings at the now abandoned secret bunker and morale was slightly low as a result. The various members were lacking in their previous zeal and were now moving at a much slower pace between each of the tasks they had to complete – most of it being admin and reporting, which was generally the least favourite task for most of the staff.

Sue and Kate had pulled the leader of the taskforce, Oliver, into one of the interrogation rooms for a quick debriefing on what they had found upon arrival and searching of the bunker. Oliver was a highly skilled and trained, plus exceptionally valued team leader, who took his role seriously and commanded respect, but never at the expense of the team members under his instruction. He was tall, thick set and built of solid muscle – there wasn't an ounce of fat on him as he clearly spent a great deal of time taking care of his physique. His dirty blonde hair was shaved very close to his scalp and he had a handsome, clean cut face that looked remarkably youthful with kind, light brown eyes that at this moment in time looked quite sorrowful.

"I can tell already from your demeanour that you didn't get the desired outcome today, Oliver," Sue began, "That's no reflection on yourself or your team, I just want to remind you of that."

"Thank you, Ma'am. It's always a bit deflating when you get yourself and your team all pumped up and ready to tackle a raid, particularly when we know the stakes are so high. I was hoping for as big a success as the team had on the abandoned farm, but alas, it was not the case today." Oliver's shoulders slumped in a defeated fashion. He didn't normally take these things to heart; he was an incredibly resilient man and had been part of the force for more than two decades now – this was not his first time at the rodeo.

However, he had been working on this case from the very beginning and had seen so many of the raids come up fruitful, with multiple arrests being made, weapons and drugs seized, people rescued from being illegally trafficked elsewhere or put into slave labour in this country. He'd seen it all. Yet today's raid had produced no criminals, next to no evidence and no leads to follow up whatsoever. The man they were hunting knew exactly what he was doing and how best to cover his tracks. It made Oliver furious but he also had a begrudging amount of respect for someone who could pull that level of stealth off so comprehensively.

"That's perfectly understandable," Sue reassured him and Kate nodded along to her words. "Make sure you let the whole team know that they're doing an outstanding job and they are all highly valued for the efforts and extra hours they've been putting in."

"I will do, thank you, Ma'am." Oliver offered a glimmer of an appreciative smile but it fell notably short.

"What did you discover at the bunker?" Sue pressed on.

"We parked a little down the street and made our way as quickly and quietly as possible to the entrance. It wasn't easy because it's so tucked away, right at the bottom of a long garden off a house that is no longer occupied – if we hadn't known the exact coordinates of where we were supposed to be looking, we would not have located it, I can tell you that much.

"We found the doorway that led downwards into the ground after removing several large tree branches that had been strategically placed there to cover it up; it was padlocked with a thick chain holding it in place so immediately my heart sank a little as I knew it was unlikely there would be anyone inside if it was locked on the outside. But you just never know and considering we found a huge basement absolutely full of illegal immigrants less than two weeks ago, we weren't gonna take any chances, ya know?" He seemed to be struggling with some internal issues whereby he felt the need to prove his worth, despite all of his notable achievements regarding this case so far, plus his entire work history that reflected a man who was both excellent at and wholeheartedly passionate about his job. It seemed like any type of failure regarding this case was hitting him in a very personal way.

He shuffled his large, muscular weight in his seat and continued, "We cut the chain and entered the bunker single file under torch light only to find it empty and it looked like it had very recently been vacated. It had been set up to hold multiple occupants but it was clear that there had only been one individual using the space for a short time. There was no rubbish in the large bin but there was a fresh bin liner in it, so I'm assuming he took a full load out with him when he left and was intending to come back because why else would he bother getting a roll of bin liners and tidying up after himself? He also must have been travelling light and taken all of his personal effects with him as we didn't find anything left behind other than what was left of his food, water and scotch. He appears to be a keen drinker as the brand of scotch he left behind costs a pretty penny and there were a few unopened bottles as well as a half drank one.

"We searched the entire place from top to bottom to see if we could find *something* of some use but he was almost admirably thorough in leaving nothing behind for us to be able to track him with. There was no phone line or internet connection; he was sensibly cut off from the outside world for a short time as he waited for the dust to settle, then he made a move when he felt like enough time had passed. Either that or he went stir crazy. After we cleared out, the next team had been waiting on standby for the all clear to go in and dust the place for prints and do a wide-ranging, in depth search for any evidence whatsoever. We've now got the place under twenty-four-hour surveillance and it will remain that way until we see fit that it no longer serves a purpose."

"It sounds like you've done a wonderfully thorough job, Oliver. Thank you very much for taking the time to go through it with us," Sue replied, smiling warmly at him, "As soon as you've filed your report I'd like you to hand over any of the follow up to the next team on shift and go home to your family to get some well-deserved rest. Same goes for the rest of your team. Understood?"

Oliver nodded but looked distracted, then let out a long sigh. "I just really wanted to get the bastard," he said, shaking his head.

"I know. We all do," agreed Sue, with Kate once again nodding enthusiastically next to her, "And mark my words, We Will."

After dismissing Oliver so that he could recuperate from such a long stretch of overtime hours, Sue and Kate remained in the interrogation room so that they could talk privately and openly.

"This is certainly not ideal," muttered Sue, rubbing her chin and furrowing her brow.

"You know, there's every chance he came back to the bunker, saw the raid taking place and scarpered?" Kate asked rhetorically.

"If I was a betting woman, I'd put money on it," Sue agreed, "If he'd have been back in the interim, he would have been spotted by the surveillance team now in place and we'd have heard about it already. He must have got there at just the right time to get spooked and still be able to turn around, unseen."

"He's a slick one, for sure." Kate had stood up and was pacing a little agitatedly across the width of the room. "I don't like him still being out there because I don't like the idea of him acting upon some sort of hideous personal vendetta against Christie."

"What do you mean?" Sue stopped rubbing her chin and looked directly at her work sister with a bemused expression.

"Think about it." Kate tapped the side of her temple. "This is a highly trained, ex-military, top ranking member of an organisation that has basically been running the entire underbelly of Barking and Dagenham, plus a few of the surrounding areas, completely unexposed for *years*. Christie's escape from the farm was the event that sparked a chain reaction of further exposures that ultimately brought that organisation to its knees in the blink of an eye.

"During the process his brothers were arrested, his best friend killed in the line of trying to protect his mother, his mother was then arrested and we've essentially closed in on him from all angles. So, he hides away in his little secret bunker for a while, cut off from the outside world – you heard what Oliver said. There was no phone line or internet connection down there and we already know his registered personal phone hasn't been in use since a couple of days after the initial raid." Kate's voice was speeding up exponentially with her increasing excitement.

"He leaves the bunker on what he thinks will be a short expedition because as far as he knows, his mother made it out safely with the best friend and has now got her own secret hiding place. All he has to do is call them and make plans to either hide out separately for a while longer or to meet up and move somewhere entirely different so that they can eventually start rebuilding everything they've lost. But no, when he makes the call, it leads nowhere, then when he gets a Wi-Fi connection and reads up on what's happened since he went into hiding. It sends him into a vengeful rage. Who do you think is gonna be the person he targets first?" Kate spread her arms out waiting for a response.

"Christie," Sue confirmed through tight lips. They both let that sink in for a few moments.

"We need to get a protection detail put in place immediately. The fact that he's still out there, God only knows where, is like sitting on a ticking time bomb and only bad can come of it," Kate stated with a grim expression.

"Agreed. Let's get straight on it." Sue pushed her chair back so that she could stand and they both exited the interrogation room with a clear goal of protecting the victim they had both come to care for so deeply.

Christie herself had been a bit of a mixed bag of emotions for the past couple of weeks but she understood that was totally normal and wasn't about to put any type of pressure on herself to snap out of it and bounce back to her usual bubbly, vivacious character. She was allowing herself the time and space to be weepy or angry or over analytical or whatever emotion she needed to work through at any given moment.

Ultimately with every passing feeling she ended up returning to one of sheer gratitude that things hadn't gone far worse for her, that she'd made it out in one piece and even managed to help rescue twelve others in the process.

She was currently at Len and May's place in Maidstone as they had driven to come and pick her up for a night of escapism away from Dagenham, where everything was still so chaotic. On their travels they'd put in a call to Dale to see if he fancied it too and he said he had a few hours to spare before his dad duties kicked in, so they'd swung by and picked him up too.

Their house was very new to them and was still a little bit of a work in progress where they were redecorating from top to bottom, but at the very least, Len had made sure the TV, sound system and all entertainment related gadgets and gizmos were in working order because clearly that's where his priorities lay.

May had given them the grand tour of each and every room with full explanation as to what each would be transformed into over the coming weeks, plus a slow walk around the beautiful, scenic garden, coupled with descriptions of what seeds she would be planting where and the type of space they wanted to create for their future offspring.

Christie felt utterly refreshed hearing about something other than her recent traumatic ordeal and the banter between Len and Dale had them all in hysterics. It was exactly the break she had been desperately needing. Conversation was flowing all afternoon and they all collectively grew hungry and decided that ordering pizza was the best option so whilst May took down everyone's requests and called up the local Domino's pizza to place their order, Len, Dale and Christie migrated to the living room to settle in for the next couple of hours at least. The couches had been covered over with protective sheets whilst Len, May and several of their family members had been tackling the walls with paint rollers the previous day, so Dale and Christie set about uncovering those, whilst Len went to business setting up what to watch on TV.

As soon as he switched the display on it came up with the latest BBC news update and a story was being read out about one of the latest victims to be discovered and reunited with her family in the ongoing case surrounding the criminal organisation that had been terrorising innocent citizens in Barking and Dagenham for far too long. As always, the wording was over the top and sensationalised to try to grab the viewers' attention.

"Sorry, Chris, I didn't mean to switch it on to this. I'm sure you must be fed up of hearing about it by now," Len apologised, with a humble shoulder shrug.

"Hang on, don't turn over yet," Christie interjected. "I don't think I've seen this update. I don't recognise her," she said pointing at the screen where Tara's beautiful face was now taking up the prime position. She was being interviewed regarding her return to the UK after being held captive against her will in Northern Portugal for roughly six months.

The interviewer was now hidden from view and could only be heard prompting Tara with gentle questions about her situation. "What can you tell us about what happened to you?"

the female reporter asked politely.

"The last six months of my life have been the stuff that nightmares are made of. It's hard to describe the constant fear, anguish and levels of disgust, anger, revulsion that I went through and am still going through now every time I replay what has happened to me. I will never look at life or at the world in the same way ever again, what I've seen is some of the absolute worst parts of humanity you can even begin to imagine." Tara's face looked genuinely traumatised as she spoke and every so often she would pause to let a shiver run through her body, clearly letting her mental images get the better of her.

"It sounds horrific, my dear. If you feel comfortable enough to do so, would you mind talking us through your ordeal?" The reporter's eloquent and soft tone was akin to the kind of voice you would expect to hear reading out children's bedtime stories on an audiobook; it was so soothing and gentle. However, this particular tale could not be further from the type of content one would read to a child at bedtime.

Tara went on to describe what had taken place to the reporter and camera operator in full detail, leaving nothing to the imagination. Her abduction from Mayesbrook Park when she had been walking home from a busy, late shift had an involuntarily triggering effect on Christie and her subconscious took the opportunity to flash up several memories in her mind's eye from the night when she was taken from Old Dagenham Park. She shuddered noticeably and Dale reached over to place his open palm lightly against her back.

"You OK?" Dale asked softly, a look of concern in his eyes.

Christie snapped out of the graphic mental images that had

taken over her vision for a moment, looked over at him and nodded sheepishly, "Yeah, I'm OK, it just hit home a little quicker than I was ready for."

"Can I turn over now?" Len asked "I don't wanna upset you and ruin your night." Now his face was full of concern too.

"In a minute, I just wanna hear a little more about what happened to her when she got to Portugal," Christie replied, then added, "Sorry, it's just that this is the first story I've seen of anyone brought back that was actually shipped out from the farm. I've kinda been curious as to what happened to them when they reached their final destination."

"OK, but if it gets too much then just say so and I'll put something funny on to take your mind off of it," Len offered.

"Cheers, love." Christie smiled at him briefly and then focused back on Tara's appalling tale.

She had gone on to describe her transportation overseas and all of the trauma related to that – being blindfolded, gagged and bound the entire time and suffering sea sickness along the way. Then she got on to the part about waking up in a sex dungeon, wearing a revealing PVC outfit and being sprawled out on the bed with her limbs strapped to each of the four corners. Her voice was shaking as she spoke as it was clearly the worst thing that had ever happened to her and putting it into words was like trying to describe something that you would only ever imagine happening in your worst nightmares.

Tears rolled down her cheeks and the reporter handed her a box of tissues, which she gratefully accepted, but bravely and defiantly continued with her story. It was obvious that she felt an obligation to let the world know just how menacing and deranged some of its inhabitants could be. She didn't want to gloss over anything or tone it down so as not to offend people; she wanted them to hear the hell that she'd been through and been forced to endure for the last six months.

Christie's tears were now running almost as thick and fast as Tara's and Len decided that that was more than enough viewing time on that particular story. He switched it over to a music channel but turned the volume down so that he could address his dear friend, who was in a tremendous amount of pain. May had just walked back in from the kitchen area to find Christie crying and being comforted by her fiancé and their mutual friend.

"What have I missed? This is supposed to be a cheering up mission guys. What have you done?" May looked accusingly at Len and then Dale.

"It wasn't their fault!" Christie blubbed, "It was mine. Curiosity killed the cat and all that jazz."

May's expression grew even more puzzled and Len filled in the gaps, "You remember the Filipino looking chick we saw briefly on the news last night? She's doing a frank and honest interview as we speak about exactly what happened to her and she's not holding back. It's had a triggering effect on Chris." He placed his hand gently on Christie's knee and gave it a couple of gentle jiggles, followed by three gentle taps before retracting it. Dale kept his hand on her back but had proceeded to start running it up and down.

May, the most affectionate of the group, came and kneeled down in front of Christie and pulled her in to a tight, warm and incredibly comforting hug. They remained there for at least two minutes whilst Christie gently sobbed into her shoulder, her breath catching slightly with each inhalation she took. When May pulled away to look her in the eyes and to wipe away the floods of tears with a tissue that Len had covertly slipped into her hands, she said, "This is a one hundred per cent normal reaction and you have every right to be upset. Don't feel silly about letting curiosity get the better of you – you're only human, I probably would have done the same thing, I'd wanna know. But right now, it's probably just a little bit too much to take, right? You're probably still feeling wounded from your own suffering, let alone adding anyone else's distressing stories to that mix." She rubbed the sides of Christie's arms up and down to comfort her as she spoke.

"Yeah, I know, it was silly thinking I could handle it right now, when I clearly can't. It's just, when she spoke about the outfit she woke up in it brought it all back to me." She swivelled in her seat to look at Dale. "You remember what I was wearing under the massive waterproof jacket when you found me, right?"

Dale cringed and nodded. "Yeah I remember."

"I think it's fairly safe to assume that my fate was going to be very much like this poor woman's based on that fact alone. Or who knows – it could have been even worse," Christie surmised.

"But you know what Christie?" May asked. "It's not. You're here right now, sitting with people who adore you. You're not in some unknown location being subjected to anything horrible by anyone else. You're here with us and that's all because you took the initiative and had the *unbelievable* courage to fight your way free. That says a huge amount about just how incredible you are."

Christie blushed a little and mumbled a shy thank you.

"It's true. And not only that, but you helped prevent what

happened to that poor woman from happening to any of the other twelve victims that were rescued because of the extensive evidence you provided. You really are a hero." May wrapped Christie up in another, briefer hug, stroked her hair and rocked her from side to side a few times. "I know it's hard at times, but try your very best to focus on the positive outcomes of all that has happened thanks to your bravery and it will hopefully make this whole ordeal slightly less painful."

"Top notch advice, babe," Len gratefully commended his fiancée, rubbing her shoulder as he spoke and smiled warmly at Christie, "Now let's put something funny on to lighten the mood, eh?"

Christie laughed, nodded and excused herself to go and wash her face in the bathroom. The room was a little bit of a mess where they had only recently finished tiling and there were tools, supplies and reminders of the work still pending scattered around at various points, but it was still a functioning bathroom so Christie made full use of the facilities. When she gazed into the mirror after wiping away any wayward, escapee mascara, she reminded herself that she was safe, cared for and that she had nothing to worry about in this space. She had no idea of the imminent threat of vengeance hanging over her head like a thick, black, thunderous cloud.

She re-joined the group in the living room to continue with the festivities as none of the four friends had any idea about the twisted, evil plot that was being formulated in the mind of a highly skilled, deviant, ex-military man roughly sixty miles away from where they were enjoying their cosy get together. Their pizza and obscene amount of side orders arrived and they got stuck into the delightful spread whilst watching a variety of stand-up comedy sets on Len's prized entertainment system.

Any worries that Christie had previously had seemed to evaporate and she allowed herself to sit back and indulge in the merriment around her, letting the happiness and feeling of comfort and ease soak through to her very core.

She had already happily accepted the offer of staying over for the night, but Dale had to leave and take care of his fatherly responsibilities so he ordered an Uber to whisk him away just as the day started to turn into nightfall.

Before he left he pulled Christie into his arms and wrapped her in a tight bear hug for several minutes and they both comfortably melted into each other's warmth, breathing slowly and deeply, truly appreciating the moment. Eventually he loosened his grip a little so that he could look into her deep, ocean-coloured eyes.

"You need me for anything, *anything* at all, you just let me know, OK?" His expression was a mockingly stern look. "Don't make me wag my finger at you."

Christie cackled loudly at the mental image of him making such a gesture. "I certainly shall. Thank you – for everything. I mean that," she said, sincerely.

"Any time." He pulled her back in close for another couple of minutes and kissed the top of her head.

Mere moments later, Len and May appeared from having tidied up all of the takeaway containers and washed up the plates and they gave each other a knowing look before they both dashed forwards and yelled out "Group hug!", then simultaneously wrapped their arms around Dale and Christie. They all laughed and enjoyed the silliness together until the Uber pulled up to take Dale home.

It wasn't too long before Len, May and Christie retired for the evening in their separate rooms after wishing one another a peaceful night's sleep. As Christie closed her eyes she replayed the glorious scenes from the second half of the afternoon where she had felt utterly carefree and jovial. She had missed feeling that way and wanted it to continue, unhindered for as long as physically possible.

Chapter 14

Miles away, Gabriel had been busy packing his meagre possessions into his large, utility backpack at Mary's beautiful, quaint country cottage. Overnight she had washed all of the clothes he had with him, tumble dried them and left him with a clean, fresh smelling supply. She'd even offered him a couple of his father's old shirts that she had held on to for sentimental value and he had accepted one of those with a humble amount of gratitude but told her to hang on to the other one seen as though it had meant enough to her to keep.

He had slept better in her guest bed than he probably had in years – he couldn't actually remember the last time he had had that many consecutive hours of unbroken sleep. The concept was pretty alien to him. Mary and her surroundings must have had the calming effect on him that he craved so badly. He didn't really know what to make of that. Was it appropriate for his father's ex-lover to bring out such feelings of safety and security in him? He quickly shrugged away that thought as he knew overthinking things was not remotely useful and he had more important things to worry about.

He was recently showered and smelling better than he had in at least a fortnight, he had a mission set in his mind and there was nothing that was going to stand in his way of accomplishing what he set out to do.

In a completely out of character fashion, Gabriel had overslept and Mary had allowed him the privacy to do so, knowing that he very much needed the rest after the enormous amount of upheaval he had just been through.

He wandered through to the kitchen in the early afternoon with his backpack on his shoulder where he found Mary brewing some expensive smelling coffee and frying up a full English breakfast. She too had had a luxurious lay in after consuming a little too much wine the night before and was still dressed in her long, fuchsia, silk dressing gown that was synched in at the waist and highlighted her curves in all the right places. Her back was to him as she went about the business of making his breakfast food to be served as more of a brunch, so she was unaware of his presence and he took the opportunity to just stare at her for a moment and etch the scene before him permanently in his more delectable memory bank.

After a couple of minutes of silence he stepped forward to properly immerse himself in this delightfully homely scene, placed his backpack on the ground, close to the door and made his presence known.

"Good afternoon." He spoke to the back of Mary's figure and she spun just her top half around to smile broadly at him in response.

"Well, a very good afternoon to you too, my dear." She beamed. "I hope you're hungry."

"I'm absolutely famished," Gabriel replied with a hungry gaze both at her and at the feast she was lovingly preparing.

"Great. Pour yourself some coffee and sit yourself down as it will be ready in two shakes of a lamb's tail," Mary instructed and Gabriel laughed at the Pulp Fiction reference.

They sat down to enjoy their meal, exchanging only minimal conversation about how well they had both slept and how the weather was looking nice outside. Gabriel cleared up the plates afterwards and placed them into the dishwasher, wiping down the surfaces as he went and leaving everything in a pristine fashion, just how he had been trained to do so.

"So I take it from the fact that you have packed up your things that you will be leaving shortly?" Mary enquired.

"I shall, yes," Gabriel confirmed, "I received a text from an ally last night with the address of a safe place I can go to remain unexposed for a little while, whilst I figure out my next move."

"That's great news. You must be so relieved." Mary's words didn't reflect the expression on her face and Gabriel could have sworn he saw an ever so faint glimmer of a tear forming in her right eye, which she quickly blinked away and attempted to smile.

"I am," Gabriel agreed, "The last thing I would want to do is overstay my welcome and inadvertently get you in any trouble whatsoever. You've been gracious enough letting me stay overnight and I do not wish to test the boundaries of your generosity."

"Of course." Mary nodded in apprehension and swiftly turned practical. "You can take my old car. It gets no actual, meaningful use anymore but only last week I made sure the battery was still running in it by taking it for a little spin around the country lanes. My intention was to put out an ad for it and sell it on very soon as all it's doing is wasting space in my garage, so you may as well save me the bother."

"That's incredibly kind of you, Mary, thank you." Gabriel still couldn't wrap his head around how wonderful this woman was being to him and how much she was putting at risk just by having him here. "I wish I could better put into words how much I appreciate everything you've done for me in less than twenty-four hours. You were the last person I ever would have expected this from. You really are something else."

Mary noticeably blushed and tried to shrug off his compliment. "Think nothing of it. It is what your father would have wanted."

They ventured over to the separate garage building on Mary's property together so that Gabriel could exchange the current number plates on her old car for the ones he had taken off the stolen Ford Focus. Her supposedly old sky blue Audi TT was in fantastic condition and looked as though it had been freshly polished and hoovered, leaving Gabriel even more humbled by her generosity.

They exchanged a long and lingering hug before he departed from the cottage and though neither of them would dare to admit it, something stirred deep down inside of both parties – something carnal and passionate. It wasn't remotely appropriate but the extreme desire was both shared and undeniable.

"From the bottom of my heart, thank you." Gabriel gazed a little too eagerly into her sensual, luminous green eyes, then realised his faux pas and gently started to pull away from the embrace.

Mary felt him extracting himself and had to forcibly remind herself that it would not be a good idea to cling tighter and pull him back towards her, so instead she gave him a quick, sharp squeeze, smiled broadly and allowed him to let go. "You're most welcome."

She made no attempt to enquire as to where he would go from there –she already knew that the less information she had about him, the better for all concerned. So despite the growing hollow feeling in the pit of her stomach, she stepped back to watch him drive away, waving goodbye as he did so.

Gabriel's mind was set on one thing and one thing only now. He had received a text from Sandor with the address of one if his good friends and a former college roommate in Southeast London. He had been given strict instructions to arrive there under the cover of night, as covertly as possible and to keep himself hidden away from the public for the duration of his stay at this property, which Gabriel was all too happy to oblige.

He had quite a few hours before darkness would start to prevail and he had the perfect plan in mind as to how he was going to spend those few hours.

It had been all too easy to find out where Christie lived thanks to the extensive amount of news coverage her story had received ever since she escaped from the organisation's clutches and waltzed back into society with zero consideration for the snowball effect that her actions would have on the people who had sacrificed a huge amount of time and effort into turning that business into a well-oiled machine. It had produced so many great triumphs throughout its operation and kept many mouths fed with all of the profits it had generated, then this one feisty, unbridled beast of a woman had come in, trampled all over it and torn it to shreds from the inside out.

Gabriel wanted nothing more than to teach her that her actions had consequences. He wanted to look her in the eye and tell her exactly how badly she'd wrecked everything for him, before watching the colour leave her face as he throttled her to death. He could feel a warm feeling of satisfaction deep in his inner core as he pictured torturing her to the absolute extent that her feeble body could take, then stopping just long enough for her to recuperate slightly and catch her breath, lulling her into a false sense of security that he would let her live, then finishing her off for good. Before any of that he would plant nightmarish seeds in her mind that once he was done with her, he would go after her family too and destroy them all.

He wouldn't actually need to bother going through with that once he'd exterminated Christie, but for her to meet her end believing that her actions had brought hellish consequences to all those she cared about was too delicious an opportunity to waste. He licked his lips in anticipation of the sheer agony he was going to cause her.

He parked Mary's former Audi TT several streets away from Christie's house, but still close enough for him to easily sprint back to if he took the right route, then headed towards her house on foot with his hood pulled over his head and his hands in his pockets, keeping his head lowered but also keeping a keen eye on all of his surroundings as he briskly walked.

The traffic was flowing freely on the busy road she lived on and he could see numerous witnesses through the railings of the park he was walking alongside. Even if today wasn't the day he would be able to get his bloodthirsty hands on her, this would serve as a decent amount of recon for him to take away and put together a more extensive plan of action. He located the right house and began to mentally size up the structure and position of any windows and doors that looked like they may be easily accessible. Just as he was circling back to the front of the property from having checked out the rear, a gentleman who was much taller and broader than himself, but also roughly twenty years his senior, came out of the front door and spotted him.

"Who are you?" The large man was not shy about asking him for his identity and didn't seem at all intimidated either, which threw Gabriel a little, given the man's age. He merely shook his head in response, spun around and immediately began power walking back in the direction of where he had left the car parked.

Chapter 15

It had been a little while since Christie had bothered checking her phone. She had been relishing in the company of her treasured friends at their delightful work-in-progress of a new house. When she did, the first notification that grabbed her was a WhatsApp message from one of her housemates, Winston.

"I don't want to alarm you Christie but there was a man outside our house earlier looking suspicious. I've alerted the police who are looking into it but I thought it best to let you know too," Winston had written.

There were also three missed calls from Kate at Romford Police station, a voicemail from her asking Christie to call her back as soon as possible and also a text to reiterate that message. Christie's stomach felt like a giant pit, slowly filling up from all possible entry points with a feeling of complete and all-consuming dread. She pressed the call back option to return Kate's earlier one.

"Hi Christie, thanks for getting back to me," Kate answered after one and a half rings, "Are you OK? Whereabouts are you?"

"I stayed overnight at my friends' place in Maidstone," Christie replied, feeling like an anxious school girl who was being checked up on by her suspicious and over-protective parent, "Has something happened? I also had a message from my housemate saying he'd seen someone suspicious outside our house. Is this what you're calling about?"

"Originally it wasn't, but since hearing that report come through, it very much relates to what I was calling about in the first place," Kate confirmed.

"Sorry, I left my phone in my bag and didn't bother checking it until now – I've been having a really nice time here not thinking about the case twenty-four-seven for a change," Christie explained sheepishly.

"Hun, there is *no* need to apologise whatsoever," Kate assured her, "I totally get it and I'm genuinely happy that you are where you are– a.k.a. out of harm's way for a little while. See the thing is..." Kate took an audibly large breath at that point as though she was bracing herself to deliver some awful news. "There's a third brother related to two of the suspects currently in our custody and their mother is also now being held in relation to the ongoing case. This brother is currently at large and there has been a huge manhunt for him with a distinct lack of results thus far and we have reason to believe that he may want to target you in order to seek revenge for all that has happened to the family business since your escape. This man is a highly skilled and dangerous ex-military man with a drinking problem and a tendency towards violent behaviour, so you can understand our concern for your safety."

Christie gulped loudly and tried to speak but it mostly came out as a stifled, gasping, gargle-like sound.

"I know that's tough to take in right now and I hate to be the one to deliver this dreadful piece of information to you, my dear," Kate explained apologetically, "It's just that we need to put measures in place to keep you guarded on a twenty-four-hour basis until we can find and arrest this man. Do you understand?"

"Yes," was the only word that Christie's panicked brain

could formulate in her mouth.

"Good. Now, I need you to stay where you are, with your friends until we have both a protective team in place and a secure location for you to be temporarily accommodated in. Is that feasible?" Kate asked, all business and practicality.

"Definitely. When my friends hear about this I know they will be happy to help." Christie replied with confidence.

"Perfect. Try not to let this drag you down into a pit of anxiety, lovely. I know that's much easier said than done, but the most important thing to remember is that these measures are preventative and thorough. We will put every necessary step in place to assure your safety at all times," Kate offered sincerely, "I will call you back with further instructions, for now, just sit tight and stay calm."

It wasn't just a case of trembling hands when Christie hung up the phone. It was like her entire body was vibrating and the breath caught like a hard lump in her chest. From out of nowhere, Len came up behind her and placed his hand gingerly on her shoulder.

"Everything OK, mate?" His look was pure concern as he caught a glimpse of her own panic-stricken expression. "I couldn't hear much of the conversation from your side…not that I was trying to ear wig or anything."

"Not exactly," Christie stammered, "You know the two brothers that were arrested as a result of the voice recordings I got Dale to send the police when I woke up in hospital?"

"Yeah, I remember. You punched one in the throat, right? That's how you got out." Len gave her a little playful punch on her shoulder, trying in vain to make her smile, but it fell flat.

"There's a third brother. And he's pissed. At me."

Christie's entire body shuddered. "That was Officer Kate on the phone – one of the two chicks that interviewed me and have been supporting me since then. She said they have reason to believe that this third brother wants revenge and is gonna come after me, so they want to put some protection in place to prevent anything bad happening. Just before I saw her missed calls I saw a message from my housemate, Winston, who said he saw someone acting suspicious outside our house and he'd let the cops know. So it looks like their predictions are already coming true and he's found out where I live."

"Oh, mate, that's heavy." Len closed the gap between them and wrapped his arms around her for a moment, gently stroking her back in a comforting gesture. "Obviously I'm no iron clad henchman, but I'll take care of you whilst you're here and you can stay here as long as you like. You know that, right?"

"Yeah, I know, thank you." Christie tried her best to smile but it wasn't anywhere close to her usually cheerfully bright grin. "I told Kate that I would stay here until she gives me further instruction. But the absolute last thing I would ever want to do is risk him finding out where you guys live too. Apparently this dude is highly skilled, ex-military and a nasty motherfucker with it. You know how good soldiers are at tracking people? I'm not willing to put you two in the firing line so the second I receive the go ahead from Kate, I'm outta here."

"Well I want you to promise me that you will at least allow us to get you to wherever you need to go when she does and that you will stay in touch on a regular basis so that we know you're safe. I hate to sound all parent-like on ya, but it's only 'cause I care." Len gave her shoulders a squeeze and then pulled her back in for another quick hug.

"I promise." Christie's voice came out muffled from her

face being pressed against his shoulder and she sighed into his embrace for a moment.

Gabriel had made it back to the Audi TT in a flash and driven aimlessly for at least an hour with the adrenaline coursing through his veins like wildfire. He hadn't been able to do any prior research on the other inhabitants of the house that Christie lived in before he'd made his way there to scope the place and being spotted by the large, old and clearly not easily spooked man had thrown a bit of a spanner in the works.
Getting to her wasn't going to be as simple as he had envisioned, especially not since he knew all too well that he could potentially have been reported to the cops for his peeping-Tom-like behaviour. Even if the old man had only suspected him of being just a member of the public who was a little gossip hungry and wanted to get a sneak peak of the star of the current media circus, he would be well within his rights to alert the authorities and ask that people respect their household's privacy.

He mentally reprimanded himself for not thinking things through and assuming that he could just waltz up to the house in broad daylight to get an idea of how he would later be able to break in. What had he been thinking? His head was all over the place after the events from the last few weeks and it was taking its toll on how he conducted himself. He was usually so much more tactical and prepared for every worst possible outcome, yet he felt like he hadn't lived up to his usual standards at all since the raid on the abandoned farm. Perhaps the emotional baggage associated with how much he had lost in such a short space of time was catching up on him and hindering his judgement. Perhaps he was finally getting what he deserved after decades of doing whatever he pleased with little regard for the laws that governed this land.

All of this introspection was doing him absolutely no good whatsoever and he decided to pull into a service station to get some refreshments and hopefully a Wi-Fi connection for a little while. He needed to sit peacefully and get his act together before making his way to Sandor's friend's place in South East London.

Chapter 16

The team at Romford police station had been busily putting plans in place to ensure Christie's safety for the foreseeable future, at the very least, until they had all three of the Balan brothers in custody, ready to be tried for their multiple crimes against the system. It was agreed that the safest place to keep her on a short-term basis would be the Travelodge that was situated very close to Dagenham East Police station so that the team there would be close by to keep an eye on her and because there were security guards regularly patrolling the building, as well as twenty-four-hour CCTV cameras that could be logged into remotely. Kate had put in the call to Christie and made her aware of all the steps that had been put in place and when Christie had let her know that she had means of transportation to her new room via her friends, she had agreed to meet her there to brief her on the emergency protocols necessary to keep her safe.

Kate waited outside the entrance to the Travelodge patiently for Christie's arrival. It was getting close to lunchtime and the sun was beaming down on her from almost the highest, middle point of the sky. For a moment she closed her eyes and tilted her head back, allowing the vitamin D to soak into her pores and rejuvenate her, breathing slowly and deeply and appreciating this moment of simplicity and peace.

Ever since this case had broken it had become the central focus of her life and everything else seemed to revolve around it so moments like this one, where she could take the time to be present in both mind and body, were extremely few and far between. Thankfully she had an incredibly understanding partner and they were able to schedule their shifts so that they could take it in turns to care for their two young, beautiful and precocious daughters.

Her partner, Matt, knew and respected how dedicated she was to her job because he felt the same way about his position as a trainee surgeon at Queen's hospital. Though they were both ambitious and compassionate, they were also incredibly family orientated and ultimately would sacrifice anything they needed to for the sake of their young ones and making sure they were properly looked after.

She drifted away into a sweet memory of Matt and the girls at the park, where he was expertly tackling both sides of the swing set in order to push each of his daughters, one after the other, dashing back and forth with ease and never leaving one un-pushed. The girls were whooping and hollering gleefully, enjoying every second of their dad's undivided attention.

Kate had been leaning against the fencing that surrounded the little playground and watching from the side-lines, feeling pure contentment and pride. It was one of her absolute favourite memories to replay in her mind whenever the world around her started to grow too heavy or chaotic. It brought her back to a sense of inner peace and tranquillity like no other topic on the planet could, reminding her always of what was most important in life – her treasured family.

The nearby sound of a car pulling into the car park brought Kate back to reality and she immediately recognised the two faces in the front seats as Christie's friends from the hospital the first day she had met her properly and not been completely buzzed out of her mind. May was driving and pulled into the closest parking space to the front door as she could and all three of May, Len and Christie exited her dark grey Hyundai. They exchanged a few words and meaningful hugs before they all walked in unison over to where Kate was standing.

"Thanks very much for driving her all the way here." Kate addressed May and Len as a pair. "You guys are great friends."

"It's absolutely our pleasure." May beamed back. "If there's anything else we can do, *anything* at all, please let us know. We'll be happy to help."

"That's very kind of you, I'll bear that in mind." Kate nodded at the warm gesture and then turned her attention to Christie. "Are you ready, hun?"

"Ready as I'll ever be." Christie's attempt at casual, dry humour wasn't even a tiny bit sincere and the rest of them knew it but allowed her the dignity to play it out. Len and May came in for one final hug and instructed Christie to pass their phone numbers on to Kate so that they could be easily contacted if necessary, both gave her heartfelt kisses on the cheek and said their farewells before making their way back towards May's car.

"Let's get you checked into your new temporary home." Kate put an arm lightly around Christie's shoulder and directed her through the doorway and went through the motions of signing her in, retrieving her room key and escorting her personally to her room. It was on the ground floor and very close to a fire exit so that if the worst-case scenario were to become a reality and the third Balan brother got wind of where she had been placed by the authorities, she would be able to easily make a break for it and any security guards or police officers would also be able to quickly and effectively have access to her room. They had done their utmost to keep this location on a strictly need-to-know basis and warned any staff members that had been privy to this information to not even divulge it to their closest family members.

The room itself was large and well-lit thanks to the sizable window on the wall furthest from the door, the bed was far too big for Christie's slim frame and freshly made with bright, white sheets and a blue, red and green striped throw across the middle to add a splash of colour.

"Sue called your mum earlier to let her know what's been going on and what steps we have put into place to keep you safe," Kate informed Christie, "She was understandably worried at first, but the more she was told about our safety precautions, the more she eased up. She's offered to go to your place and pick up some things for you if you feel comfortable with that? Obviously we won't allow her to go alone; she will be provided with a police escort and then once she has collected your stuff, it will be taken to the police station first, just in case anyone happens to be watching your house and takes it upon themselves to covertly follow her anywhere. She will then be transported back to her place and your belongings will be brought here to you by someone from our team. Does that sound OK to you?"

Christie squirmed uncomfortably. "The last thing I'd wanna do is put anyone at risk just for the sake of a few personal items. It just doesn't seem worth it." She hugged herself as a shiver passed through her body at the thought of anything bad happening to her mum.

"I totally get that." Kate rubbed Christie's left arm up and down a couple of times in a reassuring gesture. "I'm happy to explain that to her and if you like; I have absolutely no qualms about going to your place myself and picking up some bits for you. You'll just have to give me your key and a list of where everything is." She shrugged light-heartedly to portray that it wasn't a big deal and smiled broadly.

Christie's eyes welled up. "Thank you so much." She blubbed.

"Heeeeeey, don't you worry your pretty little head about it, Hun." Kate wrapped Christie into a warm and genuine hug, stroking her back up and down and murmuring, "Sshhhhhhh." She pulled away and gently brushed the stray hairs away from Christie's face, tucking them behind her ear, "Everything's gonna be OK, we're gonna take good care of you until all of this mess blows over." Though she truly meant what she said, she knew it was a rather sugar-coated way of describing the precariously dangerous situation this brave and strong young woman had found herself in. Of course she wanted to do everything she possibly could to comfort Christie, but she also wanted her to remain alert and cautious at all times.

"Now, here comes the serious bit. I want you to keep your stay here an absolute secret from everybody who doesn't need to know. That means no photos or tagging yourself on social media, don't mention it online or even over the phone, unless you trust the receiver implicitly. I know this all may sound like common sense, but I wouldn't be doing my job properly if I didn't take the time to drill into you just how important it is to keep yourself unexposed." Kate was doing an exceptional job at sounding strict and unwavering in her instructions; it was a side to her that Christie wasn't used to seeing but she was incredibly grateful for the fact that her safety was being taken so seriously.

"Understood." Christie nodded and kept her expression focused and attentive to show her comprehension of what she was being told.

"I'm going to sit here with you and download an app to your phone called Solo Protect. This is something I want you to leave switched on and keep open in the background at *all* times because it had GPS tracking enabled so that wherever you are, we will be able to easily locate you if you find yourself in any danger. Once it has been installed on your phone it turns it into a protective, smart device so that if you need to quickly send out an emergency alert, all you need to do is press the power button five times in quick succession. There is a response team at the other end twenty-four-seven, who will be able to listen in through your phone as to what is happening at this end without making any sounds and thereby alerting any potential intruder or attacker to the fact that they are being listened to."

"That sounds like something out of a spy movie." Christie had a look of amazement on her face as she listened to the description of this app and its capabilities.

"It is very clever. We've had a lot of success in using it with people we need to keep safe at all times so it's certainly worth the service charge the Met forks out for it." Kate only very briefly digressed before continuing with her instructions, "Ideally, I would like you to remain in this room as much as physically possible, but I understand that would be a little bit like serving jail time and will slowly start to drive you a little bit potty. When you do feel like you need to go out for whatever reason, I want you to press the amber alert button and simply talk into your phone as though you were leaving a voicemail– preferably give a postcode of wherever you are at that moment as well as wherever you are intending to move onto next, then hang up the phone. Also, there is an option to send out a device check at the touch of a button and you will get fairly regular notifications about this whenever your phone has been left inactive for a certain amount of time. Please make sure you follow the instructions when they come through.

"As a further safety measure, please send a text to either myself or Sue when you want to go out so that we can make sure a squad car is not too far away from your location at all times and please don't go on any long walking expeditions by yourself. I know that's something you normally love to do, so I know it will be hard but it's only temporary and only a precaution to keep you safe."

Christie took a long, deep breath and let out a measured and steady sigh. "I get it. I really, truly appreciate everything you're doing for me and I'm not gonna do anything reckless or risky that will basically negate all of your hard work. Please do me a favour and pass that same message on to the rest of your team. I want them to know that I'm sincerely grateful for everything they've done so far and are continuing to do for me," Christie said, humbly.

"I certainly, shall my dear, they'll be happy to hear it," Kate assured her. "I'll take your key now and head over to your place. Text me instructions of what you want picking up and I'll bring it back in a jiffy," she said before heading out of the door, leaving Christie alone in her new abode.

Chapter 17

Gabriel had driven into South East London and followed the directions he had scribbled down after googling the address of Sandor's friends' place whilst refuelling both his own stressed out body and the Audi TT at the enormous service station facilities. He didn't know the area at all and had stuck to the instructions to arrive under the cover of nightfall to the luxury apartment building in a rather affluent part of Southwark. He had sent a text to the number provided by Sandor to let the recipient know he had arrived and found himself being buzzed into a concealed underground carpark that was for residents only. He eased the Audi inside with extreme caution, his pulse slightly heightened and a rush of adrenaline coursing through him as he realised he knew nothing about who was going to be greeting him and the type of people he would be staying with.

He hated going into any situation unprepared and right now he felt like a lamb being led to slaughter as he was completely clueless as to how well he would be received by these total strangers.

The large iron barrier, made of multiple thick bars that stretched all the way across from one side of the entrance to the other, closed behind him, technically sealing him inside with little room for a speedy escape. His pulse quickened even further as he gently coasted along through the car park, not knowing whether or not he was going in the right direction or if perhaps he should stop completely and wait to be approached.

A very tall, trim white man in his late forties, dressed in

slim fitting black jeans, a black polo neck and smart, shiny, black dress shoes appeared from a stairwell and waved in Gabriel's direction so he headed towards this black-clad figure and parked in the nearest parking space.

As he exited, the giant of a man made no move to come over and greet him, he merely held open the door to the stairwell and motioned for Gabriel to go through, ahead of him. They walked up three flights of stairs in silence and all Gabriel could hear was his heart pounding against his chest and a slight ringing in his ears.

A deep voice with a slight Hungarian accent sounded behind him as they reached the third floor instructing him to take the door on the right, turn left and go to the end of the hallway so he obediently followed each instruction with precision, whilst also silently planning out a sequence of defence moves in his mind if he needed to fight his way out of this situation at any stage. He was well versed in a variety of martial arts and planned to use a mixture of all techniques in his repertoire in order to catch any potential assailants off guard. It was the one thing keeping him grounded and sane at this particular moment in time.

His senses were heightened so he heard the sound of shuffling fabric from behind and every single hair on the back of his neck stood up, then he heard the jingling sound of a set of keys and the Hungarian voice let him know that this was the correct apartment: number sixty-six.

Gabriel stopped next to the door and spun around to take in more of the giant's appearance. He had a fairly faint goatee beard, as though it was something he had only just started trying on for size, which matched the colour of his hair– mousey blonde with flecks of light brown running through it from all angles. His cheek bones were extremely pronounced and his face so slender that you would be forgiven for assuming he was either a little unwell or a catwalk model, yet there was something classically handsome about him and his eyes were the lightest, brightest blue Gabriel had ever seen in a set of eyes before. The handsome giant opened the door silently and motioned for him to enter first, then slid in after him, keeping the sounds of the door opening and closing to an absolute minimum.

The lights in the room were low-lit in such a way one would expect to see in a romantic movie scene, which only served to intensify Gabriel's alertness as he took in the layout of the expensive looking furniture and sized up the ornaments that were placed artistically around the room for their potential use as a weapon.

"My apologies for being so cloak and dagger." The handsome giant spoke slightly more loudly, but still in a muted tone as it was so late in the night. "I just wanted to keep your entrance to an absolute minimum in terms of witnesses. You understand." It wasn't a question, he didn't seem to particularly care how uncomfortable he had made his new guest. "My name is Vilmos." He didn't offer any handshake by way of introduction.

Gabriel nodded back at him, a little unsure of how to communicate with this man, "Gabriel," he replied.

"I know who you are. Your face is all over the news. It's quite the predicament you seem to have found yourself in, no?" Vilmos smirked as though the whole situation was a big joke to him and that immediately put Gabriel's guard back up so he just glared back at Vilmos, silently.

A few moments passed where neither of them said anything

and Vilmos must have realised how callous he had sounded. "Forgive me, I did not mean to make light out of your personal dilemma, that was inconsiderate. My wife often chastises me for not being particularly sensitive of other people's feelings."

Gabriel nodded his acceptance. With anybody else and under any other circumstances he would have squared up to the offending party and put them in their place immediately. In this scenario he felt very much like he was at this man's mercy and his options were so slim on the ground these days that he would take whatever opportunities he could get, no matter how begrudgingly.

"Your wife?" Gabriel asked.

"Yes, my wife Elena. She'll be through in just a moment," Vilmos explained and as if his words had summoned her up from another dimension, she breezed through an archway from an adjoining room that Gabriel could not guess the size of due to the low level of lighting.

Either way, it didn't matter because at this moment in time Elena's entrance was the only thing that commanded any attention. She was absolutely breath-taking and could easily be mistaken for a pin-up model. She was about the same height as Gabriel, so tall for a woman but considerably shorter than her husband, had voluptuous curves in all of the right places, yet a tiny waist; her figure was like an hourglass. Her hair was a resplendent shade of red that could only have come out of a bottle and styled to perfection in a glamourous, retro, 1950's style wave and she wore her make up to match that style. Her figure-hugging, knee length dress was sapphire blue and she was surprisingly barefoot, but even her toe nails were as polished as the rest of her. Between her and Vilmos, they looked as though they were either getting ready to leave for a suave night out amongst high society, or had just come back, not like they were planning to invite a violent fugitive into their home.

Nothing about the scene made sense.

"Hello, Gabriel." Elena's voice was smooth as silk and her accent much milder than that of her husband. "Welcome to our humble abode." Her words also made very little sense. This abode was far from humble; it was clearly worth a fortune. What kind of reality did these people live in?

"Thank you," Gabriel said politely, keeping both his words and his expression to a bare minimum for the time being until he had had more of a chance to gauge what type of people he was dealing with. So far, though they were very attractive people on the surface, something about them seemed borderline psychotic – he couldn't quite put his finger on it. Or perhaps that assumption was a projection of his own state of mind? He felt lightyears away from his usually methodical, well prepared self and completely out of his comfort zone.

"You seem tense, my dear," Elena noted from Gabriel's statue-like stance, "Why don't you boys sit down and make yourselves comfortable whilst I go and fetch us all some drinks?" Both her sensual voice and the suggestion of drinks was enough to entice Gabriel out of his shell just a tiny bit and he glanced over to see what Vilmos' next move would be.

"Fabulous idea, my love." Vilmos practically congratulated her on her suggestion, then he side stepped towards a long, sleek, black leather platformed couch and sat himself down, leaving enough room for at least two more people to be comfortably seated. Gabriel looked behind him and opted for the matching two-seater that faced towards where Vilmos was seated and lowered himself into a seated position, yet remained prepared to jump up quickly if the situation called for it.

"What's your poison?" Elena purred at Gabriel.

"Ah... Scotch if you have any?" Gabriel asked politely.

"A man after my own heart," Elena replied, winking at him before she spun around elegantly and sashayed back towards the area from whence she had appeared, glancing at her husband en route to meet his approving smile.

Once she had left the room, Vilmos turned back to face Gabriel, keeping his pose open and friendly – one arm was stretched outwards across the back of the couch, the other comfortably resting on the couch arm, his left ankle rested on top of his right knee, making his legs look even more enormous.

"We've both been looking forward to your arrival, Gabriel. I must admit, it was a complete shock to hear from Sandor after all these years," Vilmos began to explain, "He and I go *way* back to our college years; we went through an enormous amount of upheaval together back in Hungary and then I managed to make a break for it and settled here in the UK, whilst he remained at home, where he's made a very powerful name for himself. We've only stayed in touch sporadically over the years and it's very rarely been for the purpose of asking each other for favours."

Gabriel nodded but was far from comprehending what was being said. It surprised him enormously to hear that they had been looking forward to his arrival. "I wasn't expecting to be so well received." He opened his palms, suggesting that he wanted Vilmos to explain further.

"Ah, yes, I can imagine you would be feeling that way, given the manhunt that's currently on your tail." Vilmos wore that smirk again and Gabriel failed to understand what he found so amusing about the whole situation.

Elena returned carrying a tray with three tumblers on top, a bottle of Glenfiddich, a bottle of Grey Goose vodka and a tiny ice bucket, which she placed carefully on the black coffee table that sat in between the two opposing couches. She delicately poured scotch into two of the glasses, handed one of those to Gabriel and poured out some vodka for her husband. Before she took her own seat she aimed her glass towards the centre of their mini-circle and said, "Here's to new friends." She flashed a megawatt smile as she did so. Gabriel and Vilmos leaned forwards to meet her glass with theirs and a loud 'clink' sounded as they all called out "Cheers" in unison, before taking a sip of their beverages – Gabriel's gulp being decidedly more eager than that of his hosts'.

"Now, where was I?" Vilmos seemed to be asking the question of Elena, despite her not being in the room when he had been addressing Gabriel, almost as though they had spent time rehearsing their lines before his arrival: "Ahh yes." He turned back to Gabriel. "You're surprised to be so well received. Well now, when Sandor called and explained who it was that he was asking a favour on the behalf of, my heart sang because we have been following your story on the news ever since it came to light and I let Sandor know that we would be more than happy to accommodate you.

"He too, was incredibly surprised by this – apparently I was the fifth number he had called because everyone else he knows in London had flat out refused. He said mine was the last number he was going to try before calling you back and letting you know he couldn't be of service after all. I mean unless you fancied a little boating jaunt over to Normandy." At the point Vilmos let out a strange, melodic chuckle and glanced over at Elena, who also giggled but in a far sultrier, more appealing way than her husband.

Gabriel shrugged, shook his head a couple of times, still feeling utterly baffled by what was so amusing to the couple that sat before him. He took another large sip of his drink and realised that he'd practically drained the glass in two gulps. Elena leaned forwards seductively and refilled his glass for him, to which he nodded his thanks.

"You're far better than that Gabriel," Vilmos began selling his proposal, "You needn't run away and hide out in some little holiday home on the coast of France when you have far more important issues to attend to here in the UK. What you should be doing is formulating a plan to get your organisation back up and running again once the dust has settled and people have forgotten the catastrophe that unfolded in Barking and Dagenham. You obviously won't be able to return there and pick up where you left off, but why would you even want to? You don't know who you can trust there anymore and your family is sitting behind bars. There is nothing in particular tying you to that location, so why not start again here?" Vilmos stretched out his long arms to portray his meaning of rejuvenating the organisation from their present location.

"And you guys want to be involved?" Gabriel asked, full of doubt.

"Why yes." Vilmos smiled broadly. "Yes, we do."

Elena chimed in at that moment, "My husband and I are *very* well connected and will prove an extremely valuable asset to you and your business." They glanced knowingly at one another and Vilmos nodded his appreciation at her.

"You see, Gabriel, my wife and I have both been very successful in our careers and made a fortune for ourselves separately and of our own accord. We've been looking for a new, joint venture to channel our ambitions and creativity into, something we can do together and maximise our full potential." Vilmos made the organisation sound like a light-hearted, whimsical art project they were thinking of taking up as a couple, just for fun.

Gabriel couldn't keep the furrowed look out of his brow as he tried to wrap his head around what was being said to him and he was extremely suspicious of the sanity of the people who had invited him into their home. Surely they'd seen how his name had been dragged through the mud by the British media? The stories about him had indeed been sensationalised for entertainment purposes, but at the core of all that drama there was truth behind what he had been doing underground for so many years completely off grid.

Yet instead of being repulsed by any of it, they actually seemed to be a little turned on and wanted a piece of the action for themselves. Were their lives really *that* dull that this was the only means they saw fit to inject some excitement into their schedule? How desperate did you have to be to even consider taking on such a deviant, immoral business venture? It had been different in Gabriel's case – it had been handed down to him through his heritage and there had been an enormous amount of expectation placed on his shoulders as he was the oldest of the three brothers and also the most depraved.

His moral compass had been skewed a long time ago by the horrors of war, followed by multiple stints in prison when he returned because he just couldn't control his PTSD symptoms and violent temper. It had been his family's organisation that had ultimately been his salvation and he had been able to channel all of his energy and skills into something productive instead of self-destructive. His reasons for taking part had been perfectly logical, the reasons being explained to him by this borderline lunatic couple seemed flaky at best.

"Let me get this straight." Gabriel leaned forwards and placed his elbows on his legs, his tumbler of scotch nestled between his palms as though he were warming his hands on a mug of tea. "After all that's happened to my family and our organisation, all that's unfolded so nastily on the media for the world to see, you wish to rebuild a new and improved version right here on your doorstep?" he asked, incredulously.

"I'm not saying immediately, that would be foolish," Vilmos replied, all matter-of-fact, "I'm merely putting it out there that you have the opportunity to utilise our skills and resources to start a fresh in a new area and with a new team at your disposal and ideally with a rebranding involved so that nothing can be traced back to the original organisation. It will ultimately mean that this new and improved version, as you say, will remain unexposed and be able to remain that way for a very long time. We are experts in flying under the radar and can extend that same privilege to you and whomever you decide to trust with your employment." He let that statement hang in the air, awaiting Gabriel's thoughts.

"This is the last thing I expected to hear upon arrival to your home." Gabriel laughed slightly uneasily and took another large gulp of his scotch.

"Of course, I understand this has been a terribly stressful, and no doubt heavily emotional, time for you too, my good man." Vilmos leaned forward and mimicked Gabriel's body language. "We don't expect you to make any decisions right here, right now. This is your first night here. You must make yourself at home and recharge your batteries. I just wanted to plant the seed and let you know that you have options once all of this mess has subsided. You may now consider us your allies and we are very keen to support you in whatever decisions you make going forwards."

With that, they all eased back into more comfortable positions in their relative seats and the conversation flowed as they got to know each other better, sharing war stories and life experiences, goals and aspirations, before eventually retiring in separate bedrooms. Gabriel discarded his backpack at the end of the bed, telling himself he would unpack his meagre possessions tomorrow, when he had a clearer head and a better idea of how long he would be staying in these parts. He laid back on the sprawling double bed in the guest room, enjoying the sheer comfort of the fancy, Egyptian cotton sheets and numerous pillows. Over the last two days he had slept in better conditions than he had done in years, possibly decades.

Despite the fact that his former role had brought him and his family an obscene amount of wealth and power, he had never taken the time to lay roots in a comfortable home. Instead he chose to live and rest in the same way he had during his military days – with bare minimal attention to properly recharging his batteries as he much preferred to be on the go, making more money to pass back to his family. How ironic that it had taken him becoming a fugitive and going on the run from the law for him to improve his standards of sleeping apparatus and conditions.

As he let his eyelids droop his mind wandered over the events that had brought him here and he could focus on one vision and one vision only – that of getting his sweet revenge on the precious little Christie.

Chapter 18

Christie herself had been trying her damn hardest to stay put inside the Travelodge at Dagenham East, not only out of consideration for her own safety, but the safety of those around her too. She felt like her actions had brought about a huge weight hanging over the heads of those she cared about and she couldn't bear the idea of endangering anyone else.

Much like she had done when she was being held in captivity on the abandoned farm, she took it upon herself to do work-out routines in order to keep herself both sane and in decent shape, except this time around she had the luxury of music to work out to, which hadn't been the case in her previous cell. She relished in the glory of Spotify and the ability to switch from one playlist to the next depending on the state of her mood at any one time.

At this moment she had opted for one entitled 'Metal Workout Music' and found herself pumped full of energy as she performed a variety of squats, sit-ups and fire hydrants. At one stage she took her energy to the staircase situated a few doors down from her room and ran up and down them three times. That was enough to expend all of her pent-up frustration and she felt slightly giddy by the time she made it back to her room to collapse on her bed.

Kate had retrieved her iPad, Mac laptop, some books and her journal to keep her occupied, as well as some clothes and toiletries to make herself at home for a little while. Christie flipped open the iPad and logged into her various social media accounts to see if she had any messages to catch up on.

Ever since she had returned from captivity she had grown accustomed to people from her past getting in touch to wish her well and say they were happy she had made it home safely. It was really nice of them to go to that effort but also seemed a little contrived and she wasn't sure whether people actually cared that much or if they were gossip hungry and keen to know more about what happened to her whilst she was gone. So many of the other stories from victims of the same case had gone viral and they were still taking part in interviews about their experiences, whereas all Christie wanted was to get back to a sense of normality and anonymity. She missed her private life being ever so private, as it had once been and more than anything, missed the ability to blend in, un-noticed.

Her Instagram account flashed up with a notification of a direct message and she clicked on it.

"How you getting on over there?" It was Dale checking up on her and her face lit up like the Cheshire cat.

"Trying my best not to lose my mind!" Christie replied and added in a crazy face emoji for good measure.

"Yeah, I spoke to Len earlier and he explained what happened," Dale explained, "You know, I'm here if ever you need to vent about anything."

"I really appreciate that, love." Christie was still beaming as she typed.

"My afternoon is wide open tomorrow in case you fancy a little company, keep that mind of yours from slowly melting and dripping out your ears." Dale painted a vivid picture and Christie half chuckled, half grimaced. "I know you and being cooped up indoors must be driving you a little loopy. I could be your chaperone and take you for a walk some place? Only if you're up for it though." Dale wanted more than anything to cheer her up but also didn't want to put any unnecessary pressure on her.

"I'd really like that." The smile stretched so broadly across Christie's face as she typed, she wondered if it might split her head in half, then laughed at the fact that she clearly *was* going a little loopy.

"Cool. I'll swing by your new gaff after lunch time tomorrow then, but I'll message you first to let you know I'm on my way," Dale said, casually.

"Awesome. I look forward to it," she replied with a smiling emoji.

"Me too. Just so ya know, I think you're handling all of this like a total badass." Dale felt compelled to lift her up without getting too soppy and sentimental.

"Ha!" Christie literally let out a loud mini-cackle and typed it exactly how it had sounded. "Thanks love, I really needed to hear that right now," she replied, gratefully.

"Just speaking those truths innit?" Dale wrote and added in a winking emoji.

They both signed off at that stage and Christie couldn't wipe the still colossal smile off her face as she closed all the open apps on her iPad and laid backwards onto the enormous hotel bed.

Who would have thought that her treasured friend, confidante and amazingly skilled tattooist would be the one to come to her rescue that day that felt like it was much longer ago than it actually was, where so much had happened in between?

She certainly wouldn't have, but she was so glad it had been him. It didn't even bear thinking about where on earth she could have ended up had her subconscious not taken her to that specific spot outside the Vogue Vintage shop, like a homing beacon. Everything had aligned perfectly to get the best possible outcome in her case and she would never stop being thankful for that fact. She had had an extremely near miss in terms of still being here, safe and able to tell her tale as opposed to ending up being shipped off to some distant land, potentially under the command of some hideous, beast-like owner who would expect her to perform the most grotesque of duties in order to satisfy him.

It was no lie that right now things were tense and frightening because she had a violent ex-military, ex-con, gangster-style lunatic out there thirsty for her blood and nobody could predict what his next move would be. But things wouldn't always be this way; she had a huge amount of protection around her and eventually they would catch him and bring him to justice too. They had to. It's not like he could be on the run forever.

For now, she simply had to remain cautious and alert, follow the rules for not going out alone and texting her whereabouts to Sue or Kate at all times and keeping her Solo Protect app open and functioning on her phone.

"Everything's gonna be all right," she said out loud to herself and took a long, calming breath, then decided it was a good time to watch something light-hearted and care-free on Netflix so she fired up her Mac.

Back at Vilmos and Elena's plush apartment in Southwark, Gabriel was, for the second day in a row, allowing himself the totally out of character luxury of a long lay-in, enjoying the sheer comfort of the guest bedroom he had been allocated for the duration of his stay there. The three of them had stayed up far later than he had anticipated – in fact dawn was breaking and the birds were already tweeting as they had made their way to their rooms and he didn't exactly have a heaving schedule of things to attend to for the foreseeable future so he figured, why the hell not?

Eventually it got to almost noon and he could smell the distant aroma of something fragrant and delicious coming from the kitchen so he decided to get up and make himself slightly more presentable before making an appearance in front of his hosts and newfound allies. He was both impressed and incredibly appreciative to find that even the guest bedroom in this unbelievably spacious and luxurious apartment had an en-suite attached to it. These people really were living a grand lifestyle and yet they wanted to further expand their enterprise by going into business with an exposed criminal gangster with a penchant for trafficking in all its forms? They must either be supremely bored with their lives or deranged in a big way; he had no idea which, but then again, who was he to judge?

He washed himself quickly and efficiently in their power shower, stocked with the highest named brands of cleansing supplies, spritzed himself in aftershave and dressed as smartly as he could manage with the few items of clothing that he had packed in his heavy duty, camping-style rucksack.

Once satisfied with his appearance he made his way down the hallway towards the enticing aroma of Moroccan food, being whipped up expertly by Elena in the kitchen, whilst Vilmos sat in the adjoining lounge area, browsing the news on his iPad.

"Ahh good morning... well should I say, good afternoon to you, my friend." Vilmos rose from his seated position and greeted Gabriel with a handshake and a pat on the back, the way old chums who hadn't seen each other for a while would.

"It is later than I anticipated getting up; I was just so damn comfortable in that bed," Gabriel admitted, sheepishly – another trait that was completely out of character on his part. What was this place doing to him? He felt totally off-balance.

"Not to worry; it's not like you have a busy timetable right now, is it?" Vilmos chuckled and lightly elbowed Gabriel in a jovial manner.

"I had that exact same thought when I woke up, you know?" Gabriel rubbed the back of his neck and pondered his lack of an agenda. "I'm not used to it at all. I'm a man who conducts himself to a tight schedule, with minions at my beck and call. This whole mess has thrown me off my game and left me feeling out of sorts. It's like I don't know who I am without the organisation to run."

Gabriel surprised even himself by being so raw and frank about his feelings in front of anybody, let alone someone he had known for less than twenty-four-hours. He surmised that he must have been needing to vent to *someone*, for fear of all of the recent upheaval driving him officially insane. Then he chuckled slightly anxiously at the thought that if he were, in fact going insane, he was certainly in good company.

"I get it. We both do," Vilmos responded, motioning towards the kitchen at his use of the word 'we', then he nudged Gabriel towards the opposing couch to the one that he had been sitting on. "Though we have clearly not been through anything anywhere near as dramatic as what you are currently going through when it comes to our careers and overall life plans, we can absolutely relate to that feeling of being lost and not knowing what comes next. We have felt that way for a very long time and have tried our hands at a variety of business ventures in a vain attempt at achieving fulfilment, yet nothing has helped us get there. When the news broke of, first of all, the exposure of *your* organisation, followed by its catastrophic crumble and stories of the activities you had been taking part in came to light, Elena and I both looked at each other and said that *this* was the sort of activity *we* would be interested in exploring."

"That type of thing entices you?" Gabriel tried his very best to sound doubtful and pessimistic, but in reality he could totally believe it because it had enticed him too from a very early age when he had secretly spied on the types of business transactions his father was undertaking. In hindsight, he was about ninety per cent sure that Marius had actually been aware of his lame, childish attempts at being a covert spy because his father had much later on groomed him for taking over multiple aspects of the organisation after his return from serving in the military.

However, at the time he had felt a little smug because it seemed like he had been privy to an entire underworld of dealings that he should have no clue about whatsoever for such a young boy.

"It does, yes. For both of us," Vilmos confirmed without batting an eyelid.

Seconds later Elena emerged from the kitchen carrying two large serving dishes loaded with delicious smelling food, one resting on each of her forearms, which were both covered in the fanciest looking black oven gloves Gabriel had ever seen. Literally everything about this couple and their home was sumptuous.

"Vilmos, my love, would you mind helping me set the table?" Elena asked. "Apologies for the interruption," she added, smiling at Gabriel. Her cheeks were rosy from the heat of the kitchen but there wasn't a hair out of place, zero sweat and no flustered appearance about her whatsoever – she seemed to take any situation in her stride.

"But of course! How silly of me to have not thought ahead." Vilmos lightly tapped his forehead as if to scold himself, but in a mock gesture. Sure, he had skipped a beat by not setting the lunch table, but judging by this man's abode, he was clearly anything but silly.

"Is there anything I can help with?" Gabriel offered.

"Why thank you, Gabriel, you could grab the drinks. I've already laid them out on a tray through there." Elena nodded towards the kitchen, where Gabriel gladly exited to and found the tray containing tall glasses for each of them and a pitcher of what appeared to be homemade lemonade, which he retrieved and carried back towards the dining area. The table was black mahogany and large enough to host dinner parties, which he had no doubt that they regularly did. They didn't seem like the type of couple to keep themselves to themselves.

They all sat down together and Elena dished each of them up with a helping of Rfissa, cooked with a variety of meats and couscous, blended with different types of vegetables. Vilmos poured each of them some lemonade and before anybody could tuck into their meal, Gabriel raised his freshly filled glass to the middle of the table by offer of a toast.

"I just want to take the opportunity to thank both of you, from the bottom of my heart, for your kindness and generosity in keeping me here as your guest. I know that it is a huge risk on both of your parts and this enormous favour will not go unrepaid," Gabriel announced, solemnly.

"You are most welcome, we are *very* happy to have you." Vilmos nodded and clinked his glass against Gabriel's.

"Indeed we are," Elena added and clinked her glass against the other two whilst smiling seductively, "Now let's eat before my masterpiece goes cold."

"So, to continue with the previous conversation." Vilmos had just chewed and swallowed his first mouthful of food and wanted to pick up where he and Gabriel had left off. "I completely understand your trepidation, or should I more accurately say, extreme doubt about my wife and I's interest in becoming a part of your next venture. After all, the stories that are all over the news at the moment are incredibly hateful and paint you and your family out to be the most vile types of barbaric creatures to ever grace this planet." He didn't mince his words.

Gabriel gulped loudly at the description, took a moment to process what he had just heard as he wasn't remotely accustomed to anybody being in a position to put him in his place and slowly nodded his comprehension at what was, in fact, an accurate portrayal of his image in the media.

"I apologise for my husband," Elena interjected, glancing scornfully at Vilmos, "He's not one for sugar coating things when he talks and not everybody is ready to hear what he has to say." Vilmos merely shrugged unapologetically in response.

"No need to apologise," Gabriel took over, "He's right." He faced Vilmos. "You're right– that is how we've been painted and quite frankly, I'm beyond pissed off about it. I mean, I can handle my own name as an individual being dragged through the dirt. Hell, I can even handle my brothers' names being tarnished – we all had a part to play, none of us are innocent bystanders. But my mother?

"That's crossing a line. She's a good woman, a faithful woman and she doesn't deserve *any* of this." Gabriel shovelled a large forkful of scrumptious food into his mouth and chewed each morsel with precision in an attempt at distracting himself from his bubbling rage.

"You mean, she knew nothing of what was taking place under her very nose?" Vilmos asked rhetorically, with one eyebrow raised comically high to demonstrate his obvious and extreme disbelief.

"Of course she knew and technically, *technically*, she was considered to be the overall head of the organisation in succession of her husband, my father, who passed away a little more than a year ago now." Gabriel bowed his head gravely for a couple of seconds before continuing, "She may have had her name at the top, but she took *no* part in *any* of the transactions that took place on a daily basis to keep the organisation running. At the absolute most and only ever in the worst case scenarios, I would call upon her to make a decision if something had gone wrong or had changed. She was more of a wise and experienced advisor to me than anything else when it came to the business side of our relationship, but I largely liked to stay on top of things myself and keep her out of it. She's very old and getting more and more frail with each passing year. She's still one of the toughest females I've ever had the privilege to know, but my father's death hit her hard and it seems like she's merely counting down the time until she can join him," he explained with a grim and mournful expression on his face.

Both Vilmos and Elena had respectfully placed their cutlery down as they listened to Gabriel open up about his mother.

"And now, she's sitting in a holding cell, waiting to be tried for crimes against humanity. And there's absolutely nothing I can do about that." Gabriel slammed his own cutlery down and his voice grew more hostile. "I had everything planned to get her out as soon as the first raid on the farm happened and the media circus began. Everything was set. Every single step had been put into place and it was supposed to go off without a hitch. My dear friend and most trusted ally, Stefan, was supposed to pick her up and transport her to a location only he and I knew of in the midlands. He would keep her there safe and completely hidden off grid until I could later join them and we would all move on.

"Stefan died in action trying to uphold his end of *my* plan. I lost my best friend for good and my mother to the authorities in one fell swoop." An unwanted tear trickled down the side of Gabriel's face and he brushed it away angrily. "It should never have happened that way – it should have been me that was captured instead and my mother that had escaped. But here I am now, the only person able to salvage any of this mess and rise again like a phoenix from the ashes. I will not let my father's legacy die in vain," he stated his intention resolutely, looked Vilmos in the eye, then met Elena's eyes to firmly make his point, then re-focused on his meal and continued to eat.

Vilmos nodded his apprehension of Gabriel's pent-up emotions and reinforced his earlier suggestion: "Now that we have come to be in your life, your wishes to continue your father's legacy will be easily accomplished, when the time is right and the dust has settled. In fact, we are here at your every whim, to utilise to the maximum of our capabilities and to bring a whole new style of organisation into fruition – one that is infallible and resilient in every way possible.

"We will help you put all of the necessary steps in place to learn from previous mistakes and make sure that they never happen again and that we remain unexposed. The fact of the matter is that humans, by their very nature, have a tendency to air towards the mercenary and we have an extreme amount of wealth to enforce our plans. We are very well connected amongst the highest-ranking members of our local community and even beyond that. We can exercise a great amount of power by using those connections wisely, with your guidance, to set up a similar, yet entirely freshly staffed organisation with unlimited resources at our disposal.

"We can unite the best of both of our worlds to create something unstoppable and more powerful than we can yet comprehend. The fact that we have brought you into our home when nobody else would demonstrates how loyal and trustworthy we are to your cause. I realise that actions speak louder than words and that we still have a lot of work to do in order to fully gain your trust, but it certainly is a great place to start and we have no qualms about proving our worth to you. The fact that you're even here, completely unexpectedly, says it all. We had no idea that a *very* old friend of mine was connected with your organisation when we first saw the story on the news and made our own independent decision that we wanted a piece of the action. It's as though the cosmos aligned perfectly to deliver you to our doorstep, like it was written in the stars for our paths to cross. Whether you're a believer in fate or not, you have to admit, it's a pretty gargantuan coincidence, no?"

"I don't believe in coincidences," Gabriel stated, "I believe everything about our existence on this planet is preordained. Our destiny has long ago been decided and we are playing out a part that was already written for us."

"It seems we are on the same wavelength, my good man" Vilmos replied and once again raised his glass for the three of them to clink together, "I believe this is going to blossom into a *very* fruitful, powerful and profitable relationship." He beamed and they all toasted each other.

"I'm certainly not going to argue with that." Gabriel's grin faded after a moment. "I just wish there was something I could do for my mother." He scraped the last few morsels of food off his plate and finished off his deliciously satisfying meal wondering what the food was like where Olga was being held and how she was being treated by those in charge of keeping her there.

It was such a hard emotion to deal with because it felt like he should mourn her; after all, even if she somehow lived longer than whatever horrendous sentence she was served after her trial, it's not like her life would ever be the same as it once was. She'd basically lost everything the moment she was exposed and captured. He wasn't sure if even Olga was tough enough to withstand all of that at her age. Gabriel felt caught in a devastating state of limbo between grieving for his mother's loss and wanting to do anything in his power to break her out.

"I'm not going to lie to you, Gabriel, I'm afraid that will present somewhat of a moral dilemma." Vilmos switched his expression to pure seriousness. "Pretty much the only assistance that can be provided for your mother at this point in time is highly priced, top-notch legal aid in order to get her the absolute best possible outcome for any and all of the crimes she will soon be put on trial for.

"If you or I were to have any hand in that then our names could be traced back from providing that to her, we would be inviting an extremely undesirable amount of suspicion onto our radar and you can guarantee we would be put under immediate surveillance. This would not bode well for both our future business ambitions and certainly not for your current state of freedom." Vilmos was further cementing the knowledge that he wasn't one for sugar coating things or telling people what they wanted to hear; he was a straight talker with everybody but felt it of the utmost importance to be painfully honest with his future business partner about how much and how badly this would affect them. "It will be absolutely essential for you from now on to cut all ties from any family members that had an involvement with your former organisation. In fact, ideally, you would cut ties with any of your remaining family altogether. I know that seems harsh, dreadfully harsh, but if you are going to survive and rebuild then it will be necessary."

His words hung in the air for what seemed like a much longer stretch of time than it actually was, none of them feeling particularly sure where to go next with the conversation and Gabriel slowly digesting the concept of severing all connections with his family. It was heart breaking and infuriating all at the same time. They had survived so much as a unit and even though he regularly came to blows with his brothers over one thing or another, they had always stuck together and had each other's back.

Loyalty to his family had been the major constant all throughout his life as it had been drilled into him by Marius from day one, as soon as he was old enough to understand. He did not appreciate being forced to suddenly walk away from a life-long habit.

There was only one person he blamed for all of this. It wasn't him, his family, the lifestyle they had chosen to lead or the terrible crimes they had committed. No. It was Christie and her obnoxious, haphazard and clumsy escape that were the cause behind all of this wreckage and destruction. Who the hell did she think she was? Why couldn't she have just known her place and done as she was told? And even if it was her fate to break free, why couldn't she have just slunk away and crawled under a rock somewhere? Why did she have to lead the authorities back to where she had been held captive and tear the entire operation apart from the inside out?

Gabriel loathed her and he could feel the rage burning in his chest the more he pictured her sickly sweet face, like butter wouldn't melt in her mouth. He wanted to do abhorrent things to her before taking the life right out of her body and he had played out a variety of different means of doing so in his mind ever since he very first found out of her escape.

He had only encountered her in the flesh on one occasion when he had paid a visit to the abandoned farm where all of the women that had been abducted by the organisation ever since he had taken over much of its day to day business had been held for various amounts of time. The abduction and trafficking of women had grown exponentially over the last three years after he had converted the farmland with the introduction of the discarded shipping containers. That had taken him a great deal of time to organise and set up exactly how he had wanted it and he felt a connection to it as his own creation, like it was his baby, but he had handed the reins over to his brother Augustin, who had hired a number of his very closest allies as well as their youngest brother, Luca. The youngest of the three had always been a little questionable in terms of resilience and strength, but there was zero doubt about his loyalty and respect for his brothers.

After that Gabriel had taken a step back to focus on other things like arms dealing (which was his speciality) the buying, cutting and selling of drugs, plus trafficking of Eastern Europeans into the country for slave trading. It was only on the rare occasion that he felt the need to drop in and pay his brothers a visit and the last time he did, Christie had been brought into her new cell very late the previous night. There had been so much interest in her and whispers amongst the other men about how much they would gain from her sale that he hadn't been able to resist taking a peek at her. He had slowly eased the door to her cell open when no one else was looking and allowed only the top portion of his head through the gap at first. She was comatose on the bed and he had stealthily eased his entire body into her room and stood over her bedside for a couple of minutes, examining her beauty as she unconsciously breathed heavily, her chest rising up and down slowly and invitingly.

He had felt overwhelming and unwanted urges to do unspeakable things to her from that very moment and had had to grit his teeth together and force himself to leave immediately before the temptation became too much to bear. Now he still felt those urges but they were forever tainted by his uncontrollable need to end her life. He wanted to tear her body apart from the inside out in the most beastly way imaginable, having his way with her whilst also inflicting enormous amounts of pain and essentially splitting her open. Then he wanted to tell her exactly why she had deserved it, tell her he was going to do vile things to everyone she cared about, before ending her life as barbarically as possible.

"There is just one thing that I simply will not be able to give up." Gabriel squeezed the words out of his tense jaw, trying to keep his tone steady and the venom out of his voice. He knew he had to appear somewhat rational and in control of his faculties if he was going to make a case for his argument.

"What's that?" This time it was Elena who had spoken, clearly concerned for all three of their fates but mostly for that of her and her husband.

"My goal to end Christie's life." It was out there now; there was no taking it back. His intentions were set and they were either in or they were out – no matter what, he was going to put his money where his mouth was.

Neither Vilmos nor Elena needed any explanation or elaboration on who Christie was and why their fugitive houseguest held so much contempt for her. They had had their own little private jokes about her as they had watched the story unfold all over the British media.

Whilst they had agreed upon and been captivated by her beauty, they had also felt utterly baffled and almost enraged at the fact that someone so puny and feeble had brought a colossal and breathtakingly powerful organisation to its knees. It had been like watching the most unlikely character on a soap opera cause the most unfathomable amount of damage completely unexpectedly and they had exchanged heated debates over how on earth she had been able to pull it off and what they would have done differently if they were the ones in charge. They could fully understand Gabriel's need to repay her for the irrevocable problems she had ignited the day that she had fled and left a trail of breadcrumbs back to where she had been held prisoner. There was no doubt in either of their minds that they would both feel and behave in the same way if they were in his shoes.

"That can be arranged." Vilmos let that sink in as Gabriel brought his gaze to meet his directly for at least a minute. "We will put together a step by step plan to make sure it happens at exactly the right time and with zero risk of it coming back to bite us later."

"I want it to be sooner rather than later," Gabriel

announced.

"Then it shall be done just like that," Vilmos agreed and Elena nodded her concurrence.

Gabriel could not believe how little argument he had needed to make in order to get the two of them on board. They truly were his newfound allies in all of this and he felt a vast amount of gratitude for how he had come to be in their home so surprisingly and all at once. There was no other explanation for it than that it was meant to be and the three of them were destined to achieve things bigger than he ever could have imagined in his wildest dreams.

"With your permission, I'll go ahead and put in a call to my comrade in the police force?" Vilmos suggested. "That way we can exert extreme caution when putting your plans into place – we can make sure everything is timed to perfection with the absolute least chance of being caught."

"You have a connection in the police force? Won't contacting them at a time like this be a little risky and potentially arouse suspicion?" Gabriel asked dubiously.

"Oh, yes, we have several connections in pretty much any authoritative body and all aspects of the government." Vilmos shrugged as though it was no big deal when in actual fact he felt gleeful at being able to report this back to his newfound friend and colleague. It made him feel like he was a kid again and he was bringing something to class that would immediately turn him into 'Teacher's Pet'. "This contact in particular won't be surprised to hear from me trying to gain more intel on the whereabouts and routine of little miss Christie – he's had his ear to the ground on this case at my request ever since it first came to light. He's fed me all of the inside information I have in my repertoire from day one and is more than happy to do so because I line his pockets so generously. As I said before, it is very fortunate on our part that the human condition is to sway so committedly towards the mercenary lifestyle. As long as I pay out, I get what I want—" he stated, resolutely.

"In that case, yes, please do." Gabriel beamed back at him and Vilmos took that as his cue to go and make the necessary call with absolutely zero hesitation.

Elena had been taking in the entire exchange wordlessly and with fascination at how seamlessly the relationship was developing between Gabriel and her husband. Vilmos was the kind of man who many people were drawn to as they found him captivating and appealing in all manners thanks to his looks, his eloquence and sizeable presence in any room. Yet Vilmos had very little interest in trying to impress other people – he did it so naturally that it seemed to almost bore him and he certainly wasn't willing to bend over backwards for people unless it somehow benefited him in the grand scheme of things.

Yet with Gabriel he looked like an excited puppy, eager to seek validation and love from his master. Elena was rather enjoying seeing this new side to the man she had loved so dearly for so many years. It was like embarking on an entirely new adventure with him that was full of passion and excitement – even their love making in the early hours of that morning, after they had bid goodnight to Gabriel and retired to their marital bed, had been something out of this world. It had been as though a tiny ember that had once been a blazing fire had long ago started to withdraw and die out and though they had both been draining themselves trying to spark it back to light, they had been fighting a losing battle.

Now suddenly that tiny, dying ember had received a raging

boost of ignition and burst into insatiable and multiplying flames. She was surprised by the fact that she could even stand up straight afterwards; he had ravaged her so greedily and she had relished in every single moment of it until they had succumbed to exhaustion and truly restorative sleep. She felt like a lovesick teenager all over again and it was thrilling.

"Allow me to show my gratitude for such a fine and satisfying meal by clearing the table." Gabriel's unexpected voice interrupted Elena's mesmerised daydream about the passionate love making between herself and Vilmos mere hours ago and she blushed slightly.

"That would be lovely." She accepted his offer. "Let's make it a joint effort," she said as she began picking up plates and glasses, then led the way through to the kitchen. He followed her lead as she rinsed each item first, handed them over to him and he placed them in the dishwasher, then they both set about clearing the counters together as she had utilised almost every inch of each surface whilst whipping up her culinary masterpiece for the three of them to enjoy.

"You know, I'm really happy you're here and that things seem to be gelling so nicely between the three of us," Elena confided in Gabriel, "It still feels a little surreal, because we were so avidly enthralled by the case and its developments from the very beginning. To have you standing here in my kitchen, helping me tidy up is a bit like having a celebrity in your house, but actually better because I've met a *lot* of celebrities in my time and they never live up to my expectations. I'm always left disappointed." She placed a delicate, feminine hand on his left forearm. "But with you, you're surpassing all of our expectations and I can see this being a lifelong friendship."

Again, she blushed a little before removing her hand.

"That means a lot to me." Gabriel smiled warmly back at her. "I find it incredibly hard to trust people and my time in the military taught me it was better in the long run to not get too attached to people either as, ultimately, bad things happen to good men and I'd rather save myself the anguish. Plus my father taught me from a very early age that when you are in a position of power, you must learn to be suspicious of all those around you until the day they have physically proven to you that they can be trusted and that they're worth more than just the words that come out of their mouth." Gabriel chuckled a little at the fact that he was being so raw and opening up to Elena.

"Since the moment the two of you welcomed me into your home, despite all of the horribly degrading stories about me and my family all over the news right now, I've felt more at ease with you than I have with others I've known my whole life. I feel like I can be honest with you both and you won't judge me for it and that is a very, *very* rare thing for me indeed."

"I'm certainly glad we all seem to be benefiting from this new bond and that it's not just one sided or all about business; it seems to go much deeper than that from all of our perspectives," Elena evaluated. "As my husband described to you yesterday, we have been searching for something that will bring us greater fulfilment than any of the multitude of avenues we've explored. We've literally tried our hands at *everything*." Elena rolled her eyes for dramatic effect and shook her head. "We both decided at a very early stage in our relationship that we do not want children so that was never even a consideration. We were searching for what would make us feel completely accomplished elsewhere and nothing was working."

"You don't ever want kids?" Gabriel asked, a little surprised by that as they both seemed to be so in love and in tune with each other, surely that would be the natural order of things.

"No. Never. I find children to be unlikeable, annoying and pest-like. Vilmos has never seen what the fascination with them is either. Do you?" Elena challenged.

Gabriel took a moment to quietly ponder this but he made that obvious to Elena by gently rubbing his chin as he thought. Finally, he concluded, "Having kids with someone is a *huge* commitment and I don't think you should bring a child into this world unless you feel you're ready to make such a commitment. I think that's selfish and irresponsible." His eyes then drifted upwards as though he was trying to recall a memory "I can't remember feeling anything close to that level of commitment to another. My life has always revolved around whatever mission I was faced with at the time and the overall running of the organisation after we lost my father became my baby, I guess."

Gabriel had never put those words to the evolution of his role in the organisation because he had never put too much thought into it. Everything had just naturally gravitated that way because he had been the right man for the job and he had seized the opportunity when it was offered to him by the one man he respected and admired the most on this planet. Nobody else would have been able to handle it and frankly, he didn't want anyone to.

"You've never been in love?" Elena purred at him.

Again, Gabriel needed a moment to ponder this – no one had ever questioned him on matters of the heart and whether or not he felt any desire to procreate so he felt a little caught off guard but in an interesting way. He didn't want to shy away from it; he wanted to explore these subjects and analyse why things in his life had transpired the way they had and he genuinely felt like he could open up to this woman.

"I've felt loving feelings towards women in the past- I've cared for them deeply and wanted what's best for them. But ultimately, what has been best for them is to get the hell away from me!" He let out a booming laugh at his own summary of himself and the type of influence he was on other people. "I'm not exactly husband or father material. I don't fit that mould – I'm far too drawn to things that I shouldn't be doing and I like to push the boundaries and see how much I can get away with for my own gain. I do take care of my loved ones, my family and my most trusted friends, but even doing that is of great risk to all of them." He bowed his head as he recalled watching the news stories of his brothers being arrested, then later his trusted ally, Stefan, being shot by police so that they could unceremoniously cart his mother off to jail too. "The events of the past few weeks are evidence of that fact."

They both bowed their heads respectfully for just a few seconds before Vilmos reappeared and clapped his hands together to snap them out of their humbled trance. "Well that was a delightfully productive phone call indeed." He smiled broadly, seemingly oblivious to the current temperature in the room due to the seriousness of Elena and Gabriel's previous conversation. "There is going to be an enormous amount of planning to do in order to make sure this goes off smoothly, *but* I have some outstanding intel that I can't wait to share with you." Vilmos could barely contain his excitement. "Elena, my dear, sweet Elena, won't you fetch us some beers and bring them through to the lounge so that we can all plot together?" he commanded in a pantomime like fashion.

Elena was beyond grateful for the lively interruption and immediately proceeded to retrieve three bottles of Hofbrau Original, expertly poured them into tall glasses, leaving just the right amount of foam sitting on top, placed them onto a tray and followed the two men to where they had situated themselves in the plush lounge. Vilmos was obviously eager to get started and Gabriel now had a look of extreme intrigue painted on his face as they courteously waited for her arrival.

"So, my comrade – Mickey in case you're interested." Vilmos gave Gabriel a conspiratorial wink. "He tells me that little miss Christie has been temporarily placed in Dagenham East Travelodge after your appearance at her house spooked one of her house mates and he filed a complaint."

"He didn't seem spooked to me; he was pretty ballsy and straight up asked me who I was," Gabriel huffed.

"Well, regardless, a complaint was made but Mickey said they had already started to think about a protective detail for Christie *before* that even came through due to the lack of any arrests being made off the back of the raid on your secret bunker. It seems they had already predicted your temper getting the better of you once you found out about your poor mother's arrest and your friend being shot in the line of his duty trying to protect her. And the obvious conclusion is that you would go after Christie."

"Then clearly they all know how much she deserves my rage!" Gabriel's sudden outburst surprised even himself and he paused for a moment to take a large, deep breath and a long sip of his crisp, refreshing beer.

"No one here is judging you, Gabriel," Vilmos assured him, "I'm simply quoting Mickey's report." He took a sip of his own beer and continued, "Now, he said that ever since she arrived there two days ago after being dropped off by her friends, she hasn't set a foot outside the building. She must have had it drilled into her that her safety is at threat and rightly so, she is probably terrified. She has been visited by one police officer to both greet her upon her arrival and also to drop off some of her belongings after collecting them from her house. She has also been visited late on the first night by her mother, who dropped off some shopping to her, mostly food supplies apparently – now isn't that sweet?" Vilmos said with a mocking tone and a playful eyeroll.

"So sweet I could vomit," Elena said sarcastically and let out an evil sounding chuckle before taking a swig of her beer.

"There are no names or further details about the two friends that dropped her off, however I was able to get an address for Christie's parents if it happens to prove useful at any stage," Vilmos continued, "Mickey says that they are not intending to keep her there for a huge amount of time and that they are now in the process of figuring out something more secure and lasting for her, at least until they have you in custody." Vilmos looked directly into Gabriel's eyes at that point. "The manhunt for you is relentlessly persistent despite them drawing a blank on the last raid – as we speak they are examining evidence with a fine toothed comb in the hopes of finding someone with some clue as to where you could be."

Gabriel interrupted, "I don't suppose he mentioned how they found my bunker did he?"

"I asked actually – turns out it was an autistic kid that had been trafficked here earlier this year. He overheard one of the guards at the basement he was been held in give the coordinates to another guard after the news broke of the raid on the farm.

This little kid memorised the coordinates and told them to his beloved Ol' Pa, who in turn handed them over to the police once they'd finally got a translator involved and managed to process all of the witnesses they found in that basement." Vilmos was undoubtedly enjoying being able to feed this juicy piece of gossip back to Gabriel. "You can thank your lucky stars for the language barrier getting in the way on this occasion, or they would have snapped you up already."

"That must have been Stefan giving the coordinates to his right-hand man just in case anything fell through or didn't go to plan," Gabriel said and then grimaced at the memory of his friend's mug shot flashing up in the news story about his shooting. "An autistic kid, you say?" he asked, incredulously.

"Who would have thought it, right?" Vilmos closed his eyes and shook his head to display the inconvenience. "Anyway, as it stands it appears that we need to act quickly, which I know you will appreciate, because she isn't likely to stay put in the hotel all day every day forevermore so we must seize the opportunity whilst she is still gripped by fear. Our best and least risky time of attack will be during the day as security is tighter and more vigilant at the hotel during the night, especially since their new arrival took up her temporary residence there – they would easily be able to pick up on any intruder to the premises. If it were to take place during the day time, you could break in with military stealth, perform your deeds and get back out again relatively swiftly and hopefully unseen."

"I like the sound of that." Gabriel had a sinister smirk on his face as he rolled his now empty glass back and forth between his hands. Elena took note of how quickly he had drained his beer and took the glass out of his hands before scampering off to fetch him another one. She returned to hear the rest of Vilmos' proposed plan of action.

"My friend at the council will be able to get blueprints of the layout of the Travelodge and send them directly to me so that we can plan your entry point ahead of time. What I recommend is that my beautiful wife accompany you on this little jaunt because let's face it, you driving around the area alone is going to do nothing but arouse suspicion." Vilmos looked over to Elena to seek her approval at his suggestion and she nodded her apprehension and acceptance of her duty. "If it looks like the two of you are a couple then no one is going to think too much of you being in the hotel's vicinity – it will just look like romance or even a scandalous affair." Vilmos performed an over-the-top gasp for dramatic effect and giggled at his own frivolity.

"Only if you're sure you don't mind?" Gabriel posed the question to Elena.

"I don't mind at all. I have several wigs in my wardrobe; it will be nice to take one out for the day." Now it was Elena's turn to giggle at her own whimsical attitude towards an activity that could potentially land her in serious and irreparable trouble. "We will take the Volvo, as it's the least conspicuous of our cars."

Gabriel laughed. "How many cars do you have?" he asked, swigging his beer merrily.

Vilmos mimicked Gabriel's light-hearted beer swigging. "Five." He shrugged like it was normal behaviour to have five cars between two people. "We'd have more if we could but storing them is an issue around here."

"I can quickly and easily switch the plates over from the ones I drove in with onto your car to lessen the chance of anything being traced back to you guys," Gabriel offered by way of reassurance.

"Brilliant. And you can borrow some clothing items from me – anything you like and that will fit you, just to heighten the disguise." Vilmos was half addressing Gabriel and half tapping away on his phone to request the blueprints of the Travelodge from his contact at the council. He was surprisingly good at multitasking and didn't seem to miss a beat when transferring his attention between the two activities.

The three of them spent the rest of the afternoon and early evening planning the trip for the next day down to a tee, leaving Vilmos and Elena feeling motivated and fulfilled for the first time in years; it was like they had found what was missing from their lives and they grasped hold of the opportunity with zeal.

The plans left Gabriel feeling excited that he was going to get the revenge he so desperately wanted on the little bitch that had taken everything away from him. In a perfect world he would love to have more time with her to perform utterly wicked deeds and let her know how much she deserved every single one of them before ending her pathetic life for good.

But this isn't a perfect world. He knew that all too well and he would seize any opportunity he could to both pay her back for the extreme havoc she had caused him and to also send a message out to the rest of the world that he was a force to be reckoned with. He had always valued his infamy and reputation for being capable of performing the most heinous acts against his fellow man that anyone could possibly imagine without even batting an eyelid.

He wondered what the people he used to command or do business with thought of him now after being in hiding for a few weeks. Did they judge him and think him a coward? He couldn't bear that thought; it was incredibly damaging to his ego and he would relish in the chance to prove to any outsiders that he was still capable of the worst types of evil, even when he had an entire governing body out hunting for his capture. It would be like sticking a finger up to society and letting them know he was above *any* rules and regulations they tried to impose on him. He could barely keep the smug grin off his face as he imagined the furore that would no doubt be the result of his imminent repugnant actions against the nation's current sweetheart.

After switching from beers to much heavier doses of alcohol and laughing wickedly as a collaborative threesome for a couple more hours, taking enormous amounts of joy in working together to come up with something so dastardly and despicable, they decided in unison that an early night was the most appropriate idea ahead of their systematic plans for the next day. They would all sleep soundly with the knowledge that tomorrow's actions were exactly what they wanted and needed to happen for each of their own fulfilment.

The next day they rose at a fairly early hour to put the finishing touches on their preparations for the day's tasks, each of them as animated as a child would be when waking up on Christmas day. They ate a hearty breakfast together, chatting enthusiastically about what lie ahead and complimenting one another for their brilliance in each of the roles they were playing.

Vilmos had decided he should remain at the apartment and be keeping tabs on both Elena and Gabriel as well as Christie's movements via his police contact, Mickey. He had asked Mickey to provide him constant updates whenever they came in regarding the ongoing case and the manhunt for Gabriel, which Mickey was all too happy to provide as he had mouths to feed at home and Vilmos was lining his pockets generously for such vital intel.

Elena had gone through an entirely transformative process that looked as though it must have taken her hours to perfect. She was now sporting a bronzed tan as though she had just stepped off a returning flight from an extended trip to a faraway, exotic location; her wig was made of golden ringlets and hung beneath her breasts, which she had strategically concealed underneath a high rising, slightly baggy t-shirt, so as not to draw attention to her stunning figure and she coupled that with jogging bottoms and trainers – a look that she would never normally wear outside of her local gym. The idea was that she would hopefully blend in amongst the locals of Dagenham if at any stage she was forced to exit the vehicle, but she was hoping she wouldn't have to do that.

Gabriel had selected only the top half of an outfit from Vilmos' wardrobe due to the considerable height difference between the pair but thankfully part of that get up was a baseball cap and sunglasses to help conceal his features that had been plastered all over the British media for weeks now and also help him blend in amongst the locals.

He went about effortlessly switching the number plates over from Mary's former Audi TT onto Elena's considerably unexceptional white Volvo V40 – yet another one of the many skills his father had taught him as soon as he was old enough to do so. Then he shoved one of Vilmos' sports bags filled with breaking and entering supplies, concealed underneath gym clothes and a towel, onto the back seat and they were ready to set off.

He allowed his new allied couple the privacy of an intimate farewell by waiting in the passenger seat of the car for Elena to come and join him when she was ready. The two of them seemed to have rekindled a large amount of the scintillating passion that had originally drawn them to each other many years ago and whilst he found that quite admirable for a couple who had been together so long, he had very little desire to bear witness to its side effects.

Soon enough they were on the open road, heading towards Dagenham East with what should have been only one thing on their minds, but in reality it was a whole cascading and continuously overflowing multitude of different things swirling through both of their heads at any one time. The result was complete radio silence between the two of them for at least the first thirty minutes of the journey as they each processed and compartmentalised their separate barrage of thoughts. Eventually it was Gabriel who broke the silence.

"I must admit, I'm a little surprised you're both on board with my plans to execute my revenge on Christie and also willing to play your own role in something that many people would be utterly repulsed by." He looked over at her in the driver's seat, trying to gauge her reaction as he spoke.

"Why so surprised?" Elena asked. "Is it because of my gender?"

"Well, yeah." Gabriel admitted, "I thought women were all about sticking together these days? Ya know, after the whole 'Me Too' movement a little while back? I thought that had brought around a fresh wave of feminism and that women were supposed to do everything in their power to stand up against the men who pushed them around or took advantage of them. This is taking chauvinism to an absolutely extreme level and yet you're willing to assist me in my expedition."

"I find those that follow trends in such a fashion for the sake of social cohesion and assimilation to be quite pathetic and borderline pitiful," Elena stated matter-of-factly.

"Only *borderline* pitiful? You have no sense of pity for people like that?" Gabriel was fascinated by Elena's response.

"I reserve my pity only for those that truly deserve it." Elena explained, "You yourself make an excellent case for that point." She looked over at him briefly to check his reaction, then adjusted her eyes back to the road ahead. "When the news first broke of the raid on your former place of business and then we watched as reports kept coming in about how much you had lost – your brothers, your trusted friend, your mother, the organisation itself... from a distance I felt a great deal of pity for you, my dear Gabriel." Once again she checked his reaction but he didn't appear to be angry, he looked more shocked and intrigued than anything else so she continued, "Then as I've gotten to know you over the past couple of days, I've come to realise that it's not my pity you need whatsoever, it's my support. Because with the right support from myself, my husband and any other allies we can trust with this along the way, you will be more than capable of bouncing back from this, stronger than ever." She reached over and gave his arm a quick, gentle squeeze. "I wholeheartedly believe that and am on board with helping you achieve your goals in any way that you will allow me to."

"I certainly feel that fate brought me to your doorstep and I couldn't be more grateful for that fact," Gabriel replied with an appreciative smile.

"I feel exactly the same way." Elena beamed back at him.

"I look forward to seeing what amazing things we can accomplish together."

In her temporary home at Dagenham East Travelodge, Christie had just completed her newly devised indoor workout regime, where she'd changed up a few of the moves after checking out @homesquatvideos on her Instagram page and decided that it was a good lead to follow. She felt herself aching in all of the right places and enormously accomplished as a result.

"How's it going?" Dale's name popped up in her direct messages and the wide grin spread across her face instantaneously.

"Not too, shabby thank you," she typed back eagerly, "How's it going with you?"

"All good over here, thanks," Dale replied and placed a thumbs up emoji. "Still up for hanging out today?" he asked.

"Sure am." Christie was very purposefully trying to play it cool but on the inside she was beyond ecstatic at the prospect.

"Cool. I'll leave shortly then and message you when I'm close by," Dale confirmed.

"Perfect. See ya real soon." Christie clicked off of her Instagram page and opened the Solo Protect app on her phone just to do a quick device check and make sure everything was in order, then she sent a text to Kate to let her know that Dale would soon be on his way over to meet her and would essentially be acting as her chaperone for the afternoon to prevent her from going stir crazy.

Kate replied mere minutes later to thank Christie for letting her know and inform her that she would make arrangements for a squad car to be in their vicinity once she had more details on where they would be heading to. Christie took a deep, calming breath and felt blissful in the knowledge that so many people cared about her wellbeing. She felt safe and protected from all angles, completely oblivious to the pending danger that was flying down the motorway in her direction.

She took a cleansing and refreshing shower to wash away the workout sweat, then put her 'Vibey' Spotify playlist on whilst she went about making herself presentable for the day's activities. She spent extra time perfecting her eyeliner and picked out one of her favourite dresses, a mauve coloured mini number with black rose patterns embroidered onto it, paired that with black tights and the only other pair of Dr Marten's from her collection that Kate had grabbed for her when she went to her house, a black pair with skulls and roses printed in patterns on each outer side.

She felt an overwhelming urge to look 'just right' for her outing with her treasured companion who had played such a fundamental and heroic part in her story and she made a promise to herself to let him know just how much she appreciated everything he had done for her when he arrived. If it hadn't been for the fact that he was the one who found her in Romford the day that she fled chaotically from captivity in the confused, hallucinogenic state she was in, she didn't want to even think about what might have happened to her. There were some colourful characters in Romford, she knew this all too well, and any one of them could have taken advantage of her cluelessness as to who and where she was.

She thanked her lucky stars that it had been Dale and that he had not only taken the time out of his day to make sure she got the help she so desperately needed, but he also cancelled important plans to stay by her side (which he didn't brag about).

She had only found that out later when it was discussed on their joint breakfast show interview.

Plus, he made sure her closest friends and family were informed immediately of her discovery outside the Vogue Vintage shop and subsequent hospital stay, then stayed with her for hours on end when she was barely coherent enough to form a sentence. When she listed all of these things off in her head it made her feel a little emotional, but mostly full of the utmost gratitude for having him in her life.

Elena and Gabriel were nearing the exit on the A1306 that would ultimately lead them onto Rainham Road South and headed straight towards Dagenham East Travelodge.

Gabriel could feel his pulse quickening and his heart starting to thud in his chest, the same way it always had every time he was deployed on a fresh military mission and was about to enter hostile territory. The same sweat returned to his palms, his mouth felt as parched as a desert and his chest began to feel tight and constricting. He pulled at his seat belt to ease the tension but it made next to no difference so instead he leaned over into the back seat and retrieved the hip flask he had stashed inside the sports bag he had packed in there earlier.

"I hope this doesn't bother you," he said politely to Elena but made no effort to pause and wait for her response before taking a generous gulp of the scotch inside.

"Not at all actually," Elena responded with genuine empathy in her tone. "Does it, by any chance, have something to do with post-traumatic stress?" she asked gently, not wanting to come across as nosey or intrusive.

Gabriel was thrown for a moment that she would be so intuitive.

He swallowed hard, wiped his mouth and asked, "Do you have experience of this?"

"My brother was ex-military. He was never quite the same when he returned from the forces," Elena explained, her voice starting to sound a little thick but she managed to keep her emotions at bay for the sake of focussing on the number one task they had to do for the day. "He would drink heavily to combat the symptoms but ultimately the booze just exasperated them."

"Was?" Gabriel questioned Elena's use of the past tense when describing her brother.

"He took his own life about five years after returning from his final mission," Elena replied with the kind of monotone that made it sound like she had had to repeat that same sentence many times over the years. "That was twelve years ago now and there isn't a day that goes past where he doesn't cross my mind."

"I'm so sorry." Gabriel felt a surge of guilt that he wasn't even a tiny bit accustomed to feeling as he glanced down at the treasured, engraved hip flask in his hands.

"Don't be." Elena looked at him directly in the eyes for a second just to make the point that she was serious, then refocused on the road. "I get it. PTSD is a fucking terrible thing to go through and you need to do what's right for you in order to stay on top of it. *Especially* considering how essential it is to have your head in the game at his particular moment in time."

"You know, I never speak to anyone of this," Gabriel confided, "Stefan – my friend who was recently shot whilst trying to protect my mother – was the *only* person who had any idea about it and that was because he was right there with me, side by side, when it all started. He knew and he understood but we never got all touchy feely about it, ya know? We were best friends and brothers in arms but we never discussed what we were going through mentally or psychologically at any one time. We just threw ourselves into our work and taking care of our loved ones in the best and only way we knew how."

"You must miss him," Elena stated, sympathetically.

"If I'm honest, it hasn't quite sunk in yet that he's gone. We had the kind of relationship where we didn't need to see or speak to one another daily and depending on what was going on with work, we could occasionally go weeks without so much as a text message," Gabriel explained, "But it didn't matter, nothing ever changed between us, we would simply pick up where we left off the next time we did talk." He took another generous swig from the hip flask and then replaced the cap tightly, before returning it to its pocket in the sports bag. He had a nice, warm feeling in his belly now and the anxiety beating against his chest had subsided. "I suppose there's a part of me that keeps expecting to hear from him with some banter-ridden explanation as to why he's been M.I.A for the past few weeks and one of these days it will hit me that he's gone for good."

Elena mulled that over for a few seconds, considering her response before saying, "There's no denying that when it does hit you, it will be an extremely painful process that you will then have to face. But I want you to know that I am here for you. You *can* discuss your feelings with me in a way that you couldn't with your friend and I don't want you to keep anything bottled up because all that will do is eat away at you and slowly drive you insane. That being said, I also don't expect you to feel comfortable opening up so don't for one second think that there's any pressure on my behalf. Just talk about it when it feels right for you and we can work through it together." She turned to offer him a comforting smile.

"Thank you, Elena," Gabriel replied, "That means more to me than you can possibly know, so thank you."

They pulled into the carpark of the Travelodge and parked close to the edge so that Gabriel would be able to exit the car and stealthily creep around the carpark's edges, which were helpfully lined with tightly packed trees and neat hedges for him to conceal himself amongst.

Elena had skilfully turned the Volvo and parked it in a position to make for a swift getaway once Gabriel had performed his appalling, vengeful deed and returned to her side. She pulled out her Samsung Galaxy from where she had stored it in the side compartment in her car door and quickly typed a WhatsApp message to Vilmos to let him know they had arrived and asking him if there had been any updates from Mickey.

Then she pulled up the blueprint of the Travelodge that he had sent to her earlier so that she could figure out exactly where they were sitting in relation to where Christie's room was. They had gone through all of the details the night before as to how Gabriel should creep around the edge of the building and break in through Christie's window, as they had placed her very close to the fire exit in their efforts to try to keep her safe but that had in fact worked in favour of her approaching attacker. She held the phone out to Gabriel so that she could indicate on the screen where he should be heading for. As he left the car, he took one quick glance at it, looked back to the scene in front of him and to the side and nodded.

"Just over there, right?" He pointed in exactly the right direction that had taken Elena several moments to figure out by looking at the blueprint in her palm. "Don't worry. I've got this," he said resolutely.

Vilmos responded to Elena's WhatsApp with an update from Mickey about Christie's pending movement from the hotel on a little trip out with the same friend who had found her the day that she escaped. He warned that the friend was already on his way so Gabriel would need to conduct his task quickly and get out of there as smoothly and swiftly as possible.

"That's my cue." Gabriel already had the sports bag slung over his shoulder and he grabbed the door handle to swing his legs out and get moving. "I'll be back before you know it." He reassured Elena with a confident wink and had disappeared into the hedges before she had a chance to properly catch her breath.

She shakily sent a reply to Vilmos, "He's on the move."

"Perfect. The second I hear anything else from Mickey, I will let you know," Vilmos replied within seconds.

Dale was approaching the Travelodge from the opposite direction to how Elena and Gabriel had done and, in his case, in an Uber. He had toyed with the idea of getting public transport and then quickly abandoned that idea in favour of his most used form of travelling from A to B. He took his iPhone out from his jeans pocket to send an Instagram message to Christie and let her know that he would be with her momentarily and asking her which room he should go to.

Christie was happily prancing around her room to her playlist when his message came through and as soon as his name flashed up on her screen she pounced on her phone to message him back with instructions of how to get to her room from the reception desk. She switched over to her metal playlist as she knew he would have a greater appreciation for the tracks she had handpicked for that one and turned the volume down slightly so that she could hear him knocking upon arrival. She felt a little giddy and had unmistakable butterflies in her stomach knowing that he would be there any minute now.

Dale got out of his Uber at the traffic lights next to the turn off to the Travelodge, simply to save his driver the effort of having to turn back around before heading to his next job – instead he could simply carry on going straight down the main road. He thanked the driver and waved cheerfully at him as he drove away, then started walking casually towards the hotel entrance.

Across the carpark he spotted a white Volvo with a blonde woman sitting in the driver's seat and he couldn't shake the feeling that something about the picture looked very wrong. He had a noticeable churning feeling in his gut and when he'd had that same feeling in the past it had never let him down as a clear warning sign that trouble was imminent and he quickened his pace towards the front door.

Meanwhile Gabriel had crept rapidly and practically silently through the hedgerow that lay next to the building. He could hear music coming through an open window and the nearer he got to the sound the more obvious it became that it was coming directly from the very room he was aiming for. He whispered thank you out loud and glanced up at the sky, feeling as though his father was watching over him like a twisted, demonic guardian angel, clearing the pathway for his son to commit the most vile, disgraceful deeds imaginable. He crept past a fire exit to his left, with a tiny pathway that led round to the front of the building and beyond that to the exact spot he needed to be in to carry out his mission.

Just below the window there was a small patch of clear ground for him to rest his sports bag; the rest of the area was completely surrounded by greenery, allowing Gabriel's shadowy figure to remain completely concealed as he prepared to manoeuvre himself unknowingly through Christie's window and into her room.

As with all modern hotel rooms, the window had been fitted with a restrictor that only allowed it to open a certain amount but this was not an issue for Gabriel. He had brought various different types of equipment with him but he only needed one tool to easily allow him entry because he had performed this task many a time in the past so he knew exactly what to do and how to do it quickly. The biggest dilemma for him at this moment in time was making sure he wasn't seen doing it from the inside; he had to be sure Christie was either not facing the window when he disarmed the restrictor or ideally, in the bathroom.

He slowly moved his face to the left-hand side of the window frame and peeked through the glass with his right eye, moving cautiously and making no sound whatsoever. He couldn't believe his good fortune when he searched the entire space for any sign of movement and discovered none – the bathroom door was in fact closed and that was the only place she could possibly be considering the music was still blaring from her phone, which was sitting on top of a small chest of drawers next to the bed.

Even better than that, he could see that the bathroom door didn't directly face the window; it opened out so that the back of the door would face the window when she came out, allowing him an even greater element of surprise if he acted swiftly enough.

He pulled his Swiss army knife out of the side pocket of the sports back and expertly unscrewed the friction hinges so that the restrictor came away from the window frame completely. Within just one minute he had eased the window open far enough to allow his trim, muscular figure to manoeuvre its way inside the bedroom. He looked around at all of the open surfaces, taking note of what was there and whether or not anything could be used as a potential defensive weapon if she were to lunge for it and use it against him. The only notable item was the set of still warm but now unplugged hair straighteners sitting on the desktop nearest a large mirror, which he grabbed by the cord and tossed behind him as quietly as possible. He tested a nearby lamp to see how heavy it was but it was actually glued down to the surface to deter thieves so that was not going to be a problem.

He heard the toilet flush and a few seconds later the taps in the sink running so he knew it wouldn't be long now and his heart beat faster in his chest. He could barely contain his excitement and could even feel himself getting notably aroused; he knew he was going to enjoy every moment of this and he flexed his fingers with delight, preparing them for the task they were about to undertake.

The bathroom door swung open and Christie appeared, completely oblivious to the man in her room and the danger that was about to befall her. She had a silly smile on her face as though she had no worries or fears and was seemingly off in her own little world daydreaming about things that brought her happiness.

She didn't see Gabriel coming until the very last split second and by that time it was too late. The smile disappeared from her face to be immediately replaced by a look of sheer horror mixed with confusion and Gabriel wished he could hear out loud what thoughts were running through her mind at that moment in time. He wanted to hear how terrifying he looked to her, wanted to know whether or not she was aware of how much agony and suffering he could inflict on her if only he had more time on his hands.

Her mouth gaped open as though she were about to let out a blood curdling scream but he had already grabbed the thick rag he had put in his pocket earlier and shoved it into her mouth, then covered that over with his palm before she could make a sound. He spun her around so that her back was pressed against his hard chest and wrapped his arms around her as she struggled against him, making muffled, flustered sounds through the cloth in her mouth and struggling to inhale through her now moisture-filled nose.

Though he had toyed with the idea of using a weapon on her, he much preferred the method of using his bare hands to exact the most intimate amount of pain and revenge.

The sudden surge of adrenaline that ran through her slim, not particularly muscular body meant that she was able to put up some resistance and the complete blind panic that had shocked her system meant that she didn't hold back on her attempts to break herself free from his vice-like grip.

However, his mass was too overpowering and he simply tightened the stronghold he had on her as he dragged her away from the bathroom and towards the ground, where he could flip her onto her back and pin her down whilst straddling her. She was entirely helpless against him now, there was no going back.

This was the end for little Miss Christie and Gabriel couldn't wipe the look of absolute pleasure from his face. He wished he could freeze frame this moment and watch it on play back whenever he wanted to get himself off – it was even better than he had imagined.

His knees were pinning down her arms on either side of her and the look of anguish on her face let him know he was causing her a great deal of pain at that moment, making him feel powerful, deadly and hugely turned on. All she could do was whimper as the tears ran down each side of her cheeks and her eyes darted around, not knowing what to do or where to look. He wrapped his thick fingers around her delicate neck and began to press against her windpipe, feeling the muscles beneath his fingers getting tighter and tighter, constricting her air supply and he leaned towards her to breathe in the heavenly scent of her fear and desperation.

Christie was pinned helplessly beneath this hulk of a man with inhuman strength, who she only recognised from the mug shot she had seen plastered all over the media for the last couple of weeks as the ongoing manhunt for him continued to come up with zero results.

This was it. He had found her and he was going to take everything she had fought for away from her in one fell swoop.

She looked hysterically around the room, trying to remember where she had left her phone because she knew if she could get to it, she could hit the power button five times to raise a red alert on the Solo Protect App that would bypass the regular system of having to dial 999 in an emergency. Instead the police would be on their way to her within just ten minutes. Pure devastation hit her like a drop-kick to the face when she realised that the phone was out of her reach, on the bedside set of drawers, still blaring out her metal playlist that she had been so cheerfully tapping her feet to just mere moments before heading into the bathroom.

Images flashed through her mind of her rollercoaster of a life up until that point and all of the people she cared about the most. She felt an overwhelming wave of sadness as she realised she would never see or hold them ever again, never tell them how much she loved them or how much they meant to her. Her emotions ranged from bewildered to terrified to angry to devastated in what seemed like a matter of seconds and though she tried to struggle against the mass that held her down, it was totally pointless and she could feel her windpipe closing in on her oxygen supply, that was also constricted by the rag he had shoved into her mouth.

She knew it was only a matter of time until it was over. She begged internally for this not to be it, for this not to be the last breath she ever took at the hands of a vengeful mad man. She wanted to live and grow old, go on adventures, make treasured memories, fall in love, achieve wonderful things and see the people she cared about flourishing around her. She didn't want to be just another victim that this lunatic could count off on his ever-growing list; she knew she deserved better than that.

The only saving grace that she could possibly think of in those last seconds was the idea that at least she had helped save the other twelve victims on the day of the raid and hopefully prevented any more from being taken.

Gabriel was leaning in towards Christie's sweaty, tear-stained yet still glowingly beautiful face and slowly, very pointedly stuck his entire tongue out like a lizard and licked from her jawline up to her cheekbone in one of the most grotesque and degrading actions he could perform on her as she lay there, petrified.

"Mmmmmmm," he groaned in pleasure as she tasted like salty terror, "This may be the end for you, you little whore, but it isn't quite yet for the rest of your family. I want you to know

I'm going to take my time and hunt down every single person you love and care about. I'm going to do worse things to them than you can ever even conjure up in your puny little brain and then I'm going to take them out. One. By. One." He chuckled bitterly, "It's only fair, seen as though that is what you have done to me. I'm just better at it than you."

Dale had practically sprinted through the hotel reception, leaving the woman occupying the front desk shocked and afraid, which then led her to immediately dial for security as he ran past in a blur and headed towards where Christie had instructed him to go. He didn't care if he looked like some sort of mad terrorist; it was actually better that way because it meant that the authorities would be called and that meant more protection for Christie.

He still couldn't shake the feeling that something was terribly wrong and just hoped and prayed that he wasn't too late. Even if it did turn out to be nothing, he would rather look like an over the top, dramatic fool that cared a little too much about her welfare than just shrug off his gut feeling and leave it to chance.

He stopped for a brief second to check the signs displaying the room numbers that each corridor led to, picked the one on the right as that was the direction he needed to head down and sprinted towards the end, where Christie's room was supposed to be.

When he got to her door he barely paused to catch his breath before banging loudly against the thick wood and shouting out, "Christie?" He waited for just one second before banging again and shouting louder, "Christie, it's me. Open up!" He pressed his ear against the door and all he could hear on the other side was rage against the Machine's 'Killing in the Name Of'.

The sudden, sharp and repetitive banging sound against the door to Christie's room, coupled with the faint sound of a male voice shouting at her to open up sent a jolt of adrenaline through Gabriel's body and he tightened his grip against Christie's windpipe, trying to squeeze the very essence of her soul right out of her body.

She gulped and gargled against his fingers and tried as hard as she possibly could to make any sort of recognisable sound but was failing to produce anything. Yet she refused to give up; she wasn't going to give this psychopath the satisfaction and she couldn't bear the thought of him going after her loved ones once he was done with her. It was getting more and more difficult to get any air at all into her system. Her ears were ringing and all the shapes around her were growing hazy as she tried desperately to hold onto her consciousness but could feel it slipping away from her, inch by inch.

Dale rapidly gave up on his intense door banging and shouting, looked around frantically for something hard to bash the door down with and then abandoned that idea too when his eyes fell on the fire exit just to his right. He slammed his body weight through that, setting off all of the building's emergency alarms and ended up on the outside of the building, with a tiny pathway leading to his right-hand side that he should obviously follow if there was in fact a fire.

Instead, he allowed the door to close behind him and ran to his left, where he had envisioned that Christie's bedroom window would be. There was a sports bag on the ground in front of him so he quickly deducted that someone else must have broken in just before he had arrived as the window was still ajar enough for him to climb his way through. Every part of his system was fuelled on adrenaline now and he surged forwards to launch himself through the open window, not knowing what he would find on the other side and simply hoping that he wasn't going to run face first into a weapon of some sort.

As he tumbled onto the carpet and tangled himself slightly in the curtains, he noted the scene before him – the monster whose face he recognised from the news as the fugitive third Balan brother was straddling his dear friend Christie and he couldn't tell whether or not she was still breathing.

It looked like she had struggled against him but now he could see no movement coming from her and she looked so small and fragile underneath the bulking man that had pinned her to the floor.

Dale stood up at the same time as this despicable madman rose from the ground before him and he felt blind rage as he stared at Gabriel's smirking face. Though he had heard on the news reports that the fugitive Balan was a highly skilled, extremely dangerous ex-military man with a tendency for violence and he also knew all too well of the types of activities his organisation had ran their business on, he wasn't going to shy away from giving this sick son of a bitch what he deserved.

Years ago, Dale had been very close friends with a member of the motorcycle club known as the 1% who wasn't just all about the bikes; he also had a flare for the Krav Maga fighting system and had relished in teaching some of those moves to Dale. Though he hadn't seen that friend for a long time, suddenly his booming instructional voice came roaring back into Dale's ear drums and he poised himself ready for the onslaught he knew was about to head his way. Though he was usually a calm, gentle man, he felt the most revulsion and pure contempt he had ever felt in his lifetime for the man that was turning towards him at that very moment and he wanted nothing more than to tear him limb from limb.

Gabriel was taking a moment on his feet to size Dale up. They were roughly the same height and breadth but Gabriel knew that his own physique was made of pure muscle. He worked extremely hard to keep it that way as it was just as good for his mental health as it was his physical health and pursuits.

Dale, on the other hand, appeared to be in a fairly good shape, but a little soft around the edges and approximately three or four years younger than himself as far as Gabriel could deduce in spite of Dale's tendency to opt for slightly baggy, skater style clothing items that men half his age would generally wear. The copious amount of tattoos on Dale's body clearly meant that he wasn't a stranger to pain and didn't shy away from it so that was something to bear in mind when choosing the moves he would inflict upon this otherwise boyish looking man that stood before him.

He also noted the glaring anger that seemed to be radiating from Dale's body at that particular moment in time as he had entered the scene just as Gabriel was completing his mission.

There was no more time to spare. An alarm had been set off, most likely by his opponent or perhaps a startled member of staff. Gabriel needed to make his move and swiftly escape before the authorities descended upon the hotel and thwarted his plans with Elena and Vilmos altogether.

Gabriel took a calming and steadying breath, then lunged forwards and ran at Dale as though he was about to tackle him on a rugby pitch. He did not expect that Dale would be remotely prepared in the slightest. In his mind's eye he already had Dale on the ground and was punching the life out of him but he was totally incorrect in his prediction of how this was going to go.

Dale waited until Gabriel was just mere inches away from colliding with him and threw his entire strength into an upper cut that hit Gabriel directly in his stomach, forcing him to convulse backwards and onto one knee on the ground. The look on the attacker's face was priceless: pure shock, coupled with agonising pain at first, soon to be replaced by sheer rage at the fact that he had been temporarily incapacitated by a man whom he had misjudged as inferior to himself.

It didn't take him to long to recover and he rose again to his full height, flexed his muscles so that the sound of several joints cracking in unison was audible even over the top of the ongoing playlist still blaring out of Christie's phone. The current song was Limp Bizkit's 'Counterfeit' and the pace of the beat was quite fitting for the current violent activity they were partaking in.

Dale glanced over at Christie's lifeless looking figure that was laying on the carpet slightly behind and to the side of Gabriel. He wanted so badly to go to her and see if she was still breathing and it was breaking his heart to think that perhaps she wasn't.

Gabriel took full advantage of the split-second distraction that he noticed had registered on Dale's face and this time sprung forward a couple of steps with his fists elevated to chest height. Dale's attention snapped back into place and he attempted a heel palm strike against Gabriel's chest but the skilled ex-military man saw this move coming and lunged his stance sideways and slightly backwards in order to avoid being hit completely.

With his right side still leaning forwards he quickly jabbed Dale straight on his right cheekbone, then swung his left arm back around in a hook punch to Dale's other cheek. The two hard blows in quick succession left Dale utterly dazed and he stumbled backwards, trying to find his balance and failing to do so. He leaned his hand against the windowsill and heaved in as much air as he could, attempting to clear the fog that was now clouding his line of vision.

Gabriel was beginning to lunge for him again but Dale used his own instability to grab onto Gabriel's shoulder as a balance, pull him forwards and knee him directly in the groin faster than even he could have known that he was capable of considering how off kilter he felt.

They both fell to the ground in a total shamble: Dale trying to shake some sense into his ringing, pulsating ear drums and Gabriel holding onto his groin in agony. Dale kicked out with brute force, his heel cracking loudly against Gabriel's chin and knocking his entire upper body backwards so that he was now flat on his back with his own legs curled underneath him.

The pain in his jaw was splittingly intense and he wondered if it had cracked open entirely. He wiped his palm against it and checked for any bleeding through his hazy vision and thankfully there was none so he placed both palms on the ground and performed a move similar to something out of a menacing and vicious breakdancing routine in order to free his feet and kick back at his opponent.

Dale had managed to find his own footing very briefly before Gabriel swung both his legs out in a semi-circular motion so that they whipped Dale's legs out from underneath him and he came crashing loudly to the ground. Gabriel then pounced on top of Dale like a ravenous lion hunting down a gazelle and threw a hooked punch straight into his left cheek, making his head jolt roughly to the right.

Dale, with his head still facing away from Gabriel reached backwards, grabbed hold of the scruff of his neck and tried to pull him into a headlock but it was futile and Gabriel managed to wriggle his way free before being snared by Dale's enraged grip. They both rose up onto their knees and grabbed hold of each other by their clothing: Dale trying his hardest to wrestle against Gabriel's brute strength but coming up short. He attempted to push against Gabriel's face with the palm of his hand as he felt himself being pushed to the ground but before he knew it, Gabriel had manoeuvred his arms to each of his sides and was now kneeling on both of them– the same way he had been doing to Christie when Dale had tumbled into the room to try and stop him.

"Not so tough are you now, *mate?*" Gabriel's poor attempt at a cockney accent whilst he accentuated the word 'mate' was both degrading and mildly infuriating. "Did you really think you were gonna burst in here and save your little girlfriend?" He spat on the ground directly next to Dale's head. "Pathetic."

"Get *off* of me!" Dale continued to struggle against Gabriel's immense strength, refusing to give in and stop fighting. He bucked his shoulders upwards from the ground and rocked his waist from side to side, trying to knock Gabriel off balance and it looked as though he was almost successful a couple of times but Gabriel just about managed to catch himself and re-adjust his weight to keep Dale fixed in place.

"Make me." Gabriel sneered back at Dale and then back handed him across the face in what was intended to be the most humiliating action he could perform on his opponent in order to exert his own dominance. Dale could only see stars for a few seconds and saliva involuntarily came sputtering out of his mouth as his face was flung to one side and pressed down against the carpet. As he slowly turned his head back into an upright position, his focus was starting to return and he could see the smirk on Gabriel's evil face as he raised his hand again to repeat the same move.

A loud, sharp banging on the door made Gabriel pause in his tracks and look in the direction of where the noise had come from with an expression of complete alarm on his face.

"*Police! Open up!*" came a bellowing male voice on the other side of the door. There was a moment's pause, followed by four louder bangs. Gabriel sprung to his feet and immediately ran towards the window. Before Dale could let out a sound or even attempt to make a grab for his ankles, Gabriel had lifted himself back out of the open window, shoved the sports bag back over his shoulder and ran as stealthily through the bushes back towards the car as he could manage.

Elena had started the engine and opened the door for him, ready to make an instant getaway.

Three police vehicles were outside the entrance to the hotel but all of the officers were either inside the building or facing towards it, clearly expecting the assailant to be brought out in an arrest. Elena slipped the Volvo purposely slowly and very quietly past them and onwards to exit the carpark.

Gabriel had returned the baseball cap to his head, placed his sunglasses back on and sank his body downwards as far as it could possibly go in a seated position.

"Stay low until I say it's all clear," Elena murmured in Gabriel's direction, whilst carefully surveying the roads from all directions. "Vilmos has already arranged for another car to be dropped off at a different car park not far from here but I will need your help in figuring out where we can abandon this one and then proceed to the next one on foot."

"Roger that," Gabriel stated and the two of them continued in silence for another ten minutes until Elena was sure they hadn't been tailed.

"You can come back up now. I don't think we were followed," Elena said a little breathlessly to Gabriel and he cautiously moved himself back upwards into a regular seated position and scanned the roads around them in all directions.

"Find somewhere away from the main road to pull over and let me have a look at what Vilmos sent you. I can figure out an escape route from there," Gabriel instructed, his heart rate beginning to slow down somewhat. In his mind his mission was complete and now all that was left to do was to get himself and his new, trusted ally back to safety, leaving as little as possible to trace them back there.

Chapter 19

Back at the Travelodge, the very moment Gabriel had flung himself out of the window, the main concern on Dale's mind was to check whether or not Christie was OK. The police were still banging loudly on the door but he ignored that for a moment to clamber up on to his knees so that he could kneel next to where his friend lay on the floor looking limp and lifeless. He pulled the rag out of her mouth, grabbed both of her shoulders and began to shake her.

"Christie? Christie, please wake up." There was no movement from her whatsoever and he shook her a little harder. "Christie?" The banging on the door sounded three louder and slower times.

"Last chance now. *This is the police!* Open up!" The male voice shouted out his final warning.

Dale wrapped Christie in his arms and held her against his body, rocking back and forth, still saying her name over and over again. He couldn't have lost her, not after all this, but she felt so uncharacteristically still in his arms and he wondered if he had just got there a minute too late to save her. The crushing wave of devastation swept over him and a tear slipped out of the corner of his eye as he looked down at her unconscious face.

She looked so peaceful and beautiful, as though she had just slipped into a light slumber and was dreaming happily about things that brought her serenity.

For a brief moment he was mentally transported back to the first time he had met her. She had come to him after he was recommended by their mutual friend, Len, who was ecstatically pleased with the work Dale had done on his very first tattoo. Christie's deep and meaningful explanation as to why she wanted that particular tattoo and what it symbolised for her had touched Dale right to his inner core and they had developed a profoundly trusting bond as they opened up to one another about their own various life experiences whilst she was sitting in his tattooing chair.

She had returned to him for many more masterpieces after that and their connection had gone from strength to strength, both parties seeking advice from one another and telling each other things that nobody else knew. It was a relationship that ran far deeper than that of client to service provider from the very beginning and he had taken it a lot worse than he cared to let on to those around him when news had emerged of her disappearance. Being the one who had come to her aid the day she escaped and returned to society had filled him with an unfathomable amount of joy and he wasn't ready to give up on that feeling yet.

"You can't leave me, not yet." He sniffed loudly, wiped away a stray tear and gave her one final hard jostle whilst calling out her name again.

Miraculously, her eyes slowly started to bat open and she heaved a wheezing breath and spluttered against his chest. Her instincts forced her to fight him off for a few seconds and he patiently waited for her to subside, a look of confusion taking over her features as she began to register the man who was holding her.

"Oh my god, Christie!" Dale exclaimed and relaxed the grip he had on her, allowing her some space to breathe.

At that moment, four armed police officers came charging into the room after being let in by the young and terrified woman that had previously been sitting at reception using one of the housekeeping keys. They each took a minute to examine who the occupants of the room were and then the commanding officer at the front of the party addressed Dale, who was still cradling a dishevelled looking Christie gently and rubbing her back.

"What's going on here?" he asked accusingly of Dale but at the same time feeling incredibly confused as he recognised the man on the ground in front of him from all of the news reports surrounding the case.

This man had found and helped Christie the day she had escaped from the abandoned farm, yet was now on the ground with her in her bedroom, looking as though he had just broken in and attacked her? It didn't make the least bit of sense.

She looked notably upset, breathless and bedraggled so it was clear something bad had happened to her in the last few minutes, but she was also gripping tightly on to the man he recognised from the news as opposed to fighting him away. He was holding her only as if to comfort her, not contain her so he did not seem to be any sort of a threat as had originally been feared and reported by the receptionist.

"The man you're looking for just escaped out of the window." Dale motioned towards the open window by nodding his head. "I can't be sure, but I think his getaway car was a white Volvo with a blonde woman as his driver," he explained.

The commanding officer nodded to his subordinate to his right-hand side and motioned for him to proceed to the window. The second in command followed orders and crossed the floor over to the window, with one hand on his gun, ready to pull it out if he were to come face to face with an attacker.

The other two officers headed back out into the hallway to question whether or not the receptionist had seen anyone else trying to enter the room after she had called for help.

"No, I saw no one else," the still shocked and trembling receptionist replied, "Just the skin head, tattooed guy with the beard."

The officers guided her back down the corridor and towards the reception desk, where she sat down and waited for them to head outside, survey the entire car park and return to ask her some more questions.

"Do you have immediate access to the CCTV footage from the last hour?" The officer that addressed her was a stocky white woman with brown hair, slicked back into a ponytail and large, bright blue eyes that seemed to be perpetually alert.

"I don't but I can call the manager and ask him to come and provide it to you?" the young, flustered receptionist replied, tucking her ginger curls behind her ear and trying to sound professional.

"Please do that," the female officer instructed whilst her male colleague was speaking into his police radio updating the rest of their team to be on the lookout for a white Volvo heading in any direction down Rainham Road South, containing one IC1 female driver and IC1 male passenger. The lack of information about either a number plate or where they were headed made the update sound vague at best but certainly worth sending out, regardless.

The jittery receptionist immediately set about putting a call into her manager, who was off site at present but lived near Dagenham Heathway, so didn't have far to travel at all when the necessity presented itself. He answered after just two rings, sounding gruff on the other end as though he had his hands full. In the background there were sounds of multiple children squealing with excited delight and it quickly became clear that he was tied up with parental duties.

"Is everything OK?" the ruffled manager answered without so much as a hello.

"Hi, Dominic, it... it's Penny. So... s...s...s...sorry to bother you." The receptionist was still clearly full of anxiety and stammered over her own introduction. "Can I p...p...p...p...pass the phone over to the p...p...p...police officer I have standing in front of me so sh...sh...sh....she can explain what's needed, please?"

"Yes, of course." Dominic immediately softened his tone after hearing how distressed his member of staff sounded.

The female officer gladly took over, offering Penny a sympathetic smile as she accepted the telephone receiver and introduced herself as Abigail to the hotel manager. She professionally and efficiently explained the situation that had just taken place in his place of business and asked for permission to view the CCTV footage as quickly as possible so that they stood a chance of catching the suspects in their tracks.

She was all too aware that with every passing minute the assailant and his potential getaway driver were less and less likely to be caught before they could go into hiding and she couldn't stress that fact enough to Dominic, who seemed to be contending with a number of small, excitable children in the background. Though she felt an intense urge to invoke her inner drill sergeant and start barking orders at him down the phone, she managed to restrain herself and keep an even, calm tone to her voice.

The clock kept ticking and what seemed like an unnecessarily long amount of time later, Dominic was able to free himself from his entanglement with the miniature humans in his vicinity and give both permission and instructions to Abigail over the phone as to how she could access the recording. Abigail motioned to Penny with her hands, mimicking writing with a pen in the air and Penny helpfully handed over some hotel stationery for her to be able to note down what she was being told.

All the while, back in Christie's room, Dale helped her up off the ground and sat her down on the edge of her bed, fetched some tissues from the adjoining bathroom and handed them to her as he sat down next to her, gently rubbing her back up and down. The commanding officer remained in the room with them to get their statements, whilst his second in command had gone out through the fire exit next to the room to see what he could find.

"Hello Christie, my name is Rohit." The commanding officer, a tall, broad Asian man with very short black hair and a precisely barbered, substantial beard, had gotten over his initial confusion and was now addressing Christie with a gentle tone as it became clear to him that she'd suffered a terrifying and life-threatening ordeal at the hands of an enraged, exceptionally well trained fugitive who had thus far managed to outsmart the police force at every opportunity. "In your own time, could you explain to me what happened here today? An ambulance is on its way so that you can be thoroughly checked over but I just wanted to get your perspective on what took place."

"He...he...he just came out of nowhere!" Christie was struggling to keep her voice even as she spoke: "I was in the bathroom and I came out." She sniffed and sobbed slightly when she inhaled so Dale handed her another tissue. "And he grabbed me before I could even register the fact that there was another person in the room." Her entire body shook as she replayed the scene in her mind.

"Can you identify the man who did this to you? Have you seen him before?" Rohit asked, though he was already about ninety per cent sure he knew what her answer was going to be.

"Yes. I've seen him before but not in person until today." Christie confirmed, the strength returning to her voice as she calmed her breathing down. "His face is all over the news right now as you guys have been trying to hunt him down in relation to my case. He's the third Balan brother that's been on the run ever since his organisation was exposed." She shook her head as it dawned on her just how quickly he had been able to find her despite being reassured at all stages that her location was only privy to those whom absolutely needed to know. "He knew how to get to me. I don't know how but he knew. And he said he's going to go after everyone I care about." Tears rolled down, thick and fast from either side of her eyes as she vocalised her worst nightmare. She couldn't bear the thought that she would be the reason behind why any one of her loved ones would suffer or fear for their own safety.

Dale continued to rub her back up and down in a comforting manner. "Sshhhhh, no one is gonna let that happen." He attempted to reassure her but in reality, he had no way of knowing himself what steps the authorities were going to put in place in order to keep everybody safe.

So far, they had failed to capture this mad man and protect Christie. She had been close to losing her life today and they had shown up too late to do anything about it. It had taken a civilian to take it into his own hands and step in, putting himself in danger in the process. He turned his attention to Rohit. "What happens now? You guys must be able to grab him now that you have a rough idea of his whereabouts, right? Are your colleagues going after him as we speak?"

Rohit was nodding along to demonstrate that he was listening to Dale's questions but also trying to listen in to any updates that came through his police radio, attached to the collar region of his padded vest. "My colleagues are currently trying to track down the white Volvo that you mentioned earlier, but without any number plates to go by or a clear idea of which direction it was headed, that makes the task far more difficult."

His expression was not one of hope as he knew that with every passing minute they grew less and less likely of catching their assailant as he attempted to flee the scene and he had also encountered fugitives with military training in the past- they were a nightmare to go after as they were so damn good at covering their tracks and evading capture. There was no doubt in his mind that the man in question had received some of the best training he had had the displeasure of having to go up against, coupled with a long history of criminal activity, this guy knew how to fly completely under the radar and remain that way for lengthy periods of time.

"We're currently trying to get our hands on the CCTV footage of the outside of the building and the carpark; once we have that we can get a better idea of where we need to be looking and formulate a more cohesive plan of action." His attempt at sounding sure of his task force's capabilities fell a little flat considering the gravity of the situation and how little prepared they had been upon arrival.

Dale had an overwhelming urge to yell at the officer that stood in front of him, to stand up, grab him by the shoulders, try to shake some sense into him and let him know just how close he had come to losing Christie because of their extremely lacking protective detail for her. They were supposed to be keeping her safe and yet when he had shown up and had to force his way inside, the one man they had been tasked with keeping away from her had been straddling her in her own room, strangling the life right out of her. It wasn't good enough in his eyes and he wanted reassurance that this was never going to happen again.

However, he couldn't vocalise any of that right now in front of Christie. She had already been through enough without him adding fuel to the fire and losing his temper at those in charge of her protection. He could still feel her trembling and pulled her even closer towards him so that he could warm her up and help her relax a little. She leaned her head into his shoulder and sniffed, wiping her face with the tissues he had given her and his heart melted at just how fragile and terrified she looked. He could tell that, emotionally, she was hanging by a thread right now and her nerves were more fraught than they had ever been. She hadn't deserved any of this from day one and it seemed like the nightmare was far from being over.

The second in command returned to Christie's doorway after having searched the entire hotel grounds for any evidence and coming up empty handed, then checking in with his colleagues at the reception desk to see how far along they had gotten with checking the CCTV footage.

"Sir, we've checked the CCTV recording and got a number plate," he addressed Rohit in an urgent tone, "We now have two squad cars in pursuit."

"Thanks, Travis," Rohit replied and began to start another sentence when Kate suddenly appeared and eased herself straight into Christie's room.

"I can take it from here, guys, you both go and follow up any leads you can on tracking down the assailant," Kate commanded of the two men.

"Yes, Ma'am," they both replied in unison and Rohit turned back towards Christie to offer her a sympathetic smile before he left, but she was miles away, forcing her brain not to replay the horrific events of her day so far and instead think of how lucky she was to still be here, alive and kicking – once again thanks to Dale.

Kate squatted down in front of Christie. "Hello, lovely, how are you feeling?" She reached out and gave Christie's knee a gentle squeeze.

"Lucky to be alive." Christie replied, without a hint of irony.

"Yeah, I bet. I got here as quickly as I could," Kate said, apologetically. "The ambulance crew should be here any second now to check you over and depending on what they say, we'll either get you to hospital or over to the station if that's OK with you?"

"Sure." Christie nodded her agreement but felt lacking in enthusiasm for anything.

"I've contacted your mum and she's on standby to make her way to wherever we go from here," Kate informed her, trying to sound comforting and feeling like she wasn't doing a very good job at it.

Moments later the ambulance crew arrived and immediately set about their duties of giving Christie a full physical evaluation. Kate stepped out into the hallway to call Sue for a live update on the pursuit of Gabriel Balan.

"Any news?" Kate asked as soon as Sue answered.

"So far, he's managed to slip through the net yet again." The frustration in Sue's voice was palpable. "We've been able to tap into some brief bits of footage from any of the few traffic cameras along the route they were headed but this guy clearly knows his way around the borough and how to avoid being recorded."

"This ain't his first time at the rodeo," Kate replied dryly.

"You got that right." Sue huffed and Kate could hear her pacing up and down as she spoke: "The last trace of that vehicle was coming off New Road and into Anderson Way – it's all residential around there, so no way of following them on camera. We have several squad cars out checking the surrounding areas but no results yet."

"Keep me posted." Kate sighed and hung up. This was not what she had wanted to hear and she didn't know how she was going to shield this information from her already crumbling victim.

Chapter 20

Elena and Gabriel were now travelling down the A1203 in a different car to the one they had arrived in earlier that day and at precisely the speed limit to avoid any unwanted attention.

After leaving the Travelodge Elena had followed Gabriel's instructions and driven through a large residential area, navigating their way through multiple side streets in a maze-like fashion, before finally exiting onto a vast and largely no longer used carpark next to some warehouses that hadn't been occupied for several years. She had parked at the furthest corner of the carpark, out of sight of any witnesses and it was clear that the security cameras dotted at each corner of the warehouse site had been disconnected as there was no need for them anymore.

They had both swiftly changed clothes into completely different outfits that Elena had packed for them in a bag on the back seat before they left the apartment and Elena had removed her wig and discarded it with their used clothing onto the floor of the car. Gabriel had doused the items with a small amount of lighter fluid and then lit the corner of the bag with a disposable lighter so that it was only just starting to catch fire as they promptly jogged away from the vehicle into some nearby trees on the other side of a fence that surrounded the carpark, completely concealing their escape.

They heard the explosion of the car a few minutes later as they were surfacing from the trees onto some parkland, where they lightened their pace to a brisk walk, as though they were a couple out for some joint exercise.

Gabriel used the Google Maps app on Elena's mobile to locate the vehicle that Vilmos had arranged to be dropped off at a nearby multi-storey carpark. It was a manageable distance by foot despite the detour they had taken and he confidently led the way, tapping into his former military commanding style.

Whenever they encountered any other humans in their vicinity, Gabriel grabbed hold of Elena's hand and as they would walk past each stranger, he would engage her in jovial small talk so that they appeared far too preoccupied to look anybody in the eye or have their own features recognised. As a result, they were allowed to walk freely without anybody paying too much attention to them along the way.

Now they were in a black Citreon C3 heading back towards safer territory but were both still on edge and keeping an eye on the traffic behind them in the car's mirrors, watching to see if they had been tailed.

"Shall we call Vilmos now and get an update on what he can see on the news?" Elena eventually broke the silence, keen to both hear her husband's voice as well as get a live commentary on what was being reported about their vicious, criminal escapade.

"Yes, I think that's a good idea," Gabriel confirmed and leaned into the sports bag that he had kept with him the whole time to retrieve his all-important hip flask and take a large gulp of its contents. "I can't wait to hear what has been said about Christie's appalling and tragic demise."

He let out a wicked chuckle as he finished that sentence and Elena smirked. She was pleased that he had accomplished what he set out to do but wasn't quite ready yet to laugh and joke about it. She would reserve that for later on when the three of them could relax in the comfort of her home and let loose with some strong, celebratory beverages.

Vilmos had already put plans into place for disposing of their current vehicle too. All she had to do was keep calm enough to make it in one piece to the drop off point and then they were on the home stretch from there.

She dialled her husband and put the phone on loudspeaker. He answered after just the one ring.

"There you are." Vilmos sounded incredibly relieved to finally hear from his wife. "How are you both doing?"

"I've got you on speaker phone, my love," Elena replied, "We're both doing just fine, thank you and looking forward to being reunited with you." She smiled at the thought of being wrapped in his warm and comforting embrace. She hadn't longed for him this badly in years and the feeling was wonderful. It was like going back in time to the insatiable chemistry they had experienced during the early years of their relationship.

"My brother, I'm keen to toast with you on mission accomplished," Gabriel said animatedly and mock toasted the air with the hip flask before taking another generous gulp. Elena looked over at him with a devilish grin.

"Ah," said Vilmos, then paused for a moment whilst considering how to vocalise the bad news, wondering whether or not he should wait until they arrived safely home, then deciding it was best to get it out in the open as quickly as possible – ripping off the Band-Aid, so to speak. "I take it you fled the scene without being able to double check that you had in fact completed your mission?"

The question hit Gabriel in the chest like a tonne of bricks and the floor of his stomach dropped in a devastating blow. "You can't possibly mean..." Gabriel began and then felt as though he couldn't finish his own question because he didn't really want to hear the answer.

Elena looked over at him in confusion and decided to seek the answer herself. "Vilmos, are you saying that Christie is still alive?" she asked incredulously.

"Yes. She's still alive." Vilmos delivered the crushing news. "Her tattooed saviour got to her just in time and she apparently woke up in his arms as the police burst into her room. He's being painted as quite the hero all over the news channels as we speak."

Both Elena and Gabriel fell into a stunned silence as they tried to process what they had just heard.

A minute passed before Vilmos spoke: "I know it's not remotely what you wanted to hear, either of you. I just thought it best to know where we all stand and how we should be exerting extreme caution for the foreseeable future. I will make it my duty to assist you with a new and improved mission when the time is right. You *will* have your vengeance, my dear Gabriel, I will make sure of it, but for now we must lay low until the tide passes."

Another minute of total silence passed before Elena was the one to break it. "We're roughly ten minutes away from the drop off point. I'll send you a WhatsApp as soon as we've left the vehicle," she said in a measured tone, taking great effort to compartmentalise the chaotic thoughts and emotions that were tumbling through her mind all at once.

"Understood," Vilmos replied, "Be careful, my sweet. I'll see you soon." Then the phone cut off.

Gabriel was staring straight ahead with a demonic look of pure rage in his eyes and Elena didn't dare say a word to him just yet for fear of uttering completely the wrong thing. His chest was rising and falling in a rapid, shallow and seemingly unnatural manner as though he was struggling to catch his breath.

All of a sudden, he slammed his fist into the dashboard so heavily that it jolted Elena and she swerved unexpectedly to the right. A car horn sounded loudly next to her and she swerved back into her lane, narrowly missing being hit by another over taking driver. The gentleman in the car next to her glared in her direction as he continued past their car but was met with no reaction from her or Gabriel as they had far bigger things to worry about at that moment.

"*Fuuuuuuuck!*" yelled Gabriel, then he slapped the dashboard with an open palm several times in quick succession. "That little fucking whore!" He replaced the cap on the hip flask and sat squeezing it between his palms the way one would with a stress ball, making his knuckles turn white.

Two more minutes passed by where all he could hear was white noise and a distant ringing that slowly got louder and more intense. He employed the breathing techniques he had learned during his military days to help soldiers remain calm in the face of danger, slowly in through the nose and out through the mouth, counting in his mind with each inhalation and exhalation.

"This is *not* over," he stated.

They were silent for the remainder of the drive, Elena using the maps app to both distract herself from the heavy emotional turmoil she was feeling as well as direct her towards where they needed to drop the car off.

Gabriel had drifted off into a trance-like, meditative state where all he could picture was various scenarios in which he could finally extract the life from his victim. In his mind, that was the only thing that was going to make him feel better. He didn't just want it, he needed it and he wasn't going to rest until he had accomplished it. He never had been one to tackle any task half-heartedly and he wasn't about to start now.

The robotic female voice in the app announced that they had reached their destination and Elena pulled the car over to a standstill next to the kerb. She took a long, deep breath and slowly exhaled, then looked over at Gabriel.

"We'll figure this out, ya know?" she offered.

Gabriel looked over at her beautiful face that was filled with a mixture of sympathy, concern and an ever present need to please him. He knew that factor would serve him well in any future plans he wished to execute and intended to use it to his full advantage when the dust settled from this absolute shit show of a day.

"You reckon?" Gabriel asked, testing both her intellect and gauging how far she was willing to go to keep him happy.

"I do. Between the resources, connections and sheer creativity that I and my husband have within our remit, coupled with your experience, skill set and courage, we will come up with a far better way of executing your desires." She knew that stroking his ego was the key to calming him down and winning him over to her way of thinking. "We've discussed this before – everything happens for a reason, right? It was clearly not meant to be today and we will find a better strategy between the three of us. One that is far more fitting and fulfilling all round."

Gabriel was still seething but her eloquent words and the attractive mouth she used to deliver them were gently easing the temperature in his body to a slightly lower point and he continued to use his breathing technique to relieve the tension in his chest. He unscrewed the cap on the hip flask, drained the last of its contents and replaced it into the sports bag.

"Let's get back to the apartment," he stated firmly and they both exited the car in unison.

They hadn't spotted the young man hidden from immediate view under the shade of a nearby high rise. He had waited patiently for them to get out of the car, smoking a roll up to its very tip until it almost burnt the edges of his fingers. He always smoked that way; he enjoyed the thrill of the pain it caused him.

He stepped out of the shadows and came up to about a metre away from where Gabriel stood with his back towards him. Elena noticed him first as she was facing in his direction from the driver's side of the car.

At first her expression was sheer alarm and that caused Gabriel to spin around immediately and poise himself for an attack, then after a second or two Elena realised that she vaguely recognised the young man as one of the dogsbodies her husband had occasionally utilised in the past for the type of grunt work that nobody else wanted to do and the tension in her shoulders settled.

"Gabriel Balan, right?" The young man addressed him directly.

There was nothing shy about him in the slightest and it caught Gabriel off guard for a moment. He surveyed the stranger for a couple of seconds: he was slightly shorter than himself, slim and didn't appear to be the physically threatening type. He was dressed in an entirely individual style that looked like a mixture of punk, rock and gothic trends, with a dash of unkempt homelessness – like he had slept in a bin shed somewhere.

That was actually far from the case but he liked to give off the impression that he was a low life, lacking in any skills, ambition or intellect to throw people off the scent that he was in fact a next level kind of genius with a vast array of projects ongoing at any one time that weren't exactly legal or kosher.

He pulled another roll up out of the pocket of his studded leather jacket and balanced it between his fingers, gently rotating it because keeping himself distracted by his own dexterity helped him to keep any unwanted anxiety at bay.

Gabriel noted the chipped black nail varnish on his fingers, the tattoo creeping up from under the neck of his black t-shirt all the way up past his ear, the messy, bushy, rough black hair that hung below his chin but was tucked behind his ear lobes and the small lip ring that he kept dancing his tongue under. Underneath all of the accessories and dishevelment, he was youthfully attractive and it seemed like he was doing everything in his power to make himself less appealing to most eyes.

"Who wants to know?" Gabriel asked once he was done scrutinising the creature that stood before him.

"Big fan of your work," was all the young man offered in response but then pulled a slightly crumped business card out of the pocket of his black skinny jeans and handed it over.

Gabriel looked down at the name, AJ, and job title, followed by his phone number and website. "You're a sound technician?" he asked, baffled as to why this man was addressing him.

"It's one of many ventures I have on my books– mostly to keep the tax man at bay, ya know?" He winked at Gabriel as though they were somehow on the same page. He had a wired look about him as though he never really switched off and was always running in the background like an appliance on standby. "If there's ever *anything* you need, you just hit me up on that number." He nodded towards the business card.

Elena had walked around to the passenger side of the car and handed over the keys to AJ. He politely nodded his acceptance and then turned to retrieve a light, material shopping bag from where he had previously been standing and handed it over to Elena.

Inside was a large brimmed, beige hat for her to wear, a summery pink cardigan to disguise her current outfit and some oversized sunglasses. For Gabriel there was a bright yellow baseball cap, a white, long sleeved t-shirt and some aviator style sunglasses. They both adorned their new looks swiftly, under the cover of the building's shadow and backed up to start walking away.

"Thanks, AJ." Gabriel held up the business card in his right hand and purposely demonstrated putting it into the side pocket of his sports bag to show that he intended to contact the young man at a later stage. There was something in the man's eyes that spoke to Gabriel; he had the kind of intensely crazed and calculated stare that he himself had once adorned back before he had been conditioned by the military to focus his psychotic tendencies onto the mission at hand. As such, he felt an affinity for him and had already began planning to create a protégé out of him.

Elena and Gabriel turned and began walking briskly back towards the apartment they had left what felt like a lifetime ago to meet back up with Vilmos and attempt to wind down from everything they had been through.

AJ climbed into the vehicle and drove away to complete his assigned task of destroying it.

Chapter 21

Back in Romford police station, Kate and Sue had finished taking a statement from Christie about what had taken place at the Travelodge earlier that day. It had been harrowing listening to her replay the utter terror she had felt when Gabriel had forced her to the ground and told her all of the horrific things he intended to do to everyone she cared about whilst strangling her with the intention of ending her life.

Trying to comfort and reassure her at this stage was an exercise in futility as they both felt as though they had let her down in their attempts at keeping her out of harm's way up until this point. They knew they would have to up their game and place her into a far tighter protective custody, at least until they could get their hands on the sick and twisted Gabriel Balan.

They walked Christie back out towards the reception area, where Carrie and Dale were both patiently waiting and asked to speak to Carrie privately so they could inform her and her alone about where they were next going to be placing her daughter.

Whilst the three women were wrapped up in their deep and purposeful conversation, Christie walked over to where Dale stood, with his arms wide open to wrap her up in a bear hug, which she wholeheartedly accepted. She buried her head into his chest and began to weep softly against him. His heart bled for her and he rubbed her back up and down with one hand whilst stroking her hair with the other. Normally he was great at making her laugh through any situation but he didn't feel it was remotely appropriate at this moment in time and remained quietly trying to comfort her fraught and frazzled mind.

"I can't see myself ever feeling safe again after this," Christie whimpered.

Dale sighed and wrapped his arms around her more tightly. "It seems that way now but you'll get through this, you always do." He pulled his body weight back so that he could look directly into her big, ocean-coloured, tear-stained eyes. "You're the strongest woman I know by far and we are *all* here for you to figure out what the next steps are, OK? Never ever feel like you're alone in any of this."

"Thank you.... For *everything*," Christie replied, with a deep sniff and then rested her head back against his chest. He proceeded to gently stroke her back and they both wondered how on earth life was ever going to be the same again.

To be continued...